Born in Glasgow, Lesley Campbell used to work for a prestigious commodity broker with responsibility for Russia, Australia and southern Europe. She lives in West London with her two children. *Forged Metal* is her first novel; she is currently working on her second.

FORGED METAL

Lesley Campbell

CORGI BOOKS

FORGED METAL
A CORGI BOOK : 0 552 14570 X

Originally published in Great Britain by Bantam Press,
a division of Transworld Publishers Ltd

PRINTING HISTORY
Bantam Press edition published 1998
Corgi edition published 1999

Set in 11/12pt Palatino by Falcon Oast Graphic Art

Corgi Books are published by Transworld Publishers Ltd,
61–63 Uxbridge Road, London W5 5SA,
in Australia by Transworld Publishers,
c/o Random House Australia Pty Ltd,
20 Alfred Street, Milsons Point, NSW 2061,
in New Zealand by Transworld Publishers,
c/o Random House New Zealand,
18 Poland Road, Glenfield, Auckland
and in South Africa by Transworld Publishers,
c/o Random House (Pty) Ltd,
Endulini, 5a Jubilee Road, Parktown 2193.

Reproduced, printed and bound in Great Britain
by Cox & Wyman Ltd, Reading, Berks.

For Blake and Philippa

In memory of Peter and Robert Tauber

I am grateful to everyone who helped me, especially my mother, who never stops. Thanks to Graham Slater and David Waite for *all* the years, Gilly O'Shaughnessy, Vincent Garay-Spiegel, Broo Doherty at Bantam Press, Sue Jenkins, Helen Murdoch, Allan Pennington, Cammie Douglas, The Metal Bulletin and Martin Hayes at Reuters. To Iain MacGregor, who teaches more than he realizes. And to Gino, for so much, but above all his kindness. A fine thing.

The people I met in Russia were either loyal friends or bitter enemies. Unfortunately, it was sometimes hard to tell the difference. Dvoretsky, Patkin and Bogdanov are among the nicest people I know, but there are others whose duplicity and brute force I will never forget.

FORGED METAL

PROLOGUE

Oleg felt his breath tearing at his lungs. Suddenly he was flung against the wall of the tunnel. No-one heard his pleading with the tall man leaning against him and no-one paid any attention to his clumsy attempts to pull away from the man's grip, first to one side then the other.

Kiosk vendors selling cheap clothes, cigarettes and magazines, gypsies sitting on the concrete floor thrusting their dirty babies at foreign-looking passers-by, and old women selling their last worldly goods all watched the violent activity around them impassively.

Pinned to the wall, Oleg took a deep, uneven breath. Through the stench in the underpass of stale cigarette smoke and unwashed bodies he could smell his assailant. Since the coal miners had gone on strike, there had been no soap in Moscow and cheap, harsh perfumes were used as a substitute by the fastidious. But this man had a subtle, foreign smell. Oleg felt a sudden surge of hope: if he was not Russian he was less likely to be a killer. But he looked Russian. He had a soft face, puffed up by the toxins of bad living, his blue eyes with almost white eyelashes compressed into slits between the low forehead and the high, bulging cheeks. He wore the ubiquitous black leather jacket of the small-time Moscow gangster and held his gun confidently in the open.

Oleg felt his breath ease gradually. If the man had intended to kill him he would have done so by now.

'Oleg. You have refused to sign the contract Mr Kartchak drafted. He is not pleased at all.'

'I did not *refuse* . . . I told Kartchak I was not authorized. The contract would have been un-enforceable with only my signature.'

'Unenforceable?' The gunman laughed.

'Oh yes, I know you think you can enforce any-thing with your guns and your threats,' Oleg continued, his confidence growing. 'But the law exists. There *are* rules.'

'You've been dealing with the West too long.' The man lifted the gun until it pointed between Oleg's eyes. It was a CZ 75, made in the Czech Republic.

Oleg's attention was momentarily caught by the barrel; in the overhead light it reflected a harsh, matt blue, giving it an artificial look. For a second he wondered if it was a fake, but he had seen enough guns to recognize the authenticity of the black grip and the solidity of the trigger and safety-catch mechanisms.

'There are no rules in Russia today,' the gun-man continued. 'No system. But we still have traditions. In my gun there are six bullets and I will shoot you with one of them. Which one will it be? Russian roulette for modern Russia.' He was shaking with laugher and almost lost his grip on Oleg, who lunged to the left.

'Now, now. Don't you feel the odds are sufficiently in your favour?'

'Please.' The old man begged. 'I'll do whatever you want. Sign anything. There is nothing to be gained by killing me.'

'It's too late. Mr Kartchak only asks once. We've appointed someone else to sign the contract. He's already sitting at your desk.' With total insouciance he grazed the muzzle of the gun across the man's forehead until it reached his temple. No-one approached him and the level of sound in the tunnel did not vary.

'One shot to the head. This looks efficacious, but there have been failures. Suicides who stayed alive for hours, in agony, half their heads gone. Or like this, in the mouth. So soft.' He pushed the muzzle against Oleg's lips.

'But this . . . this is the best, of course.' He held the gun against the man's heart, having nosed his raincoat aside. 'Not too many layers here. Thank God it's spring, eh, Oleg?'

Oleg's head rolled back against the wall. It struck him that he *was* going to be killed. In spite of the delay, the preamble. The man had been playing with him.

'You can choose. But if you choose the wrong one it will be agony, perhaps the bullet will stay inside you, who knows? Certainly my advice to you would be this one . . .' He prodded him in the heart again. 'But this is your game, not mine.'

13

Oleg said nothing. His eyes filled with tears.

'If you will not choose, I will shoot you in the stomach, which causes the most pain, for the longest time.'

Instinctively, Oleg tensed his soft stomach muscles as if he could make the target disappear.

'Choose!' He was so close he sprayed the old man's face with a sudden shot of saliva.

'I can't . . . don't. For God's sake.' Oleg's voice rose. 'I'll do what you want. Stop this. Please.' He felt the barrel of the gun dig in just below the ribcage and in a flash of panic could imagine the sickening, searing pain of a shot to the stomach, the hours lying unheeded in the cold dank tunnel with the hawkers tearing at him, unmindful of the blood.

He felt a tear run down his face. Then he heard his own voice, in the high unsteady falsetto of a girl trying to be brave.

'In the heart . . . Shoot me in the heart . . . please . . .'

ONE

She knew something was wrong the minute she walked into the dealing room. She could smell it. She stopped for a moment, watching, then began to weave her way between the banks of desks, stepping over the wires, bins and piles of research reports which could somehow not be accommodated in Wellington's million-pound dealing room.

It had become a party trick; she would arrive at her desk and reel off the prices, without having looked at the screen. She could cheat, of course, filtering one voice out of the general brouhaha, but today she didn't have to. There would be a note of panic in the dealers' voices if the prices had fallen and a certain assurance if they had risen. Somehow, rising prices were more *natural*.

The sounds she heard today were the unmistakable signals of a bear market.

She swung her briefcase on to the desk and scanned the Reuters screen, her eyes moving quickly over the numbers, evaluating them in a couple of seconds. When she spotted the copper price her heart tightened. The futures price had dropped fifty dollars over lunch. And she had a huge position.

'Damn it. What happened?' she asked her assistant, her eyes running down the news head-lines.

Libby shrugged. 'Nothing. No news, nothing.'

Alex could see the tension in Libby's face. Hunched at her desk in the harsh shadows of the fluorescent lights, she looked drained, as if every colour except grey had been leached from the pale skin and dark hair which were usually a striking combination.

Alex's biggest client, The Kid, had bought copper. It had been Alex's idea; she had expected a strike at a German plant, but now the position was showing a substantial loss. With the price now at $1900, he was losing nearly $100,000 – not much for The Kid, but the position was still open; he would lose another $10,000 for every dollar the price fell.

She looked around again, hoping for a clue. There was a tension in the room she recognized; the market was inexplicably going the wrong way.

Suddenly, Alex's eye was drawn to a scuffle in the opposite corner and she saw the managing director's secretary hit one of the dealers in the face. It had not been planned, but her fist was closed and it was bone that smashed into his face, not the flat of her hand. She saw him take a step forward, his own fists instinctively clenching.

'Jason!' she shouted warningly. He turned to look at her then sat back down, scowling. Louise smiled at her in gratitude but Alex could not bring herself to acknowledge it. If Louise was so bloody touchy she should stay out of the dealing room. On a day like this, with the dealers prowling around looking for trouble, she had no sympathy for the girls from the back office who wandered in looking for a chat. They should be able to read the signals. They were certainly clear enough today.

She looked down at her papers but immediately picked up the sound of another dispute behind her. Two dealers were leaning over from their central bank of desks to watch the spectacle and the whole room had somehow shifted into a different pattern, one movement in a complicated formation routine.

She saw Larry, the analyst, lean suggestively towards Marcus, then watched as he bounced his index finger off his thumb and flicked it against Marcus's pale forehead, another sharp painful meeting of bone on bone, the taut skin on Marcus's forehead instantly showing a red tattoo.

She knew she should have intervened, but she recognized that there was something irritatingly precise about Marcus; the way his tailored shirt tucked into the perfect girdle of his waistband, neatly secured by a discreet little buckle. Nanny's clean little boy.

He was a bully and she was inclined to leave Larry to it. In addition, the dynamics of the dealing room on a day like this were immutable.

'Alex! What about this bloody position?'

Alex immediately turned back to her assistant. Libby rarely raised her voice. Another warning bell, another signal.

Obediently, she dialled The Kid's number.

'Hi, it's Alex. Copper's down. I don't know what's behind the move but it looks shaky.' As she spoke she watched the price dip on the screen to $1880. The copper dealer sat back in his chair, shaking his head.

'What's my position?' The Kid asked.

'You're long four hundred lots. Showing a loss of around $300,000 at the moment.'

'What do you think?'

Alex had two seconds to come down on one side or the other. $1875. She was paid to make this kind of decision, but nonetheless she hesitated. This was The Kid and this was a lot of money. Last year, The Kid had paid Wellington over $7 million in commission – as big as all her other customers put together. She was the company's biggest earner, but it was a precarious position with so much riding on one customer.

Her heart beat fast and strong, and she was aware of an unusual pulse in her throat. She looked round and saw one of her colleagues yelling an order to the dealer, his face almost purple, his eyes bulging as he strained to be heard. He was leaning over the desk with the phone held in his hand behind him, a pose which suddenly reminded her of a sprinter's position in the photo finish of a disputed race – chest forward, arms back, lungs bursting in a mad second of fury. Two more beats of her heart like small explosions. Then she registered that the noise level was exceptionally high, everyone yelling, strident angry voices. Why?

18

Jesus. She could read the signs. Something *was* going to happen.

'Dump it. Close out now,' she said into the phone.

'Do it,' answered The Kid.

Alex threw down the phone. 'Vinnie!' she screamed over the competing orders and instructions. The dealer turned to face her. Heaven help those whose voices didn't carry. 'Sell four hundred at market. The Kid wants out.'

Copper and aluminium were traded in 'lots' of 25 tonnes and this was a substantial order, the final straw for Vinnie, whose demeanour showed her clearly that he was losing money. His grip tightened on the phone in his hand and Alex braced her feet against the desk, easing the chair backwards, away from him. In a sudden surge of fury Vinnie smashed the handset against the top of the desk, breaking it into twenty pieces.

'That bastard! Had my eyes out to get into that position, screwing me again now.'

$1860. Something had gone badly wrong. Alex shut her eyes and listened to the noise.

Fear, tension, anger. And not a buyer in sight. Somebody knew something she didn't. The loss on The Kid's position was ticking up like a taxi meter and Alex despaired.

'Answer those phones!' she shouted. In exasperation she picked up one of the flashing lights on her section of the board.

'Wellington.'

'Alex? It's me. What do you make of all this?'

'I don't make anything of it!' she snapped irritably. 'What do you want, Sol?'

19

'Aha! Caught you the wrong way round, did it? Well, let's see. I do happen to have some information, but I'm not sure it's ethical to discuss it. And I know how concerned you are about ethics.'

'What the hell is it? Hurry up.' The price was now $1850 and she could hear Vinnie's voice above the others. He had clearly not finished selling for The Kid. Sol laughed, and if he had been sitting beside her Alex would have slapped him.

'What's it worth?'

'Whatever you want, but make it quick.'

'Whatever? Anything at all?'

$1840. Her temper flared. 'For God's sake, Sol, this is important! I have a position out there and I need to know what's going on.'

'All right. But listen, this is really hot. Not a word or I'm dead. There's a press release around. Embargoed till five.' Alex looked at her watch. Twelve minutes to go.

'What is it?'

'You don't really want me to tell you that, do you? That would be collusion. But here's what I want you to do. Buy me a hundred lots of tin at market.'

Alex stood up, sending a fifty-page computer printout cascading to the floor.

Libby's composure snapped. 'Get that out of my way.' She swept at the mess, then gathered the reams of paper up into her arms and flung them back towards Alex. The concertina unfurled even more, creating a bigger volume of crumpled, useless data.

Oblivious, Alex cupped her hand round the

20

phone, desperate for a measure of confidentiality. 'You want to buy tin? Why?' She could sense the interest among the other brokers; the general hum of conversation had dipped a little as they strained to hear what she was saying.

'Just do what I say. Go to it. And if you're long of copper God help you.'

He put down the phone, leaving her with no choice but to shout his order over to the tin dealer. She heard the words pass round the room like a bizarre Chinese whisper. *Alex is buying tin.*

'What's Sol up to?' Libby asked.

'No idea. Says there's to be a press release at five but won't tell me what it is. I don't really want to know either. He's been reading documents upside down on someone's desk again.'

Anxiously, Alex turned back to the copper dealer. 'Have you filled The Kid's order yet?'

'No, I can't get in. Kerridge is selling ahead of me, dumping a bundle . . .'

'Listen to me, Vinnie,' she said carefully. 'I want him out. *Now.*'

The dealer looked at her uneasily. The combination of Alex in full throat with the financial muscle of The Kid behind her was daunting. Alex glanced at her watch. What if they couldn't close the position before the announcement? God help you . . . Sol had said. Now *she* felt the fear. Damn Kerridge, selling ahead of her. Could they have known? Surely not. Not Kerridge. What were they up to?

She could do nothing but wait and watch Vinnie, his aggressive gestures stamping out the deals, his voice strangled with rage when he wanted nothing more than to scream mindless obscenities. And he had to be cool. If the market knew he was a seller they would back off. At the very time his instincts were telling him to jump ship, he had to restrain himself.

He was overweight, but still young enough to be called chubby. Under stress, his high colour made him look as if he had been hiking in Scotland. Like most of the dealers, Vinnie had come suddenly and unexpectedly into a lot of money. His clothes were cheap but he wore three gold rings on each hand – one a massive gold sovereign in an ornate setting. On one wrist was a thin copper bracelet his mother insisted he wore, on the other a heavy gold chain. He ran his hand over his blond crewcut, aware of Alex behind him, watching him like a hawk.

With a few keystrokes Alex conjured up a copper chart on her screen. She examined it closely, smoothing out the jagged pattern, looking for the trend. Having formed a perfect alpine horizon, rising and falling rhythmically, the copper price suddenly plunged far below the previous ground level and appeared to be suspended in a void. How far could it fall? Alex went further back in time, a five-year chart now. Again she drew a line from previous lows, joining them up like a child's dot-to-dot. She had found a floor. Every time the price had fallen to this line it had bounced. She instructed the computer to extend the line into the future. Where was the floor now?

$1750. That was where the copper price would find support, she reasoned, and where a buyer, looking at the chart, would put in his order.

'Libby. Look at this. Support at $1750. It'll hold. The fundamentals are good ... Jesus. If we can get it down there the funds will come in and buy it ... It'll take off.'

Libby leaned over, her expression sceptical. Her dark wavy hair fell over her face as she examined the chart, running her finger over the screen as if she were reading braille. It was a slow, elegant movement. Alex watched her perfectly manicured nail skim over the figures and felt her impatience grow.

Finally Libby sat back. 'Down to $1750? And what if the funds don't come in? There's a black hole out there.'

'I know, I know,' Alex insisted. 'It's a risky idea. Smash it into the ground like a tennis ball and hope it bounces.'

'Or you never see your ball again.'

Alex gestured at the screen. 'If you were a fund manager and you looked at this chart, you couldn't help yourself. Moving averages, stochastics, the lot. Every one a buy signal.' Alex knew how the analysts pored over the charts, using them to understand investor psychology and be one step ahead of the next big move. Technical analysis, they called it. They used increasingly sophisticated mathematical formulae to monitor the movements and momentum of the market, to the extent that their predictions were now self-fulfilling. It didn't matter whether there really *was* support at $1750, what mattered was that the big fund managers *thought* there was and piled in to buy.

Alex hated the charts. Supply and demand dictated market moves, nothing else. She considered technical analysis to be on a par with reading tealeaves and the whole question of studying charts, which had started as a humble adjunct to traditional analysis, had become a pseudo-science which took itself too seriously.

But even those who sneered at the practice of chart-watching could no longer afford to ignore it. The US Funds in particular were easily big enough to push the market anywhere they wanted.

Libby leant over and put a restraining hand on Alex's arm. 'You may be right. But you haven't got time for this kind of thing. Just get out.'

'I'm not sure. If we don't close that position by five we're dead. And the way Vinnie's going I'll still be long at Christmas. I need those buyers, Libby. If we square up now The Kid'll lose a million.'

At five to five Alex could bear it no longer. She vaulted over her desk and up on to Vinnie's, snatching the sheet of paper holding the tally of his deals.

'Give me that!' He reached for the list.

'You've only sold half of it! Get a move on!'

'For fuck's sake, I can't. Look at the phones ringing – they're all fucking sellers. Get out of my way, Alex, let me do my job . . .'

'If you can't do it, *I* will. Mark it down. There are buyers below the market.' She looked at the price. $1830.

'Look, I'm doing it slowly. Don't want to scare off what buyers there are—'

Suddenly Alex was on her feet on his desk, holding his sheet in her hand like a weapon, threatening the other brokers.

'I'll sell at $1800!' she yelled, her voice carrying clear as a bell across the room. There was a pause. It was a bold gesture: either the market would collapse or she would flush out some buyers. But she had three minutes to go and nothing to lose. She heard her words echoed by the brokers into the phones, but there was no answering bid. The offer had fallen flat.

'At eighty I'll sell!' She swung round, addressing the whole room. Beside her Vinnie smirked. She was pushing the market down against herself. He folded his arms and waited. Alex felt a moment of cold fear. She knew that Neville Douglas, her boss, would be watching from the safety of his glass-panelled office. The dealing room fell quiet as the brokers waited for the next move in the expensive game of chicken she had created.

Alex swallowed. She'd have to go lower. Then admit one massive, costly defeat.

'At sixty,' she said, her voice quiet, challenging the marketplace. Vinnie turned his back on her in contempt. Alex looked around. No-one showed any interest. The silence was eerie.

She shivered. Nobody would buy now that they had seen her fear. Now she *would* lose The Kid's account. What had been an understandable misfortune – caught on the wrong side on a freak day, a random, acceptable happening in such an intrinsically risky business – had now careered out of control because she had decided to

25

take charge. She had tried to call the shots.

Alex looked behind her. In the glass cage at the back of the dealing room the bulky silhouette of her boss began to move towards the door. This was the kind of performance he abhorred. Neville examined every day's commission figures minutely, wanting a written explanation for every decrease. Yet he expected her to maintain her excellent results without showing any deviation from the slow, staid working patterns which had become the Wellington trademark. Thorough research, intelligent comment. Great in the days of the old school tie, but that didn't bring business in any more. Coming from the comfort of the Treasury department, Neville had no idea how difficult it was to compete with the American investment houses who wooed Alex's customers with commission rates pitched so low they could not possibly make money. But they were prepared to undercut her – and lose a fortune – to make inroads into her market. For them it was just another terrain – cocoa, coffee, oil, metals. It was all the same to them. Part of some distant corporate strategy.

Neville believed that if you worked hard you brought in business. If the figures were poor there was only one explanation. Alex felt her muscles tense as she remembered his performance as he drew his finger slowly down last month's commissions. Feigned surprise at the figure by her name, mock exhaustion as he leant back in his chair. Oh, Alex, what happened?

She looked at the door to his office. In a matter of seconds he'd be in the dealing room. He'd have her off the desk in a shot and would probably suspend her this time.

Suddenly the nervous voice of Vinnie's clerk piped up. 'Um ... the Kerridge guy says he can take some at fifty.'

Alex grinned. At least she'd been right about him. Kerridge had been having a quick punt. He didn't know about the press release, otherwise he'd be waiting. He'd sold all the way down and now he was taking his profits, buying back to close the position before 5 o'clock while there was still some liquidity in the market. Maybe he'd had a sniff of something ... maybe it was coincidence, but he'd shown his hand now. This would tempt in the other buyers.

The market stopped its freefall and gradually the noise level picked up. $1770 traded, then $1780, then straight up to $1830. The bounce.

Now the noise was what it should have been, the greedy, grabbing noise of brokers trying to generate commission, the quick-tempered answers from the dealers, the buyers suddenly clamouring to get in before it was too late. Pressure, but positive, money-making pressure this time.

Alex closed The Kid's position then jumped down and handed the dealer his sheet with a broad smile.

'Well done, Vinnie. Thanks.'

'My pleasure, Alex,' he answered and, in the way of dealing room disputes, the matter was closed. Alex took a quick look at Neville's office. The door remained closed.

Libby began to fill in deal tickets. 'Oscar-winning performance,' she observed dryly without looking up. 'You're damn lucky.'

Alex took a deep breath, her heart still pounding. Her shirt was suddenly uncomfortably tight and she pulled the silk away from her hot skin. Her hair had escaped from the tight chignon she wore and she tucked two loose strands behind her ears. 'Remind me never to have port after lunch again. How did we end up?'

The Kid had closed his long position with a $600,000 loss. At least he was a good loser. Alex had no worries on that score. And since his net worth was approximately $600 million, she had no doubts that he could afford to pay up.

She sat back and waited for the announcement, drumming her fingers on the desk. Now that she'd closed the position she had time to reflect. What if Sol were wrong ... or she'd misheard? Two seconds of quick-fire conversation while her mind was in turmoil followed by a $600,000 loss for her biggest customer. What if Sol had misunderstood? She gazed at the screen until the figures blurred.

At three minutes past five the Reuters alarm buzzed and the headline flashed in eye-catching red. Immediately the dealing room was silent, bar one angry voice telling a junior to shut up.

INTERNATIONAL CABLE COMMUNICATIONS (ICC) HAS ANNOUNCED ITS INTENTION TO IMPLEMENT A COMPLETE SWITCH FROM COPPER WIRE TO FIBRE OPTICS BY THE YEAR END. MANAGING DIRECTOR, PARKER GREENE, SAID THIS MOVE WAS A FURTHER INDICATION OF THE COMPANY'S ONGOING

The dealing room exploded in noise as brokers called their customers and competitors called to take early advantage of the news. $1790 traded, then, as if in a void, it continued to fall. Alex smiled. What did the charts say now? She typed in the new parameters and asked for the next support level where the price could be expected to stabilize. The answer flashed back at her a second later. $1640. So what had happened to the support at $1750? Washed away in a tide of fundamentals. She sat back, jubilant.

'Look at this,' Libby said without taking her eyes from the screen. 'He's done it again. Read the rest of it.'

MR GREENE ALSO ANNOUNCED THE EXPANSION OF THE COMPANY'S SOLDER DIVISION IN MONTREAL, WHICH RECENTLY SIGNED A JOINT VENTURE WITH FUJITSU OF JAPAN FOR THEIR NEW RANGE OF DOMESTIC APPLIANCES . . .

Alex's eyes jumped from the copper price to the tin price. $100 up. All that tin needed for the solder . . . She smiled and watched the pandemonium, relaxed now.

Someone yelled over that she had a call and she knew it would be him, ringing to crow.

'Hello?'

'Seen the tin price?'

'Yes, Sol, I have. Well done. Do you want me to close your position and take your profit, or are you going to stay long?'

'Close half this evening and half tomorrow. Listen, this makes the Sinco deal really sweet. Why don't you call them?'

'Tomorrow.'

'Well, I'm going to call Gabriel and see how he's feeling. Now then, if I remember rightly you promised me anything I wanted in return for the information. Dinner tonight to begin the negotiations.'

Alex agreed. 'But not if you're going to spend the whole evening telling me how clever you are. It didn't take a genius to see the tin angle. If I'd seen the press release I'd have done the same thing.'

'Oh, would you?' he asked. 'And what else would you have done to demonstrate truly creative financial ability?'

Alex racked her brains, going back over the wording of the press release. They had been sparring for years and she hated it when he scored points at her expense.

'OK,' she conceded. 'I don't know. What else did you do?'

'Bought shares in Downer Blythe. They manufacture fibre optic cable,' he announced, insufferably pleased with himself. 'They're fifty cents up already. I'll see you at La Poule au Pot at eight.'

'Bye.'

Livid, Alex filled Libby in on their conversation and together they tidied up for the day. Finally, they added up the commission they had made: $80,000.

They left at six, colliding with the copper dealer at the lift.

30

'How did you end up, Vinnie?' Alex asked.

'Not bad,' he answered. 'How does that bloke Sol know what's going on? That's about the third time this year he's had inside information. Just happened to be in the ICC boardroom, right? Jammy bastard.'

Alex picked her car up from the underground car park, drove quickly to her flat and went straight into the bathroom to run a bath. She clicked on the answering machine then got into the bath, her mind on the next day's trading opportunities.

The first message was from The Kid. Alex had been unable to get hold of him earlier and had asked his secretary to track him down and tell him what had happened.

'Alex,' the message said. 'Good work. I'll call you tomorrow. Buy some copper on the bounce if it looks good.'

He knew that the market was unlikely to fall further now that the ICC news was known, and the next thing would be a 'correction', a move up as today's sellers bought back to close their positions. Sometimes it was worth buying to piggyback with this, sometimes it was not. Alex lay back to contemplate the market, her feet propped between the taps. She slid further down into the water, thinking again how pleasant it would be to have a free-standing, claw-footed bath, an old one, long enough to accommodate all of her 5'10" frame.

She pulled her mass of blond hair into a knot on top of her head, then wound a towel round it. If there was one thing she hated it was women –

or men – who played with their hair, tossing a handful from one side to the other, leaving it in precarious positions from which it would fall, slowly and irritatingly, back into place. It annoyed the hell out of her. She clapped her hands against the towel. If it got too damp it would be a mass of unruly corkscrews.

She got out of the bath and replayed the other messages on her answering machine.

Each one had the same sense of urgency – even her friends outside the business knew they had a matter of seconds to catch her attention as Alex ran into or out of the flat. The message she had hastily recorded and never got round to changing gave them an indication of her attitude to answering machines.

'This is Alexandra Brookes. Please speak after the tone.'

Sometimes she wondered what had happened to her attention span. She had had one once.

She had done well at school and had gone on to university where she gained an upper second in politics and philosophy. After graduation, she considered several options, mostly with banks. But one company appealed to her, a company with the rare combination of tradition and aggression. The interviews were challenging and she joined Wellington Trading, member of the London Metal Exchange, three months after graduation.

One Monday morning in her second year she arrived at the office at the usual time and was surprised to find the dealing room almost empty. For a moment she wondered if it was a bank holiday. The managing director, Andrew Everington, had appeared behind her, beaming.

'Ah, Alex. A safe pair of hands at last.'

'What's going on?' she asked.

'Buggered off, the lot of them. Called me at home at ten last night. Pissed as farts, of course.'

'What, the whole team? Everyone? Everyone except me?'

'No no, we have a very competent skeleton staff left. And of course I'll pitch in. Come on, Alex, let's get going.'

Alex took off her coat and got to work. It was quite common for whole teams to move from one company to a rival, and in spite of her initial reaction Alex recognized that it offered her a great opportunity. She was now one of the longest-serving members of staff.

Andrew invited her to lunch at the Savoy. It was routine; every remaining member of staff received some encouragement from the management. Alex, the junior, got lunch at the managing director's favourite restaurant.

She had been expecting magnificence, but the reception area to the hotel was surprisingly dingy. There was a certain *gravitas* in the wood panelling and dark, muted colours of the carpet, but the art deco style made it as insubstantial as a film set and Alex stood in the middle of the lobby, disappointed. She could appreciate the smaller details, like the fluid, carved ironwork on the staircase and the gold pediments of the marbleized pillars, but the whole scene was flat. While time had mellowed some London hotels into dignity and solidity, it had made the

Savoy dusty and bland, with all the charm of an institution.

In the River Room Alex ordered an orange juice and sat back to wait.

Andrew was close to retirement then, a big, loud, confident man, one of the last of the military clique that ran the commodities markets after the war. He sat down heavily next to Alex and rearranged himself, tucking in his shirt, straightening his tie, then ordered a large gin and tonic.

'Well now, Alex. A bit unsettling, all this movement. Hope it hasn't upset you too much.'

'Not at all. But how are you going to replace them?'

'Already done. Just bought the team from Tring. Don't tell anyone yet, though, they haven't resigned.'

'But what will Tring do?'

'Buy someone else's team, I suppose. Standard practice.'

'You'll miss them, won't you? You worked with Bob for over twenty years.'

'Yes, but I've known Neville from Tring for nearly thirty years. Worked at Tring myself until I left to set up Wellington Futures. Now, what shall we have to eat?'

Alex picked up her menu. 'What a small world,' she observed. 'You all seem to know one another.'

'In the RAF you know ...' His voice tailed off. Alex could sense that he was searching for some common ground between them. She studied the menu, refusing to help him out.

'Well, Alex. You're one of us now.' He rallied. 'And we're damn glad to have you.'

'In spite of the fact that I don't know Billy and Joseph and Buffy and Rollo?'

Andrew was clearly discomfited. He'd miscalculated this little number.

'Now look, Alex. You're very good at what you do. Doesn't matter that you don't know these old coots. And you have a great future with Wellington. We'll do everything we can to help you get ahead. Here's what I suggest. Ten grand a year raise, a car and ...' he looked at her expressionless face, '... and travel. Would you like to travel? Pop over and see the boys in the Frankfurt office?'

'I'd like to go to the Metal Bulletin nickel conference.'

'Well, that doesn't sound like a lot of fun, but yes, that's fine.'

'It's in Warsaw.'

Andrew sighed. 'Fine, Alex, fine. Whatever. And I suppose you'd like a grilled sole and salad for lunch?'

'Not at all.' She'd made him suffer enough. She leaned towards him, smiling broadly. 'I want foie gras and a filet mignon, please. Rare. And a bottle of bloody good red wine.'

As part of her promotion, Andrew put Alex in charge of some bigger accounts. Sol Bergman was already an institution by then and one of Wellington's most profitable clients. He was a qualified lawyer, from a family of lawyers, when he joined a New York investment bank. Initially he had worked in trade finance and, instead of

35

moving around the bank to experience its different functions, he forged his way down the first path he had been shown. He became responsible for copper at Hartman, the giant trading house in New York, then moved to London, where his approach to business – wild, imaginative and distinctly intellectual – contrasted with the disciplined number-crunching with which Alex was familiar.

As a team they worked well. Alex was so green; all she could offer him was her total dedication. She arrived early in the morning and tracked him down all over the world to keep him in touch with prices. One whole page of her address book was dedicated to Sol: the golf club, his parents' house, his flat in the south of France, and Alex spent her day trying to anticipate his questions, trying to watch the market with his eyes. Her excellent training was continuing.

They were an odd couple – the quick-witted New York Jewish trader and the middle-class English philosophy graduate. There was humour in her oval face – good-looking as she was, she was accessible. Sol was a closed book, his dark jowls and black hair giving him a saturnine malevolence he liked to cultivate. Beauty and the Beast, a colleague had once observed, and Sol had played up to it from then on, slouching beside Alex, his permanent irritation with the fools who surrounded him etched on his face, his only other facial expressions those of incredulity and boredom.

Alex and Sol spoke most of the day on the phone, had lunch together twice a week and frequently drinks after work. Alex was sharing a flat near Sloane Square with three other girls, Sol was living in a mansion in Richmond which Alex never saw. He dropped her occasionally at her flat but never came in. He was a terrible snob and Alex knew he would probably hate everything about the building she lived in – the shared hallway with the bikes and the piles of unclaimed junk mail. The flat itself was not bad. Alex thought her attic bedroom had a rustic charm, but she knew Sol's middle-class Manhattan upbringing and college education had not led him through a Bohemian phase and he would have no time for it. It was years until Alex had the confidence to retaliate and mock his penchant for the new and expensive, calling him a philistine who had no culture and whose taste was controlled by the latest issue of the most pretentious art magazine on the market.

In the early days Sol and Alex would leave for lunch and would still be sitting in the dark cellar bar they had nicknamed the Tomb, drinking port and hatching plans, four hours later. Sol was machiavellian in the extreme. Only one in twenty of his plans ever came to anything but he and Alex would sit and he would explain them all to her, then ask her why they wouldn't work. By the time Alex had asked all her questions and he had explained, it had usually become clear to him where the flaw lay. That was her job, to go over the deal painstakingly, giving him 'what ifs'. Alex had had a good grounding by then and the questions she asked were intelligent. Having a degree was of no practical value in the City; if anything there was an anti-academic bias, and Alex herself was never convinced that her university education had improved her in any significant way. Looking back, however, she felt that she was analytical and questioning and that these were rare attributes in a business that was largely instinctive.

They became inseparable; they worked together, travelled together and, in time, slept together. The first time was in Atlanta. They had been to visit a factory and had found themselves with only one hotel room between them. Sol considered finding another hotel, but it was late and the available room had two beds. So they ordered hamburgers, Alex put on her pyjamas, he put on the television and they settled down. At one o'clock Alex made her way into the bathroom to clean her teeth.

'What time's the flight tomorrow?' she called out. There was no answer. She peered round the doorway and saw Sol apparently fast asleep.

'Up!' she called from the doorway. 'I can't sleep in the bed next to the door. Move!' He opened an eye and squinted at her. Alex expected a retort but none came. He continued to look at her as she slouched against the door.

'What is it?' Alex asked.

'You, standing there, with the light behind you . . . You know your pyjamas are transparent?'

She could have reacted in any number of ways. But she just stood there, watching Sol watching her. She could imagine what he saw: the cream silk clinging to the length of her thighs, moulding the tops of her legs and her stomach, the loose neckline exposing half of one of her breasts as she leant against the door, a tangle of blond curls in her eyes. A long crystal drop earring hung from one ear and there were smudges around her eyes. In a moment of voyeurism she shared that sight with him and began to fulfil what she knew without a shadow of a doubt he wanted. She crossed her arms and lifted the silk top over her head, allowing it to drop to the floor without taking her eyes from Sol's. She stood for a moment before moving her hands to her breasts, touching them in exactly the way she knew Sol would. She eased the bottoms off and, without thinking, rubbed the soft fabric slowly against her face, then her neck, her breasts, her stomach.

Sol had not moved and Alex knew that she could do anything she wanted. She had read that many women secretly long to be a stripper or a tart once in their lives; to know what it's like to be so openly and publicly desired and to be paid for that desirability. Alex made her way slowly over to Sol, who opened his arms, a half-smile on his face. She straddled him and reached her arms out, linking her fingers with his, leaning on him. He tensed, suspecting that the audacity of her performance would carry on in bed and suddenly realizing he was in a very vulnerable position. His smile faded. Alex was, after all, taller than he was and probably stronger.

She wrapped her legs under his knees, her weight on her pelvis and hands. In a second he was pinned to the bed. She kissed him like a man, her mouth weighing down on his, forcing the direction and the pace. Sol's response was lukewarm, neither resistant nor compliant. Alex could feel his discomfort but also the trepidation, the suspicion that he might find the experience extremely exciting. He pushed against her, testing, but could not move her at all. Alex felt the slight tremble of his hands.

She looked along her arms at the taut, tanned muscles and felt an unusual thrill of power. She could do what she liked with him. She began to move slowly on top of him, keeping most of her weight on her hands, gently rotating her hips. This is what it was like to be a man, she thought, to be in control. She dug more deeply and the movement of her hips became faster. Again, Sol tensed underneath her, then, after a moment, he responded, moving in unison with her. Alex found herself enjoying the shared rhythm.

'Now,' she ordered, rolling over. 'Make love to me.'

As soon as she released him he took hold of her, knocking the breath from her. She understood. He tore his clothes off and was on top of her in a second, his hands on her shoulders, his mouth now on hers, pushing into her. They made love roughly, building to a desperate climax which was almost a struggle between them, a competition, as if only one of them could enjoy it.

Afterwards they lay in half-sleep, just touching. Alex rolled onto her side and looked at his face. She had just committed the most intimate act, yet his body was completely unknown to her. She ran her hand over his chest, feeling the soft hair.

'God!' Sol turned to face her, feigning surprise. 'Alex! It's you. I fell asleep and I thought . . .'

She smiled lazily. 'You couldn't believe your luck and you thought you must be dreaming. I know. I *am* too damn good to be true.'

The rest of the night passed in easy camaraderie and the following morning Alex found it natural to link her arm in his as they stood at Reception waiting to pay the bill. Sol squeezed her arm in acknowledgement and she smiled to herself.

Alex ordered a cab before dressing but the traffic was heavy and she arrived at their favourite Pimlico restaurant a couple of minutes late.

'Sorry, sorry.' She slid into her seat. 'I know you hate it when I'm late and I have no excuse.'

He leant over and kissed her. 'Gave me a chance to work out how much money I made today.'

'You said you wouldn't do this.'

'Hell, let me gloat for a couple of minutes. Such a textbook case. So damn easy . . .'

'Never mind all that. Tell me about Gabriel and Sinco.'

'Ah, yes . . .'

When Alex heard his hesitation she bristled. She knew she was about to hear something appalling. And of all the deals they had done together, he knew this one meant a lot to her.

Three months earlier Alex had been called in by the management of Les Fontaines, the last remaining French tin mine, which had existed since the time of the Phoenicians. The local community had raised money for the miners, who had agreed to work for almost nothing in an

41

area of high unemployment where mining was a part of their history. Alex knew the manager of the mine and had been asked to a meeting which was the last-ditch effort to save them. She had pored over the balance sheet and looked at the tin price, but she was not capable of alchemy; it cost the mine $5500 to produce one tonne of tin and the world price was $5000.

'We need a breathing space and we need working capital,' the manager had explained. 'The reserves are fantastic; we just need to be able to get to them.'

Alex had come back to London and had sat with Wellington's research analyst, Larry. They pulled out every piece of information they could on tin. They sat until two in the morning, checking and cross-checking, drawing charts, until, exhausted, they reached the same conclusion. How could the tin price continue to fall when world production of the raw material, tin concentrate, was falling by 17 per cent every year? Larry pulled up a spreadsheet.

'Look at this, Alex. This is a classic. When a commodity is expensive producers fall over themselves to bring new mines on stream, then, eventually, the fact that there is more of the commodity around means that the price falls. See?'

Alex looked at the chart he had pulled up, correlating the supply of tin with the price.

'I see,' Alex murmured. 'But we're at the opposite end of the cycle. Prices are so low that we're losing production, miners are shutting up shop. So the supply is decreasing and we should see the price turn around soon.'

Larry moved over to another screen. 'This is not science, Alex, but I can simulate the next cycle by assuming that current trends will continue . . .' He tapped a stream of figures into the computer.

Suddenly the chart, which had shown the alarming fall in the tin price, began to hesitate, jaggedly bumping along the bottom before beginning a hesitant move up.

Alex leaned forward. 'When is this, Larry? How long?'

'It's overdue. At a guess I'd say prices will begin to pick up in another three, four months, maybe.'

'Bingo!' She could see it now. The odds were in their favour. She hugged Larry.

'If this comes off . . .'

Alex had gone back to the mine and looked again at the balance sheet. The only remaining asset was a parcel of land, not far from the main town in an area on which a massive DIY warehouse had already been constructed. It had potential. If she could use this one asset to buy time for the mine, she would have achieved her aim. Of course, they could simply sell the land and pay the overheads, but she began to see another possibility.

Sinco was a tin smelter in the Basque area of Spain. While the plant itself had good relationships with all its neighbours, two major contracts had been cancelled when banks had pulled their financing. The banks had explained that they could not continue to have exposure in a part of the country where there was the danger of terrorist action. Sinco was desperate.

Alex put Les Fontaines and Sinco together. Like two patients with the same terminal illness, they struck a deal to guarantee themselves survival for one more year. That was all both wanted. If, after this period, the tin price fell further, Les Fontaines was finished. Sinco had a year to prove to the banks that it was not a target.

Sinco contracted to buy the tin ore Les Fontaines mined, but at a better than break-even price. Les Fontaines gave Sinco title to their land. Alex sat with both parties, discussing ore grades, discounts to the London Metal Exchange price, foreign exchange conversions. The plan was simple and mathematically precise by the time it was signed. Both parties would be able to carry on for a year.

Now, with the day's massive increase in the tin price, Alex knew everyone must be euphoric.

'Gabriel was very happy. Sends you his regards.'

Alex looked at him. Something was wrong. Sol was holding something back.

'What is it?' she probed. 'Am I missing the point? I know this deal is not your usual style; no-one made a million but it was very satisfactory nonetheless.'

'How do you know no-one made a million?'

This was it. Alex sat up. 'What do you mean?'

Sol took her hand. 'Let me go back to the beginning. Sinco called me the day after the original deal was signed. Told me that they had a year to improve their reputation, a year to stay intact before the banks would consider lending money again.'

'Yes, I know all that.'

'Well, it was either success or failure for them. Survival or bankruptcy. And if you're bankrupt, well, that's it.'

'Sol. Get to the point. What did you tell them to do?'

He grinned. 'I told them to take the deeds to the Les Fontaines land, mortgage it and buy tin futures.'

Alex gasped. 'They were supposed to hold onto that land. It was to compensate them for the higher price they'd paid . . .'

'I know, I know. But what good is balancing the books if the books are closed? You're right, of course, they could have paid off a few more debts as they went under, but what the hell. If the tin price had gone down they'd've been finished. I told them that they should try to make the future a little rosier. If they were going to stay in business, wouldn't it be nicer to have a little cash in the bank?'

'Sol, I can't believe you did this. After all my work to balance this deal. It was perfect. Watertight. And you went behind my back and blew a great big hole in it. Why didn't you at least tell me?'

Sol nearly choked on his wine. 'And we would have discussed it rationally? Like hell. You would have been on the first plane to Sinco, breathing fire at them, threatening to get Les Fontaines to pull out. In fact, they begged me not to tell you.'

Alex stared at him, rigid with fury. For a moment she felt like grabbing the tablecloth and yanking it off the table, then slapping Sol hard. A wild aggressive attack to wipe the complacent smile off his face. She dug her nails into the table-cloth.

'You bastard.'

He was summoning the waiter as if the information he had given her was nothing, of no significance. Alex was aware of the quiet buzz of polite conversation that continued around them and was momentarily surprised by the fact that the torrent of pressure building in her mind could not be heard by those discreet, intimate couples sitting near her.

Her mind reeled from the fact that Sol had deceived her and that the smelter had colluded. What a fool they must think her. She had put the whole thing together and then her partner comes in at the last moment and suggests an audacious speculation. She had worked for months on the scheme, done her research, prepared the plans for the board, and Sol had strolled in with an idea of the most simplistic, risky nature. Was it worth it? Why had she bothered?

'But what if the tin price had gone down and not up . . . ?'

'Alex, how many discussions could we have like that? If the zinc price hadn't gone down . . . If the copper price hadn't gone up . . . I played the odds.'

'*You* played the odds, but it wasn't your game. You played with somebody else's money. That kind of decision is easy to make.'

'You should know,' he said casually. 'It's what you do for a living.'

Alex drew in her breath, shocked.

'My advice concerns minimizing risk, not increasing it.'

'Come on, Alex, you're beginning to sound like a textbook. Be honest. You exist to generate commission. You make a dollar on every tonne of business your customers do. Don't try to pretend otherwise.'

'What good is a dollar's commission if I lose a bundle on a bad debt? Do you think I take on just *anybody*? And then encourage them to do just any old trade? You know that makes no commercial sense. If Sinco had been a customer of mine and I had advised them to do what *you* advised them to do, I would have been hauled in front of the Wellington board like lightning. It was incredibly reckless. And even if you think today, with hindsight, that it was a good bet, I'm still not convinced.'

What kind of partnership was this when he felt he could intervene in her plan, completely undermine the rationale of the exercise and thwart her with the collusion of one of the parties? She was furious with both what he had done and his careless admission of it.

'I think it's time we recognized that our approaches to business are not compatible,' she finished.

'I admit I was wrong,' he began, picking up her hand and holding it against his cheek. 'You know how I am, I can't resist the lure of the quick buck. I had to really persuade Sinco, they wanted to stick with your plan . . .'

'So you had to work on them! Why did you do

it? I just don't understand. You had enough deals on your own, why not stick to *them*?'

'Oh, Alex.' His shoulders sagged comically, as if he had exhausted himself with this inner turmoil. 'Your idea was so neat, so precise, I just couldn't resist adding a flourish . . . spicing it up a bit.'

'*Spicing it up?*' she repeated, her voice rising and beginning to attract the attention of the other diners. She looked over her shoulder then composed herself.

'Spice up your own deals,' she snapped.

'I went too far,' Sol conceded, his head to one side. 'I meant to jazz it up but I admit that I almost blew the whole thing. That's why we're such a good team, Alex. I promise I'll never do anything like that again. I need you.'

'In future,' she sighed wearily, 'if we do a deal together, or if you involve me in one of your deals, you do not go behind my back. Do not compromise me. Is that agreed?'

Sol reached over and ran his hand up and down her spine. 'Don't go behind your back? *This* back? This gorgeous back?'

'Sol, leave off. I've forgiven you, but I'm not ready for a *rapprochement* yet.'

'Probably just as well.'

Alex froze. 'What now?'

She looked closely at him, trying to guess the tone of his announcement. But it was so dark in the flickering candlelight that Alex could barely make out where Sol was sitting.

'Sol, for once, just tell me what you have to say.'

He sighed and Alex knew it was bad news.

'I'm going back to New York. Ben wants me to open an office there, primarily to deal with some Brazilian business but also to do some West Coast copper.'

Alex said nothing but she was stunned, both from the anticipation of life without him and that he could consider a move that necessitated leaving London.

'I'm on the main board of Fischer Green now and have sole responsibility for the US. It's too good to pass up, Alex. You understand that.'

'Don't tell me what I understand,' Alex answered quickly. 'In fact I understand something completely different. I understand that you must have been discussing this for quite some time and that you have brought me to dinner tonight for a brief farewell and that you have probably booked your flight already.' Alex looked at him and watched for signs of embarrassment. There were none. In the half-light of the restaurant he was particularly handsome. Dark-skinned, dark-eyed, he was somehow very *male*. Alex knew she could bruise her hand if she stroked his face, yet she longed to do just that. He stared back at her, his eyes unblinking under the annoying fringe of poker-straight, gleaming black hair. She reached out to brush it back then stopped herself.

'I couldn't tell you about it,' he continued quietly. 'You know Ben. Fischer Green is still a private company and he doesn't like his business discussed outside the boardroom.'

The waiter appeared at the table and it was the

49

moment for her to make up her mind. Either she left the restaurant or she ordered and committed herself to another hour at least. She hesitated, then reached out for the menu and ordered a glass of red Sancerre.

They were silent for a couple of minutes, ostensibly studying the menu, but Alex was wondering which way the emotional dice were going to fall. She was aware that she was close to tears, that her face was hot with anger and that she was hurt. Three competing, strong emotions.

'Come and see me every weekend,' Sol continued. 'Or I'll come back to London. We'll see each other all the time. We'll speak every day and we'll still travel. In fact, let's go to Brazil next month.'

'Maybe,' Alex answered. 'But it won't be the same. No more lunches, no more afternoons in the Tomb.'

'Alex, you obviously haven't noticed but it's three weeks since we had lunch together. It's a month since we sat in the Tomb all afternoon. We're all grown up now. We have big jobs, big budgets, we do big deals. You're in charge of fifteen people at Wellington, it's a senior position. You're not an awkward little kid any more.'

'What is this?' she snapped. 'The introduction to "The Ugly Duckling"? Are you about to burst into song?'

He smiled. 'Listen, we see each other once a week now, if that. We're busy people. My being in New York will make virtually no difference. And it's a new challenge. We'll go to Brazil and do this deal. Wait till you hear about it.'

Alex found herself caught up in his description of the deal. Dinner came and went and they left the sensitive subject of his departure alone. Alex gulped down her wine and by the time they left the dice had fallen and the tears were glistening in her eyes.

'Why aren't you upset?' she demanded as he casually paid the bill. 'Aren't you going to miss me?'

'I am,' he answered calmly, his tone irritating her even further.

'This is an important issue, you know. We've been together for years. And New York is not next door. This is ... significant.' She could not envisage her working life without Sol; her whole concept of business was intertwined with an image of him.

'Come on, Alex. You're going to come over and see me, and when you're in London you'll be so busy you'll forget I'm not there.'

'Platitudes.' She was disappointed. 'You sound like a mother talking to her five-year-old on the first day of school. Let's go.'

She sat hunched miserably in the front seat of the car until they reached her house. When they drew up outside he turned off the engine and leant forward, his familiar face now smiling gently. He kissed her softly then drew back, his rough cheek grazing hers.

'Sol!' Alex yelped in pain. 'You're a lethal weapon!'

'Can I come up?' he asked.

She sighed. 'Of course. But I have to know one thing first. When *are* you leaving?'

He frowned as his fingers stroked her cheek slowly. 'Tomorrow.'

'You bastard,' she said quietly. 'And how long have you known?'

'Not long, Alex, it all came up kind of suddenly.'

'Uh, huh. Well, bon voyage, Sol. Thanks for dinner.' She got out of the car and slammed the door. Sol clambered out of the driver's seat and leant on the roof.

'Alex, I would have told you earlier if I could have, but Ben—'

'I know,' Alex interrupted. 'I know what Ben's like. But your relationship with me is as important. You've respected Ben's way of doing things at my expense. You know you could have trusted me. I should have known . . . You should have told me.' She knew how strange Ben was and it was plausible that he would have sprung this on Sol. The timing of the Brazilian deal was nothing to do with him but she nonetheless suspected Sol's silence had been as much the result of negligence as of confidentiality.

'I guess you won't be taking me to the airport, then.' He smiled and straightened. 'I'm sorry. I had no choice. Maybe I could have done things differently but . . . well, I gave Ben my word.' He reopened the car door. 'Take care.'

He drove off and Alex stood for a moment outside the house, shivering slightly. She watched the car disappear, then turned into the house.

He was gone.

In one evening he had thrown her emotions around as if they had no significance, then, in that infuriating, jaunty manner, had announced that he was leaving her. New York was a great opportunity for him and he had assumed she would share in his enthusiasm. This was what Alex found so totally unacceptable, that he expected her to suspend her attachment to him, to rejoice in his success and celebrate his departure. Why was he going? Was this an indication of his lack of commitment to their relationship? She had had no warning of this and began to trawl through the memories of their last weeks together looking for signs that he was losing interest in her. She drew a great breath, hoping to find some equanimity. Her body suddenly felt leaden.

The door was about to shut behind her when she heard the car brakes and she knew that he had stopped abruptly around the corner. Quickly, she reached for the door, trapping her fingers as it swung heavily back into place.

She winced. Was this the apology, finally? Or yet another announcement? She could see him walking slowly back to the corner of Draycott Place, jiggling the car keys in his hand.

He stopped at the bottom step and grinned up at her. 'Forgot to give you one piece of really great news. Went right out of my mind. A compensation for all this grief.'

'Well?'

'Ben knows this guy in Chicago, Bartling. Big copper book. Wants to talk to someone on the LME. I gave him your name. He's expecting your call.'

Alex shook her head slowly. For a second she

considered telling him how she really felt. But one look at his exuberant face silenced her. He wouldn't be able to understand that she could be depressed at a time of such great opportunity. Blowing on her bruised fingers, she trudged back up the steps and let the door crash into place behind her.

In spite of herself, she thought about Bartling. Neville would be pleased with an account like that. Get him off her back for a while. Another major account down to Sol. And then what? How much new business would she be able to generate on her own? She stopped. Her concern for her future was a genuine one; the competition was making the game tougher and tougher, but had she, like Sol, mingled her personal and professional feelings? Was her sadness partially driven by economic force and the regret that a successful business partnership had come to an end? If so, it was the height of hypocrisy to resent Sol's delight in leaving.

As she made a cup of strong black coffee she calculated the commission from the Brazilian brass deal he had described. It was an extremely long shot, but if it paid off it would be a massive coup. And if not? She'd lost two good customers to the competition and had a couple of very bad months. Neville was breathing down her neck, making it clear that he expected her to turn the tide. She sipped the coffee.

She could be facing a major problem.

In his Mayfair office, Professor Vichevsky snatched up the phone to his assistant. 'Arkady, get me Kartchak.'

He waited, drumming his fingers nervously on the desk. There was no doubt in his mind that Kartchak was doing well; he was a true opportunist who had lived very comfortably in the Soviet era and would continue to flourish under the new regime. But there was something about his manner – and his appearance – that Vichevsky found particularly unsettling. Something beyond the overt threats and the suppressed aggression. Something unhealthy.

Before the end of communism Kartchak had been an army officer, an occasional neighbour of Vichevsky's in the shabby muscovite housing estate. Now he lived in glorious splendour in a fortified flat next to the Palace Hotel in central Moscow.

Kartchak's temper and his taciturn nature had proved ideally suited to his main business of running a team of contract killers. His was one of the first 'new Russian' businesses to employ a Western accountant, since he was aware of the fundamental flaws in his bookkeeping – fifty per cent of the hits his men achieved had to be followed up by the execution of the original client for refusing to pay. Kartchak had to pay his workers twice and still collected nothing, although some of his boys would do the follow-up for nothing.

The first kill would be straightforward, but for the second they took their time. With a small-calibre pistol, a .22 or .32, they would work up from the ankles, the knees, through the pelvis, to the wrists, elbows and shoulders. They knew both where the most painful points were, and the points of irrational psychological vulnerability – not just the genitals but the armpits and insteps as well. The best shot was often the first, when the cold muzzle of the pistol was gently warmed against the skin on the sole of the victim's foot.

Kartchak implemented a commission scheme, passing on the responsibility for collecting payment to the men themselves. In return he insured their families and guaranteed support in the event of the employee's death.

Soon Kartchak had Russia's best killers on his books, ex-army officers who were both professional and detached and for whom the army was no longer a viable employer. For the first few months he made a fortune. But then the competition appeared, gangs of Chechen and Georgian warriors who fought for pleasure and killed each other as often as they killed for money. The army officers were lured away by long-term contracts as security experts with Western corporations, and Kartchak had to take what he could get. For a while he depended on Fyodor, an ambidextrous Siberian who could shoot with both hands.

Vichevsky heard a click on the line and Kartchak's abrupt 'Yes.'

'Hello! This is your faithful research assistant here with the information you asked for on oil refining.' He hoped he'd done enough research.

'Not now, Vichevsky!' Kartchak snapped. 'Things in Moscow are deteriorating. The Chechen are ruining my business and every male over the age of fifteen thinks he can be a contract killer. The Western companies go for big names they recognize, but these companies cannot operate in Russia.'

'But your other businesses? They're good, aren't they?'

'Fine,' Kartchak answered wearily, 'but the contracts – they were my mainstay. Low overheads, good cash flow, you know?' Having learned about accounting he used the jargon with ease. He spoke no English but used economic terms in English since no Russian equivalent existed, although his accent often made them unintelligible to Vichevsky. 'Nowadays I can't keep the men with me and I can't guarantee a result. What do you expect of a contract killer in Russia? I have guys who can slide an Uzi from under their coats without wrinkling the backs of their cashmere jackets, kill a man, and from the back look like they're fucking ballet dancers. Pirouette. Gone. Then I send other guys, so-called professionals, who screw up badly, lash out, miss. Victims run away dripping blood over old ladies, pulling them down as they go. Goddamn mess. Happened last week, just off the Arbat. This woman, hysterical, went for my guy and managed to get the knife from his hand and she's waving it around, screaming . . .'

Vichevsky shuddered. He had never shown any interest in this aspect of Kartchak's business yet Kartchak insisted on talking about it in repulsively calm terms as if he were discussing grocery deliveries. Vichevsky didn't like the implied collusion.

'. . . and she manages to stab him in the eye. So now she's still got the knife and he can't see anything.'

'Terrible. But about the oil and gas . . . Are you still interested? Do you need me to speak to my people here?'

There was a pause and then, 'Soon. I'll call you when I need you. Roman hasn't come back from Tashkent with the report yet.'

'Well, just call me,' Vichevsky said brightly. 'Banks, brokers, I have contacts. Just tell me when and I'll set up the whole thing for you.'

'I said I'd let you know!' Kartchak snapped.

'Fine. I thought I'd mention it because I'm rather busy at the moment. I'm doing some metal business . . .'

'Are you? What, precisely?'

Vichevsky had not expected such a forceful expression of interest. He knew almost nothing about metal, other than what he had heard on a radio report about falling copper prices. Something about cables. 'The usual. Couple of plants . . . exporting, raw materials . . .'

'You?' Kartchak laughed. 'But this is big business. You have that kind of money?'

'I don't need it. There are banks for that kind of thing.'

'Oh yes? There are banks in the West who will give you money to buy from Russian plants?'

Vichevsky felt the ominous descent of the conversation into unsustainable lies. He had no idea whether a bank would consider this kind of transaction. And he suspected that Kartchak probably knew that. He drew a deep breath before trying to close the conversation enigmatically. 'Kartchak. There's always money available. And if the bank will not lend to Russia, then you simply don't tell the bank that the money's for Russia.'

To his dismay, Kartchak took the fictional bait. 'Excellent. How do you do it?'

'Oh, there are ways . . . holding companies, you know the kind of thing . . .'

'Vichevsky. There are excellent opportunities in metals today. I'll call you when Roman is back with the pipeline report and then we'll talk. Oil and gas are tricky, too much bureaucracy. Now metals interest me.'

'Of course, of course. Perhaps you should come to London.'

'No, you come to Moscow. I'm too busy. I'll send you a ticket.'

Vichevsky felt another surge of annoyance. He had made it quite clear to Kartchak that he was busy too; this was clearly something that Kartchak wanted, yet *he*, Vichevsky, had to travel to Moscow. But the lure of a free ticket overrode his anger.

'Perhaps. I've some more work to do. I'll let you know.'

'Vichevsky, this could be worth a lot of money. I will be very angry if you do not bring this business to me. Do you understand?'

'Of course.' When Vichevsky put down the phone his hand was shaking. He had to find out about the metals business. He'd call his friend Ivan at Moscow Bank. Quickly he dialled the number. He had lied badly to Kartchak and he was scared.

TWO

With a deft gesture Libby slipped Neville's memo to the bottom of the pile. The second, insistent request for Alex's business plan would put her in an unbearable mood for the whole day. Everyone's commission figures were down, but Alex's had plummeted. Her high-profile clients were easy targets for the new banks that were aggressively elbowing their way into the business and there was nothing she could do about it.

Libby dialled Metco's number for the fourth time. There was no answer from Spike's extension. He had left the flat at six a.m., ostensibly for the office, but had been uncontactable all morning. She let the line ring for a long time although she knew that if Spike had been there he would have snatched it up on the first ring.

When she saw Alex coming she put the phone down. There was no love lost between her boss and her lover.

'Morning! How was dinner?'

'Sol's gone back to New York. For good.' Alex

looked at her watch. 'In fact he'll have taken off by now.'

'What do you mean, *for good*? He's working out there?'

'Yes. Head of Fischer Green US. Main board. Too good to be true. Apparently.' Alex was shaken and the effort of control made her abrupt. For a moment she stood by the desk, running her index finger over her upper lip.

'Coffee?' Libby asked brightly.

'Please.'

Alex looked at her diary. At ten thirty she had a meeting scheduled with Starling's Bank, at six an interview with a journalist. She flipped over the page. At ten the following morning a meeting with Neville Douglas to discuss business development. She knew she was supposed to have done the projections for the overheads of her unit but she was reluctant to face up to the figures. She snapped the diary shut. She'd wing it. She dialled Larry and asked him to gather up the most recent nickel research reports, then went into her office to read what he had put together.

At ten she made her rounds of the vast dealing room, looking over shoulders, asking how business was. Libby watched her. Even in repose, standing upright and perfectly still, listening to the long, convoluted story of a trade missed or a deal gone wrong, there was a sense that she was not only *listening* but *feeling*. Her expressions were easy – a smile of collusion with one colleague, a small gesture of delighted surprise that the new junior had traded; all natural and unforced. While Libby had become an expert at concealing even the strongest emotions, Alex was completely transparent.

She caught Libby's eye as she returned to her desk for her bag. They looked at one another for a moment.

'I'm fine,' she answered the unasked question. 'See you later.'

Starling's Bank had made the transition that Wellington could not make; it had carved a niche for itself and had stayed out of direct competition with the big banks. Where Wellington clashed head on with Goldman Sachs and J.P. Morgan, Starling's had pulled back, concentrating on the specialist knowledge they had acquired over three hundred years as a leading finance house of the British Empire. Malaya had been their stronghold. Rubber and tin. Now the country no longer existed and the commodities were moribund as cheaper substitutes had been discovered, but the bank's name still had enormous cachet. Alex was intrigued and eager to learn how they had done it – it was a feat she longed to emulate at Wellington.

She had been waiting for barely a minute when her friend William appeared. Small and anxious, he took Alex by the arm and led her across the marble-floored hallway.

'Alex, you're going to hate me,' he began as he hurried her up the ornate staircase. 'The bank has a special interest in this project at the moment, and I mean *really* special. Lord Ingles felt it would be sensible for everyone involved to hear what you have to say at the same time.'

'Lord Ingles?'

'Our chairman. He's fine, Alex, don't worry. But the rest of the board will be there. Sorry. Question-and-answer session if you can face it.'

'Of course, William, but I'd have appreciated some notice. And perhaps a clue about what this *project* entails.'

'Oh, God, Alex. *I* can't discuss that. I'm just an analyst.'

The main boardroom of the bank was exactly what she had expected, old English oak panelling, good oil paintings. William opened the door and stood back. For a second Alex hesitated. Ten men were seated round the table, examining her in total silence. She felt a sudden urge to retreat, then almost immediately a desire to shrug off the challenge. Another performance of corporate theatre, the small charades aimed at establishing commercial supremacy and the upper hand in a negotiation. The English establishment and the Japanese were both past masters at the game, in very different ways. As soon as Alex recognized the intention to intimidate, she was composed.

William pulled out a chair for her, then began to introduce her round the table, a largely unnecessary exercise: two former cabinet ministers, one peer of the realm and two high-profile financiers. Alex nodded, keeping her face expressionless. She would not give them the satisfaction of seeing the slightest tremor. It was no great effort.

After the introductions, Lord Ingles stood up. His angular face was as familiar to her from the gossip columns as from the financial pages, and he had just married his third wife, a former model thirty years younger than he.

'I'd like to echo William's words and say how glad we are that you could join us today – albeit under slightly false pretences.' He smiled. 'We need your assistance in a very large transaction we're considering. First, would you give us your views on the nickel market?'

Alex spoke fluently about the nickel market – production costs, consumption growth, the impact of the fall of communism on Cuba, a major nickel producer. She enjoyed herself. Occasionally she was interrupted by a question or a request for clarification. Lord Ingles asked about storage costs, an accountant asked about the Russian domestic market – a long, convoluted question Alex felt was designed more to impress the board than to elicit an answer. After twenty minutes Alex had told them just about everything she knew. She was pleased with her performance and felt that she'd come across as knowledgeable and confident. Then the tone changed; a couple of the men leant back slightly and Alex registered this subconsciously as the winding-up process. Mentally, she prepared to take her leave.

'Thank you, Miss Brookes,' Lord Ingles responded. 'I believe you have covered every aspect of the market. Well done.'

Alex inclined her head in acknowledgement of his praise.

'Just one more point . . .' he smiled again. 'Are you preparing any research on the nickel market at the moment? Something that will be published?'

'No, I'm not, but I'd be happy to write a special report for you setting down the facts and views I have put forward today.'

Lord Ingles shook his head. His tight smile was pure condescension and Alex stiffened.

'That's not what I meant,' he answered slowly. 'We would very much like to see your report and we're particularly interested in your overall view, if I paraphrase correctly, that the nickel price may fall dramatically within the next two years.'

'I would anticipate a small oversupply if Russia continues to produce at current levels, but there are too many wild cards to be able to draw that conclusion with any conviction.'

There was a slight shuffling from round the table.

'Of course,' Lord Ingles continued, 'it is our view as well that the price will fall, and if global perceptions confirm that view our deal would be all the more interesting.'

Alex's mind raced. How was their deal structured? Why was it so necessary to believe that the price was going to fall? She looked round the table again. The patronizing insincerity of Lord Ingles galled, as did the tight smile, almost a smirk, on the plump face of the accountant. She could just imagine him afterwards nursing a large gin and tonic before lunch in the bank's dining room, gloating over her inability to grasp the theme of the meeting.

'Lord Ingles. What is it you want from me?'

The smile faded for an instant and Alex could sense the quick calculation he was making. She glanced at William, who was looking uncomfortable; presumably he had recommended bringing her in.

'Fine.' Lord Ingles stood up and gripped the back of the chair. 'Let's not beat about the bush. After all, what we require is nothing out of the ordinary and I'm sure it's standard practice for you. If the bank approves this project they'll have need of you and Wellington, not just on nickel but on several similar projects currently under consideration.'

The carrot, the pay-off if Alex complied with whatever he wanted. And not a bad carrot at that. The bank was very wealthy and this was exactly the kind of business all the brokers in London dreamed of. Apart from the huge commission earnings, the kudos was immeasurable. Neville would be impressed with this name.

'I'm still a little in the dark . . . This is a Russian mine, is it? You're looking to finance their production?'

'It is indeed a Russian mine. May I introduce an old friend to you.' He gestured down the table and a tall, heavily built man, whom Alex had not noticed, stood awkwardly to attention. 'Mr David Macneice works for the European Bank for Reconstruction and Development and he has brought this project for our consideration. His organization wants to smooth over the difficulties resulting from the turmoil in the former Soviet Union. To integrate Russia into the global marketplace, as it were. He'd like us to provide some working capital.'

Alex nodded. 'I see. You lend the Russians the cash, they pay you back when the nickel has been sold. And the EBRD underwrites part of your risk. Will you need to trade on the London Metal Exchange?' she asked, mentally assessing the value of the commission.

It was Macneice who answered, his voice surprisingly high-pitched. 'Not at all. We are all bankers, not speculators. This deal is directly between the Russian mine and the bank—'

Lord Ingles interrupted. 'It's really very simple. We've structured the deal in such a way that it would be very advantageous to us if the mine were to believe that the nickel price will go down. You have been quoted frequently in the press, Miss Brookes, and your opinions carry considerable weight. Were you to write a report on nickel, saying exactly what you've said to us today – perhaps stressing the downside potential of nickel – it would make our job much easier.'

Alex almost laughed out loud. She really hadn't expected such an austere group to come up with such a blatantly manipulative plan. How Sol would have laughed at their clumsy efforts. He would have devised a much better – and subtler – ploy. Starling's wanted her to publish a report, talking the nickel market down, frightening the Russians and improving their bargaining stance.

How amateurish. She looked around the table, aware again of the oppression of the situation; the group of men, Eton and Oxford most of them, she'd guess, in a boardroom that had hosted trade finance discussions for over three centuries. But she found their tactics laughable; the hints, the circuitous discussions, the discreet allusions to future business. Above all, the half-baked plan they had smugly presented to her as if it were a major coup.

'I understand exactly what you want, gentlemen,' she spoke slowly. 'You are financing a mine in the former Soviet Union. You have structured the deal so that you are selling the metal on their behalf. You want them to believe that the price will fall and that you are, in fact, going to give them a very good "floor" price for their metal. Of course, we all know that nickel is a very volatile metal and that you will probably have the opportunity, at some point during the life of the contract, to sell at considerably higher prices than today.'

She stood up, balancing the power held by Ingles, who was standing at the other end of the long table.

'Research is not infallible. Even mine.' She smiled, hitting her stride. 'Why depend on such an unreliable medium? Such a feeble instrument. Let me suggest something a little more dependable.'

She knew from the silence that followed that they were hooked. Reticent and suspicious, but hooked. There would be a resistance to her plan – in the same way that she had instinctively reacted against *their* suggestion. She moved away from the table and walked to the window, glancing outside for a second, knowing their eyes were following her.

'Prices are historically very low. You want to buy the metal at today's prices and make a profit if they rise. Absolute common sense and a very interesting deal. But so many imponderables. Now *you*,' she turned to Macneice, 'believe that trading on the London Metal Exchange is for speculators, yet this deal you are contemplating seems to me to be one massive speculation. When I talk about trading, I'm talking about hedging – off-setting risk, not increasing it.'

She moved away from the window, enjoying herself enormously, aware that Macneice had blushed. 'Gentlemen, I'm sure you're all familiar with financial instruments, futures and derivatives. Let me suggest the following plan. In the same way that you have insured this wonderful building against fire or a bomb or other hazards, I suggest you buy an insurance policy to protect you against a fall in nickel prices. Simple. I'll even write you that policy myself. Then you can, with total confidence, guarantee your producer today's prices. He has the security of knowing that if prices *do* fall he'll be paid today's higher price. You, on the other hand, can afford to do this – and,' she moved back to the table, 'if the price of nickel *does* rise, you can reap that benefit, dollar for dollar, into your own bank account. No risk. No downside. A simple put option.' She smiled. It was a clever idea. Neat, efficient and safe.

Macneice answered her, his tone mocking. 'What an excellent sales pitch for your Exchange – and for Wellington! But I rather think the intention is to sell direct to consumers – steel companies and so on. No need for intermediaries – or futures and derivatives.' He used the terms with distaste as if Alex had solicited for business in some sordid underworld.

She turned on her heel and was gratified to notice a small movement of recoil as she advanced on Macneice. 'Excellent. You've managed to tie up an erratic demand with an even more erratic supply. The day your producer produces, you are confident you will have a buyer. Well done. No financing of unwanted material in a warehouse until Germany, for example, recovers from the summer lull, no panic buying of supplies from another seller when France suddenly finds itself with an un-seasonal boom. All the traditional problems of long-term contracts between producer and con-sumer solved. Excellent.' She stopped a foot short of Macneice and looked down at him, stretching the moment out. 'I'm surprised, though, to find that a trade financier with your expertise and experience should consider a financing operation with a producer that has – to date – defaulted on over thirty per cent of their contracted deliveries. I wonder how the French steel company will like that. Or British Steel for that matter.'

There was another pause and Alex wondered if she had gone too far. Perhaps it would have been better to make a slower proposal, leading them gradually towards her conclusion, letting them think they'd come up with the idea themselves.

William stood up and began to gather his

papers together. 'Well, Alex, thanks for coming in. That was most . . . interesting and I'm sure I speak for everybody when I—'

'Just a moment.' Ingles walked round to Alex and she thought for a moment she was about to be dismissed. She drew herself up and turned to meet him. Three feet from her he extended his hand, his expression of amusement the first convincing expression she had seen. Alex found herself smiling in response as she took his hand.

'I've been put in my place, I think,' he said eventually.

'That was not the object of the exercise.'

'Maybe not, but a welcome by-product.'

'Maybe . . .' Alex conceded, still smiling.

'These options . . . the put options. Will they solve the problems of default? Late deliveries and so on?'

'Yes. Like any insurance policy you use it if you need it, if not you've simply wasted the premium. No commitment. Options are ideally suited to this kind of transaction, Lord Ingles. They have a cost, but they leave you free to do what you like in the event that the Russians perform in an exemplary fashion.'

'Will you come back and tell us more about all these financial instruments we should know about?'

'Of course. But perhaps you'll come to *my* office?'

Lord Ingles laughed. 'Should we not meet on neutral ground?'

'I think we should have lunch to discuss terms, Lord Ingles. My treat.' She bent to gather up her

71

bag, at ease with him now that she had forcibly broken the ice. She looked round the table for the last time. Macneice was shuffling his papers, frowning. For a second, Alex considered a special farewell for him, but he half turned away from her, his shoulders sagging, and she suddenly felt sorry for him.

'I'll be in touch. Thank you.'

William escorted her to the front door where he stood aside to let her pass.

'Alex, I . . . well done. I'm sorry I couldn't warn you the whole bunch was going to turn up and I'm sorry . . .'

Alex smiled and looked at her watch. 'Nothing to apologize for, William. I need a cab, I'm due at the Ritz in fifteen minutes.'

Six hours later Alex and Libby sat in the deserted dealing room, playing poker. Alex glanced in the mirror when Rory Freeman's arrival was announced. At some point she had rubbed her eyes and the soft line of black kohl, which had given her eyes definition in the morning, now looked like the product of several sleepless nights. She clicked her tongue with annoyance and wiped away the smudges, then became aware of Libby smiling at her. She smiled back.

Rory Freeman was the best-known financial freelance journalist. He had made his name five years earlier when he had interviewed the president of a South American country that had been uncharacteristically dumping copper onto the market. Rory had spoken to several disgruntled bureaucrats who had told him of the president's fears of a military coup. Members of the president's inner sanctum were busy feathering their nests, selling the country's riches and sending the proceeds to their Swiss bank accounts. None of this could be printed, of course, but Rory pushed on, sending back export figures, foreign trade data and central bank information which revealed the full story. Rory's report was published in *The Economist*, causing shock waves in international banking circles. Loans were called, investigations launched and the military coup promptly took place. Since then, Rory had regularly filed reports from Papua New Guinea, Zambia and even, on one occasion, Afghanistan.

'Mr Freeman, Alexandra Brookes.' Alex smiled and extended her hand. He shook it warmly and smiled.

'Good of you to see me,' he said.

Alex looked at him as he preceded her down the corridor. There was something about his appearance that did not seem to fit; somehow, he just didn't look right in a suit. Grimy, bloodstained khaki would be more in his line. Alex smiled at the image and ushered him into the boardroom.

Relaxed, she settled at the table and crossed her hands expectantly. She didn't have long to wait.

'What's your view on the Korean steel scandal?' he asked.

She stiffened. The company concerned was one of Wellington's biggest customers.

'The matter is *sub judice*. You know I can't talk about it. Is that what you've come for?'

He riffled through papers in his briefcase, his expression pleasant, unfazed.

'I want personal views, not gossip. There's a difference.' His tone was mild, a gentle reproof, and his nonchalance irritated her.

'I don't know you well enough to be sure *you* know the difference,' she snapped. 'I'm the one going on record here and I won't be goaded into indiscretion.'

'It doesn't matter,' he murmured as he straightened the documents in front of him. 'I spoke to the chairman ten minutes ago. Now.' He smiled at her calmly. 'Who's trying to corner the copper market?'

Alex gasped. She'd been wondering the same thing. The copper price had risen only marginally, but pointers were beginning to emerge and she had a suspicion – no more – that there was a scam in the offing. Someone was buying copper and holding it, forcing higher prices and panic. Alex had seen it all before, but the trick was to see it happening before anyone else did. Small movements of metal from unusual places, sudden demand for immediate delivery to inaccessible ports, big buying orders early in the morning or in the evening. There was enough evidence for her to warn her customers that they should take cover.

She went back to Rory's question. She could handle it in any number of ways, including telling the truth, but she was limited by client confidentiality. Her suspicion was that it was Achille, the flamboyant head of a huge Italian trading house and one of Wellington's biggest customers, who was trying to manipulate the market, and she could reveal neither that he was a client nor that he had been buying.

She chose righteous outrage as her defence. 'Come on, I don't have time for this. My answer to this and any other similar questions you may have is "No comment."'

'Any off-the-record thoughts?' he continued, unperturbed.

'No!' Alex barked, her voice rising. 'And I've had enough. I would never have agreed to see you if I'd known you were putting together some kind of gossip column.'

'Perhaps you could give me your views on the new legislation? Will it clean up the futures industry?'

Mollified, Alex spoke for five minutes about the problems facing the Exchanges and the regulators. When she moved onto the Japanese markets Rory held up his hand.

'I have enough,' he said slowly, as if considering more questions. 'More than enough.'

For a moment Alex hesitated. He had enough? What did that mean?

'Look . . . what's this all about? Just about every question you've asked me has been inappropriate, questions I can't answer. Apart from a couple of things on legislation all I've been able to say is "No comment."'

'And you said it very nicely.' Rory stood up. 'Thank you.'

Alex tried again. 'Maybe I'm missing the point . . .'

'I'm sorry, I really have to run.' He glanced at his watch. 'Thanks again.'

Alex watched as he marched down the corridor towards the lift. A determined man, calm and focused.

Damn. There had been a hidden agenda and she just hadn't picked up on it. She went back over his questions. Perhaps she should have been more forthcoming. Perhaps she should have been more careful. One article, read by the whole industry, could have an enormous impact on her career.

When Libby asked her how it had gone, all she could do was shrug. 'I just don't know.'

The following day at ten o'clock Alex stood in Neville Douglas's office, a polystyrene coffee cup in her hand, tapping her foot with impatience. Conversations with Neville were invariably a series of cross purposes and misunderstandings and Alex felt she and Neville communicated more efficiently by memo. But Neville had wanted a meeting.

He was poring over Alex's commission figures from the previous year, although they both knew that he was already familiar with the figures.

'Neville, shall I come back when you've had a chance to look at the numbers?' she asked briskly. 'I'm very busy.'

'Just a second, please, Alexandra,' he answered without looking up.

Alex found Neville and his insistence on forecasts and projections exasperating and he, in turn, had no idea how to deal with her and her insubordination. Alex knew how Neville hated to have to appease her; not only was she

Wellington's biggest commission earner, but as senior broker she kept a room full of volatile prima donnas more or less under control.

He was a big man, but his size was a handicap; it made him awkward when dealing with the nervous, agile dealers who danced around the office all day, throwing things at each other and racing their chairs round makeshift circuits, and it also made him uncomfortable with women – Alex in particular, who could never seem to sit still in his office. He glanced quickly in her direction. She had undone her hair and was deftly arranging it into a chignon on the back of her head while looking out onto the dealing room. Efficient and casual and very beautiful.

He looked back at the figures which danced in front of his eyes. Neville Douglas was the first trading director to have come from the Treasury department. The Wellington balance sheet showed an erratic history – spectacular successes one year, appallingly bad debts the next – and the board felt that control was the key. But Neville was aware of the resentment among the traders, who had to report to someone with no first-hand experience of trading.

'Alex,' he managed, 'these figures just don't tie up. More business, less revenue? How can that be?'

Alex's shoulders sagged. How could Neville be unaware of the fact that no fewer than three banks were members of the Exchange while two major international investment houses were now trading actively in metals. 'Oh, Neville, we've talked about this. We have to cut commissions to compete—'

'No question of that, Alex, unless you cut your overheads.'

'We *have* cut our overheads. We're doing no entertaining this summer, no Ascot, no Glyndebourne. Nothing. And I haven't replaced Ashton. How can I keep my clients when we're being undercut? Chase will deal for half a dollar. We're charging a dollar!'

'You're still over budget.' Neville ploughed on to the next page without looking up.

'Over *your* budget, not mine,' she flashed back. 'These figures are ridiculous. Absolutely unattainable and just because the board ratified it, it doesn't mean they can be achieved. They don't have a magic wand, you know.'

'Alex. Calm down. We need to have these targets to focus our efforts. I see you haven't completed the business plan I asked for.'

'No ... well, I've been busy,' she acknowledged, then rallied. 'No significant changes from last year, anyway.'

Neville picked up his pen. 'So, shall we say a ten per cent increase?'

'You can say anything you like. Listen, Neville, the marketplace is changing. Unless we look at the structure of the markets, our competitors and counterparts, we're making blind assumptions. Up or down, ten or twenty per cent. It's not my decision. Neither is it directly linked to my efforts. I believe that revenues will be lower this year across the board – not because of our laziness but because the same amount of business is being spread between more brokers.'

'We've always had competition, you know. Do

you think we used to have a monopoly?'

'No, but—'

'Well, this simply cannot be, Alex. We can't have a drop in revenues. The new computer's performance has been very disappointing. We've had to contract out to an agency ... very expensive and labour-intensive.'

Alex envied his simplicity. There was no point arguing with him. All he wanted was to be able to report an encouraging increase in proposed revenues to the board. Then he had a whole year until he had to explain the discrepancies – or during which to hope that a solution would appear. But Alex was refusing to co-operate. How much simpler if she just said fine, up ten per cent. Then he would, on paper, be able to compensate for the computer department's loss.

'Neville. We will all do our very best ...'

'If you did the business plan, as I asked you to, we might be able to solve this issue, rather than making what you refer to as "blind assumptions". Where is your new business going to come from this year?'

'I have a major project in the pipeline in Brazil. And the former Soviet Union is, of course, the biggest new market we've ever seen. Starling's bank is already in there and ...'

Neville picked up a third sheet of paper. 'New accounts? I see you've signed up Bartling.'

Alex smiled. 'Yes, and a very nice account too, Neville. No question of them going bust.'

She could see Neville's annoyance. In the minefield of their relationship credit was a large issue. Trading for her clients meant, in effect, lending them money. And she needed to compete with other brokers, but Neville invariably threw up his hands in horror when he saw her requests. Measured risk. Her business, yet Neville acted as if she were trying to give away the shop.

'Need I warn you that the former Soviet Union is hardly bankable? If we are depending on business from this source we certainly are in a very precarious state. You need more mainstream business, Alex. More Bartlings.'

Alex bit her tongue. It was no good stating her case, again, that the facilities offered by the banks would top anything Wellington could offer and that most of the *mainstream* was lost for ever. She sighed.

Neville stood up. 'We can talk around this issue all day, Alex. I take your point about the marketplace, but we have to do our best. Business has always been difficult. What we need from you is consistency, Alex. And a consistent *improvement*.' He took off his glasses and Alex knew he was preparing to dismiss her. 'Let me see your figures up to target this month, please. Do you think you can manage that?'

Alex hated the tone of his voice, the unctuous voice of the schoolmaster to the rebellious schoolgirl.

'I'm worried about Achille. And we've lost Hartman this month,' she began. 'Gone to Swiss Bank. Two million credit line . . .'

'There are other Hartmans out there.'

Alex sighed. Surely he could see that any other company would be lured away by the massive credit lines that were way beyond Wellington's means. Did he really believe Hartman was an isolated case?

'I need—'

Neville raised his hand. 'We'll review the situation in exactly four weeks' time. I have a board meeting the following day and the matter will be raised. The board are seriously concerned. The whole situation may have to be reviewed.'

Alex looked at him. Reviewed? What did he mean by that?

'Neville, if we have to compete—'

'Submit your report to me by the end of to-morrow, please, Alex. Any other recom-mendations should be made to the credit committee meeting next Tuesday, as usual. Now, I have to go.'

Alex sat in Neville's office for ten minutes. He had cut her off twice, refusing to allow her to make her point. The man came from the Treasury department, for God's sake. He understood about credit. He must be able to see the position the company was in.

She stood up, suddenly understanding his fatalism. If he did report to the board that Wellington was no longer able to compete for metal business since it did not have a big enough balance sheet, what would happen then? Close the shop and go home? Much easier to bury his head in the sand and blame Alex – or Marcus, or Alan – then hope that the market would shift, the big banks lose interest so that Wellington could somehow recover their old clients and go back to where they had been.

Alex gathered up her papers. Not a chance.

Vichevsky dialled the number of the Moscow International Bank, London.

'Belayev, Ivan.' In his distraction he forgot that he was calling a London bank and reversed the names.

'Putting you through to *Mr Ivan Belayev*,' the receptionist answered tartly.

After a moment he heard a voice.

'Belayev.'

'Ivan, I need your help.'

'Who is this?'

'Vichevsky. I need your advice. Can we meet? Can I take you for lunch?'

Belayev sighed. 'I'm busy, Vichevsky. Year end, I have to get the books sorted out—'

'Please, Ivan. A lot depends on this. You have to help me.'

'Not lunch. I'll meet you for a quick drink. Twelve thirty at the Bull and Bear.'

Vichevsky was about to complain that he already had a lunch appointment and suggest the following day, but he stopped himself.

'Thank you, Ivan. I owe you.'

He arranged the papers on his desk, packed his Filofax into his briefcase and then put on his coat. He closed the office door behind him and locked it, negotiating the narrow staircase with care. At his age a fracture could be fatal and he was not sure he could depend on the British National Health Service to look after him.

Out on the pavement he looked down Curzon Street towards Park Lane. He considered taking a cab. It was twelve o'clock, the weather was fine and the traffic should not be too heavy, but he was reluctant; a cab could cost him £25 to get to King William Street if he got stuck in traffic, and he would rather spend that money on getting Ivan drunk and picking his brains. He took the tube to Monument station and emerged just before twelve thirty.

Ivan was late. Vichevsky had retrieved an abandoned copy of the *Telegraph* and was ensconced in a corner, sipping a mineral water, when he arrived.

'I'm only staying for one. This is an extremely bad time for me,' Ivan announced as he took off his coat. Vichevsky noticed yet again how *foreign* Ivan looked. Somehow his skull was proportioned to some alien blueprint, the forehead too heavy for the small chin, the eyes too wide for the small mouth.

Vichevsky took his coat. 'Well, sit down, have a nice drink and relax. I only want you to unravel some of the mysteries of the banking world for me. It's second nature to you, utterly incomprehensible to a poor old fool like me. Vodka?'

'And tonic, just a splash.' Ivan settled down, soothed by Vichevsky's solicitous manner in spite of himself.

Vichevsky brought back the drinks – a large vodka and tonic for Ivan, a plain tonic water for himself – and sat down.

'Now then,' he began. 'How to borrow money? A simple question but one which I find fascinating. If I wanted to borrow money, what would you, as a banker, want to know?'

'God, Vichevsky, I could be here all day with this one. Give me a clue. What do you want to do with this money?'

'I want to trade, to do barter trade and ... investment business.'

Ivan drained his glass and Vichevsky darted to the bar again, afraid that he had lost patience. Yet again he cursed the fact that he had little knowledge of business and that it showed. Even when he tried, somehow the jargon sounded false and embarrassing.

'Write this down,' Ivan ordered when Vichevsky returned with fresh drinks.

'Ready.'

'OK. I need to know who you are. Do you have a track record? Have you ever been bankrupt? What is the business, what is its risk profile?'

Vichevsky underlined these words. This was the kind of phrase he needed to be able to throw around. Risk profile.

'I need to know where the business is. We balance our portfolio, only ten per cent Indonesian risk, fifteen per cent Mexican, for example; we spread the risk around the world so that if one economy crashes we don't lose everything. Next. Who are you doing business with? Is it a reputable company?'

Vichevsky wrote furiously. When it appeared that Ivan had stopped, he looked up. 'Is that it?'

'Yes. But getting that information and evaluating it could take weeks or months. And banks are notoriously slow to give the green light to projects in new areas, new countries or new companies.'

'But how does one get started, then?'

'You start with your own capital and when you are wealthy the bank will lend you more.'

'What about the capital to start?' Vichevsky persisted, depressed by Ivan's words.

'It depends.' Ivan finished his drink but before Vichevsky could go to the bar again he started to put on his coat. 'What is it you're looking for, Vichevsky?'

'I have some excellent contacts in Russia . . .'

'I know. Don't give me your usual spiel about Gorbachev and Kohl. I've heard it.'

'No, no, that's not what I was going to say. I know some people who have access to cheap raw materials, some metals, oil and gas, and they need money to bring it to the West.'

'Not a chance. Trade finance in the former Soviet Union is a dead issue. We'll finance the stuff outside, on a vessel, for example, but we won't lend any money if it means our money is in Russian territory.'

'But you're a Russian bank! If you won't do it who will?'

Ivan picked up his briefcase. 'No bank will touch it. Forget it.' He hesitated. 'Is this for Volkov?'

'Volkov? Maxim? Why should he want this information?'

'He's in town. He has some deal with a smelter . . . I don't know. He called me and I told him the same thing. Dead loss.'

Vichevsky stood up, his papers fluttering to the floor. 'Wait, Ivan. There must be a way, surely!'

'Maybe some crackpot venture capitalist, but

85

I can't think of any who'd be that stupid. Maybe the EBRD, but I don't know if even they would look at it.'

'What's the EBRD?'

'The European Bank for Reconstruction and Development. Try them. Thanks for the drinks, Vichevsky. Good luck.'

'Thanks, Ivan, I'll keep in touch, let you know how I get on.'

Vichevsky finished his drink, then went to the phone booth. There was no listing for the EBRD in London. He called Directory Enquiries and gave the full name. No luck. They must be based elsewhere. He would have to call Ivan again in the morning. At least he had the suspicion of an answer now; if pushed he could say he had been working on a project with the EBRD and that it had fallen through for some reason. That would sound more feasible to anybody who knew any-thing about business. He turned his mind to Maxim Volkov. Volkov had been at university with Belayev, and Vichevsky had met him on a couple of occasions. He hadn't taken to him – he was arrogant and off-hand, but perhaps he could help. He might be a useful contact in the metals business. Cheered, Vichevsky set off for the tube station and home.

Four days later Alex arrived in the office after a series of meetings.

'Any problems?' she asked Libby, flipping through the notes that had accumulated on her desk during the morning's absence.

'Can I have your autograph?' Libby waved

a copy of *Futures Trading* at her.

Alex took the magazine and flipped quickly through it. The photograph, supplied by Wellington's personnel department, took up half of the first page. Alex's eyes darted over the text.

'I'm going to read this in my office.'

In addition to the desk in the dealing room, where she spent most of her time, Alex had an office which she used for writing reports. It had a glorious view overlooking the Tower of London and she wished she could spend more time in it. The room was decorated in Wellington's usual livery, white and ochre, but she had allowed herself a little latitude and had moved in an ancient leather sofa, a remnant of the original partners' office seventy years earlier. It was relaxing to watch the Tower in the late summer sun or in sharp, bright winter light and, since the office was on the tenth floor, she could lie back on the sofa with her feet up, gazing at the Tower and the sky beyond it, her view uncluttered by the charmless new office blocks and derelict warehouses on either side of the river.

She flipped open the magazine and read the article.

The recession has brought a lull to the City of London and, with it, time to recover from the excesses of the eighties; time to throw off the legacy of yuppiedom. Today's senior traders have known the best of times and the worst of times, all in ten years. What have they learned and how will they react to the next boom cycle? And how will they deal with the waves of scandal, insider trading and rogue traders currently sweeping the markets? In a special series of articles, we talk to the up-and-coming generation, the active traders who will shape the way business is done and whose values will be the values of the financial community, and ask: Is morality obsolete in the City?

First, Ms Alexandra Brookes, Head of Brokerage at Wellington Trading, respected member of the London Metal Exchange.

Alex dropped the magazine and mulled over what she had read. This had not been the thrust of the article as she had understood it – or had Freeman ever actually said what the article was about? The issue of regulation was a topical one, with some politicians claiming that outside authorities should be in charge. It was a view-point Alex understood. She read on.

When asked about corruption, Ms Brookes acknowledges the efforts made by regulatory bodies to 'clean up' the City, but says that they are largely cosmetic. 'The ethos of the City has changed and the new trading patterns have put enormous pressures on everyone. A City dealer can speculate with the bank's money and make a fortune. And we hear about them a lot. From then on, the shareholders expect this level of success. Never mind the risk ... they want these spectacular returns. And the institution that plods on, managing consistent, acceptable returns, seems very uninteresting. Perhaps they feel they should have a go ... There are very few widows and orphans in the commodity world. It's the pressure to turn in unfeasibly high profits that causes the problems in the City today. That's where the regulators should be looking.'

Alex smiled. So that was what he was up to. After a moment she realized that Libby was standing at the door and she looked up quickly.

'The Kid's on the phone,' she said. 'Won't be put off. Needs to speak to you now.' She smiled sympathetically. 'I did my best.'

'All right, put him through here.'

At forty-five, The Kid had diversified beyond the confines of his original family stockbroking company and ran an empire largely driven by whim from his office on the top floor of the Seagram building in New York. Alex knew what his latest scheme was: he wanted to be a banker.

Wearily she picked up the phone. The Kid launched straight in.

'Listen, I need you in New York now.'

'I can't just now. I'm busy.'

'Drop it. This is big. Takeover of the century.'

Why did all her conversations have the same staccato rhythm? Alex wondered.

'If you fax me the details I'll have a look, but I really can't leave London for at least a week.'

'OK, I'm sending it now. Saw the article, by the way. Makes you look like a saint.'

'Oh, please,' Alex sighed. 'You know me better than that.'

'I do, Alex, and if you want my opinion I have to tell you that the article does you no favours. You're too damn straight. What these regulators don't realize is that we, the customers, are not all suckers waiting to be shafted by the big bad broker. We're professionals. And as such I want a broker who'll tip me the wink occasionally when Signor Achille has decided to buy up all the copper he can get his hands on ... and who'll drop a little hint when he decides to let it all go again. Scruples? Can't make money with a scrupulous broker.' He laughed. 'Don't quote me.' He hung up.

Alex walked back to the dealing room with the article. While she couldn't stop production of the magazine, she could make sure nobody else got their hands on this copy.

'Come on, it's nearly one o'clock. Let's go and have a drink,' she suggested to Libby. 'Call switchboard and tell them we'll be gone for fifteen minutes.'

They left the office and went into the building next door. Raoul greeted them with his usual affectionate mock deference, pulling stools out for them at the end of the long bar near the front. He knew they were good for business perched on the bar stools, two tall, elegant women, one blonde, one dark, but they chose instead the dark interior, the last table next to the dusky curtains leading to the dining room. In spite of the fact that Raoul had aimed for Gothic charm, somehow the bar had turned out to resemble a brothel more than anything else. The artwork on the walls, in ornate gilt frames, was a mixture of

90

misty landscapes and disturbing, distorted portraits by well-known artists. There were two naked brick walls which Raoul had decorated with black cast-iron sconces and candles – proper ecclesiastical candles of yellowish wax – and swathes of white muslin hanging on wide mahogany poles. But it was the tasselled red velvet curtains between the bar and the dining room that set the tone, and although the bar was officially known as Le Bordeaux it was universally referred to as Le Bordel.

'Ça va?' Raoul enquired, pulling up a chair, ready for a chat.

'Two glasses of red,' Alex replied.

'Right away.' He stood up quickly, recognizing the tone of her voice.

Alex flipped through the messages Libby had taken that morning. None was urgent but a couple were intriguing. Libby thought one of them was a headhunter. Another, from a Professor Vichevsky, caught her eye.

'Who's this?' Alex asked.

'I don't know. Some Russian. Said he'd got your name from Moscow International Bank. He has a heavy accent but speaks perfect English. I told him what I told the rest, that you'd call back later today.'

Raoul arrived with the wine, poured two glasses, bowed and left.

'To Rory Freeman!' Libby lifted her glass and Alex grinned.

'The man's a liar. Had me wrong-footed from the beginning. I thought he wanted to know about EEC legislation.'

'Well, you should have known what he wanted. The whole issue of regulation is so contentious. They say we're all too bent to police ourselves.'

Alex laughed. 'Well, even if I only get one new lead from all this coverage it'll be worth it. What did you say that Russian guy's name was? Vichevsky? You know, Libby, Russia's where the biggest potential is. Starling's are looking to finance a mine. I keep hearing things ... I'm going to call this guy as soon as I get back to the office. He could be a stepping stone. That'll keep Neville off my back. Give him an excuse for a four-page report to the board.' She drained her glass. 'Let's go.'

THREE

Alex suppressed a laugh. Professor Vichevsky spoke like a character from a bad spy novel.

'We cannot talk on the phone. Perhaps we could meet tomorrow?'

'Very well, professor. But can I ask you how you got my name?'

There was a pause. 'From a contact. In the banking world.'

'Who?'

Alex could sense the professor's distress at her directness. 'At the Moscow International Bank. Apparently he read an article in a magazine.'

'I see.' Alex knew nobody at the Moscow Bank. She sighed. 'OK. Let me take your address.'

At ten o'clock the following morning she stepped from the taxi in Mayfair's Dover Street. The building was impressive and Alex looked up in surprise. What kind of Russians could afford the rental in a building like this? She looked at the names on the bells and spotted Vichevsky's. Fifth floor. It was a long hike to the top and her heart sank with every step. The building had been subdivided into a large number of tiny offices and rented out to people who wanted an address to impress, but low overheads. The last staircase, from the fourth to the fifth floor, had obviously been the original stairs to the maid's quarters when the house was a family home. The carpet was noticeably shabbier up here and there was a gloom which was undiminished by the tatty travel posters tacked to the walls.

Alex rang the bell and waited. Eventually a dark head appeared round the door and asked her to come in. The protocol was difficult. The man would have liked to usher her in ahead of him but the staircase continued to rise steeply inside the door which he was awkwardly holding open. Alex eased past him and waited on the landing above. She could hear guttural Russian accents coming from inside the room at the top of the stairs – they sounded angry and she felt a twinge of unease. Her sherpa reached from behind her to open the door and she was momentarily surprised by the brilliant smile he flashed at her, revealing four gold teeth. The door opened and a wave of cigarette smoke blew out, strong enough to make her lean back.

The room, when Alex could make it out, was only ten feet square and contained a ridiculously large desk behind which sat, she presumed, the professor, the only person in the room with any space. Behind his desk and next to it were four chairs, all occupied by shouting, smoking Russians. A small window overlooked the rooftops of Mayfair. It was shut.

94

The professor stood up and introduced himself, but the general level of conversation around them continued regardless. Alex was standing some two feet away from him but he had to shout. A small, stocky man, he appeared to Alex to have started the uneven transition from Jekyll to Hyde – the thick black hair on his head was unruly and Alex noticed that the backs of his hands and fingers were also covered in hair. She shook his hand reluctantly.

'Please sit,' he offered, before realizing that there were no unoccupied chairs. The young man who had let her in was sent to fetch one, which he wedged beside the desk. Alex took a quick look round. All but one of the men were wearing unmatched suits – not just the jacket and trousers, but socks and shoes as well. It occurred to her that if they got together in the morning and distributed their clothes between them each could have a matching set.

One man, however, was conspicuously well co-ordinated, in an exemplary, fashion magazine way. The charcoal jacket hung beautifully over his white silk shirt. Alex was sitting so close to him that she noticed details – an unusual black-faced watch, his long, very new and very elegant alligator shoes. She had to lean back slightly and look up to see his face and when she did she found herself blushing as if caught in the act of theft. His dark, oriental features were impassive and composed. He was looking at her down a long, narrow nose, his black eyes set above sharply sloping cheekbones, not an inch of flesh to spoil the clean lines of his face, not a wrinkle to support the idea that he had ever smiled. A completely foreign face, alien almost. Alex shuddered.

The professor launched into a short autobiography. He had an impressive background which, of course, Alex had no way of verifying. University of Moscow ... Gorbachev ... Thatcher ... he knew them all. Alex listened impassively, thinking that this blatant self-advertising was actually quite refreshing after the insidious name-dropping of the West.

'I have had a stroke of great good fortune. My friend and former colleague at Moscow International Bank, Ivan Belayev, has introduced me to the world of metals, knowing that I am in a position to be an unusually well-qualified intermediary between Russia and Great Britain.' He beamed and Alex found herself smiling back. The man was full of exuberance and it was difficult to be unaffected by his enthusiasm.

'It was he who read a magazine article about you, Miss Brookes, and passed your name to me as someone I can trust with this business.'

Alex nodded her thanks. Perhaps the article *had* been worthwhile.

'I find myself able to put together the might of the Soviet industrial machine with the mercantile expertise of the West.'

He stood up and turned, with a flourish, to Alex's neighbour.

'May I present to you Maxim Volkov of the Russian aluminium industry. A very old friend.'

Alex leant back and managed, awkwardly, to shake the man's hand.

'Very pleased to meet you, Mr Volkov. May I ask what your interest is in the aluminium industry?'

'I sell aluminium,' he stated, turning to her. Like an obedient pet dog, Alex sat upright, alert now, her heart thumping. This was exactly what she wanted, access to the giant aluminium smelters of Siberia.

'I sell much aluminium,' he continued and Alex began to suspect that he was playing with her; he was probably aware of her enthusiasm. He leant over to the professor's desk and took a piece of paper. Alex edged slightly closer.

'I sell from here. One million tonnes per year.' He handed her the paper and Alex became the focus of attention in the room. He had written the names of the three biggest smelters in the world, legendary names which conjured up images of a great industrial power, churning out metal for the mighty military machine, heroic workers toiling for Mother Russia. Alex gasped, greedy now for his business.

'That's a lot of aluminium,' she said quietly.

'Not so much.'

'Well, not so much in Russian terms, but a lot from our perspective. Europe produces only around three million tonnes per year in total—'

'Three and a half,' he corrected her. 'You are counting also the Arabs?'

'No, well, in any case . . .' She tried to pull herself together and take a lead from his abrupt tone. 'What can I do for you and your million tonnes?'

'I need to know what you do. How to sell my

aluminium. Take me to London Metal Exchange.'

'Of course. Come to my office and I'll go through everything with you. Tomorrow. Nine o'clock. Do you have my address?' She found it an effort to contain her enthusiasm. One million tonnes. Yet she knew that this man would think less of her if she gave any indication of the strength of her feelings.

'*I* have your address,' the professor interjected eagerly. 'And I will, of course, accompany Mr Volkov.'

There was a pause and Alex stood up. There seemed to be nothing else he wished to discuss. 'Nice to have met you. Until tomorrow.' She turned to the professor and saw with amusement that her status had changed in his eyes. Alex had been accepted by Volkov. The professor stood up and reached for her hand.

'Such a pleasure,' he breathed. 'I look forward to seeing you tomorrow.' He took a timorous look at Volkov, who was looking out of the window, a cigarette held between the tips of his long fingers in a curiously old-fashioned European way. They were both dismissed.

Alex jumped in a cab and sped back to the office, desperate to tell Libby about the meeting. Her mind raced. Could this man be who he said he was? In twelve years in the business Alex had seen most of the scams and had developed, she thought, a good instinct for spotting cheats. But Russia was virgin territory. What good were her instincts in a country with no track record in the international business arena? Then she thought back to the numbers. Millions of tonnes.

She had been predicting that Russian exports would increase as the military were stood down; the communist military machine had previously consumed around 80 per cent of the metal they produced. Where else could this metal go but to the West? Some analysts had predicted that Russian production would cease without the Soviet spoonfeeding of raw materials, cash and expertise. They had forecast a huge increase in the world price, but Alex had gone the other way. The producers *had* to stay in business. And they would find a way to sell their metal. And the price would go down, not up.

Now it looked as if she had been right. Certainly stocks of Russian metal in the West had gone up, but not to the extent she was anticipating. This man represented a possible solution to the problem – there was a bottleneck, no-one in Russia knew what do with the metal. And now she had a chance to tap into that massive resource, to be the first broker to gain access to the Russian market.

'Raoul's,' she mouthed at Libby as she hung up her coat.

Settled once more in the smoky depths of the bar, the story tumbled out. Libby listened without a word. The drinks sat untouched on the table as they discussed their strategy for the following day. Structured presentation, questions, buffet lunch in the Wellington boardroom, quick tour of the Exchange – from the visitors' gallery only – at the busiest time of the day when her unscrupulous competitors were least likely to try to muscle in. They filled in the programme for the day and then sat back triumphantly.

'Another toast to Rory Freeman, I think,' Libby suggested.

'I take it all back,' Alex agreed, raising her glass. 'He's a wonderful journalist. Come on, let's get started.'

For the remainder of the afternoon she prepared for the presentation, reading research and calling analysts specializing in emerging markets. At five she put the last couple of reports into her bag and left.

As soon as she got home Alex called New York.

'Fischer Green,' a voice snapped before the phone had time to ring more than once.

'Sol Bergman, please.'

'Who wants him?'

'Alexandra Brookes.'

'Hold on, Alexandra,' instructed the unknown receptionist with American familiarity. Alex sat back, savouring the anticipation of telling Sol all about Volkov and the aluminium business. She hung on for two minutes, becoming increasingly impatient, and was just about to hang up and call back when the same voice announced that Sol was out. Alex thanked her, cut the line and dropped the phone onto the floor. She lay back for a moment feeling unreasonably angry with Sol, resenting that he should be out when all this was happening. She couldn't relax now, so she quickly dialled the number of Sol's favourite restaurant. There were about four restaurants used by the trading fraternity in New York and Alex was prepared to call them all, but she was in luck; the head waiter of Smith and Wollensky told her that Sol was there. The sound of glasses chinking and raucous laughter all but obscured his voice when he finally came on the line and Alex had to shout to make herself heard.

'Sol, it's me!'

'Who is it?' he yelled.

'It's me! Alex! Can you hear me?'

'Only just. Where are you? Can I call you back later? Or can you call me in the office later?'

Alex felt deflated. She had been looking forward to this conversation so much that she was reluctant to let it go.

'How long, Sol? When will you be back in the office?'

She felt another twinge of annoyance. This was very unlike Sol. In her mind her news was so important that he should offer to take the call somewhere else, but he clearly had no intention of doing so.

'What? I can't hear you.'

'Damn it, Sol!' Alex shouted. 'This is ridiculous . . .'

'Call me later, Alex. I'm at a birthday party.'

'*You* call me later. I'll be at home.'

The line went dead before Alex could hang up on him.

Not only had Alex not had the pleasure of telling Sol about her plan, she had been deprived of his feedback; it was unthinkable that she should launch into a new venture without discussing it with him, listening to his views and developing her own stance as they talked.

The phone rang at eleven and Sol's secretary greeted her with brisk efficiency.

'Hold the line for Mr Bergman,' she instructed in her nasal Brooklyn twang, and she put Alex on hold while she went off to find Sol. A mechanical voice then interrupted the muzak with the chirpy announcement that Alex was holding for Mr Bergman's secretary and that if she wished she could leave a message on voicemail. A whole list of options followed: '. . . press seven for reconnection to an operator, press five for security . . .' Alex put down the phone and left it off the hook.

She slept soundly, which she always did before a presentation, soothed by the possibility of a major deal when other people might feel unsettled. She woke up half an hour before the alarm, at five thirty, showered and dressed quickly in her favourite pinstriped suit, and drove to the office through the sparkling, empty streets of London. The drive from her Chelsea flat to the City always delighted her – Buckingham Palace, the Mall, down onto the Embankment with St Paul's in front of her and Big Ben behind. The gardens along the Embankment were sprinkled with daffodils and the Thames looked almost blue, having been a cruel gun-metal grey for months.

Alex sat in her office and checked her paperwork. She had a script for the presentation and although she rarely used it she liked to have it on hand. She also had a selection of slides which she hated using since everything became very anonymous once the lights were off. She ran through the overnight news on Reuters, looking particularly for information on Russia. She pulled up the historical file on aluminium to make sure she hadn't missed any items of significance, then sat back. She was prepared.

Libby arrived and checked the paper, the charts, the pens. The boardroom was ready, the buffet lunch would be served at the appointed time, the coffee was made. Alex clicked the top of her pen. Her heart was pounding. The Russian market. What an opportunity. When the phone rang at two minutes past nine she jumped.

Behind the vast reception desk the burnished metal plate bearing the company's name and logo dominated the dramatically lit hall. The thick carpet muffled their footsteps as they turned the corner and met their guests, yet again an ill-assorted, uncomfortable and unprepossessing group. Volkov stood out, not just because he was head and shoulders above the other four, but because he was obviously at ease in this plush environment. Alex went straight up to him, ignoring the others.

'Welcome to our company. I'm very honoured that you've found the time in your busy schedules to come here. Please ask me any questions you want.' She stood with her hands clasped in front of her as the translator spoke, smiling benignly, not knowing what to do as heads nodded in unison. She vowed to learn Russian.

'Is the professor not with you?'

Volkov waved his hand dismissively. 'Where is he? I don't know. Perhaps he wait for us in his office.'

'Shall I call him?'

'No.'

Alex hesitated. 'Very well. Please come this way.' They went first to the dealing room, where she explained that Wellington traded on most of the world's commodity exchanges, that they also traded foreign exchange, precious metals and options. She could see Volkov, who had been standing at the back of the group, move forward, his eyes following the action as the copper dealer, like a queen bee, barked out instructions and deals to the clerks and brokers. Alex had seen this before and knew the signs. He was hooked. And he could clearly sense what Alex could, that something was happening. His eyes chased the flow of business as it snaked round the massive room like electricity, watching as information passed from one broker to another. Like a Mexican wave the tremor of a massive order began to move around the room. Alex saw the open-mouthed con-centration of Peter Maclean, half out of his chair, as he listened to the voice on the phone. She could see which line was open, she knew it was King, codename for a huge Korean corporation. Peter put down the phone and smiled. The room was silent as they waited to hear what the client wanted to do. Peter savoured the moment.

The dealer was impatient. 'Well?'

'Buy him two thousand up to forty.'

It was an extremely big order. The dealer was pleased. He was already long himself and it suited him to go out and buy more. He had am-munition now, and a game to play. In addition, if King had given *him* a buying order, he'd prob-ably given similar orders to a couple of other brokers. He rubbed his hands in pleasurable anticipation.

He half turned towards Alex, suddenly aware of the presence of her visitors, visibly delighted to have an audience. He stood with his chest out, hands in his pockets, surveying the room. For a moment he said nothing. His two clerks sat one on each side of him, looking up at him with the blind, passive obedience of gundogs. How was he going to play it? The whole room faced the dealer, in silence, waiting for him to move. Alex felt uneasy. Trading was not a spectator sport and the dealers who played to the audience, those with the biggest egos, invariably lost the most money.

The dealer nodded a couple of times, as if listening to instructions from above. Then he turned to the broker sitting behind him.

'Call Marvin!' he snapped. 'Bid him for twenty. See if he bites.'

Alex explained to the visitors what was going on; the customer wanted to buy copper and had given the copper dealer, Vinnie, the instruction to buy for him. It was a more efficient process than calling every potential seller himself. The exchange made trading quick, clean and – of enormous importance for King – anonymous.

Like a professional card player, Vinnie knew who was long and who was short, who was winning and who was losing. Marvin was a punter, a wealthy, bored punter. He had bought copper and was sitting on the position, showing a small profit. It was not Marvin's style to sit with a position for any length of time and Vinnie reckoned he'd sell some to him.

Slowly, discreetly, he began to buy. One hundred, two hundred. The noise level began to increase.

Alex glanced at the Reuter screen and noticed the price ticking down. Odd. Nearly twenty dollars down since he had started. Suddenly she felt the nervous beginnings of doubt. It was happening again, something was not right.

Oblivious, Vinnie continued to buy, his bravado increasing with the size of his position. His gestures became larger, he pointed aggressively across the room, barking instructions. Alex was tempted to restrain him but was inhibited by the presence of her guests. She looked at the screen again. The price was still falling in spite of the dealer's histrionic performance. By now the price should have been marked up by astute dealers recognizing that he had 'volume' to buy. How could the market not have read the signals? Unless . . . unless they were reading different signals. Finally, Alex abandoned her party with an apologetic smile and walked casually over to the dealer.

'Something's not right, Vinnie. Look at the price. Who's selling?' The dealer was high, the adrenalin of his position hindering any kind of analytical thought.

'It's fine, Alex. Just fine,' he mumbled. 'I'm on top of it.'

Alex put her hand on his arm, soothing him as she would a child.

'Vinnie,' she said quietly. 'You're going to get buried.' She wished she knew what was going on. She looked at Peter. He was sitting back in his

106

chair, watching silently. Again Alex felt a tremor of suspicion. Something about his nonchalance worried her. Why was the King line not ringing? Why wasn't he asking what had been done? Normally the line would flash every couple of seconds when he'd given an order of this size.

Why wasn't King worried?

Suddenly Alex understood what was happening. She grabbed Vinnie again, roughly this time.

'Vinnie, it's King! King's the seller. He's given *you* a buying order, but he's selling through other brokers.'

As if in a trance, the copper dealer held out his hands to stop his clerks buying any more. Then he turned to Alex and looked her in the eyes, dazed. 'It's King? He's selling?'

'Yes, Vinnie. Now start selling yourself,' she urged.

For a moment he did nothing, his mouth slack with disbelief and indecision. He was $200,000 down on the morning. Could he possibly bluff the market up again? He was the centre of attention again as the brokers watched, trying to lipread, knowing something was going on. Alex's presence next to the dealer had alerted them to the fact that this was no ordinary transaction. There was a twist.

Libby appeared at her side. 'What the hell's going on? Are we buying or selling?'

'We're selling. King gave him a buying order then sold ten times as much to the market. A rather clever game of double bluff. He's got his own back for last week.'

'What do you mean?'

Alex led her to the side of the desk, out of the Russians' earshot. 'I saw Vinnie front-running one of King's orders last week. I knew he'd get revenge. Vinnie's none too subtle and King is very well connected.'

To enhance his profits, Vinnie had bought copper for his own account before going to the marketplace to buy on behalf of the customer. Alex had seen it but had bitten her tongue. Now she wished she had intervened.

Still the dealer did nothing, standing as if hypnotized. Alex went back over to him and nudged him. 'For God's sake, Vinnie, get a move on.' She looked at her watch. She had no time to supervise the liquidation of his position. She would dearly have loved to shake him.

'Do you want to sell some to Brightman?' one of the clerks asked quietly.

'Yes!' Vinnie burst out, surprising the whole room. 'A thousand, sell him a thousand.' Alex groaned. What little finesse Vinnie had had was now gone. The self-confident dandy who had strutted around the room ten minutes ago was now out of control. He had lost $250,000 in addition to the humiliation of having been set up by a customer. Now his face was ashen as he listened to the voices giving him bids. Terrible bids. Lower every time.

Alex began to usher the Russians from the room. So much for the display of slick professionalism she had planned to show them. She looked quickly into Neville's office as she passed. How was she supposed to bring in new business *and* keep control of the dealing room? She smiled

at the Russians. Although they probably understood little, there was no point in allowing them
to witness Vinnie's continued humiliation; his
anguish was obvious to all.

Volkov stood motionless as she held the door
open, watching the game as intently as a
Wimbledon final, his eyes darting around the
room. Alex was struck yet again by the absolute
concentration on his face; she had the impression
that this was not an idle pastime – he was absorb-
ing and learning.

She coughed to attract his attention.

'I want to know what they do,' he said.

Alex smiled. 'And I will tell you.'

'Tell me now.'

'Come to the conference room. I'll explain
everything.'

Still Volkov did not move. 'Why is he selling
now? Before was buying.'

Alex took a couple of steps towards him.
'Look, come now. The rest of the party have
already gone.' She gestured to the doorway. 'It's
difficult to talk in here . . .'

'Tell me what they do,' he repeated, his tone
cold. He turned to face her and they stood, head
to head for a moment, unsmiling and
determined. Around them the chaos of the dealing room continued, phones ringing, traders
passing between them in irritable impatience,
but neither moved.

Alex felt compromised by the dealer's behaviour. Had he not been acting improperly she
could have given vent to the anger she felt
towards Volkov, but she hesitated. Righteous

indignation seemed a little hypocritical in the circumstances. Before she could react, Libby appeared. She looked from one to the other and immediately understood the situation.

'Mr Volkov!' she began brightly. 'Your translator needs you! We have a language problem and only you can help.'

Reluctantly he moved away from his observation point in the dealing room. Alex led the way down the corridor, wondering how she could possibly have explained that the dealer had been caught with his fingers in the till and had been given a resounding smack by one of the market's most influential customers. So much for regulations.

The boardroom had a broad bank of windows, all of which were open, but it was already filled with smoke in spite of this. Alex coughed and made a face at Libby. She rolled her eyes in sympathy and fought her way to the windows, hooking the curtains back in an effort to increase the flow of air.

Alex took her notes out of the folder, laying them neatly on the table in front of her. She waited until every cup of coffee had been stirred and every teaspoon put back in the saucer. She waited and waited. There was a low hum of Russian and Alex found herself tapping her foot. She looked up expectantly but the conversation continued. How bloody rude, she thought. She coughed. Libby, at the other end of the room, shrugged.

Eventually Alex turned to the translator.

'I have a schedule. I will begin now,' she

110

snapped. 'If anybody prefers to have a meeting with another agenda I can make another room available.' Diplomatically, the translator tried to soothe her by saying that this was not necessary, but Alex insisted that he translate out loud. The group could not be said to come to heel. The looks remained sour, the body language quietly threatening.

As soon as she had begun Alex saw that her usual presentation was completely unsuitable. In order to explain risk management, Alex felt there should be a logical sequence. To Wellington trainees, brought up in the West, Alex asked them to imagine that they owned an umbrella shop and then asked them questions about the price of umbrellas, which they could answer with their only rudimentary knowledge of economics. But this basic common sense – of interest rates when money is borrowed, of prices rising and falling as supply and demand fluctuated – was clearly not something she could take for granted in her Russian guests. Alex simplified further, so far that Volkov lost patience. But instead of asking her to move on he began to speak to his neighbour. They seemed to be telling each other jokes and Alex carried on for as long as possible in spite of the laughter. The translator began to fidget. He knew Alex was about to explode again and his eyes darted nervously from her to Volkov and back again. Alex stopped speaking. No-one seemed to notice for a very long time and Alex blushed in a combination of humiliation and anger. Libby looked out of the window and the translator picked his nails intently.

'Would you like me to finish now?' Alex asked. To her horror Volkov turned slowly towards her, utterly unmoved by her sarcasm.

'Let's drink.' He stood up and the others followed suit, smiling now that the ordeal was over, looking forward to a drink, clearly assuming that Alex would comply. Volkov had spoken. The fact that he was a guest in her office did not diminish his authority. Alex stood at the board as they put their jackets on and gathered up their briefcases, feeling that she should make a stand, that now was the time to make the rules, have the head-to-head and mark out their territories. Her heart was thumping at the prospect. The problem was that any subtlety would be wasted. In English, her dissatisfaction would be clear from her tone or the implication of her words, but in a foreign language she would have to be direct.

'Stop,' she said quietly and they all did, more in surprise than obedience.

'I have arranged a buffet next door. Perhaps you will all join me for a drink?' She smiled graciously. While Alex did not wish to confront Volkov, or attempt to diminish him in the eyes of his colleagues, she could still assert her own status.

There was a moment of hesitation.

'Libby, perhaps you would lead the way to the dining room?' Alex busied herself with her papers as Libby led the group past her and into the hallway.

'I'll join you in a few moments,' she called after them. 'I have one or two calls to make.'

She pulled the door shut behind them, sat

down and put her feet up on the boardroom table, her hands clasped behind her head, satisfied with her performance. All she had to do now was wait for a couple of minutes, then march into the dining room as if she had done a multi-million-dollar deal. She smiled to herself as she examined her brand new suede shoes, turning her ankle to one side then the other, admiring them.

By the time she rejoined the group in the dining room the buffet had been decimated. The cocktail cabinet was open and every bottle seemed to have been opened, in spite of the fact that Alex had laid on vodka, beer and wine. Twenty small sherry glasses sat discarded on the bar. Libby came up to her.

'I don't believe it,' she gasped. 'They're each drinking one of everything – one Scotch, one Bacardi, one gin . . . I don't know what to do.'

'There's not much you can do,' Alex answered. 'What about Volkov, what's he drinking?'

'Vodka,' she answered shortly. 'Lots of it.'

By the time the group reassembled in the boardroom they had lost two members of the group. They had simply disappeared, saying nothing, and the translator's explanation was unhelpful.

'They have to do something.'

The jackets came off, cigarettes were lit and the conversations struck up. By this time Alex had given up all hope of conducting a seminar in a logical, concise fashion and leaned back against the board.

'Shall I do this or not?' she shouted.

113

The translator looked up, aghast.

'Well?' she challenged, looking directly at Volkov.

'Tell me this.' He stood up and a hush fell. 'Your dealer, there, just now. He was cheating?'

Alex reddened. She had been right to feel awkward. He *had* understood.

'Not cheating, no. An error of judgement.'

Volkov turned to the translator who uttered a few hesitant words. Suddenly Volkov laughed. 'I will remember this. Not cheating but an "error of judgement".'

'Do you want to learn about the Exchange or not?' Alex demanded.

'Tell me how price works. Why one price for today, another for delivery in three months? How to calculate this? And how to trade my aluminium. What to do?'

He listened to her explanation of interest rates, insurance and rent. Alex did not doubt for a moment that he understood every word. She forgot her notes and spoke fluently for over an hour, sometimes standing still, sometimes moving around the room, using her hands to emphasize a point, her elegant suede shoes kicked off. Alex was careful about her language and avoided colloquialisms. Occasionally he would stop her and query a term she had used. Alex wrote it on the board and he copied it onto a minute scrap of paper. By the end of the meeting she was building margins of error into his equations. His cold, mathematical approach to the markets contrasted with her largely instinctive feeling for

114

investor psychology, but their approaches were complementary.

Alex was exhausted. She knew he would have gone on for ever if she had let him, but she was afraid she would lose the edge of her concentration. She stood up and stretched.

'Let's call it a day.' Libby nodded eagerly and Alex put her jacket back on. 'We can do some more tomorrow.'

'Tomorrow we go to Moscow,' Volkov announced.

Her heart sank. Alex had no idea his visit was so short and she felt that a prize had been shown to her – close enough to touch – then snatched away. Although they had established the beginnings of an excellent working relationship she had no claim on him, he had not committed to dealing with her and there was no exclusivity; he could go off and deal with any one of her competitors now. Alex prepared to sit down again.

'Well, let's finish off tonight, then.'

'No. You can tell me in Moscow.'

'You'll call me?'

'You come also.'

Alex shivered. Her first instinct was to say, 'Don't be so ridiculous.' She looked at him and saw again the names of the three giant aluminium smelters he had written down. Millions of tonnes.

'Do I need a visa?'

'Yes. I send Sergei to embassy. Call him now.' He scribbled down a number which Alex gave to Libby. She dialled quickly and spoke for a few minutes.

'Sergei says that if they send someone to the embassy tomorrow with your passport, four photos, an application form and a letter of support which he will send you, they'll give you a visa immediately.'

Alex had no more questions. 'I'll go home and pack. What time is the plane to Moscow?'

'Five. I take your ticket.' He put his jacket on calmly, apparently finding nothing surprising in her unquestioning acceptance of his plan.

At the door he bowed slightly and left without a further word, taking the remaining two members of his team with him.

For a couple of seconds Libby and Alex stood at the door, unmoving. Then Alex looked over her shoulder at the debris. 'Let's go.'

They went to Raoul's, settled into their dark corner and went over the day's activities. They were high, adrenalin coursing through their veins; they knew they had within their grasp not only the biggest deal of their careers, but a deal that would rank pretty highly in the textbook of futures trading. If they could sign a deal with Maxim Volkov, trading to protect the price of the metal he was exporting, it would be a massive coup.

For half an hour they basked in the euphoria of anticipation, calculating potential commissions on the basis of the latest export figures. Then Alex began to calm down and take stock of her position.

'I've just agreed to go to Moscow, Libby.' She paused. 'What do I know about this man? Only that he has some nebulous contact in the Russian

116

Embassy and that he knows an odd little Russian academic who lives in a dusty old garret in Mayfair. Hardly triple-A rating, is it?'

Libby shrugged. 'What do you want me to say? You're going, Alex, I know you.'

'I don't know anyone there. Not a soul.'

'That's the whole point, Alex, you said it yourself. The returns on business in Russia are excellent – because of the perception of risk. If every bank and broker sets up in Moscow what will happen to the returns? Rock bottom. Might as well invest in T-bills. If Russia *were* triple-A rated you wouldn't want to go there.'

'You're right. God, Libby. One million tonnes. And think of the caviar, the vodka, the champagne . . .' she raised her glass '. . . the icons and the palaces. To glorious Russia!'

Kartchak strode impatiently down the corridor of the Moscow Central Hospital. An imposing figure, he dressed well, favouring black, and was pleased with its resulting intimidating effect, his short black hair brushed forward, his dark eyes expressionless. His face and skull had joints like knuckles; between the prominent cheekbones and the jutting blade of his jaw was a slash of dark, indented shadow. From a distance he looked like an apache, the two sinister black streaks like urban war paint.

He listened to the screams of pain and despair from the rooms behind him. It was impossible to tell the sex or the age of the sufferers by the sound alone; only the appearance of the anguished mothers gave any clue to the occupants of the cubicles. Kartchak felt no sympathy for the children, or for their mothers. In a few minutes he would suffer agonizing pain as his dislocated shoulder was wrenched back into its socket. He could anticipate the nauseating wrench and the crack as the bones ground over each other and the swollen, tender tissue.

For some people, repeated manipulation made the exercise easier the next time. But for Kartchak it was the opposite. At first they had made him lie face down on a trolley with his arm hanging over the edge, to allow the dead weight to pull the joint back into position, but this no longer worked.

Once, in the army, the assistant had simply put his foot in Kartchak's armpit, grabbed him by the wrist and pulled sharply with all his might. Kartchak had passed out. It was typical of medical care in the army. He remembered the army dentist and the extractions he had endured at his barbaric hands, the agonizing abscesses and infections his men would suffer rather than go to him. But this didn't stop Kartchak doing business with the soldiers he had formerly commanded, buying anything they could steal and depleting their stocks of drugs even further. Some of the men had not been paid for months and Kartchak knew how desperate they were to strip the base of supplies, which would make them even more vulnerable. There was an increasing predictability to the course of a Russian ailment. A leg injury invariably led to amputation, an eye infection to blindness. Everything to its logical conclusion.

Unless the patient died.

Kartchak couldn't bear the smell. It was not the normal antiseptic odour of a well-run hospital, but the thick stench of decay as untreated bodies, like sweet pieces of fruit, slowly rotted. He looked round impatiently. There was a body in the boot of his car and he knew he had to deal with it soon.

He had been returning to Moscow that morning after a weekend of drinking at his dacha and had been up earlier than normal. His eyes were bleary and sore and he was driving negligently down an uneven country road, one hand loosely on the wheel. Suddenly, there was a jolt and the interior of the car was thrown into darkness. He swore. When he drew his head back and focused on the windscreen, he swore again.

His first thought had been that he had collided with a dog; there was a pack of wild dogs near his dacha and he had shot some of them the previous weekend. But it was not a dog. It was a small child, a girl of about five. The impact must have killed her instantly. Her lifeless eyes stared at him through the glass, her face pressed against the windshield with the blank intensity of a hungry child gazing through a sweetshop window. Her arm was bent at an awkward angle between her torso and the glass, the small palm pushed forward as if trying to protect herself.

Kartchak stepped on the brakes a little too heavily, causing the body to slide down the bonnet, leaving a trail of bright blood as the car jolted to a halt. The dead girl fell lightly to the ground. Kartchak sat still, gathering his thoughts. For someone used to death he'd felt a strange reluctance to confront the body.

After a moment he opened the door and stepped out into the pitted lane. A sod of frozen earth suddenly crumbled beneath his weight and he stumbled heavily back against the car, one arm instinctively extended to break the fall, and he knew instantly from the hot, searing pain that he had torn the damaged ligaments in his shoulder again. He drew a deep breath. There was nothing he could do until he reached Moscow and the hospital.

He lit a cigarette, staring dispassionately at the child's body, cradling his injured arm. He was himself again – hand in hand with and a friend of death.

After a moment he ground out his cigarette then picked the body up easily with one hand, holding it away from his own body, careful not to soil his coat with the girl's blood. She was as limp as the doll that lay beside her on the cold ground. He carried her to the rear of the car, laid her down, opened the boot and placed her body on an old piece of canvas, again careful not to let the blood stain the carpet. He picked up the doll and threw it in next to her. Then he got a rag from inside the car to wipe the blood from the bonnet.

When he had finished he climbed back into the car to deal with the windscreen. He pressed the lever for the washer. Nothing happened. The water in the container under the bonnet was frozen. For the third time Kartchak swore. He rummaged around and found a soiled handkerchief in his pocket. It was barely adequate for the job. By the time he was finished, the hand-kerchief was saturated and Kartchak's hand wet with the girl's blood. He put the sodden cloth back into his pocket and wiped his hand on his suit trousers. The suit would have to go as well. He looked down at the streaks of dark blood. He had dealt with the whole thing like an amateur.

His next priority was to tend to his shoulder. He turned on the engine and moved forward slowly. Every time the car bounced he clenched his neck and back muscles, trying vainly to absorb the shock and protect his damaged joint. After fifteen minutes he joined the motorway and headed for Moscow.

He was told by the nurse on the door that he would have to wait. Clumsily he drew a wad of notes from his pocket and handed it to her, trying to smile. He could buy her co-operation but he also needed her compassion.

Kartchak turned his mind back to the girl's body. What the hell was he going to do with it? It was broad daylight and he was right in the centre of town. He would have to wait until evening, then tell Vladimir to take the body and dump it in the suburbs somewhere.

He paced the corridor, an idea slowly forming. Perhaps he could use this accident, turn it to his advantage and lay the blame at someone else's door. Plant the body and inform the police of its whereabouts.

Who should he implicate?

A moment later he knew what to do. He went to the public phone and called his office, holding the receiver between his cheek and shoulder, dialling with his left hand. 'Tanya. Get Vladimir to go to the Ministry for Metallurgy and follow Mintov's driver to his home. I want to know where he lives.'

'You want to know where Mintov lives? I can find that out for you.'

'No, no!' Kartchak snapped. 'Not Mintov. His driver. Tell Vladimir to call me when he finds out. No matter what time it is.'

Kartchak had never met Mintov. Knew nothing about him except that he was the number one in the Ministry for Metallurgy and that he had enough wealth squirrelled in the West to make him immune to any offers. So corrupt he was no longer corruptible. To have access to the head of the Ministry would make Kartchak unassailable in the metals industry and now he had a weapon. He would call his contact in the police department who would launch an investigation then write a report on the finding of the child's body in Mintov's car. Photographs, forensics, the lot. Kartchak would fabricate a witness statement testifying that Mintov had knocked the child down, then arrange for the report to be suppressed. If Mintov ever became an obstruction to his plans, he would threaten to produce it.

Kartchak smiled. He was two steps ahead as usual.

FOUR

Professor Vichevsky laid his hands, palms down, on top of his closed diary. He pressed lightly, reassured by the slight spring as the pages and pages of phone numbers, press cuttings and business cards yielded under the weight of his hands.

He turned the diary over and examined the gold-embossed name in the fine-grain leather. Filofax. He had seen so many Western businessmen carrying these heavy objects, a cross between a diary and a briefcase, and he had understood early on that contacts were his business; who else in the former Soviet Union had the same level of commercial sense allied with a wealth of Western contacts?

Had Vichevsky known that the commodity broker was a woman, he would have hesitated to ask her along to the meeting. Alex. What kind of name was that? He remembered looking at her as she walked in, her eyes travelling round the room, taking them all in, calmly summing them up. She was so assured. He had introduced himself, trying to establish his background, and she had sat quietly as he spoke, smiling at him, knowing exactly what he was doing. Allowing him. Then she had focused on Volkov and the two of them had excluded everyone else.

Vichevsky picked up the phone, dialled zero and waited for Arkady, his assistant, to pick up the line. His office, perched above the well-maintained roofs of Mayfair, was tiny; that of Arkady even smaller with only a flimsy partition between them. He tapped the phone impatiently.

'Yes, professor?'

'Have you had any success in tracking down Maxim Pietrovich?' In the traditional Russian fashion, he used the first name and 'patronymic', the father's name.

'No, professor, he seems to have checked out of the hotel.'

'What do you mean, he *seems* to have checked out? Either he has or he hasn't.'

'The hotel manager says he left things in his room, but he hasn't been seen for two days.'

'But what about the bill?'

'It was paid in advance for a week. In dollars. Cash.'

Vichevsky put the phone down. Maxim Pietrovich Volkov was potentially an enormous resource. He had access to Russian metal producers, pathetic, tawdry little men who had degrees in thermal engineering but who knew nothing about anything else, or the brothers of government officials who had more interest in distilling their own liquor in the plant than producing metal. He, Vichevsky, had dreamt of these plants and how he could take them under his wing and guide them into the West, but he knew he could not for a variety of reasons. His background in academia did not impress these greedy upstarts, and neither did his lack of capital. While some of his compatriots had stumbled upon fortunes in the early days of confusion, he had been working diligently in London with the British Chamber of Commerce. The first barter trades had been offered to him and he had been unable to participate. Sometimes he went back over the deals – copper for sugar, aluminium for shoes. He had failed to come up with the cash to buy the goods in the West and had ceded his place immediately. Maxim Volkov had bought copper from a Russian producer who had put the decimal point in the wrong place. Had the producer erred on the other side, increasing the value by ten rather than decreasing it, Maxim would have bought it anyway. But he had made his fortune and established himself.

As usual, Vichevsky felt his blood pressure rise when he considered the random fashion in which Russia yielded its riches. Why should he, a professor from Moscow University, be patronized by a parvenu trader who spoke appalling English and understood nothing of Western ways, who could afford to pay a hotel bill of 400 dollars per night and not even stay in the room?

He wondered whether he could put Volkov and Kartchak together, but instantly saw the inadvisability of the plan. Once they had met each other they would simply decide to get rid of him. Or each other. No, they would never work together. He would keep them apart and try to develop each relationship separately.

Kartchak and Volkov. Vichevsky shook his head, wondering how he had ended up with two such partners. Both uncompromising, both arrogant. Clearly that was where he, Vichevsky, was different. He was too refined. Reassured, he stroked the Filofax again.

At nine the following morning he called Wellington and asked for Alexandra Brookes. Barely a second later a female voice answered. Her assistant. She informed him that Alex was not in the office, but that if he wished she would ask Alex to call him. The professor agreed, adding that it was very urgent. Ten minutes later the phone rang.

'Professor Vichevsky. Alexandra Brookes here. I understand you need to speak to me urgently?'

'Ah! Good morning, Miss Brookes. And how are you today?'

'Fine, thanks, fine. I was sorry you couldn't make the meeting yesterday. What can I do for you?'

Vichevsky hesitated. On the phone, she was very brisk. 'You heard Maxim talking about one of my little babies in the metal business. I have another, but I do need your help with some technical information. Could we meet?'

There was a pause. Then, 'I'm going to Moscow later today, professor, but I could meet you for coffee at, say, ten o'clock?'

'Fine. My office?'

He heard her sigh. 'Professor, I have a very busy day. Either we meet near my flat in Chelsea or we wait until I return from Moscow.'

Vichevsky recognized her tone of voice and quickly conceded. 'Anywhere you like. Just name the place, I'll be there.'

'There's a café near Sloane Square called Cappuccine. Holbein Place. Do you know it?'

'I'll be there.'

Vichevsky arrived at the café early and sat smoking a small cigar and reading a wrinkled copy of *The Times* he'd found on the table until Alex arrived. He stood up and pulled out a chair for her with a bow.

'You are very kind to come and meet me, especially when you're travelling later today. And to Moscow!'

'Don't worry,' said Alex, smiling. 'Since you were my first taste of Russia, I can certainly spare you half an hour.'

They ordered coffee and waited in awkward silence until it was served. Then Vichevsky pulled out a notepad and pen. The question he wanted to ask was too basic; he knew she would be shocked and embarrassed, but he couldn't think of a way to lead in gently. He fumbled with the top of the pen.

'Ah, technology,' he started irrelevantly, since the pen was a basic plastic ballpoint. Alex waited. 'Great thing. My country was great, but we have fallen behind in some ways. I wanted to ask you . . . about aluminium . . . the production of aluminium in Russia . . .'

'What? From a technological point of view? Russian smelter technology versus Western?'

'Yes, smelters.' He wanted to ask how

aluminium was made but knew that that would reveal the depth of his ignorance. He had looked aluminium up in an encyclopaedia, but the information had been either too vague or too specific. He knew that four tonnes of bauxite made two tonnes of alumina and that two tonnes of alumina made one tonne of aluminium, but the processes involved in the conversion were a mystery. He had copied a sentence from a textbook, hoping to use it as a cornerstone of his questioning. He read it again. *Lateritic bauxites, consisting mainly of alumina trihydrate, are sedimentary rocks and low silica igneous and metamorphic rocks.*

'Miss Brookes, bauxite . . .'

'Yes?'

'I'd like to know about conversion. Lateritic in particular.'

'Lateritic? Professor, I think you need to talk to a geologist. I can tell you about aluminium, but . . .'

'Oh, please do!'

'What exactly do you need to know, professor? If I have to tell you everything I know, we could be some time. And I have a plane to catch.'

'Actually, I want to know how to arrive at the final product. Aluminium. What exactly do the Russian smelters do?' He waited for her laughter but she showed no surprise at his question. Without a moment's hesitation she launched into an explanation.

'Electrolysis. Alumina is put in a cell – known as a pot – with a catalyser, molten cryolite. In the tank is a cathode and an anode, which is either a prebaked carbon block or a combination of unbaked petroleum coke and coal-tar pitch . . .'

The professor held up his hand. There was no point in trying to take notes since the words were unfamiliar to him and he could not be sure he would even approximate the spelling.

'Sorry, my English is not good enough to follow you. In Russian, of course, I could discuss this technology at the highest level, but in English . . .' He shrugged.

'OK.' Alex reached over, took his pad and began to draw a diagram. 'This is a pot – like a small bath. At one end is a cathode – you know, negative and positive? Cathodes and anodes?'

'Yes, of course, please go on.'

'In the bath instead of water is cryolite. Into the cryolite we drop the alumina and it is heated. Then we put a very high charge of electricity into the pot. It passes from one end to the other. Oxygen is separated from the alumina and sticks to the anode. The pure, molten aluminium is drawn off from the cathode at the other end. That's it.'

Vichevsky tore off the drawing and folded it carefully. 'So simple!'

'Actually, professor, it's not.' She smiled. 'And it's extremely energy-intensive. That's why the big Russian smelters are in Siberia. There's an abundance of hydroelectric power there.'

'It *seems* simple. What can go wrong?'

'Any number of things. The most common – and most disastrous – is when the pot lines freeze.'

'Ah yes. And so common in Siberia.'

'No, professor. Not frozen in that sense. If the electricity supply is disrupted, the molten aluminium solidifies and the pots are unusable. We call them frozen because they can't be used, not because they're cold.'

The professor blushed. 'Different terminology,' he muttered. He was making a mess of this.

Alex looked at her watch. 'I really must go. I have so much to do,' she said, rising from the table.

'You've been very kind. Thank you. And I absolutely insist on paying for the coffee.'

Alex looked momentarily amused, thanked him profusely and was gone.

Back in the flat Alex selected a bag, a Mulberry overnight grip made of tough hide, which stood a good chance of surviving the rigours of Russian travel. There were practical considerations in addition to the aesthetic; she had been told that the temperature in Russia at Easter could fluctuate by 20 degrees.

She thought about Professor Vichevsky. There was not a single indication that he had anything but the most coincidental link with the metals business. Certainly he seemed to know absolutely nothing about the subject. She assumed he was a small-time fixer with the whiff of a potentially lucrative deal. Still, he'd introduced her to Maxim Volkov. Perhaps he'd continue to be useful.

She pulled out a basic wardrobe, neutral colours, with a bright Hermès scarf to dress up if need be. She opened her jewel box and slowly picked out the crystal drop earrings she had worn the first time she had made love with Sol and held one in each palm, half caressing, half assessing. Where the hell was he? She tossed them lightly back into the box and snapped it shut.

She left a message on Fischer Green's answering machine then dialled her parents.

Alex knew that she had benefited from the best of both worlds with her parents; her father, a doctor, was both pragmatic and humane. Her mother, a historian, had a brain that operated like a sophisticated zoom lens, putting the minutiae of Alex's early problems into a perspective that defused even a self-obsessed adolescent without denying the legitimacy of her stance.

Alex could still remember the day she had come back from school, aged thirteen, fired with indignation at what she had learned of animal vivisection. She had hurled the words of hurt and anger at her mother as if her mother were responsible; since her mother was an adult, she was, by definition, part of this unspeakable conspiracy. She had ranted at her for ten minutes before demanding an explanation. Her mother, who had listened without a word, had begun by agreeing that Alex had a point and that she admired her sense of commitment. If people did not feel indignation, then the world would never change to reflect this sense of fairness. Mollified, Alex listened.

'I admire your strength of feeling, Alex, and I can only tell you how I would feel if I knew that my child,' she smiled at Alex, 'if *you* could possibly be saved by a vaccine that had had to be tested on animals. My feelings do not detract from your argument, in fact we're talking about the same thing on different levels, but sometimes even the best theoretical argument can fall down when someone like me has to make a choice between the good of all and the good of someone you love. I hope I never have to make that choice.'

Alex hesitated. The issue of vivisection was the first to be brought home like a ticking bomb to be defused by her parents, and when the passion faded Alex was left with the same ability to stand back from an issue and examine it on different levels. Nowadays, at dinner parties, she was the consummate devil's advocate, taking the opposite tack to any stance with what appeared to be total commitment before rounding on former allies and attacking their opinions with equal ferocity. As a party trick she recognized its value, but sometimes she regretted that the passion had indeed died, choked by objectivity, and that she would never feel that sense of outrage again. She had views and beliefs, but they were based on practicality rather than aspiration.

'I'm off to Russia this evening,' she announced to her mother, 'so don't worry when you get no answer from the flat.'

'Russia?' her mother queried. 'For how long? Are you going on your own?'

Alex realized that she had very few answers to give her mother and was caught by another moment of doubt.

'I'm going to Moscow with a client. I'm not

sure how long for and I've left the phone number of the hotel in the office. Libby'll call you and give it to you.'

'Well, what's the hotel called, then? I can find out the number myself.'

'I don't know. The agent booked everything for me because it was such short notice. Honestly, don't worry. Everything's under control.'

'Why don't I believe you?' her mother asked. 'Is there something you're not telling me?'

'No, no,' Alex insisted, hoping she sounded righteously irritated by her mother's insistence. 'Routine business trip, that's all. Don't worry. Moscow is a very civilized place these days.'

'Now I know you're lying. I read an article about organized crime and corruption in the police force yesterday. I won't worry you with the details but I can tell you that Moscow is most certainly not a "very civilized place these days".'

'Point taken. What I meant was that it is a normal business trip in that I will be picked up at the airport, chauffeured around, taken from hotel to meeting and back again. No wandering the streets, I promise.'

'Alex, you know I trust you. I don't think you'll get mugged coming out of a sleazy night-club at three in the morning, but I do think you might get involved in a political discussion in some housing estate ten miles out of the centre of Moscow and find that no-one's got any petrol to get you back to your hotel.'

'Perfectly plausible in Madrid, but not in Moscow. I'm not leaving the hotel other than for a couple of well-chaperoned meetings. I'll call you when I arrive if I can. Otherwise I'll be in touch with Libby.'

'What would I do without Libby? How is she?'

'Oh, fine. Still with Spike, unfortunately.'

'You'll have to get used to that, I think. How long has she been with him now?'

'Must be six years, but to all intents and purposes he's not the same guy. I remember when I first met him. He was cocky, certainly, but now that he's making money he's insufferable. And he's so dismissive of Libby, who's worth ten of him. Anyway. I have to pack. Give my love to Dad and I'll call you as soon as I can. Don't worry.'

By one thirty, couriers had delivered the visa and the air tickets. Alex examined the visa, then thrust it into her bag, having understood nothing. She was quick to pick up languages but the Cyrillic alphabet defeated her. After a last-minute round of calls, which failed to unearth Sol, she left for the airport.

In the dingy half-light of Heathrow's terminal two she checked in for the Aeroflot flight, mentioning Volkov's name to be sure she was allocated a seat next to him. She took the card entitling her to access to the VIP lounge and made her way through passport control. She recalled Volkov as a tall, dark spectre, imposing and controlled, and was not prepared for the surly welcome from an unshaven man who was clearly wearing the same shirt, now badly creased, as the day before. While Alex had enjoyed eight hours' sleep it was obvious that Maxim had allowed the momentum of the early evening to carry on and he had arrived in the airport unwashed and having had no rest.

Maxim stood up and kissed her hand perfunctorily. She had seen little expression on his face during the whole of the previous day and his face in repose had an inbuilt severity; the thin lips seemed pinched in disapproval even when the conversation was neutral and his flaring nostrils permanently conveyed contempt. The black hair, which had been swept back the previous day in sleek uniformity, now hung in greasy disarray. Alex examined him as he ordered and swallowed a beer, trying to remember the intellectual compatibility she had felt the previous day. While she knew she should not allow herself to be affected by his appearance, he looked so dissolute, and so comfortable in his dissolution, that she began to reconsider the whole project.

There was no doubt that she needed to be taken care of in Moscow, a novel experience for someone who had manoeuvred her way out of many awkward situations in Europe and South America. In addition to her inability to master even the most basic phrase in Russian, she had no first-hand knowledge of how the system had worked nor how it worked today. Were there taxis? How would she recognize the police? *Were* there any police? Like her mother, she had read only the most dispiriting stories of life in Russia in its transition from a communist to a capitalist regime, and by all accounts there was no support system for Russian nationals, let alone stranded foreigners.

'Tell me,' she asked hesitantly, 'where am I staying in Moscow?'

'I don't know. Only my secretary book this. Driver will say when we come to Moscow.'

'Your driver will pick us up at the airport?'

'Of course.'

She had not expected any recognition from Maxim that she had dropped everything to come on this trip, but nonetheless she was surprised by the way he continued reading his Russian newspaper, drinking his beer, paying her no attention at all.

She sat back and pulled out a map of Russia. Nothing could detract from the excitement of the trip. Tomorrow she would be in Red Square, looking at the Kremlin, watching the changing of the guard at Lenin's Tomb.

On the plane Maxim began to question her and Alex reluctantly stowed away her maps and guidebooks.

'So, now I understand market,' he began, 'what do you do? What is to do hedging?'

'Hedging,' she began, 'hedging is simply dealing with risk. When the London Metal Exchange first started—'

'Quickly. I have other questions here.'

Alex smiled. 'When the Exchange first started, it was to deal with the problems of merchants who were bringing copper into Britain. Copper which was produced in Chile, for example. The London merchant would do a deal, agree a price with the Chilean company and then wait. It took three months for the copper to arrive in Europe. And during that time the merchant was nervous. What happened if the world price of copper fell while his metal was at sea?'

'Yes, yes, yes. He lose money.'

'Exactly.' Alex ignored his sarcasm. 'And the same thing can happen to you. You have what we call price risk. If the world price of aluminium falls while you have aluminium in your hands, you will lose money.'

Volkov looked out of the window, pretending to ignore her.

'So these early merchants decided to sell the metal even before it arrived. Agree the price and wait for the metal to arrive some time in the future. All the buyers and the sellers got together in one place and agreed prices with each other. See? A futures contract. A contract where the delivery takes place in the future.'

'This is your job? All you do? So easy?'

Alex laughed. 'Well, there is a little more to it than that, but you have an idea now of how it works.'

'Pah,' he said again and ordered another drink.

'Are you sure you understand?' she queried, willing to try another tack. He ignored her and after a moment drew out the tiny piece of paper on which he'd written notes the previous day.

'Question.'

'Yes?'

'What is integrated producer?'

Alex launched into an explanation of how business worked in the West and Maxim sat impassively, either staring straight ahead or out of the window. In spite of his obvious hangover, which he seemed to have successfully treated with beer, he began to drink vodka almost as soon as the plane took off. He refused the food which was offered by the pretty but scowling stewardesses and barely allowed Alex the time to start hers. When she stopped to eat in the middle of an explanation of currency fluctuations, he simply lifted her tray and called loudly for a stewardess to take it away.

'I hadn't finished.'

'Not good food.'

Alex looked at him. Whether the food was good or not was not the issue and she debated discussing with him at this early stage just how they should deal with each other. She was the broker, he the client, but the gap between them was likely to be magnified by the fact that he was a Russian man and she a Western woman. She decided to mark out her territory now, before he began to believe that he had the remit to take control. She had already seen him dig in his heels the previous day by refusing to leave the dealing room.

'Mr Volkov – Maxim. *I* decide if I want to eat. Not you.'

Like a shot he called the stewardess back and spoke angrily to her.

Alex attempted to interrupt. 'Don't fight with *her*. I don't want any more food. I just don't want you to decide for me if I'm going to eat or not.' The dispute with the stewardess continued and the senior steward was called. He looked at Alex then gesticulated angrily. Alex picked up her book. After a moment another tray of food was brought and slammed down in front of her.

Angrily she turned to Maxim. 'For God's sake. This is so childish. I said that I don't want you to tell me what to do. The food is irrelevant. Take it away.'

Maxim was furious. 'Now you don't want? After I fight with stupid bitch to bring more, now you don't want?'

'OK. I'll eat some more. But listen. Do not shout at me. Do not make decisions for me. Understand?'

'Eat.'

They sat in cold silence until Maxim fell asleep. As the plane began its descent the same stewardess attempted to fasten his seatbelt, but he woke with a start and slapped her hand away.

In Moscow airport the passengers, fanning out to a throng twenty wide, were funnelled into one lane for passport control. There was a great deal of jostling and Alex regretted having taken her bag as hand luggage. It was heavy and as she was reluctant to drag it along the filthy floor she was obliged to keep it cradled in her arms. The guard who examined her passport was a handsome blond boy in military uniform, who tapped some information into his computer terminal then sat, impassive, for three minutes until a signal indicated that she could proceed. He glanced at her suspiciously as he handed back her visa and did not respond to her pleasant smile and muttered thank you.

Maxim ignored her until they were in the baggage hall. Although the airport had always been used for civilian, commercial flights, it looked to Alex like a military installation. All the personnel wore uniforms and the only relief on the olive-green walls were black and white signs in block capitals.

The airport hall was full of people and Alex had to struggle to keep up with Maxim as he pushed his way towards the door. Several times hands grabbed for her bag. Unheeding, Maxim forged through the crowd which immediately closed in around her.

Alex knew how conspicuous she was and hugged her shawl around her. She was aware that she looked very Western and very wealthy and regretted her choice of clothes. The beige cashmere shawl had seemed like a good, all-weather garment to take, but in the dark-grey morass of the Sheremetyevo airport she felt that its expensive, self-satisfied glow sent out signals of luxury like a beacon. It was as if a coloured image had been cut out and stuck onto an old black-and-white photograph, or a bauble hung from an unadorned Christmas tree. Alex regretted the obvious opulence of her appearance.

She was uneasy. The looks of the men jostling her were uninhibited. They gestured towards her and talked to each other, nodding in her direction. One spat on the floor and wiped his mouth slowly. The women looked at her with open animosity. Alex felt both afraid and revolted by the intensity of the crowd, which seemed to want to move in on her and obliterate her. She could understand nothing, everything was totally alien and incomprehensible, but the crowd seemed to move towards her with a common purpose. She suddenly felt extremely vulnerable and began to run. She caught up with

Maxim at the edge of the hall and stood for a moment by the open door. But there was no respite; the smell of tobacco mingled with petrol fumes overwhelmed her.

Maxim ignored her until his driver arrived, then snatched her bag and threw it into the boot. He got into the front seat, seeming to forget Alex, who had little choice but to scramble into the back of the slowly moving car. Maxim and Boris shouted at one another for ten minutes, then lapsed into silence as they drove towards the motorway.

Alex's eye was caught by Boris's hands on the steering wheel. At first they appeared smaller than normal, gnarled and stunted. But then she saw that both his index fingers were missing and his thumbs had been severed at the joint halfway down. She shuddered with revulsion and looked away.

Navigation along the motorway was not easy; few cars respected the lane system and queues appeared inexplicably as armed policemen wearing belted greatcoats and fur hats stepped into the road and flagged down passing cars. Alex wondered how they picked their victims since all the cars she saw on their way into Moscow were identically dirty and battered, emitting foul-smelling smoke.

After miles of bleak apartment blocks the architecture changed and the buildings took on a monumental air; huge Stalinist monoliths where nobility was tempered by severity, each gracious curve topped by a spike, each arch truncated. Intimidating buildings, designed to be awe-inspiring, now seemed only threatening. Alex leant forward and stared out of the window, excited by the simple fact that she was in Moscow, a place unlike anything she had seen before. The streets were deeply rutted, each pool filled with filthy rain which splashed the unheeding passers-by. As they tore down the Arbat the scene which flashed past Alex's eyes like a magic-lantern show was overwhelmingly grey, but occasionally, behind an ornate wrought-iron gate, a building in warm ochre would catch her eye like a flash of light and on one occasion a small church with impeccably gilded domes burst between two dark office blocks like a small firework.

The street layout confused Alex, who had a fair sense of direction. Inner Moscow seemed to be constructed like the maze at Hampton Court; the one-way system appeared to reroute cars half a mile in order to take them up a street parallel to the one they wanted. The final lap of the journey was around Djerzinsky Square, which Alex recognized from news bulletins, and past the famous blank, forbidding façade of the Lubianka prison.

The Magyar Hotel had been the home of a prominent Russian family before the revolution. The common areas had been relatively sympathetically renovated by a Russian/Swiss joint venture and retained many of the original features. But there was still a dustiness in the dark red velvet of the chairs in reception and a sense of fatigue in the heavy folds of the damask curtains at the window that could not be dispelled by the brightly coloured brochures and the gaudy *matrioshka* dolls offered for sale in the display cabinet.

Maxim led Alex to the reception desk and waited until the conversation between bellboy and receptionist was over. Alex was surprised at his patience and was sure that she would not have been accorded the same favour had she been chatting to Boris. She was given a key and the bellboy disappeared with her bag. Maxim bowed and turned to the door.

'Wait a minute!' she called after him. 'What happens now? Do we have a meeting in the morning?'

'I send driver for you.'

'When?'

Maxim frowned with annoyance. 'When you want.'

'Ten?'

He shrugged. 'OK.'

The lift, an original with a gilt filigree screen and Persian-carpeted floor, was out of order. Alex admired it for a moment, then trudged up the three flights of stairs. Her bedroom was small, barely accommodating the double bed, but the furnishings were brand new and the room was clean. The bathroom was magnificent, with pristine white walls and grey-veined marble slabs on the floor. Alex ran a bath immediately, dropped her clothes on the floor and sank down into its welcoming depth. As she lay in the neck-high foam, she looked up. There were two fire sprinklers on the ceiling and she wondered whether they were cameras. She laughed and pulled the plug. In an instant the bathwater gushed up from grilles on the floor, soaking her clothes, rising to an inch in depth, flooding under the door to her bedroom. Wrapped in a towel, she called reception and asked for help. Half an hour later an engineer appeared, adjusted a valve and left.

She asked for her parents' number and waited to be connected, not sure if her request had been understood. It took only a few minutes until the line rang and her mother answered.

'Hello?'

'Hi! It's me. I'm in Moscow!'

'Well, what's it like? How was your journey?'

Alex dragged the phone over to the bed and lay back. 'I've only just arrived . . .' Quickly she described the flight and the journey to the hotel, giving the phone number and address, finishing with the bathwater episode.

Her mother laughed. 'And d'you think he's fixed it?'

'To the very best of his ability,' Alex assured her. 'Whether or not the resources are available to execute the task is another matter. We shall see. My first impression of Russia, based entirely on the Magyar Hotel, is that Swiss perfectionism may not have found the perfect bedfellow in Russian implementation. The place has charm, it looks great, but I would sacrifice the craftsmanship of the marble sink for a lift that works, or wastepipes that are connected to each other.'

'Would you really?'

Alex laughed. 'Maybe not. What's the point in coming to Moscow to stay in yet another sterilized hotel belonging to an anonymous chain?'

'How right you are. Now look after yourself, and don't forget what I told you. Stay indoors.'

'I will. Bye.'

She hung up and dialled the operator again, this time asking for Libby's home number.

'You made it! How is it?'

'Yes, I've made it and it's ... interesting. Maxim had me explaining hedging on the plane and we seem to have had a falling out. I've a meeting with him tomorrow morning, though. Tell me, what's happening in the markets?'

Libby reeled off the prices, describing the day's activity on each. Alex listened silently, taking notes.

'And gold ... the Dow?'

'All steady. Business is fine, orderly. I've booked you a lunch with Triasco for next Tuesday but I've warned them you may not be back. They wanted to take the chance. They're going for a listing and want to hedge the whole of next year's output. Do you have any idea what your schedule is?'

'No, but I should have a clearer idea tomorrow. Today's Wednesday ... so I'll probably come back on Saturday.'

'Keep me posted. One other thing. Professor Vichevsky called. He said he knew you were in Moscow, but he wanted your number there. I said I'd ask you to call him. D'you want his number?'

'I have it. Anything else?'

'Well, I hate to mention it while you're in

Russia and you can't do anything about it, but Neville's looking for your business plan.'

'Shit! Did I do any notes? I can't remember. Have you got the commission figures there?'

'Yes, I can certainly put something together, but it'll be lacking your inimitable style. And Monty said he was expecting you to do a presentation on Chile.'

'I'll fax some notes to the office number in an hour or so. You can pick them up in the morning. There're a couple of crucial credit issues I have to put to the board before the beginning of April. OK. That's that. Anything else?'

'Couple of messages, but they don't seem too important.'

'No word from Sol?'

'I'd have told you. He's probably still settling in, you know, living in a hotel . . .'

'I know. Look, Libby, make sure he gets the number here if he calls, and the room number as well. Now, I'd better get on with this report. I'll call you tomorrow.'

Alex opened her bag, took out a pad and began to draft the outline of the plan she had been mulling over for the previous three weeks. She wanted to establish an agency in Indonesia and needed the board's green light for the initial expense. Secondly, she wanted to develop an Islamic fund to take advantage of the huge amounts of Arab money that could not be channelled into conventional Western investment vehicles.

By one o'clock she had finished the outline, called reception and delivered the fax to the bellboy. Her final task was to calculate the costs and projected commissions from her trip to Moscow. Neville had asked for the figures before she'd left. He had a point. If the numbers did not justify the trip, the trip should not take place. Alex laughed. The numbers were massive on the basis that she would charge commission of at least a dollar a tonne, but they were pure fiction. Who knew what the Russian market would yield?

If successful, she would reap millions of dollars in commission.

But there were undeniable risks.

Although she had shrugged off her mother's fears, she was not insensitive to the link between opportunity and greed. In a society with no enforceable legal system, there were no deterrents and she knew that the prospect of an income stream, worth millions of dollars, would transcend many moral codes. And the newspaper reports were extremely alarming. Crime in Moscow seemed to be conducted almost exclusively in the public arena. In a country with a submissive population, no-one interfered. The violence was brazen and casual.

Yet the size of the country and the scale of the industry excited her. No rules meant greater opportunity, open doors. She filled in the numbers on the form with insouciance. If she were successful with only one smelter she would repay her costs a thousand times over. And if she didn't, her expense account would be the least of her worries.

FIVE

She was waiting downstairs when the car came the following morning, driven by the stony-faced Boris. The journey took ten minutes, the car winding down narrow backstreets until it stopped outside a newly painted white building. Boris switched off the engine.

'Is this it? Am I here?' Alex asked. Boris waved his hand in the direction of the doorway and grunted.

'Thank you very much.' She got out and squinted up at the small windows with the black grilles across them. The blank façade of the building resembled a prison, clean and renovated but a prison nonetheless. The narrow doorway led to a small, dark hall where decorators had abandoned their unfinished task. There were sheets and overalls draped across a couple of old-fashioned desks, and scaffolding ran around the room at ceiling height. At a small table an armed watchman sat reading a newspaper. He did not look up when Alex approached him, and she waited a moment before saying, 'Excuse me?'

The man looked up and pointed towards the staircase on the left. Alex did not thank him, but made her way across the hallway. At the foot of the staircase, covered in dusty tarpaulins, she hesitated. She had been brought to a building in the backstreets of Moscow by a man she did not know, who spoke no English and did not seem inclined to be overly protective of her. There was nobody else to be seen and not a sound to be heard. Surely there should be some office sounds, a typewriter, some phones? How could she have been so foolish to have laughed at her mother's warning and ridiculed the scenario she had painted.

She considered making her way back outside and asking Boris for confirmation that Maxim was here, but when she looked out the car had gone. She was stranded. Suddenly a door opened above her. A young woman wearing obviously Western clothes appeared from the doorway opposite the staircase and held out her hand, unsmiling.

Every feature of her face seemed to have been drawn with the aid of a little compass – the huge gobstopper eyes with semi-circular shadows above and below, the flared nostrils either side of the small fleshy marble at the end of her nose. Her mouth was short, round, the upper lip with virtually no definition, the cheeks round, high and red. It was the face of a Russian doll, a face to look out from under a shawl, an old Russian face before cheap make-up and disastrous peroxide hair colour took over.

'I am Maria.'

'Alexandra Brookes.' Relieved, she ran up the steps and took the woman's hand. 'Am I in the right place? Is Maxim here?'

'Yes, he is here. Come this way.' She led Alex to a door at the end of the corridor, knocked then waited, her hands clasped demurely in front of her. There was a sound from inside and the secretary opened the door, gesturing for Alex to enter.

Inside, Alex smelled the distinctive odour of fresh paint and her interest was caught by the surprising modernity of his office. The white walls and blond wood formed a benign show-case for the few decorative pieces in the room – a massive Buddha, a gracious Italian standard lamp and a print of what appeared to be a Rorschach test. It was an odd collection of pieces, which seemed to Alex to have been picked for their size. She noticed a huge map of Moscow.

'Where on earth did you get this, Maxim?' She turned to face Maxim sitting behind an immaculately tidy desk. Alex examined the mid-eighteenth century map with interest. 'Did you find it here?'

'You want to buy it?'

'I almost certainly can't afford it. But I'm interested in where it came from.'

'You want to take it back with you?'

'For God's sake, Maxim. I don't want it,' she snapped. 'I want to know where you got it, that's all. Why is that such a difficult question?'

'Not difficult. I know the answer. But I tell people is very rare Russian map. Discovered in old building in Moscow.'

150

'And people believe you?'

'Russians, no. But tourists, yes.' He rose from behind the desk and opened a cupboard.

'Look! Many maps found in Moscow during building.'

Suddenly Alex understood the scam. 'You buy these in Europe and ship them to Russia? Can you do that and still make money?'

'Oh yes. And tourists take back to Europe with them. Is only small business but very funny, I think.'

'It's a great game.' She had seen it before. The Kid was the same. No matter what they owned – art, horses, books – it was business. Even when there was an attachment they never forgot the possibility of a deal.

She sat down and pulled her briefcase onto her knees. 'Now, do you want to talk about hedging?'

Again, Maxim was ahead of her.

'Give me form for trading.'

'An account-opening form? You want to fill it in now?'

'Yes. I want to trade.'

'You want to hedge the risk on your aluminium?'

'Bloody hedging. Two weeks ago I never heard this word. Now all you say is hedging ... hedging. Yes, I want to hedge my aluminium. And play maybe. Give me paper.'

Alex brought out the five-page document Libby had insisted she bring and drew out her pen.

'I don't think you'll be able to answer some of these but we can try.'

'Why not answer? You think too difficult for me?'

'No, but this form is designed for Western companies.'

'And Western companies more clever than Russian companies?'

Alex stood up. 'Look. Do we have to have a fight over every little detail? I have work to do in London and I did not come here to sit in your office and discuss the merits of a Western company over a Russian one. It is not an issue.'

'Sit. Give me form. What to tell you? What is auditor?'

'Now you see what I mean. There is a different system in the West. Not better, not worse. Just different. If I do a lot of business in Russia, I will design a new form. Now,' her voice rose as she leant across the desk and snatched the form back, 'can we please proceed with the damn thing?'

Maxim clicked his tongue in disapproval and Alex blushed at her lack of self-control. She sat back and drew breath.

'Let me ask the questions,' she said slowly. 'I can explain as we go. It's not necessary to fill in every section. Company name?'

For forty-five minutes they worked through the form. When they had finished, almost all the sections were left blank. As Alex had feared, there was no company law in Russia since the concept was a recent one, no accounting practices, no banking history. Nothing whatsoever to go on.

'It gives me very little information, Maxim.'

He opened a drawer. 'What do you need to

know? How much you want to start trading? Three million, five million?'

He waved the chequebook ostentatiously in front of her, showing the logo of a prestigious Swiss bank.

Mesmerized, Alex watched him pull the top from his pen. 'It's not how much *I* want. It's what you want. How much aluminium do you have?'

He ignored her. 'Give me number of Wellington account. I send money today.'

'Maxim, why are you doing all this so suddenly? I need to send you a copy of our terms and conditions . . .'

'You so bad businesswoman. Why you don't take my money now? Maybe tomorrow I don't want.'

Alex sighed. 'I'm not selling you a car, or a . . . map. It's not an object. I'm selling you a . . . relationship. There are plenty of brokers who would take your money and let you lose it all on unsuitable trades.' As soon as she said it she knew she had made another gaffe. She waited for him to protest that he would not make an unsuitable trade, but he said nothing.

'Anyway. Thank you for the money. I'll call my assistant and ask her to fax you the banking details. She'll take care of the rest of the paperwork and we can trade as soon as the funds have cleared.'

'OK. How I trade?'

Alex described the process from the initial phone call right through to the conclusion of the deal, followed by the fax confirmation and the contract. Maxim wrote down the terminology, then checked it out on her.

'Fine. You're ready to do a deal now. But before we begin I'd like to ask you some questions about the Russian metal industry.'

Alex's patience in describing the London Metal Exchange was not reciprocated. Maxim was an impatient and frequently unintelligible tutor.

'Tell me about the giant aluminium producers in Siberia. Chaika, for example. How does it operate?'

'How? You want me to explain all about technology? How to make aluminium?'

'No, no. I know all that. Tell me about their overheads, that sort of thing.'

Maxim sighed in irritation. The implication was that she ought to know all this already – a Russian, doing her job, would certainly have done her research.

'OK,' he began. 'You call this thing, Chaika, a producer. Is true, but is just an . . . oven. You not give it raw material – alumina – it not make aluminium. Like if you not have eggs and things, you not make cake.'

Alex took notes. In his attempt to explain a complicated business with his limited English, he had managed to encapsulate the essentials of the business in a clear, understandable way.

'And where do these raw materials come from?'

'Before, from State. Like magic. Still now some from Russian government but system is poor, unreliable. Most now from Western merchants.' He paused. 'Not like magic.'

'So the Western merchants sell you the raw materials, then what?'

'No, no. You understand nothing at all. How you think Chaika pay for raw materials? Write cheque like me? Maybe pay cash? They have no money. This you should know.'

Chastened, Alex ploughed on. 'So why do the Western merchants deliver all this stuff to a plant which can't pay them?'

Maxim cocked his head. '*Here* is magic,' he taunted. 'Chaika plant turn raw materials into aluminium then give back aluminium to Western merchant.'

'I see! The merchants pay a fee to the smelter, to Chaika, to convert raw materials into aluminium. Chaika can do this more cheaply than a Western smelter, so the merchant has a bigger profit!'

'So clever. Now we drink.'

'Wait a minute, Maxim, just a couple more questions. What do you need from the West?'

'Everything we had previously from government. Finance, transport, everything. I have metal and the plants trust me. They tell me to take care of them. I need to do everything the Russian government do before.'

'When you say finance . . .'

'You know what is inflation in Russia today?'

'Yes . . . three hundred per cent per annum.'

'So you know how much to borrow money inside Russia. The plants cannot do this. Too expensive. I want to find Western bank to lend money – cheaper. Then with this money we buy alumina and electricity and make aluminium.'

155

'I see, and how much spare capacity is there?'

'Later. I talk to you in hotel at eight.'

Dismissed, Alex gathered up the account-opening form and her notes and made her way back downstairs. Her mind was full of the opportunities Maxim presented. She had already drafted the deal she would take back to the West and offer to investors.

She was confident Starling's Bank would look at the deal; she would suggest a consultancy and they would pay Wellington a fee for the introduction. And then the whole deal would be hedged on the Exchange. If she could put all the parties together, the scope was immense.

She realized how much pressure she was under, how much Neville's irritating demands had affected her. She was already sufficiently aware of the decreasing commission figures, and she didn't need the additional burden of Neville's irrelevant, time-consuming charades and the implication that somehow *she* was responsible for the decline.

Boris was waiting for her outside. He remained silent throughout the journey back to the Magyar. When she got out, she thanked him and he inclined his head half an inch.

The pattern was set for the three days Alex spent in Moscow. During the day she worked in the hotel on reports for the Wellington board until she was summoned by Reception to the car. Boris drove her to Maxim's office and they discussed the markets. Then she was delivered back to the hotel when Maxim had had enough.

They ate in a different restaurant every night. Alex's favourite was in an alley two blocks from her hotel. Originally a Turkish bath, the vast, pillared room was lit by candles in carved and gilded torchères high up near the ceiling, illuminating the plump smiling cherubs nestling in the corners. Surprisingly, she discovered that the food was the best she had ever eaten – caviar, crab and thick black rye bread, whole suckling pig, garlic stems, all served on fabulous chipped Fabergé plates. Throughout the meal they talked, Maxim asking questions one after the other, Alex attempting to learn more about business in Russia.

At the outset it was an interesting exercise to re-examine the mechanics of what she did; sometimes she would move ahead without any explanation of what was, to her, a simple case of cause and effect. But he would stop and challenge her.

'How you know price go down when interest rates go up?'

'Because people buy less, the manufacturer cannot afford to keep metal in his yard, so he sells it, then the price goes down . . .'

'Metal is now cheaper, so people buy to make profit.'

'No. They don't buy until the economy is better, until people's confidence is revived and they start spending money. Then they will buy more, the manufacturer will use more metal and his yard will be full.'

Maxim took out his paper with questions. 'And bonds. Floating-rate note, what is this?'

Alex put down her knife and fork and began the next lesson. Bonds took her over an hour as Maxim threw more and more esoteric terms at her, picked out of a book which he'd found on Western economics. Since the book was in English he had understood little but had been interested by the terminology. He grasped everything with startling ease, picking up inconsistencies when Alex tried to cut corners in her explanations, relating one issue to another.

When Alex finally finished her explanation of mortgage-backed bonds, he folded away his paper and she sighed with relief. Before she could pick up her spoon, he leaned across the table, asking her a question of such simplicity that she laughed.

'Why prices go up and down?'

Having understood how economic force, like a tide, moved backwards and forwards, he wanted to know why. And what created that force? What made a country change from burgeoning economy into an over-heating economy? What made people decide to buy or to sell?

She laughed. There was no doubt in her mind that she was dealing with a genius, but a genius with no groundwork. In terms of economic knowledge, he was an *idiot savant*.

On Friday, as Alex was making her way up to Maxim's office, she met him and a guest coming down.

'You late, no time to meet Chernikov,' Maxim growled.

'How can I be late? I just wait for Boris and leave as soon as he arrives.'

'I told you be here at two. Is three now.'

'You never told me anything. If you want me to come earlier, send Boris earlier.'

'Boris wait one hour for you today.'

It was possible. Alex could readily believe that Boris would wait before summoning her, especially if he knew how Maxim would react.

'I came as soon as Boris came,' she reaffirmed adamantly. 'Why did you want me here at two?'

Maxim turned to the man standing behind him on the staircase. 'Is Chernikov, boss of Chaika plant. You could ask him all stupid questions, not me.'

'Damn. I'd have loved to have some time with him.' She held out her hand. 'I have so many questions to ask you.'

The small, grey-haired man shook her hand and spoke a few words to Maxim. Then he turned to Alex with a warm smile, anticipating her response to his words.

'He say he have more stupid questions about your business than you have about his. This I do not believe. I tell him you very, very stupid and think he have much money.'

Alex reddened. 'Maxim, please don't say that kind of thing. You'll ruin my reputation. Anyway, if you tell people about *my* stupid questions, I'll tell them about *yours*.'

Maxim looked coldly at her for a moment. 'Alex. You so stupid. You know, I understand what you say, but you do not speak Russian. With another man, I take money from you, make a deal, say yes. I say only good things, you also only good. Then I say what I like in Russian.' He

159

laughed and turned to Chernikov to prove his point. He gestured to Alex and spoke rapidly. At the end of his speech he laughed, but Chernikov's only response was a faint smile.

Alex understood the racial and sexual nuances of a man and woman in their position. It was difficult for Maxim to have to ask her questions; it was humiliating to have a woman know more than he did. But he *had* to learn and he had selected her as the least painful way to achieve what he wanted. Nonetheless, he was not comfortable with the situation and was, presumably, feeling vulnerable since she could betray him and his ignorance at any time.

Maxim accompanied Chernikov to the door, leaving Alex seething on the staircase. Her intellectual recognition of his dilemma did little to soothe her embarrassment. She was very tempted to leave.

'Come, Alex.' Maxim shepherded her up the stairs. 'You angry now because I tell him you have stupid questions. You British and so you know everything. Yes? And with poor Russian men, they very bad to laugh, because you so clever. Russian men know nothing. Poor Chernikov, he not even know what is floating-rate note!'

Distracted again by the allegation, Alex found herself following Maxim down the corridor.

'Knowing what a floating-rate note is does not constitute knowledge as far as I am concerned. I do not assess your intelligence by what you know about Western economics, nor should you judge me by what I know about Siberian aluminium smelters!'

Maxim sat down behind his desk, ignoring her, which was his usual response to any sign of emotion on her part. Whether it was because he could not match her point, or whether he did not like her to be demonstrative, she did not know. But she was prepared for him suddenly to veer off onto another issue.

'Tonight we go to Belorussia.'

'But tomorrow's Saturday,' she answered automatically.

Maxim raised his eyebrows. 'You not work on Saturday?'

'Well, yes, I could, but I'd planned to go back to London tomorrow. We could be doing most of this on the phone, Maxim, I don't really need to be here.'

Maxim shrugged. 'OK. I go alone. Minsk is not very interesting for you. Produce only 300,000 tonnes a year. You have bigger clients in London.'

'You know that's not the point!' she flashed back. 'You're like a dog with a bone, you really are infuriating.'

'So you come?'

Alex thought for a moment. She was up to date on her work and Libby could spare her for a few more days. But she felt disinclined to accede to any wish of Maxim's.

'Yes. I'll come. I'm interested to see the plant and I would like to see Minsk. But I have to go back to London on Monday. Will that be possible?'

'Possible,' he confirmed.

Libby sat hunched in the back of Spike's Audi. It

was cold, since the engine had been off for half an hour. She wished she had been wearing something more substantial than a light wool suit. She rolled the polo neck of her jumper up until it covered the lower half of her face. Her breath was cold and damp.

She had eventually found Spike at ten o'clock, sitting on the step of Shelley's wine bar in an alley near Fenchurch Street, his head in his hands. She had tracked him from one bar to the next, reports of his behaviour worsening as she progressed. This was something more than just a Friday night drink. In the last bar but one his boss had taken her to one side.

'Let him be this evening, darling. He's in a bad mood . . . Don't mess with him.'

'Come on, Roger, how's he going to get home?' She tried to keep the conversation light although she understood perfectly that Roger was giving her a strong warning. 'Be sensible,' she laughed. 'He'll fall asleep in some bus shelter and catch his death.'

'Might not be a bad thing,' Roger had muttered, walking away, giving up on her. Libby wanted to run after him, to ask him not to dismiss her just because she stood by Spike. She had seen the same look in Alex's eyes, the same resigned shake of the head. And sometimes Libby wanted to belong to the other team, the normal ones, the strong ones. Roger's retreating back was upright, good-natured and sound. Spike, when she found him, would be broken and defeated. And he would want to break and defeat her.

She could hear him singing when she turned into Fenchurch Street, Irish songs, which his father had sung, and which Spike had hated.

'He's never even been to Ireland,' he had told her. 'The only thing Irish about him is his name, yet he sings these dirges and cries his eyes out.'

Libby sat down beside him. 'Hello there. You ready to come home?'

Spike looked at her and shook his head in disgust. 'What are you doing here?'

'I've come to take you home. Come on, it's cold.'

'I'm not cold. Leave me alone, I don't want to be with you.'

'Well, that's too bad,' she countered brightly. 'I want to be with you.'

'I've asked you once nicely,' he said slowly, countering the slurring of his words with excessive care. 'Now piss off.'

'What's wrong, Spike?'

He hesitated for a moment and she knew he was going to tell her but that it wouldn't help in the long run; the sharing of the information would not defuse the anger.

'Well?' she prodded.

'Bastards . . . some fund, bought eight hundred lots on the kerb . . . I was short . . .'

'Spike, come on home.'

'Home?' He turned to Libby and his face tightened in anger. 'Get lost.'

'I'll wait in the car. Look, over there.' She pointed out the Audi sitting in the square in front of the station. 'I'll wait for you there. OK?'

'You can wait as long as you like.'

Libby could not claim to have been deceived about Spike's family life. His father was a drunk who had been shunned by all the children, until he had been hospitalized with pneumonia and some of the girls had reluctantly organized a rota to look after him. After his mother's death Spike could not bear to see the old man. On the day of her funeral, they had fought. Spike had called him a murderous bastard and had reminded him of the Saturday nights when he had come home and beaten her up.

'Never beat her up,' his father had maintained. 'Gave her a couple of good hidings, that's all.'

This was not domestic violence behind closed doors, a secret vice cloaked in respectability and concealed from the outside world. Nothing was hidden. When Libby had asked Spike, gently, if his father had beaten the kids, he had answered, 'Not all of us.'

Somehow, Spike was changing towards her. While he still needed her, there was an edge of desperation to his touch, as if he knew the therapy was becoming less effective. Instead of being soothed by her, he would at best be momentarily calmed. And worst of all there had been one occasion when it had been she who had caused his fury. Until then she had been the cure, now it appeared that she was part of the illness.

She dozed off in the car and when she awoke at midnight Spike had disappeared. She got out, her cramped muscles aching, and looked up and down the deserted City street for him. After a moment she got back into the car and drove home alone.

The flight to Minsk left at five and took three hours. A group of ten men waited for them inside Minsk airport, another dreary, dark green hangar with the same makeshift appearance as Moscow airport. Maxim greeted them one by one, and instead of introducing Alex immediately he held a brief conversation with each. Although some of the Belorussians looked shyly towards Alex, they allowed Maxim to carry on uninterrupted. As she stood there, waiting, Alex wondered how Maxim had come to know these men and what he represented for them. They treated him with a mixture of deference and affection; each one had clasped him and kissed him when he arrived and now they almost stood to attention as he spoke.

Finally he turned to her and explained who she was. She was able to distinguish her name and the name Wellington. She also understood the Russian for London Metal Exchange. His speech reminded her of her vow to learn Russian and she made a mental note to organize a tutor. She smiled throughout the introduction, hoping that Maxim was not denigrating her.

'They say welcome. They will come to hotel to celebrate your arrival.'

'Fine. Thank you.'

'Come.' He led her to the car and opened the door.

Two suites had been reserved, on different floors. Alex was shown hers, then accompanied to Maxim's. The vodka was produced and a small glass put in front of her.

Maxim stood up. 'I will make toast to say

welcome and I will talk for you also. I say thank you to them and that we so happy to be here . . . All these things.'

Alex smiled as he made the toast, gazing into the middle distance, waving his glass, occasionally thumping the table. Finally, he lifted his glass and the toast was drunk. Alex sipped a small amount of the vodka and coughed.

'You have to drink vodka like Russian,' he explained. 'Look.'

He lowered his head until his chin was against his chest then exhaled noisily. He lifted his glass and drained it, still holding his breath after swallowing the vodka, his face contorted as if in pain. He took a long gulp of mineral water then exhaled, waiting for her appreciation of his performance.

'I wonder why you drink it if you hate it so much?' she asked.

'Don't hate. Love. But is alcohol.'

Alex laughed. 'OK. Let's have a go.'

Another glass was poured and she took it in her hand, breathing out with theatrical vigour. With a quick flick of her wrist she upended the glass and swallowed the ice-cold shot of vodka, suppressing a cough as the spirit hit the back of her throat. She snatched up the water glass and drank. The sensation was pleasant, warm and tingling. She smiled at the group who applauded her, grinning at her willingness to participate. Only Maxim remained impassive.

'You should not drink alone. Very rude.'

Immediately the glasses were refilled. The youngest of the Belorussian group stood up and began to talk. At first Maxim translated with vigour, protesting when the speaker went too fast and he could not keep up. Alex was charmed.

They were pleased to see her, Maxim reported, and appreciated that she had taken the time to come to their country where conditions must be very unsatisfactory for someone used to Western standards. She began to protest but was over-ruled. A toast was drunk.

Then the plant manager, Belkov, stood up. He was a tall man, far too thin and uncomfortable in his thinness, as if he had until recently been fat. He had a kind face, soft and shy, and when he got to his feet the others stopped talking. In his quiet, pleasant way, he had authority.

As he spoke, the awkwardness of his demeanour and ill-fitting clothes was forgotten.

'My English is very bad,' he began. 'I want to drink toast.' He lifted his glass, and Alex, still slightly breathless from the previous toast, began to have an inkling of the ordeal ahead. She prayed for a long toast to give her some respite.

'All my life I worked hard. Because I must. I know I must. And I stay in Belorussia, because I must. And I speak Russian,' he nodded in apology to Maxim, 'I do not want, but I must. Now, you live in England. And you can do what you want. Not what you must. And you are here.'

He lifted his glass to Alex and the others stood. 'If I live in London and do what I want, I not come to Belorussia. Is not easy for you and is not . . .' He turned to Maxim, who presented him with the word.

'. . . it is not *convenient*. We know this.' He stopped for a second to translate briefly. The others nodded.

'Forgive my bad English. We have saying here that we recognize your soul like old friend. We all feel this and we are very glad you have come here.'

Alex felt deeply moved. She knew nothing about these men and the conversation had not, until now, gone beyond the initial pleasantries, but she knew exactly what Belkov meant. She was comfortable with them. She glanced at Maxim, who looked back, his expression neutral.

'Will you translate for me?'

He shrugged.

Alex stood up. 'There are no such sayings in English and so I cannot return the compliment. I ask myself *why* we do not have ideas like this in our language. I feel perhaps we did have them once, but we have forgotten them. There are differences in our cultures and there are things which one culture does better than another.' She swallowed. Suddenly she felt tears in her eyes. 'I can only say that I am glad today to be in a country where the soul is not forgotten.'

After Maxim had finished the translation, she lifted her glass.

'*Nasdarovya, ee balshoi spaseeba.*' Your health and many thanks.

There was a pause as the Belorussians lifted their glasses to her and simultaneously drained them. It was an emotional moment which was almost immediately defused by Maxim, who snatched up the bottle, talking rapidly in Russian.

He took Alex's glass and looked at her, his lips tight in the ferocious disapproval she had seen on previous occasions.

'So now you want to marry Belorussian and live in Minsk?'

'Don't be stupid, Maxim,' she laughed, forgetting how careful she had to be. 'It was a lovely thing to say and I am very moved by their warmth and feeling.'

'Pah!'

'I am,' she confirmed quietly, looking around. These were foreign faces, different in construction from the European features she was familiar with, with foreign mannerisms and language. But she felt comfortable with them and saw something which reminded her of the faces in 1945 newsreels in Britain, optimism, innocence and well-meaning. She looked from one face to another then stopped herself. Maybe it was the vodka, she rationalized, but she was feeling very emotional.

After the third toast, traditionally devoted to God, the conversation started in earnest. Belkov wanted to explain to Alex how his business worked and how conditions had changed since the end of the communist regime. Initially, the plant workers had had no idea how to proceed. There was no-one to look after them, no-one to support them. Without pathos, he managed to convey the sense of desperation they had felt when they realized that they were entirely on their own with no idea how to procure the raw materials they needed or even how to arrange transport to deliver the metal they had in the factory. Belkov laughed. They had tried to contact potential buyers in the West and their first letter had been addressed simply to 'Pirelli, Italy.' In Russian script, he added.

Then the first Western merchant, Trademin, had arrived. There was a prolonged discussion to find the right word to explain how the plant workers had felt when these people had appeared, finally accepting Alex's suggestion that they were perceived as a 'godsend'. They brought raw materials, food, medicine and clothes. They had taken the place of the Soviet authorities, leaving the plant to get on with the business of aluminium production. While Alex was pleased that things had worked out well for the plant, she was somewhat uncomfortable with the portrayal of Trademin as angels. It was a bizarre thought, that a Western merchant, part of the most aggressive and cut-throat sector of the market, could be 'helping someone out'.

Belkov continued and Alex's worst fears were confirmed. The so-called benefits offered by Trademin could not possibly cost as much as the enormous discounts the Belorussians were offering. Even the roughest calculation revealed that they were making massive profits. But if she pointed this out, she knew what the answer would be. They had no choice. With no infrastructure left, Trademin was better than nothing. Alex bit her tongue. She would speak to Maxim about this later; they would do some sums and she would suggest a fairer way to do business. And as Belkov had offered to take her round the plant and the town, she would wait until she had

170

seen the conditions herself before deciding what to do.

As the vodka flowed Maxim's translations became sporadic. He argued in rapid Russian with each member of the party in turn, slapping the table and allowing no interruptions. Some of the Belorussians tried to include her and form a group apart from Maxim, but he would permit nothing but full attention. Finally, Alex tapped his arm.

'Maxim, I have to go to bed now. I'm exhausted.'

His answer was immediate. 'No.'

Alex laughed and stood up. 'Gentlemen, I'm very sorry—'

Suddenly Maxim stood up. '*I* say when you go.'

The room was quiet. Alex looked at Maxim's face. He was ugly. The nicotine-stained, irregular teeth, the bad skin, the etching of deprivation. Alex thought back to the façade he had presented on the first day in Vichevsky's office – a façade she had never seen again. He still wore obviously expensive clothes, but they could do nothing to lift the aura of deliberate neglect. His tie was invariably loose, the small greasy knot obscuring the sheen of the silk, his jacket showing that it had been carelessly thrown off too many times.

Alex was frightened. There was something in his rigid immobility she found particularly threatening. She felt that if she moved he would pounce, lash out and bring her back to order with one sharp blow. One harsh reprimand to bring her to heel. She flinched at the image. He was almost waiting for her to do it, wanting her to provoke him.

No-one else moved. Alex heard her own breathing and felt her unsteady legs begin to weaken. Suddenly Maxim's hand shot out and grabbed her wrist, slamming her right hand, palm down, onto the table, pinning it beneath his own.

'Why you do this all the time?' he spat at her, rubbing his index finger along his upper lip in a cruel parody of what she recognized to be her own behaviour. There was no explanation for it. She did it when she was thinking – or when she was scared.

'It make me mad, all the time, doing this,' he continued and to Alex's horror he reached behind him with his other hand and produced a knife from the dresser. Carefully, he laid the long blade on the soft outer edge of her hand. Alex screamed and tried to pull back her hand but he held it fast and drew the blade once, quickly, across the back of her knuckles. A thin red score appeared on her skin and she stared at it in shock. Either he was very skilled or very lucky – the skin was hardly broken. She snatched her hand back and tucked it under her arm protectively, tears of pain and humiliation welling in her eyes.

Maxim laughed and put the knife away casually, breaking into Russian, ignoring her. He poured another round of drinks and placed a glass in front of Alex, filling it to the brim. The table fell silent.

Alex reached for the glass, noticing that her

hand was shaking badly. She tried to compose herself. After a moment's hesitation she knocked back the vodka, knowing that this was the demonstration of obedience Maxim required.

She had learnt her lesson. The next time she took issue with him she would wait until they were on their own. Furtively, she examined the back of her hand. At least she still had all her fingers. She thought of Boris and his ugly deformed hands and with a sudden jolt of fear wondered how it had happened.

Vichevsky stood on the forecourt of Moscow airport in the biting wind, his one small suitcase tucked under his arm. His assistant, Arkady, had promised to arrange for his cousin to be at the airport, but there was no-one. Vichevsky was bitterly disappointed. He had told Arkady to ask the driver to hold up a card with his name on it and had been looking forward to this fleeting moment of fame for days.

He plodded back into the terminal building and allowed himself to be swept off by the first driver to spot him.

Kartchak's combined office and apartment was in a renovated block next to the Palace Hotel in the Tsverskaya. Vichevsky gave the driver the address then sat back and pulled out the notes he had taken from his meeting with Belayev and a small clipping from the *Evening Standard* which mentioned the EBRD. He also had a file of random cuttings from the financial pages of the *Telegraph* – since Kartchak couldn't speak or read English it didn't matter that they were nothing to do with aluminium. Finally, he had brought the article from *Futures Trading* magazine on Alexandra Brookes.

A very good friend, he intended to say with an enigmatic smile.

With any luck, he would run quickly through the concept of venture capital, talk about the British banking system, then aluminium production. He fingered the return part of his ticket. While he was uneasy with Kartchak, one quick meeting was a small price to pay for a free trip to Moscow. He should be in and out in less than an hour. Then he would go to his former home where his mother and sister were expecting him.

It was after six when he finally paid the taxi driver a massive sum in roubles, which he automatically translated back into sterling. Only nine pounds! And the driver had shouted a jubilant obscenity as he had driven off; no doubt this was twice the normal fare.

The door to Kartchak's apartment block could have been a service door at the back of the hotel; there were no signs, nameplates nor even a number. Vichevsky walked past it a couple of times before deciding that this must be the place.

He vaguely recognized the man who unlocked the heavy door and ushered him in but there was no invitation to talk. Three armed guards were standing in the foyer, their rifles on show, watching Vichevsky closely.

'Wait there.' The doorman indicated another door to the left of the main hall.

Vichevsky found himself in a narrow, plushly carpeted corridor, lit by small spotlights. Five doors led off to each side. Vichevsky was impressed. An apartment of this size and opulence so centrally located would cost a fortune. He sat down in a flimsy canvas chair by the door and pulled his suitcase onto his knees, prepared for the wait which Kartchak would indubitably inflict on him.

Kartchak walked slowly from one side of the bedroom to the other. A girl lay sobbing on the bed. He had not touched her and had no intention of doing so; he was not interested in anything 'unusual', but obviously the girl did not know this. All she knew was that she had been called by the doorman of the Palace Hotel and told where to go. She had made a little remark about Kartchak's appearance and asked him if he was Russian – his clothes were Western and the eye-catching newness of the furnishings in the flat led her to believe that he might be a foreign businessman.

Kartchak turned suddenly and looked at her from a new angle. She sobbed more loudly, burying her cheek against her outstretched arm. He allowed this, although it spoiled the perfect symmetry of the X formed by her arms and spreadeagled legs. As he watched, she tossed her head from one side to the other, and her knees crept towards each other. He touched her ankle lightly and they flew apart again.

'Hands,' he said quietly and she instantly let go of the bedhead, unaware that she had been clutching it. Satisfied, Kartchak resumed his walk across the room.

The girl's muscles must be hurting by now. She was in an unusual position, even for a girl like her, and Kartchak examined her carefully for any little movements that would indicate that she was trying to ease her discomfort. Apart from the exaggerated movement of her ribcage there was nothing, and he sat down, delighted with her. Anyone coming into the room and looking quickly at her would assume that she was tied to the bed by her wrists and ankles and that she was crying through fear. Only Kartchak knew her embarrassment, that she was there, exposed, because she was obeying his instructions. Even a girl like this could still be humiliated.

Kartchak remembered the first time he had shot someone for money. He had tied the man's hands, then made him kneel down as he had been trained to do. Suddenly, it had seemed ridiculous. At that moment, he had the most authority a man could ever have, to be able to decide whether to kill or let live. If you could make a man do just about anything by wielding this power, surely you could make him kneel down voluntarily and keep his wrists together as if tied?

The first man had been confused. He had knelt down, facing Kartchak, and begun to plead for his life. Kartchak had shot him quickly since he was close to hysteria and had missed the point. But from then on he had teased the moment of ultimate power to the maximum, spinning it out like a thread of glass, afraid that it could break crudely and the keenness of the moment would be lost.

He had discovered that you could do the same with women. Here he had a different kind of power and the game was subtler. But the satisfaction was as great.

'Up,' he said gently. The girl closed her legs and drew her arms around her body as she stepped off the far side of the bed. Kartchak walked round and looked at her face. Her cheeks were red and he drew his finger softly across the hot skin. He had done nothing to her, yet she would never forget him. He paid her and let her go.

At first Vichevsky thought the girl walking towards him down the corridor was a Western catwalk model. Her carriage was unnatural – her head back, her chin up and her arms crossed over her chest. But as she approached he noticed her red eyes and realized that she was trying to control her tears, that she was bravely holding her head up with a semblance of dignity to counterbalance the humiliation of whatever had happened to her. Her tightly crossed arms held her coat in place over her shoulders but also gave her comfort.

Vichevsky stood up and tried to open the door for her. It was locked. He heard the girl sob quietly and knocked on the door. The doorman opened it and let the girl out. Vichevsky sat down again, disturbed.

Kartchak appeared ten minutes later and gestured to Vichevsky. 'Come in here.'

Vichevsky gathered up his bag. He was unsettled by the girl's appearance, and the sight of Kartchak, after two years, brought back memories of the appalling life he had led in Moscow.

'Sit there,' Kartchak ordered and Vichevsky marvelled at how objectionably authoritarian the man could be. He did as he was told.

'Do you have a business plan for your aluminium venture?' he began, and Vichevsky bridled. If Kartchak felt that he did not have a realistic business plan would he demand the return of the ticket he had bought and leave Vichevsky stranded in Moscow?

'My accountant is working on the cashflows. Let me fill you in on the concept.'

Kartchak ignored him. 'Do you have the funding in place?'

'I have ascertained that there is funding and I can assure you that it is no mean feat to find money in the West for a Russian project. You have to have extensive contacts. I did not wish to proceed until I had spoken to you, but everything is in place.' He knew his face was red and made a show of taking out his handkerchief and waving it in front of his face. 'Hot in here,' he explained.

'Tell me about the deal ... the *concept*,' Kartchak sneered.

Vichevsky explained how aluminium was made, having learnt Alex's explanation by heart. He had thrown in a couple of technical terms from the book. He wondered if this was enough.

Kartchak leaned forward. 'Answer my question, Vichevsky. Yes or no. Do you have the money for this?'

'Yes,' Vichevsky lied.

'I'll be in London in two weeks. Set up the meetings. Now, I understand the government may impose export duties on metal.'

Vichevsky's heart lurched. He knew nothing about export duties and was appalled to learn that Kartchak did.

'Well, that may be . . .'

Kartchak smiled. 'You can go now, Vichevsky. I'll see you in London.'

Chastised, Vichevsky stood up quickly. 'Fine. Call me and I'll arrange everything. No problem.'

Kartchak left the room by a second door and Vichevsky scuttled down the corridor and out onto the pavement as fast as he could.

It was not the first time he had promised Kartchak something – anything – to keep him happy. But this was getting out of hand. And now it looked as if Kartchak was already seriously involved in the metal business inside Russia.

Breathless with fear, Vichevsky leant against the wall. He would have to find some money soon.

SIX

Libby arrived with two polystyrene cups of black coffee and they moved into Alex's office.

'Tell me everything.' She settled behind Alex's desk.

'I don't know where to begin. Let me tell you about the plant first. God, Libby, you cannot imagine the conditions. All around the plant the vegetation is dead, stunted bushes, tufts of yellow grass, decay ... trees that look like skeletons. Everything covered in fine grey ash. Even the people look as if their skin is ingrained with this stuff. They look ill. They smile and they have teeth missing, there are so many with amputated limbs ...' She stopped for a second to compose herself. 'The plant is like a scene from hell. Black, with sudden flashes of light when the molten aluminium is poured out. The heat is unimaginable. The noise is deafening. I saw women driving forklift trucks, lifting and stacking the ingots, pouring with sweat, their faces filthy. There are huge signs on the factory walls exhorting the workforce to work for peace, as if somehow producing metal is a *cause*, or something worth dying for. When you think that eighty per cent of what they made went to the military, my God, the futility. Walking around, I felt . . . ashamed.'

Libby watched her face, utterly still.

After a moment Alex carried on. 'The plant manager is responsible for the whole community – the school, the hospital, such as it is; he has to feed and clothe his workers. Life expectancy, Libby, is *forty-five*. People are dying of tuberculosis and diphtheria, things we just don't have here any more. People die of post-operative infections, there's no blood, no antibiotics, no needles. They have to wash the bandages and reapply them before they're dry or even before they're clean.'

Alex stood up and looked out of the window at the misty view of the river.

'Somehow, we accept the concept of suffering as part of the necessary process to produce. We know it's tough in a smelter – or a mine or a chemical plant. But this is so *extreme*. I looked at the aluminium price on the screen this morning, Libby, and I thought that for all these years we've been dealing with a number – this clean, sanitized product – without having any idea of what it takes to produce it. People are killing themselves to produce something which we casually turn over for a commission, sitting here in our offices.'

'So?' Libby challenged. 'What are we going to do about it, then?'

'Investment. The great leveller.' She picked up

her calculator. 'The margins are amazing – all because in the West there's a quite unreasonable perception of risk. We can undercut Trademin and still make around 100 per cent per annum. I think Starling's might go for it. And I think I can sell it to them. It's a damn sight better than the nickel mine the EBRD were trying to drag them into. And if Sol ever reappears he'll go for it too.'

'Go for what?'

'We'll buy the Belorussian aluminium. Provide them with the raw materials. Give them working capital. I need twenty, maybe thirty million to get the whole thing going.'

'So why *are* the returns so fantastic? Why are no other banks doing it? Why is it just a handful of merchants?'

'Jesus, Libby!' Alex snapped. 'Am I incapable of unearthing a good opportunity? Don't you think this might just be the reward for trailing off to Moscow and Belorussia?'

'Hey, calm down. I was just wondering how difficult it was going to be to get that kind of money. Don't be so touchy.'

Alex smiled and rubbed her eyes wearily. 'I'm sorry. I *am* touchy. This is the first time I've tried to put something together without Sol. And Neville's getting to me. Sorry.'

The phone rang and Alex picked it up.

'Alexandra Brookes.'

'Sol Bergman,' a sleepy voice murmured.

Alex looked at her watch. 'Talk of the devil. Why are you calling me so early?'

'I missed you. How was your trip?'

'Fine. I tried to reach you a hundred times.

Hey, you must have missed me a lot to be calling at three in the morning. Or have you just got in?'

'I'm in London. I'll see you at six in the Savoy. Night night.'

Alex spent the rest of the day at her desk in the dealing room, answering messages, dealing with problems – strikes, delayed shipments, aluminium contaminated with asbestos – the usual. Finally she wrote a trip report to keep Neville happy. At five she packed up.

'Want to join us for a drink?' Alex asked Libby. It was a casual question, but it dropped between them like a flare.

Libby sighed. 'No. I'm seeing Spike later. Thanks, but I think I'll just go home.'

Alex recognized the signals. In the past she had tried to talk to Libby about Spike, because she hated to see Libby hurt by him and also because she wanted to understand the attraction. But Libby would leap to his defence: 'He doesn't mean it. It doesn't matter. Leave him, you can't stop him and he'll be worse if you take issue with him . . .'

Alex would shrug, feeling that there should be a way to deal with him, not only for what he did to Libby, but because he was a vicious, un-principled cheat. Even the sight of Spike irritated Alex; he stood, rarely sat, his chest out, legs splayed. Occasionally he would shudder, his shoulders tensing in an expression of annoyance, or he would shake his legs as if his clothes were uncomfortable. He jingled the change in his pocket when he spoke and scratched his crotch with bold insouciance when he talked to women.

He chainsmoked, dragging each cigarette to the bitter end, holding the butt curved inside his palm like a tramp.

Had he been smaller he would have been almost pretty, his mouth curving naturally into a pout and his long eyelashes giving him an effeminate softness. But Spike was tall and his pout became a permanent warning signal of his temper.

He would frequently boast of how he had skimmed the price on a customer's order, which he regarded as a skill. He had been reprimanded on a number of occasions by Metco but had survived since he was an aggressive, successful punter; his 'book' made money and his irregularities were disregarded.

Alex shrugged. The last thing she wanted was for Spike to join them. She and Libby had successfully avoided a foursome for years.

'We'll be at the Savoy. Try to make it.' Both of them knew that the invitation stood if Spike failed to turn up. Another part of the unspoken code.

Libby smiled. 'You've got enough to worry about. I'll be fine . . . He'll be fine as long as the market was kind to him today.'

Alex turned quickly. Libby never made direct reference to Spike's temperament and she was surprised to hear the comment.

'So you look at the screen to see if you're going to have a pleasant evening?' she began. 'You could ask for a balance sheet before seeing him, establish a threshold – you know, if he's made less than fifty thousand on the day you put it off. I really don't understand, Libby.'

'No, you don't,' she answered angrily. 'It's not an equation, Alex, or a foreign language. It's not something to *understand*. God, you can be so analytical, so bloody methodical.'

'Jesus, Libby. Can't you see? Spike's a bastard. A complete bastard. And he always will be because you let him get away with it.'

'What the hell do you mean?' Libby burst out. 'It's a relationship not a training course.'

Alex looked at Libby for a second before answering. 'I'm not criticizing *you*.'

'Yes, you are.' Libby squared up to Alex, her face tense with anger. 'That's exactly what you're doing. Now leave off.'

They stood for a moment, looking at each other, each angered indirectly by the other, the issues much greater than the one they had addressed.

After a moment, Alex softened. 'Call him up and tell him you'll be late. Go on, just this once.'

'Not tonight.' Libby turned away. 'You're going to meet Sol anyway. But thanks.' Another unspoken convention. Libby had occasionally had dinner with Alex and Sol and they made a civilized, polite threesome. But somehow the relationship between Libby and Sol lacked momentum; they were bound together by their shared friendship with Alex but they seemed to have to start from scratch every time, as if the warmth was artificial and had to be rekindled every time they met.

It was all so unsatisfactory. Alex gathered up her papers, reluctant to leave Libby with the issue still hanging between them.

'I'm off, then.'

'Have a nice evening.'

Alex hesitated then shrugged. She'd done her best.

She took a taxi to the Savoy and made her way through to the American Bar. Sol and Alex usually sat at the back, near the bar, in a dark corner where they were aware of the music from the piano, but cushioned against the participation of over-enthusiastic amateurs late in the evening. Here there was a quirky elegance, unlike the tepid *hauteur* of the lobby and reception area.

Sol was already there when she arrived, ensconced in the corner, a whisky sour in front of him, reading *The Economist*. He looked up as she sat beside him, his hair still in his eyes, his smile warm and full of genuine pleasure. He put down his magazine and kissed her.

'Tell me everything.'

She laughed. 'How much time do you have?'

'No, I mean it, Alex,' he urged. 'Start at the beginning and take me right through.'

For an hour and a half she spoke about her experiences, prompted by Sol. Unlike Libby, he asked questions, interrupting her when her descriptions moved to areas he did not want to hear about, keeping her on the economic track. He picked her up on small details and was annoyed when she could not answer.

'I have no idea what kind of plane it was, Sol,' she snapped. 'A small one, with only two seats on each side of the aisle. Listen, I've flown all round the world and I could not identify a single plane. What does it matter?'

'It doesn't *matter*. It's interesting, that's all. Carry on.'

'Shall we go for dinner? I want to tell you about this deal.'

Sol hesitated, then took her hand. 'Let's go back to your place.'

Surprised, Alex looked at him. 'What? And go to bed, do you mean?'

He laughed. 'You are a passion killer. I'm attempting seduction and you are being very down to earth.'

'Sol, this is the first time since I've known you that you've suggested missing dinner to make love. Had *I* suggested it, you would have answered that you wanted to have dinner *and* make love. Plus – and this is not a complaint – spontaneous seduction is not your style. You're not a back-of-the-car or a lift man. Or am I wrong?'

'I'm not suggesting we do it in the back of a car.' He paid the bill. 'I'm suggesting we go back to your warm, comfortable flat and make love in your bed. I've missed you. Is that so strange?'

'No ... it's not strange, but ... never mind. Let's go.'

Once inside her flat, Alex felt almost shy with him.

'Drink?'

'No.'

He led her into her bedroom where he undressed her with unusual care, unfastening each button slowly, running his fingers along the lace edge of her bra, telling her how beautiful she was and how much he wanted her. Then he made love to *her*, restraining her when she reached for him, forcing her to be passive. With her hands stretched above her head, she luxuriated in the sensation.

She closed her eyes. There was something different in his touch; like listening to a familiar voice speaking a different, unknown language.

She fell asleep then woke with a start. Sol lay beside her.

'Relax. It's only ten o'clock. At night. You don't have to go to the office yet.'

She smiled. 'I've lost all track of time. What a compliment!' She rolled over and pushed her head under his arm.

'You closed your eyes and fell asleep like a shot. I've never seen anything like it. I guess you must be exhausted from your trip. What's the time difference?'

'Three hours.'

'Listen, I've a couple more questions. Let me get them off my chest, OK?'

Alex sighed. 'Is this the best moment? I do want to talk about it more, but not now.'

'Russian banks. Don't they finance this guy's operation?'

'Sol, could we talk about this tomorrow?'

'I'm going back to New York tomorrow. I'm only here for a meeting. Tell me how Maxim operates.'

Alex sighed. 'Well, he's a merchant. He takes aluminium from the plants and he sells it. End of story.'

'How does he buy it? Does he pay in advance?'

'He pays thirty per cent up front, the rest six weeks later.'

'Cash? Is that fixed? What if it takes him longer to sell the metal?'

'Oh, I don't know. You'll have to ask him that. I'll introduce you some time.'

'When's he coming over?'

Half asleep, Alex wanted nothing more than to lie in his arms, but he was leaning on one elbow, not exactly prodding her awake but nudging.

'Alex! When's he coming over?'

'For God's sake, I don't know!' she snapped finally. 'What's this all about, Sol? Is this all that matters? I've hardly spoken to you since you went to New York, you don't return my calls and now, when we do finally meet up, all you can talk about is business. Is that why you're here?'

'No, of course not, Alex, although I admit to being interested in Russia. This is a good time for me . . .'

'Well, I'm glad I could help. I'm honoured to be part of your corporate strategy.'

Impatiently, he grabbed her arm, pulling her round to face him. 'Alex, you should listen to yourself. All these years discussing schemes – tin and Nigeria and Cuba – remember? All those years when you picked my brains then went right out and got yourself a new customer. Remember the German zinc deal? How much did Wellington make on that? Half a million?'

'Why does everyone keep pushing me around?' She snatched back her arm. 'You always could turn an argument round. Maybe we *did* make half a million on the zinc deal, but you didn't lose it. Maybe I *did* learn from you, but you learnt from me. You're too undisciplined.

189

You'd pay back every dollar we made in legal fees if I didn't stand behind you making sure you'd signed the right bloody bit of paper.'

'Damn lucky my brother's an attorney . . .'

'For God's sake, grow up.' Alex got out of bed and pulled on a T-shirt. 'Yours is not the only way to do business. How dare you sneer at anyone who does things differently? Who do you think you are to patronize me just because I make sure the contracts are in order? Maybe you can just stuff the bad contracts in some drawer and forget about them, but I've got bloody Neville and the compliance officer poring over every clause of every deal I do. They have to be right. One bad debt, one single default and I'm out. That's not easy to live with in a business like this.'

'And who gets these contracts for you to check, Alex? Who brings in the deals for you to go over, pick holes in and criticize?'

At the bedroom door Alex turned back. 'Well, maybe things are changing, Sol. Maybe you'll have to start checking your own paperwork.'

'Perhaps you could give me an explanation for the outstanding items, Alex? Otherwise . . .'

Alex snatched up the paper and ran her eye over the list of items. God, how had she managed to run up her expense account this far? A company credit card was an insidious way to pay.

'As soon as I can, Marge.' She saw the doubtful look on the accountant's face.

'I need it right away, I'm afraid. Neville says I

should have the forms back from you today. If not, no more . . . no more use of . . .'

'What are you saying? That I can't use the card? That I can't travel any more?' Alex's voice rose and she had the satisfaction of seeing Marge shrink away from her. 'Before the end of the day I have to take care of a new account, two compliance problems and interview three potential new employees. How do you suggest I prioritize, Marge?'

'Alex, I'm only telling you what Neville told me . . .'

'Yes, well let's make this a two-way communication channel. You can tell Neville from me to get stuffed.' She snatched up her bag and wrote out a cheque for the total amount.

'Here. Now *you* owe *me*. And I'll do the explanations when I have time.'

There was only one thing worse than dealing with Neville and that was dealing with someone acting under instructions from him. It wasn't Marge's fault, but the thought of spending twenty minutes going through the card statements item by item was intolerable.

As Alex walked back through the door the credit controller, Monty, shouted across the dealing room at her. 'Hey, Alex! Got a minute?'

She made her way across the room. 'What is it, Monty?'

'You know a company called Fleck?'

'Yes, it belongs to the Russian I saw last week.'

'He's sent us ten million dollars. Look.'

He held out the faxed confirmation to her.

She gasped. 'My God, that was quick. And

I thought he was going to send us five.'

Her eyes skimmed across the words. This was it. The first Russian customer. The beginning. Suddenly all the talk had become reality.

She looked over at Neville's office. Damn, it was empty. She would have loved to storm in there and slap the fax down on his desk. Not much risk if you're holding ten million dollars of the client's money, is there? Ought to be able to make some commission out of this.

'You done the paperwork for this account?' Monty asked.

'Yes.'

'Well take this to Compliance, then, Alex.' He handed her the sheet of paper. 'He should be able to trade tomorrow.'

'Thanks, Monty.' She ran across the dealing room and waved the paper in front of Libby, a broad grin on her face.

'We have a new customer!'

Libby looked at the fax. 'Ten million? Bloody hell. There must be a lot of aluminium in Russia we don't know about.'

For a moment Alex hesitated, uneasy. This was all too quick. But then she dismissed her fears. If you have a spare ten million dollars sitting in a Swiss bank account, why wait? God, she would love to use this money to start off with the Belorussians, but Maxim refused to have his nest egg repatriated. He had no acceptable explanation for how he had managed to accumulate his wealth outside Russia and did not want to attract the attention of the tax authorities. He wanted to use it to hedge his aluminium and to speculate, but these illicit dollars could never go back to Russia.

The phone rang again five minutes later. Alex picked it up and recognized the hollow, distant tone of a Moscow call. He started speaking before she could tell him about the account.

'Come to Moscow now. To see Russian government.'

Alex felt a familiar surge of excitement. 'The government? What for?'

Maxim sighed. 'What else. How to hedge. Also we go to Siberia. Is good you meet plant managers. Fedorov have big problem.'

'Maxim, we've been through all this with the Belorussians. Let me try and put together a deal here. I have to go and see the banks, make a presentation. I can't help this Fedorov – or anyone else – until I've sorted out the financing.'

'Fedorov is biggest aluminium producer in Russia. We go there, then to Moscow.'

The implication was clear. She couldn't do one without the other and Alex was desperately keen to meet the Russian government. She craned her neck. Neville was back in his office. She grinned.

'OK, Maxim. I'm on my way.'

Kartchak put the phone down. Another very nice business, sending blood down to the Crimea, where Moscow's *nouveau riche* were spending their dollars in the casinos and nightclubs, enjoying their freedom – unless one of them became ill and required hospitalization. Then they were uncomfortably reminded that they were still in *Russia*.

He examined one of the new disposable syringes he had bought in bulk from Romania. Poor quality, but very cheap. He put it back into his drawer, took out the cuttings Vichevsky had brought him and put the article from *Futures Trading* on top. The photo of Alexandra Brookes had caught his attention. Good looking. Unusual.

The paper was glossy and Kartchak ran his index finger along the line of her jaw. He looked at the immobile face again, so composed and confident, such a fearless expression.

Kartchak felt a moment's excitement. Then, carefully, he began to trace the whites of her eyes with the sharp nail of his little finger, carving the crescent shape, cutting into the paper. The image of Alexandra Brookes buckled and Kartchak smoothed it out again, then put it back in the drawer with a smile.

Libby sat in the deserted dealing room with the phone in her hand. She wanted to call her mother and tell her she was coming home for the night because there was a problem with the central heating, any story to explain why she had to move out of the flat she shared with Spike, but she knew she would not be able to do so without crying.

She had called Spike to tell him that Alex had gone back to Moscow and that she would be working late. He had been calm and she recognized the sound of his measured, restrained anger – the worst kind.

'And how long will she be away this time?'

'I don't know. Couple of days, maybe.'

'She'll let you know?'

Libby could see where he was leading and tried to head him off. 'Spike, I chose this business. I work long hours but I get well paid. I really can't complain.'

'No. You really can't complain, can you?' His voice dropped to a whisper and Libby blushed, knowing that every dealer in the Metco dealing room would be straining to hear his words. 'She screwing this Russian, then? Is that it? Is that why she keeps going off to Moscow? Is he good, then?'

'Oh, Spike, don't.'

'"Oh, Spike, don't,"' he mimicked in a high falsetto. '"Don't say nasty things about Alex. She's wonderful. So nice and clever." And I can just hear you telling her what a bastard I am. No wonder the bitch can't stand me.'

Libby had no answer. 'I've got to go. I'll see you later.'

'No, you won't. I've got some of the boys coming round later.'

'Well? That won't bother me.'

'It might, all that noise. I suggest you go and spend the night somewhere else.'

'Wait a minute, Spike. I live in that flat. You're not going to tell me that I can't sleep there, in my own bed, just because you've invited some friends round. Come off it.'

'I don't need you hanging around turning the music down, emptying the ashtrays, offering to make coffee. God, the last time you were a real pain in the arse. Ah, here's cheeky little Cheryl from the back office.' His voice dropped. 'Got your coat, darling?'

195

'Spike, this is ridiculous. Of course I'm coming home. And I'll stay out of your way – nothing would give me greater pleasure.'

The phone went dead.

Libby opened her drawer and took out the key to Alex's flat, hoping that Spike would not try to find her at midnight, drunk and contrite, and call her mother who would then be alerted to the fact that her daughter was missing. She was tempted to call her own flat and leave a message on the answering machine to tell Spike where she was but then, suddenly, everything seemed un-reasonably complicated.

She knew she was crying and that she would not be able to stop. The tears had begun of their own volition, a simple reaction to the humiliation of her situation and to the longer term futility of her relationship. She took a deep breath and dialled Spike's office, hoping that it had been a joke and that he was still there, playing cards. But the line rang, unanswered.

A flashing light on the board caught her eye and she felt her mood lift in a sudden surge of hope. By the time she picked it up the line was dead. A wrong number. She sat for a long time in the deserted room, the receiver pressed to her ear, tears streaming down her face, finding some companionship and comfort in the purr of the dial tone.

SEVEN

Boris picked Alex up at Moscow airport wordlessly and drove at his usual breakneck speed back into town. She was checked into the Magyar Hotel by the same receptionist as before and her bag carried by the same bellboy. Neither acknowledged her.

There was a message from Maxim, informing her that she would be picked up at eight thirty the following morning. In her room Alex pulled out a book on Siberia. She was amazed by the distance – Irkutsk was three-quarters of the way across Russia, down near the border with Mongolia. In the middle was Lake Baikal, the largest freshwater lake in the world. Alex doubted she would get to see it.

When Maxim arrived the following morning, she began her questioning immediately.

'Tell me about the plant. What's the capacity?'

'I have no figures.'

Alex looked quickly at him. He **had** done this before, doggedly withheld information simply because he did not wish to discuss it.

'Maxim,' she began slowly. 'I've come from London. I'm flying to Siberia. I think I should have a little background. What is this meeting about? At least tell me something about Fedorov.'

Maxim shrugged and looked out of the window. 'Is plant manager. Good man.'

Alex gave up.

On the plane, she read more travel books, ate a spartan meal, then fell asleep, waking as they were about to land in the pitch dark.

She sat bolt upright, confused. 'What time is it?'

'Eleven o'clock.'

Alex glanced at her watch. 'What's the time difference? Is that eleven o'clock local time or Moscow time?'

'Pah! Is eleven o'clock here.'

The centre of Irkutsk was a classic clash of Russian culture – the ugly 1960s blocks of flats, stained by damp and dirt with jagged cracks running from top to bottom, next to log cabins sitting snugly in the snow with their ornately carved shutters mimicking the expensive masonry effects of early Muscovy. Ironically, it was the cabins that had the greater sense of permanence.

The hotel was a bizarre mixture of styles. Many official environmental groups had stayed there and there was a simulated log cabin reception area with maps and posters showing areas of ecological interest. In one corner was a wishing well surrounded by a picket fence, which contrasted oddly with the garish signs advertising the nightclub in the basement. Japanese tourists were lured to the in-house Japanese restaurant and Coca-Cola signs decorated the remaining walls.

Alex was shown to her room. It was basic and a little tatty, but it would do. She took a shower and sat down with a book, wondering what Maxim was doing. She considered calling him and suggesting dinner but changed her mind. They could do with a respite from each other's company.

She woke the next morning and looked at her watch, but could not remember whether she had set it to Moscow time, Irkutsk time or whether she was still on London time. Disorientated, she dressed hurriedly, starving, hoping she had not missed breakfast.

She found Maxim in the reception area. 'We go to Fedorov's house in the country,' he announced.

'Not to the plant?' Alex asked. 'Is it far?'

'Not so far. Go and pack.'

The trip took three hours on roads, then single tracks, then pathways barely discernible in the snow. Alex sat huddled in the back, determined not to give Maxim the pleasure of complaining. In fact, the scenery was spectacular. She recognized that having wanted to see unspoilt countryside she could not have done better.

Maxim slept and the driver spoke no English and as a result she felt cocooned, alone in the wild, in spite of the harsh growl of the underpowered car's engine as it fought to maintain traction on the icy ground.

Fedorov was waiting for them at the door to the cabin. A small man, he stood in a challenging open-legged stance, arms folded, barrel chest out, head forward, double chin prominent.

For a moment Alex was daunted. She worried that he had not been warned of their arrival and resented the intrusion. She roused Maxim and gathered her coat around her, more for self-protection than against the cold.

As Maxim emerged, Fedorov's expression changed and he chastised Maxim in mock disapproval – in English – for not having visited him for so long and for not having told him that he was bringing a guest. Before Alex could protest, he laughed.

'Since I have only one room, it does not matter if I have three or thirteen guests. I was joking. You are very welcome.'

'This is wonderful!' Alex said. 'Is the correct term a *dacha*?'

'No,' Fedorov answered, 'it is an *izba*, a cottage rather than a weekend home or *dacha*. And it is a real one. Come outside, I'll show you.'

While Maxim settled beside the stove with a bottle of vodka, Fedorov took Alex outside to examine the walls of the cabin.

'These are logs, not planks made in a sawmill, but taken straight from the tree. Planks are much easier to handle and more uniform in size, but logs are much better, much thicker. And look – no nails, only wooden pegs.'

'It has such character, like a child's drawing of how a house should be, solid and real.' She too ran her hands over the smooth wood, as if stroking the flanks of a horse.

'But how do you keep the cold out?' she asked,

noticing that some of the uneven logs seemed to leave gaps.

'Moss,' Fedorov answered, 'but I'll show you tomorrow. It's too cold to stay out now. Let's go inside.'

The house had a classic double gable construction, with one main room and another separate, in the front. Everything was made of the same, mellow wood and in the middle of the room stood a long pine table with benches on either side. A pristine white linen tablecloth ran down the middle.

'First you must take off your shoes.'

Obediently Alex took them off, assuming this to be part of some long-forgotten religious observation. Fedorov walked over to the stove, a massive whitewashed edifice which stood in the corner on a wooden plinth, giving off a fragrant crackling heat.

'Look, I will put them here.' On the side of the stove were five small niches, each containing a pair of shoes. 'And if you are very lucky you can sleep here tonight.' He drew back a curtain to reveal a platform between the stove and the ceiling. 'It is called the *polaty*. It is the warmest place in the house.'

Alex wandered around taking in every detail, firing questions at Fedorov. She learned about the history of the house and, from there, the conditions of peasant farmers. She was fascinated.

After half an hour Maxim stood up. 'Is enough. You want to live in Siberian house now? How you get your hair fixed here? Ha!'

Alex laughed with him and sat down, allowing

him to pour her a glass of wine and begin the round of toasts.

Fedorov brought out dinner, which was supplemented by the food the driver had brought. Dried meat, pickles, black bread and some white, crumbling cheese, washed down with strong young red wine.

For a while Maxim and Fedorov spoke to each other in Russian. Alex waited with growing impatience for them to revert to English, but the conversation was becoming heated and it was fifteen minutes before Maxim turned to her, his face red with outrage.

'Pah! Is the new Tsar. Never I have heard such a decision!'

'What?' Alex queried. 'What's going on?'

Maxim looked at her. 'You not believe this. You know me. My office, my things. All I have.'

Bewildered, Alex listened to the staccato speech, the random heap of words that could have been assembled in a number of ways, with a number of possible meanings. 'I'm sorry. I don't understand what you're talking about.'

'Milk! Mr Tsar wants milk for his workers!'

'Not milk, Maxim.' Fedorov returned with a fresh bottle of wine. 'A milk pasteurization plant.'

Maxim laughed again. 'And I should do this?'

'It's in your interest.'

'Wait a minute,' put in Alex. 'I'm here because Maxim said you had a problem and that I could help. Well, can I?'

Impatiently, Maxim shook his head and reached for the bottle of wine. 'Such a problem.

He bring you to Siberia because he needs milk.'

Fedorov filled Alex's glass and smiled gently at her. 'Perhaps I should explain. It is true that I asked Maxim to build a milk pasteurization plant, but we have not received the payment from him for a delivery of aluminium from a long time ago. One million dollars.'

Maxim stood up. 'You think I will not pay?'

'Not at all. Sit down. It is a fact that you have not yet paid. So? It is like a credit.' He turned back to Alex. 'We asked a French company to build this plant for us. You must understand the significance for us if we cannot pasteurize milk. It will not last. And so there are shortages. We cannot transport so often fresh milk—'

Again Maxim snorted with disdain. 'So? What you do before? Why so sudden this problem?'

'Things are much worse than before,' Fedorov answered simply. 'So, the French company said they would build the milk plant for three-quarters of a million dollars. But we must give them the money first. Cash. This we cannot do. And so I say to Maxim. You organize to build it. This way you save money. A quarter of a million dollars in your pocket.'

Suddenly Maxim stood up, sending the bottle of wine crashing to the wooden floor. 'This is problem with Russia today! I come here to talk to you about the plan, how to see the future! A big plan! And you talk about milk!'

'You want to talk about aluminium but I cannot produce it if my workforce is ill, if they cannot get to the plant because their wives are ill and cannot look after the children. Maxim, it is all very well to have your grand schemes, but I am talking about survival here. Life and death. My workers are dying—'

'And I want to give you this life. But you want only milk.'

They lapsed into Russian again, their voices rising until Maxim took a step forward, his eyes bulging with anger. He spat one vicious sentence into Fedorov's face then hit him sharply on the shoulder with the heel of his hand.

'Pah. You know nothing.' He walked over to the narrow bed and lay down with his face to the wall, his coat pulled up to his neck.

Fedorov looked at Alex and smiled. 'Come on. It's late. We can talk about this tomorrow. Let me show you where everything is. The bathroom is attached to the house so you don't have to go outside. It is primitive, but there, you are in the middle of nowhere. Climb up here when you are ready, I have put down some blankets and a pillow.'

Alex settled down on the platform after a moment's hesitation. The fact that it had supported the weight of sleepers for five generations reassured her and as she lay in her niche behind the patterned curtain, listening to the low voices of Fedorov and Maxim, smelling the sweet smell of the wood, she knew she would have no trouble falling asleep.

It seemed a matter of minutes before she became aware of Fedorov shaking her gently. She sat up.

'Can you ride?'

'Yes, but . . .'

'Come on.'

She looked out of the window as she hurriedly pulled on her clothes. Two horses were already packed and tethered outside the door of the cabin. They were workhorses, big, broad and strong, their huge hooves planted squarely in the snow. Their manes were short and spiky and they swished their tails idly with the brutish arrogance of their famous ancestor, Przewalski's horse.

Alex stepped out of the cabin and within seconds every inch of her exposed skin ached with the pain of a prolonged sharp slap. As her lungs drew in air they felt like half their normal capacity, and she coughed as if breathing in the polluted air of inner London.

Fedorov laughed. 'You'll need more than that jacket,' he warned, throwing a fur hat at her. 'Take this and these gloves and wrap this around your neck and face.'

Alex tied the ear flaps of the hat under her chin and wound the woollen shawl tightly as far as her eyes, then cursed the fact that she had not mounted the horse first. As Fedorov laughed, she mounted with the agility of an Egyptian mummy.

'What about Maxim?' Alex asked.

Fedorov smiled. 'I asked him last night if he wanted to join us. He did not deliberate for very long. He declined. My driver is at his disposal until we return and he says he has some business to take care of.'

They took off across the flat fields, walking first, then trotting. The horse had a stoical

205

obedience, unlike the capricious mutiny of bored riding school horses, but at a gallop Alex knew that she had little authority and that her horse would continue at breakneck speed, following the leader, no matter what. They rode through woods, then across a frozen lake, skidding across the snowy surface without altering their speed. Alex listened to the crackling of the ice beneath the horse's hooves and prayed that she would not find herself up to her neck in frozen water if the ice gave way. Inside the sheepskin gloves her palms were sweating.

They stopped for some bread and cheese and it took Alex ten minutes to regain her breath.

'Where are we going?' she asked.

'To the river. A tributary of the Yanisey. Are you tired? Do you want to go back?'

'No, no! This is wonderful!'

'Then perhaps you're ready for the next stage. Your horse will go in a straight line unless you tell him to turn with your legs. But don't worry, you can trust him. If you're going over a lake or between trees, let him decide the way. He'll judge better than you or me. But if you do need to change direction, sit deep in the saddle and use your legs.'

'OK. What's the next stage?'

Fedorov went over to his horse and took a long narrow package from the saddlebag.

'Dinner tonight.' He unwrapped two shotguns and handed one to Alex.

'Safety catch, trigger, cartridges, here's how to open it. That's it. Let's go.'

'A gun! I can't! I've never—'

'Come on, Alex. It's simple. Here, take it.'

Carrying the Vostok like a grenade, Alex remounted her horse. She had never had any interest in guns and now that she held one in her hands she was afraid of its power. They rode on, Alex checking the safety catch every two minutes, pointing the gun awkwardly away from herself and Fedorov.

'Shoot!' Fedorov yelled and she fumbled with her gloves then dropped the reins. Fedorov laughed. 'Only about half an hour of daylight left. Watch how I do it.'

With surprising dexterity he knotted the reins and let them lie on the horse's withers, then showed her how to ride with the broken gun cradled in her arms.

'In earlier times you would have had a Borzoi hound slung over your saddle and when you saw your prey you threw it off then went after it. Very practical and very warm.' He laughed and Alex laughed with him.

At dusk they reached the river. Fedorov pointed to a small group of trees on the bank and they dismounted. In spite of several attempts Alex had shot nothing, but Fedorov had two rabbits. He sent Alex to collect wood and she complied, not straying beyond a twenty-foot radius of the makeshift campsite. She was exhilarated but petrified. Never had she been so much out of her element.

For a moment she stood still, listening to the unfamiliar sounds around her, watching Fedorov hunched over the fire. She thought of her skin smelling of Chanel, and her nails painted with acrylic gloss, and wondered if any wild animals had picked up her strange foreign scent. For a moment she was frozen with uncertainty. Her mother's warnings came back to her and she realized that this time she was in more danger than the usual urban escapade when a passing taxi or a policeman or even a hotel could provide refuge from the threat of a mugger. She had no skills to support her in this environment: were something to happen to Fedorov she would be helpless, dependent on her horse to get her back to the cabin. The thought of survival in one of the harshest places on the earth appalled her. She had no knowledge of even the most basic nature, how to find food, build a fire.

Maxim had been right to laugh at her for enjoying the creature comforts of the city.

She could hear Fedorov humming and the uncertainty passed in a sudden wave of optimism. She *would* crack the Russian market open, the business *would* come. She looked around at the interminable snowy landscape and the white cloud of her breath in the thin air. Jesus, she smiled to herself, if I can do this . . .

She continued her task and delivered the pile of wood to the fireside.

Fedorov did everything while Alex sat huddled by the fire. He constructed a spit to cook the rabbits, which he had skinned and filleted. He tethered and unpacked the horses, made two shelters and laid out their sleeping bags, all the time explaining what he was doing. Alex's fear dissolved. This man was safe, in control. The horses, which rolled their eyes when she approached and nipped her legs as she loosened the girth, rubbed their heads against him and strained to follow him as he walked away.

She learned that Fedorov had been educated in Moscow and Berlin. As the son of a Russian diplomat he had travelled a great deal. He had also studied in London. At fifty-five, he was totally immersed in the fortunes and misfortunes of the plant but was pleased to be able to discuss something other than aluminium with Alex.

'Tell me what you had expected, Alex,' he asked as he lit a cigar, smiling. 'Honestly. What had you been taught about Russians? That we had two heads, that kind of thing.'

Alex laughed. For a while they traded propaganda, comparing the myths of the devious, inscrutable Russians with the decadent, greedy Westerners.

'You have a kind of confidence I envy,' Fedorov said. 'You come from an island and not only do you have water to protect you, your neighbours are very similar racially to you. Above all, they have the same political system. Look at Russia's borders. Different ethnic groups, different social systems. These are threats in themselves, not to mention the threat of these differences being amplified by the self-interest of America, for example.'

'I'm not naïve. I know that we indulge in the same subterfuge we accuse you of, but there is, nonetheless, a perception that the communist regime is. . . . expansionist . . .' She trod warily but it was unnecessary. Fedorov understood exactly what she wanted to say.

209

'You are right, of course, Alex, but I would ask you to consider that there are two types of invasion, invasion to protect your own borders and invasion to acquire territory. I would ask you to consider that many of Russia's so-called invasions have been into countries where there were arms massed against us. Do you have any idea of the build-up of arms in Afghanistan, for example, before we moved in?'

He paused. 'And of course communism cannot work. It is a system based on equality. How can any system legislate for this? And if you force people to act decently, does the force negate the decency? Or is the force justified because the end result is equality? I do not know, but I know that the original idea was a good one and I cannot in my heart decry the system if the implementation was poor.'

'Poor?' Alex queried, sitting up, outraged that he could use such a word in relation to the monstrous crimes perpetrated by Stalin. 'Poor? The purges, the murder of the intelligentsia and the peasants, the sale of grain overseas which caused a famine from which millions died? This is *poor implementation*?'

'Ah, Stalin.' Fedorov stood up and began to pace round the fireside, his hands thrust into his pockets. 'I have learned of too many unspeakable acts committed not only by Stalin but by those who worked for him, Yegorov, Beria ... and even recently ... you know, there have been times when I realized how much I have been lied to, how corrupt the system was, how barbaric. It is very difficult to put these kind of

210

things into a framework, to put them in context.'

'And if you found this *context*, it would excuse the acts? There's a higher plane where these things are acceptable?'

'No, no. I'm not saying these things could ever be acceptable. It's a question of finding your own way of going on. I have had to compromise and make exceptions – even to consider that Stalin *did* kill millions, but he made Russia a great industrial country.' He held his hand out to stop her words of protest. 'Compromise. That's all I know. You are lucky to have been brought up with black and white, right and wrong. And never be asked to do the wrong thing. It has been easy for you. And it is easy for you to have principles.'

Alex bit back her anger. How orderly and comfortable her upbringing *had* been. Safe and middle class in a prosperous country. Never challenged, she had the luxury of objectivity and revelled in what she believed to be cynical good sense, sceptical of those who espoused causes.

'I sometimes wish I had been challenged a little more,' she began. 'It *is* easy to have principles in the West, but then again who needs them? We cruise along . . .' She stopped, realizing how personal the conversation was. 'It's very easy to avoid issues, even to become shallow . . .'

Sensing her unease, Fedorov smiled. 'You could never be shallow, Alex. You have too much soul.'

EIGHT

David Macneice threw the *Financial Times* onto the thick carpet where the *Futures Trading* magazine already lay, discarded as soon as he had come across the photograph of Alexandra Brookes.

He sighed. Yesterday a representative from a New York investment bank had spoken about economic cycles and the changing dynamics of the global marketplace. Kondratiev ... more money in fewer hands ... boom bust cycle. He closed his eyes.

He had been in his job for less than six months and it was beginning to become apparent to him that he was out of his depth. He looked round the huge, well-appointed office, wondering if it was obvious to anyone else.

He opened his diary. There was a reception that evening at the Russian Embassy. He smiled. The Russians were great gossips, quite at odds with the conventional image of the Russian in spy novels; most of those in the banking and industrial world were totally irreverent and if they had been privy to any information on national security they would gleefully have passed it on.

His thoughts went back to Gennady, his first contact. God, he'd been naïve. During those early days information had been limited; he'd asked for some insight into a new draft legislation debated that day in the Russian Duma.

'Ha! That's an interesting one! Half the members thought they were voting on an agriculture bill.'

'But how could that happen? There'd been a debate, surely?'

'Oh, David, you are too British even for the British!'

Macneice had smiled uneasily. 'I am not suggesting they *should* have had a debate. I'd understood that was the procedure, that's all.'

'It *is* the procedure. And since you belong to a race that plays the violin as the ship sinks, you probably cannot understand why these debates do not run on time ... Sorry, that's the Italians, I'm mixing up my stereotypes.' Gennady laughed uproariously. 'It took me a long time to learn what you foreigners say about each other. I had no idea!'

Macneice smiled to show that he was not offended. 'I believe the same jokes are used by many different nations. We have Irish jokes, but I've heard them told in other countries about other people ...'

'Let me see ...' Gennady continued, unheeding, '... cold fish, stuffed shirt, I had to learn them all, it was like school again, they gave me a list ...'

'Who gave you a list?' Macneice asked, uncomfortably aware that the terms might have been used in relation to him.

'The Americans, of course! Who else?'

'I don't suppose they joked about their own nationality,' he said stiffly.

'As a matter of fact they did. They mocked their president and their politicians, their business people . . . everyone. It was most surprising for me. And I liked it very much. With them I could talk for the first time about our political mess and our inefficiencies without fearing that they would lecture me on how to do it better.'

Macneice bristled. 'I hardly think that's a characteristic unique to Americans. In Britain we are very sympathetic to the situation in Russia. We don't consider it a joke, however, that people are facing starvation and poverty. We've great feeling for—'

'Have another drink, David.' Gennady reached for the bottle. 'What did you want to know about the vote today?'

'I don't like to pry. I'm only asking because I believe the result may have already been published in Moscow.'

'The legislation to ensure the supply of power to essential industries has been passed. This matter will come before the parliament again in six months. Until then all factories will have power even if they cannot pay cash for it.'

'I see. That's very significant.'

'Very bad for oil and gas prices in the West, and metals.'

'Yes, it is,' Macneice agreed. 'The Western

producers won't be too happy to learn that Russian producers'll be staying in business for the foreseeable future.'

'Shall we call our brokers, David?' Gennady winked. 'Sell some petroleum futures?'

Macneice looked closely at his smiling face. This was a joke, he knew, but was it a test? He wasn't sure and was uncomfortable with the ambiguity.

'I'm sure you're right. Prices are bound to drop.'

'No-one knows outside the committee – and you and me,' Gennady teased.

Macneice took a long swig from his glass. He had never been in this situation before. Gennady was right. This information – to which very few people had access – *would* make prices fall. There was no doubt in his mind that if he were to sell futures on the International Petroleum Exchange or on the London Metal Exchange he would make money.

While he was debating this Gennady burst out laughing again and clapped him on the shoulder.

'Don't go dreaming about your millions and the house in St Tropez, David. The prices have already fallen. It is too late.'

'So the news has been leaked?'

'We're the only outsiders to have learnt of the committee's decision today, but there are those who knew in advance how the committee would vote.'

It took a moment for Macneice to understand. 'You mean the vote was rigged? That it had been decided beforehand?'

Gennady shrugged, smiling. 'You obviously don't watch commodity prices very closely.'

Macneice blushed. 'Not every day, but I monitor the trends, of course.'

'And have you noticed how the "trends" change ahead of a committee vote?' Gennady asked mockingly. 'Always in the direction which anticipates the outcome of the meeting. Strange, eh?'

Momentarily compromised by his own fleeting consideration of insider trading, Macneice wanted to move the subject back onto neutral ground. This new honesty among post-communist Russians was one thing, but it could go too far.

'Ah! Look, David, there's Philippe. Shall we ask the greasy dago to join us?'

Since then, Macneice had learnt more and more about the unofficial workings of the interim Russian government and was regarded as a man with insight into the 'Russian way', which he felt was ironic since he could not identify with these methods at all.

His brief was to find a way to join up the supply lines that had been ruptured by the fall of communism – to put buyers in touch with sellers, producers in touch with consumers. It had seemed simple enough at the interview, but in practice nothing seemed workable.

Starling's Bank had seemed initially enthusiastic about co-financing the nickel mine with the EBRD, but there had been a never-ending series of doubts and queries since the disastrous meeting with the Brookes woman.

He could remember the trepidation he had felt as she had risen gracefully from the end of the table to face Lord Ingles, who had done nothing but patronize her. He remembered the mass of blond curls, her shining eyes – the whole effect was of suppressed energy, as if she might suddenly do something quite unpredictable and quite outrageous. But she had surprised them all by ambling casually across the room to the window, almost talking to herself, then executing a perfect pirouette on her stilettos before rapping out a perfect plan to deal with the issue that had beleaguered them for days.

He had blushed. She had been right, of course, and Lord Ingles had been disparaging about his performance later in the day. Macneice thanked God he had been able to escape back to the EBRD headquarters in Brussels and was spared the ordeal of the options training course.

It was certainly time he came up with something.

It took Alex over twenty-four hours to get back to Moscow, and she checked in to the Magyar tired and needing a bath.

'Tomorrow we go to government,' Maxim announced as she got out of the car.

Alex swung round to face him. 'Tomorrow! What time?'

'I come at nine.' He left with his trademark abruptness.

A sense of excitement overcame Alex's annoyance that he'd obviously known but hadn't told her. She dashed up to her room to examine her limited wardrobe. She had packed in a hurry and everything needed ironing.

As she emptied her suitcase she went back over the discussions she had had with Fedorov and Maxim about the plant. It was a depressing story. Fedorov's plant was old; its production was huge but the quality of the aluminium was erratic. There seemed little she could do for him – like the Belorussians she would find it difficult to broker a deal with the West since the technical problems would only get worse.

She hung her white silk shirt inside the black suit and stood back to assess the look. A little severe, perhaps, but severity would not be in-appropriate for a meeting with the Russian government. She called Housekeeping and asked for an iron and an ironing board.

The Export Ministry was housed in another 1950s bunker of a building, an uncompromising granite square relieved by classical columns; the multi-tiered central block finishing hundreds of feet above them in a vicious spire.

Alex hesitated as she got out of the car, looking up at the confusion of classical and con-temporary symbolism. A frieze decorating the first floor represented mining, industry and agriculture, heroic workers standing against a background of fruit-laden trees and endless forests. In the centre a man and a woman, thirty feet high, were marching forward, a sheaf of corn held high between them. Chins lifted, they strode into the glorious Soviet future, their coats blow-ing in the wind, the expressions on their handsome faces serene and confident. Every figure was adorned with the symbols of Soviet might – the hammer and sickle and the red star.

Alex rubbed the back of her neck. The scale of the building was amazing. But as she stepped onto the cracked concrete walkway leading to the front door she felt that this building, like most of the triumphalist architecture of Stalin's era, managed to make the reality of ground level even more pathetic.

People no longer looked up. Nor did they look at each other as they made their way doggedly along the pitted pavements. There seemed to be a universal sense of oblivion. Alex was alarmed by the many pedestrians, often wearing no coats in the bitter depths of winter, who simply wandered onto the road, unmindful of the traffic, unaware of the abuse screamed at them by irate drivers. She had witnessed street-corner violence where the victims seemed dazed as they were punched, robbed and brutally stripped of their possessions.

The regime had changed, but one thing persisted. From the cold, bloody, ruthless regime of Stalin to the teeming violent resentment post-*perestroika*, Russia was a country of menace. Before, it had been the anonymous fear of systematic obliteration. The silent menace of the Party. Now, it was the dirty vodka-fuelled aggression visible on every half-lit street, in every dark hungry face. Alex looked up again. Russia was still incomprehensible.

As soon as they entered the building three men appeared, clearly a leader and two minions, and in confirmation of Alex's judgement the first man clasped Maxim by the hand and embraced him. The other two were not introduced and were ignored.

'Is Alexandra Brookes, from London Metal Exchange,' Maxim waved in her direction. 'Big expert in metal.'

The man in charge took her hand and shook it warmly, clasping his left hand over hers.

'My name is Mintov. I have heard a lot about you, Miss Brookes. And read about you.'

'The article? I'll never live it down.'

Mintov had a discreet elegance which Alex had not seen before in Russia, where those who had wealth were inclined to display it. His thick grey hair was brushed back from his high forehead and his features were those considered in the West to be classically 'Slav' – high cheekbones, long narrow nose, wide mouth.

When everyone was seated Mintov began to explain the problem with misleading simplicity. Alex recognized instantly that he was no novice.

'Here is our problem. We need to produce aluminium. You understand the pressure we are under?'

'Of course. You are dependent on the revenues. Maxim has explained the situation to me many times.' Her sarcasm had no effect on Maxim, who sat at the end of the table glowering.

'Exactly,' Mintov continued. 'There is no alternative. We must produce. Before, we used to give eighty per cent of our aluminium to the military, now we cannot. We have to struggle to export. You know how difficult it is for the plants. But in spite of all their problems, our export levels have gone up.'

'I understand.'

'But worse is yet to come. As we export, so the price falls.'

Alex nodded.

'And as the price falls, we make less money. So, how can we do it? Export to the West but keep the price high?'

Alex's first instinct was to laugh. It was a classic case: in times of scarcity the price rises, in times of plenty the price falls. And an extra million tonnes of aluminium certainly constituted 'plenty'.

There was silence in the room and Alex was aware of their expectation that this London commodity broker could suggest a salvation. But the options were simple: either they sold and drove down the price, or they waited, hoping for higher prices. Waiting was a gamble and, in addition, it was a gamble which delayed their payment. Mintov had made it clear that they could not postpone payment under any circumstances – five hundred dollars was better than no dollars at all.

She smiled apologetically. 'There's no easy answer. I'll give it some thought—'

From the corner Maxim interrupted. 'Pah! No ideas.'

Instantly Mintov silenced him with a few words in Russian before turning back to Alex.

'I would appreciate it if you would think about this. We know it is not easy.' He stood up. 'The problems we have are not just the problems of an economy in transition. We are involved in commercial warfare and we are like lambs to the slaughter. Our biggest problem is feeding our workers, yet I am afraid we cannot protect them for much longer. You know of our problems, Miss Brookes. If there is an answer perhaps you can help us to find it.'

She looked him in the eyes for a moment and found his gaze clear, direct and disarming. He did not appeal to Alex emotionally or offer her financial inducements, but appealed to her intellectually, and she realized that perhaps her ego had been a little flattered by the suggestion that Russia counted on her.

In spite of the enormity of the task, Alex was intrigued. This was how trade finance had begun, before the banks had developed syndicated loans, derivatives and other synthetic tools which obscured the basic function of the marketplace, and before a whole new breed of technical analysts persuaded gullible punters that supply and demand were obsolete. Before stochastics, momentum indicators and candlestick charts.

She smiled. It was a rare opportunity to return to the economic rules that underpinned all commodity prices.

'Well, I'll certainly do my best,' she managed, shaking Mintov's hand.

'I know you will.'

Impatiently Maxim led her to the car, where he handed her a plane ticket. 'You can take the plane this afternoon. I have booking. Go to London and start work.'

Alex took the ticket from him. 'Gladly.'

Kartchak threw the screwed-up ball of paper across his office. 'It makes no sense at all. What language is this? There are more English words than Russian.'

Roman retrieved the paper containing five hours' worth of tedious translation of an article on metal trading. He sat back wearily, stretching his long legs out in front of him. He knew his demeanour irritated Kartchak, who was so fit that every action was a precise controlled exercise, while he was loose, fiddling with his pen, tapping his foot. Even the way his dark hair fell onto his forehead annoyed Kartchak, whose short hair seemed miraculously to stay a uniform length.

'What can I do? There are no words in Russian for this kind of thing. I looked some of the words up in the dictionary – the *Oxford English Dictionary* – and they don't have them. "Contango". What the hell is that? "Hedging"? Jesus, if the *Oxford Dictionary* doesn't know, how am I expected to? And all these abbreviations . . . Everything has three letters: SFO, LME.'

'Get another bloody dictionary, then. A commercial one. Don't try and con me just because I don't speak English. It's your job to translate.' Usually Kartchak would go only so far with Roman, who acted as his assistant and interpreter. Both of them knew that Roman possessed the courage and intellect to be where Kartchak was. But he was lazy. In another era he would have been labelled *decadent*; while studying

English he had developed some very Western interests and his very laziness was, Kartchak felt, the result of having spent so much time in England.

In theory, Roman's lack of ambition should make him indispensable to Kartchak; since he was no longer hungry he was unlikely to betray his employer. But he was arrogant and Kartchak suspected that he was ready to make a move – probably to live permanently in the West. His knowledge of Russian business would be very valuable to a Western bank.

Roman sighed. 'A dictionary won't help. You're missing the point. I need to understand how the business works. Constantin has got some experience of this, he worked for the Trade Delegation for a couple of years. But he did sugar, not metals.'

'Hire someone else, then. All the components are there, we need someone who knows about the aluminium industry. Get a move on!' Kartchak snapped.

Roman leant forward. 'Look, a Russian won't do.'

Kartchak opened his desk and took out the *Futures Trading* article. Alex's face smiled crookedly from the creased paper.

'Call Vichevsky. He's had some contact with this woman. Go to London. Employ her.'

Roman reached over and took the paper. He paused when he saw the two deep cuts in the paper. My God the man was primitive. He felt a shudder of revulsion as he imaged the scene, Kartchak's concentration as he carved the two defacing holes in the perfect, glossy face.

'She's not bad,' he commented lightly, folding the paper and putting it in his pocket, preferring to make no reference to the cuts. 'Who is she?'

'You say you can read English. Photocopy the article and bring the original back to me. Now. Export duties. We're supposed to register but we can get an exemption.'

'Can we? On what grounds?'

'On the grounds that I want one!' Kartchak shouted.

The violence of his response caught Roman unawares. 'OK. I'll call the Ministry and arrange to have the papers picked up.'

Kartchak smiled. 'Give them to Mintov. He'll stamp them.'

Confused, Roman said nothing. He was unaware that Kartchak had had any contact with the boss, Mintov.

'Fine. I'll do it now.'

Outside, he pulled the magazine article out of his pocket. It was unlike Kartchak to signal his interest and he knew this one must have really caught his attention.

It took him a moment to understand. There was a cool self-confidence in the face that would rattle Kartchak and this, combined with the fact that she was a professional in the West, in a language he could not understand, would make her an irresistible target. Kartchak would want to bring her down.

Alexandra Brookes. Roman wondered whether she had any idea what was coming.

* * *

225

'Well? How was it this time?'

'Great.' Alex grinned at Libby. 'A land of opportunity.' She snapped open her briefcase and began to lift out the papers. 'I'm even more sure than I was before that Russia is seriously undervalued. There's nothing to stop us walking right in there and cleaning up.'

Libby thrust an envelope at her. 'I'm sorry. I forgot to put this in the bag with the rest of the stuff. It's an invitation to the Russian Embassy. I opened it. I also accepted on your behalf – thought it would be easier to do that than refuse and try to reinstate the invitation later.'

'When is it?'

'Tonight.'

'Look, it says "and partner". Do you want to come with me?'

Libby hesitated. 'I'll see if I can get hold of Spike.'

'Right.' Alex looked around the room. 'I'm going to talk to the boys, see what's new, then I'm off to Research. Call me on Larry's number if you need me. Oh, if Neville wants me I'm doing my expenses.'

Larry smiled as Alex came through the door. Her arrival inevitably meant a crisis, a seemingly unattainable deadline and a very large fee to the company. He loved the challenge of her projects and walked round to meet her.

'Well, what do you have for me this time?'

'Russia,' she answered simply. 'What shall we do about Russia?'

For the rest of the morning Alex read all the recent papers on emerging markets, comparing their progress with European countries rebuilding after world wars. The experts were divided on the future of Russia; some said it would weather the storm, some predicted disaster, but all agreed that it was a paradox without precedent.

At four she gave up and called Libby in the dealing room. 'Are you coming tonight?'

'Yes, I think I will. I'll come to your flat at about seven, shall I? I want to hear all the news.'

'Fine. See you later.'

Alex went home, set the alarm for seven and fell fast asleep.

She was awoken by the doorbell and sprang out of bed to let Libby in. She realized she had set her clock for seven in the morning.

'Send the cab away, Libby, I need some more time. Sorry.'

They arrived at the Embassy half an hour later than planned, but they still found themselves in a queue to be announced at the ballroom door. The room was full and they moved automatically towards the bar.

'Two glasses of white wine, please,' Alex ordered, but before she could take the proffered glasses a hand reached from behind her and took one.

'Miss Brookes, please allow me.'

'Professor Vichevsky! How are you? May I introduce you to Miss Libby Archer. I believe you've spoken on the phone.'

'Many times,' the professor acknowledged. 'You've been very helpful.'

'How nice to meet you at last, Professor

Vichevsky,' Libby shook his hand. 'Alex was hoping you would be here tonight.'

Alex shot her a look of gratitude. 'I'm so sorry I was unable to return your calls, Professor Vichevsky. As you know, I've been travelling rather a lot recently.'

'It is of no consequence. I had a business matter to discuss, a small matter of ten thousand tonnes of copper, but I have a friend at Kerridge who took care of it for me.'

Alex smiled warmly. 'I'm glad you managed to settle it, Professor. And Kerridge is a very good company. A friend of mine, Michael Lashmar, is in charge there. They are especially good with smaller deals.'

The professor looked at her closely before continuing. 'Well, I have another deal, of much greater significance. I have funding available and wish to discuss the export of a sizeable amount of aluminium.'

'Of course, professor. I should be delighted. When would be convenient to talk about it?'

'I will have my assistant, Arkady, call you. My schedule is very busy. Now, one more thing. I am looking for someone tonight and I have not met him before. I saw his name on the guest list. Perhaps you know him. David Macneice? From the ERDB?'

'*EBRD*, I think, professor. And, yes, I *have* met David Macneice. Shall we walk round the room and I could perhaps point him out?'

'That would be kind.' Alex and Libby followed in the professor's wake. After a moment, Alex spotted Macneice, recognizing the solidity of his neck and shoulders and the stiffness of his demeanour.

'That is your prey, Professor Vichevsky, that is David Macneice.'

'Will you introduce me?'

Alex hesitated. Their last meeting had not been cordial. Still, she could use this meeting as an opportunity to heal the rift.

'Mr Macneice?'

'Miss Brookes? Yes, how nice to see you again. How are you?'

He had been seated throughout the meeting in the Starling boardroom and Alex had not realized that she was taller than him. As he turned, she saw the surprise in his face as he looked up at her, almost disbelieving. Then he looked at her feet. She was used to this, an indication of the forlorn hope that she might be wearing high heels. But tonight she was not. The elegant red suede shoes were almost flat.

'I'm fine, thanks,' she said, smiling. 'May I introduce you to Professor Vichevsky and to my colleague, Libby Archer. Professor Vichevsky's interested in the EBRD.'

Macneice nodded to Libby then turned to Vichevsky. The men shook hands and squared up to each other.

Vichevsky took the lead. 'I have a couple of opportunities – at government level, you understand – with an interesting risk profile.' He beamed.

'In my experience, when people use the term "interesting risk profile" they mean high risk.'

Before Professor Vichevsky could say anything,

Macneice continued. 'I'll have a look, of course, but we at the EBRD are very cautious.'

'As indeed I am. We may be very well suited.'

Silently, Alex and Libby backed away. They were on their way to the bar, surveying the scene and swapping notes as they went, when they saw Vichevsky hurrying after them. Alex groaned.

'Miss Brookes! I wanted to thank you and remind you that Arkady will call. You will be in London for a while?'

She laughed. 'Professor, I never know. I do hope so, but perhaps we should make the meeting sooner rather than later. And lunch is not necessary if you're busy. I'd be happy to come to your office or invite you to mine.'

He looked closely at her but Alex returned his gaze, unblinking, and he looked away.

'I am very afraid that you will disappear before I have a chance to discuss this matter with you. May I have a moment of your time now?'

Libby answered before Alex could. 'It's so noisy here, professor. I'm sure it would be better to talk tomorrow.'

'Over here.' Vichevsky took Alex firmly by the arm and led her to the side of the staircase. A small table was set against the wall with a chair on either side.

'I'll leave you to it,' Libby offered, 'and come back later . . .'

Alex shot a quick look at the professor. 'I won't be long. I'll catch up with you.'

'Now, Miss Brookes. Things are coming together nicely. I'm lunching with Mr Macneice and am feeling very optimistic. But I would like a little background information on the ERDB.'

Alex did not correct his error again, although any assistance now would be wasted if he opened the meeting by referring to Macneice's organization as anything other than the EBRD. She motioned him to sit down and gave him a brief history of the organization, summing up its aims and its resources and detailing some of the projects it had been involved in. She was mildly resentful; this was the second time the man had picked her brains instead of doing the research himself.

As she spoke, the professor rubbed his face thoughtfully with short, stubby fingers. She paused and looked closely at him. He was a singularly unattractive man, although she could not say precisely why. His nose pointed upwards at an unnatural angle as if pressed against a window. Its upward tilt lifted the whole of his lower face with it, his upper lip revealing his teeth and gums, giving him the dense, stuffed appearance of a man with a bad cold who was obliged to breathe through his open mouth. Alex looked away.

'Miss Brookes,' he continued obsequiously. 'Just a little clarification . . . What exactly does Mr Macneice do?'

'I don't know what exactly *he* does, but I know he works in the infrastructure unit. It's a kind of disaster management. The fall of communism is having quite a knock-on effect on the West.'

'In what way?'

'Well, take my business as an example. No-one

has any money in Russia. If you don't produce food you don't need tin cans and if you don't need tin cans you don't need tin. So they don't make cans any more, they just export the tin to the West.'

'Tin cans . . .'

'That's only one example, professor, but this is the kind of thing Mr Macneice is looking at, I believe. Since the former Soviet Union is obliged to export, he is studying how the effect on Western markets and prices can be minimized.'

'And what do you think, Miss Brookes? I value your opinion.'

'Well, I think that the EBRD has a better approach than some, but I think they should be concentrating on the former Soviet Union as a consumer . . .'

She could tell she had lost the professor. 'We should be looking to the future. Russia should be helped to continue to make the cans themselves. That'll keep the factories busy. Then the workers will continue to be paid and there will be demand for food in tin cans.'

'Brilliant! Brilliant! You are so clever, Miss Brookes. The best brains in the economic world would be excited to hear your thinking. And Wellington is privileged to have you on the staff.'

'Hardly, professor. This is all basic. I—'

'No. I will not let you devalue your contribution. But one last thing, if I may. If you had unlimited access to money, let's say ERDB money, what would you do with it? Just one example so that I am sure I understand.'

'An interesting question. What would I do?

Well, I'd begin by looking for the most profitable companies, ones that can produce at the best prices – be it copper or aluminium, or the oil and gas industry, for example. I'd look for good resources that are cut off from suppliers and from buyers. Then I'd narrow down my list to those with some kind of transport system available. Then I'd narrow even further, favouring those closer to the West, Kiev rather than Vladivostok, for example, or Belorussia—'

'—rather than Siberia?'

'Absolutely. Now there's a good example. The aluminium smelter near Minsk produces good-quality aluminium, it has a reasonable transport network, is near the West and has all sorts of other advantages. I'd look to build an extrusion plant or—'

'Extrusion?'

'The next step after the ingots, professor. What do we do with them? We have to make sheets for the building industry, window frames, or foil, for example.'

'Aluminium foil! I know what you mean!'

Alex looked at her watch. She smiled. 'Well, I'd build a factory to make aluminium foil in Belorussia. That's what I'd do, professor. But you must excuse me, I have an early meeting and I'm afraid I'm still rather jetlagged. You know, you might find the Guildhall Library in the City helpful. It's full of information I'm sure you'd find invaluable.'

Professor Vichevsky bowed. 'Miss Brookes. It is you who are invaluable. Many, many thanks.'

Alex left him quickly, making her way at

random into the crowd. After a moment, she could hear Libby's laugh and tracked her down.

'Sorry, Alex. I was going to come and rescue you in a minute.'

A voice behind her surprised Alex. 'Your assistant is very skilled at rescue missions. She snatched me from the jaws of an extremely predatory journalist.'

'Lord Ingles! How are you?'

Lord Ingles passed over the glass of wine he had fetched for Libby.

'Very well, thank you. And you? Libby tells me you've been travelling in the former Soviet Union. How intrepid.'

'Well, the banks are moving into my territory, as you know,' she began mischievously. 'I have to go further and further afield to find clients.'

'Oh, I feel so guilty. Just because I discussed the possibility of offering hedging as a part of a finance deal, you feel aggrieved. You have to take off to Russia. My, I am a terrible fellow.'

'You are. Ten years ago the banks did the finance, the brokers did the hedge. Now you think you can do everything.' She smiled. 'Well, if anything happens to me in Russia it's your fault.'

'Perhaps you should not have been quite so explicit when you came round to see us. You made us very aware that the traditional financing opportunities may even be slipping away. Quite an eye-opener.'

Alex laughed. 'I saw David Macneice a minute ago. I'm afraid I was rather ruthless with him when I came to your office.'

'Not at all. We had both been objectionably condescending, assuming we held all the cards, and were prepared, perhaps, to offer you some crumbs from our table. Frightful behaviour.'

Alex stifled a yawn and looked at her watch. 'I'm so sorry, but I have to go. Could we have lunch next week? I'd like to talk to you about financing in Russia.'

'With pleasure, although the answer is no.'

Alex felt a cold wave of fear. 'Really? I assumed you were willing to look at projects there.'

'We *did* look. We even sent two of our people to see that famous nickel operation. But we declined, even a joint venture with the EBRD. And it is now policy not to finance at all in the former Soviet Union.'

'I see. May I ask why you made this decision?'

Lord Ingles smiled. 'If I said we were appalled by the performance of the producer – the level of defaults, non-deliveries, and so on, you would hardly be surprised, would you?'

Alex tried to smile back. 'I wish I'd held my tongue. I'd been hoping you would look at an aluminium project with me.'

'Love to, if it's an excuse for lunch. But I have to tell you that there is no way the bank will invest one single pound in Russia. And I think that goes for most of the other trade finance banks as well. It's just too high-risk for everyone at this stage.'

'This project, the one I'm looking at, is completely different. Much more accessible, in Belorussia. And the plant has an excellent track record.'

'I'm sure it does, Alex, but we're fully committed in Thailand and Indonesia at the moment. These markets are really booming. Frankly we don't see the need to take on the aggravation of Russia. Did you read about the American banker shot dead in his Moscow hotel room last week? In his *own room*, for God's sake. How did they get in?'

'I read about it, but, well, perhaps I could come and see you next week? Bring some of the figures?'

'It would be a pleasure to see you, Alex. But the answer is no to the former Soviet Union for the foreseeable future.'

His decision lay like a dead weight on Alex's spirit and she found it difficult to respond to his words. Her voice was flat and unconvincing as she picked up her bag, then reached out and shook his hand.

'Perhaps I should move to Thailand, then,' she joked feebly and took her leave, nodding to Libby. 'I'm exhausted. See you in the morning.'

As Alex waited for a taxi outside the embassy she went over Lord Ingles's words. There must have been some reason, beyond the suspicions she herself had brought up, for their negative stance in Russia. She realized that she had been counting on Starling's to finance the operation with the Belorussians.

She was disappointed. But it was more than that.

Fear was contagious; there was a certain unease in being the *only* person doing something. Neville had expressed his reservations about

236

Russia several times and now Starling's had pulled out.

Alex began to walk towards Kensington High Street. Did they know something she didn't?

NINE

His superior's words rang in David Macneice's ears as he walked along Park Lane to his lunch appointment with Professor Vichevsky. *As your superior, it is my task to complete your annual review . . . I have to advise you . . . while your research work is flawless, we need to see concrete projects . . . That is what you were hired for, is it not?*

Macneice claimed to be on the threshold of a major project and had bought himself a month's grace, but if this meeting did not yield the opportunity he had promised to his boss he would have to come clean.

They arrived at the door at precisely the same moment, two minutes early. They ordered quickly, agreeing on grilled fish and a bottle of the house white wine. After some reflection, Vichevsky ordered a gin and tonic and, with the smile of a schoolboy, Macneice agreed to join him.

'Mr Macneice, I am very pleased that you found the time to meet me today. I know how busy your schedule must be.'

238

'Professor, I am acting entirely through self-interest. My sixth sense tells me that you may have a project that would be of interest to us, and if not, at the very worst I will have a pleasant lunch and learn a little more about the former Soviet Union.'

Vichevsky relaxed and ordered more gin and tonics. 'I would assume that a lot of your decisions have to be based on your "sixth sense", since there is no business support network in the former Soviet Union. I don't envy you. I have been outside now for many years and I can tell you I don't miss it. The bedlam, the confusion, I don't think I could operate in that kind of environment – although I recognize that there are wonderful opportunities and that people do flourish in that kind of "Wild West".'

Macneice smiled. He had been right about this man. As soon as he had seen him with Alexandra Brookes he had had a suspicion that he must be some central banker or a high-flying government official. Thank God he had trusted his instincts.

'I *do* have an idea,' Vichevsky continued, carefully filleting his sole. 'I have come to you because it seems to me to fit in perfectly with the aims of your organization.'

Macneice watched him. This may be exactly what he needed.

'Aluminium foil,' Vichevsky said simply, his knife and fork resting on the plate, which contained the two perfect sides of the fish and the clean, unbroken bone. He looked directly at Macneice. 'The best of the projects I have considered. I have narrowed down the list from twenty-five and have travelled extensively to do so. I believe that this is the most innovative, economically viable, politically sensitive plan to have been developed since the fall of communism.'

Macneice listened in complete silence, his meal untouched. As the plan unfolded, he saw the beauty of it.

Minsk was so far west, it was almost Europe. If he had to go there to oversee the project, he could almost do it in a day from somewhere civilized like Warsaw, or maybe even Berlin. And foil! Everybody knew what aluminium foil was, unlike some of the obscure Ukrainian titanium alloys he was expected to know about.

The professor obviously knew his stuff. A sudden suspicion occurred to Macneice and he leant forward, interrupting the professor.

'Professor, I think we have the beginnings of a very nice deal. But I should tell you at this early stage that the EBRD insists on confidentiality. So many people want to profit individually from the work we do that we have to be absolutely stringent about security. There were several people from the City at the Embassy last night, I do hope you haven't discussed this idea with anyone else.'

'No-one. I knew immediately that this was a project for you and you alone.'

Macneice sat back. His plate had been removed but he suddenly felt hungry. 'Shall we have some cheese and a little port?'

Vichevsky smiled back. 'How civilized.'

* * *

Alex spent the day on the phone. Her suspicions were quickly confirmed. Starling's was not the only bank to have decided to pass on Russian risk. Every contact she had said the same thing. Sorry, Alex, not this time. Not Russia.

She was depressed. The deal was simple. Put in the raw materials, take out the metal. Quick turnaround. An annual return of 120 per cent. How could the banks all be so determined? Most of them were financing in other volatile countries; Starling's had a huge presence in Peru, for God's sake.

She was aware of the fact that this was the first time she had tried to put together a deal on her own, without Sol. Perhaps they lacked confidence in *her*.

She had already spent a considerable amount of time – and money – on this deal, hoping to secure a huge fee from the financing bank. She'd done it before. Why was it so damn different this time? Neville had written her an uncompromising note about her figures. There was less than a week till the next meeting and she was still way below her target. She flipped open her address book. Two more banks, then she knew she was in the cold. She could still go to the venture capitalists, but they were so expensive that they would eat up most of the profit. And they wouldn't pay an upfront fee.

She'd been so confident when she'd come back from her first trip, so proud of herself for having unearthed this amazing opportunity. Now she wondered whether she should have used her time to pursue more conventional prospects.

Find another Hartman had been Neville's advice. No, damn it. She'd push this one to the limit. Too much depended on it.

At five that afternoon Libby put her head round the door with a knowing smile.

'Mr Rory Freeman on line two. The man himself.'

Alex shooed her away and lifted the phone.

'Rory. Nice to hear from you,' she began, knowing the tone was embarrassingly stilted. She was only too aware of Libby still standing by the door, smirking. 'What can I do for you?'

'I was wondering about your reactions to the article. I usually get a phone call from my victims the day after – one way or another. Am I to assume the article was what you expected?'

'Hardly,' she answered. 'And you're far too clever to think that. I've been meaning to call you but I've been travelling almost constantly since the article came out. You hid your motives very well and although I came out of the ordeal looking like a saint that does not excuse your duplicity. I hope you enjoyed your little charade.'

'Yes, I did. You were very difficult. Thought you were going to throw me out a couple of times.'

'I nearly did. Perhaps I should have done.' She found that she was smiling. There was a good-natured undercurrent to the conversation that contrasted pleasantly with the barbed, spare verbal exchanges she usually conducted. She sat down and swivelled away from Libby, putting her feet up on the desk. 'I've had more phone

242

calls since that article came out than in the whole of the rest of my career.'

'I can hardly believe that. Tell me, what's your opinion of the new SFA regulation?'

'I think we more or less covered that. It seems to me that the regulators have missed the point.'

'What do you mean?'

'Well,' Alex continued comfortably, 'the regulators look at the front row, the people like me. You wouldn't believe what I have to go through to record a trade with a client. It's a nightmare. The deal takes five seconds, the paperwork ten minutes.'

'So? Are you saying you'd like to return to the days of back-of-the-envelope trade in a restaurant over a glass or two of port?'

'No, I'm not. What I'm saying is that the regulation is not needed in the shop window, it's needed in the storeroom.'

'Great quote! Can I use it?'

'You're not doing another exposé, are you?'

'No, I was thinking of borrowing it without attributing it to you, actually.'

She laughed. 'You have my blessing.'

'Listen, with all these stories of rogue traders recently, I'd love some more insight into the mechanics of your business, how it could possibly happen. Would you be willing to tell me a bit more about it? Off the record if you prefer.'

Alex had forgotten one of the first rules in talking to journalists – to be sure to tell them what is and what is not on the record. She went back over her words, wondering if she had said anything incriminating.

'I'd love to. I find the whole thing fascinating myself. I can't tell you how these so-called rogue traders get away with it, but I can tell you why there could never be one here.'

'Great. Dinner?'

Alex was surprised and, before she could think, repeated his question. 'Dinner?'

Libby leaned in front of Alex to mime a round of applause. Alex lashed out at her in mock annoyance.

'Well, I don't know. Dinner? I suppose so . . . that would give us more time. Yes, fine, thanks.' Automatically, Alex thought of Sol. It was a long time since she had gone out for dinner with anyone other than him. Since he was still stuck in Brazil she had had little contact with him, but she knew he would be unconcerned. Rory was, after all, a journalist. It was business.

'Tonight?'

Again, Alex echoed his question, to Libby's delight.

They agreed to meet at seven thirty in the Brasserie in Brompton Road, midway between their two flats.

Forestalling Libby's questions, Alex picked up her bag. 'I'm off.'

'Night, boss,' Libby responded with a smile.

Alex lived in the same flat she had found on her arrival in London, although it had changed considerably since then. Close to the corner of Draycott Place and Sloane Street, it occupied the top two floors of an elegant red sandstone building. Originally four girls had shared the flat, but now only Alex remained, the sole leaseholder. For a central London flat the rooms were exceptionally spacious and light; the living room and bedroom both had views over the largely undeveloped, gingerbread rooftops of Chelsea and there was not a skyscraper for miles.

Alex got out of the shower with just ten minutes to spare. In the bathroom she looked at herself in the mirror then looked away quickly. To concentrate on her appearance was a minor act of infidelity and she pulled her hair back almost brutally, as if in retribution for even the contemplation of a vain gesture. She wore no make-up, pulled on a pair of loose jeans, threaded a belt through the waist and selected a white T-shirt. On her way out she grabbed a black leather jacket and zipped it up to her neck in one quick movement.

A taxi pulled up as she left the building and in ten minutes she was in the Brasserie. Rory was nowhere to be seen, so she settled at a table in the back, pulled out her copy of the *Evening Standard* and ordered a kir.

The moment she became aware of his presence she simultaneously realized that she had dozed off into the uncomfortable state where light dreams incorporated the sounds of real life around her. In a moment of confusion she didn't recognize him, thought he must be a waiter, then blushed as she saw that it was him. He was still wearing a suit, dark with pinstripes, and in the vague seconds before she finally snapped awake there was an illusory moment when he appeared much taller than he was.

He was too close. Too big. She sat bolt upright, trying to correct the scale.

'God, I'm sorry. I fell asleep. I've never done that before.'

'Don't worry. I'm glad you felt relaxed. Better than a frenzy of excitement in anticipation of dinner with me.'

'Actually, the frenzy wore me out.'

He put down his briefcase and newspaper, then took off his jacket. Something of the earlier confusion persisted. He *was* bigger than she remembered, with that same brown glow she had noticed before, the sheen of a chestnut fresh out of its shell.

Alex blushed. She pulled her T-shirt straight and dragged her unruly hair back into the pony-tail.

'Busy day. Late night. Sorry, really tired.'

'Alex, you're talking the verbal equivalent of Morse code. Would you like some coffee?'

'No, I'm fine, thanks. Bad day at the office, it sort of dulls me. Any other day I could sit in a restaurant with something like ESP, take in four or five conversations going on around me, see the waiters bickering in the corner, know that the manager can't balance the till.' She smiled. 'Not tonight, though.'

'How is business?'

'Ha! Funny you should ask. I don't know how business is.' She took a sip of her kir. 'Strange, isn't it? I seem to have been on the brink of something really big ... something major, for weeks now. But it just won't ... I don't know. It just won't happen.'

She thought of the ten million dollars sitting in Maxim's account, the only tangible result of her efforts so far. But, as Neville would say, Wellington is not a bank. Having the money there did nobody any good. She could hear Neville's voice, nasal and dense, with an annoying click from somewhere at the back of his sinuses that revolted her.

She turned her attention back to Rory. 'Sorry. Things are rather tense at the moment.'

'So I can take advantage of you tonight with your defences down? You'll be entirely truthful in answering my questions?'

'I'm always entirely truthful. Remember? I'll never be able to tell a lie again without having a vision of you like a demonic Jiminy Cricket sitting on my shoulder wagging a disapproving finger at me.'

He laughed. 'What would you like to drink? Another kir?'

'Yes, please.'

As he turned in his chair to summon a waiter Alex's eyes flickered over his body with reptilian speed. She surprised herself. She had always hated the arrogance of the sweep of a man's eyes over her body, all the more so when he finished off with her own eyes, making no pretence of what he was thinking and making her acknowledge that she had seen him. She thought of David Macneice the previous evening and how surprised she had been. Now she was doing the same thing – albeit covertly – to a man. The muscles were there for all to see and a couple of women at a nearby table *did* take a good look, summing him up before casting a curious eye over Alex. She studiously looked away as he turned back.

'What were you up to last night, then?' he asked.

'Russian Embassy,' she answered promptly. 'Cocktail party.'

'Interesting?'

'For the first five minutes.'

'Nobody killed?'

Surprisingly, Alex felt annoyed. 'You have a completely wrong perception of Russia. I can't believe you of all people have swallowed the myth that wherever there are Russians there's murder. That's simplistic and very insulting.'

Rory leant forward. 'Alex, two Russians murdered a jeweller in Hatton Garden yesterday. And an Aeroflot stewardess was found dead in Earls Court. Combined with the number of Western businessmen killed in Moscow I have grounds, I think, for the comment.'

'*A* comment, yes. But not the idea that a cocktail party at the Russian Embassy would be a bloodbath simply because of the number of Russians present.'

'Point taken.' He looked around. 'Let's have a drink and change the subject or we'll end up murdering each other. And you need something to eat to get your blood sugar up. Let's have a look at the menu.'

Alex smiled at his diplomacy. Perhaps she had overreacted, spurred by the reluctance of the banking world to put their money into Russia.

They chose their food and ordered, then talked about the markets in general before moving on to more personal subjects.

'Where did you go to university?' Rory asked when Alex complained about the wisecracks her colleagues made about her degree.

'Durham. Great place and I had a great time. What about you?'

'Cambridge. Great place too.' Alex laughed. 'And before uni?' Rory continued.

'What do you mean, before? School – that sort of thing?'

'Yes, all that stuff. Tell me something that doesn't sound like a profile from one of the business magazines – you know, "Alexandra Brookes, who graduated from Durham University, has been with Wellington trading for six years . . ." Give me some of the more interesting stuff.'

The waiter arrived with their food and Alex fussed with the pepper mill and the Parmesan, playing for time, unsure how to deal with the question. 'Well, I'm learning Italian, I love the language and I do a lot of business in Italy. You know the Italian economy . . .'

'No business talk, Alex.'

'OK. What else?' Beyond her job there was a life which she did not want to compress into a couple of conversational soundbites. 'Not much to tell really.'

'There must be. I can't believe that you are the stereotypical executive woman through and through. Beautiful, intelligent, hard as nails—'

'Whoa! How come you put these words

together like a boxed set? Intelligent and beautiful lead you inexorably on to "hard as nails". A leap of faith there, I think.'

Rory smiled and began to eat his steak. The battle was engaged. 'It's an indisputable fact that women have to be better and try harder in business. It's not unreasonable to observe that intelligence being a prerequisite, beauty cannot hurt – nor the confidence it brings.'

'That's nothing but your basic misogyny wrapped up in psychobabble. A reasonable man adopting an unreasonable stance and trying to pass it off as common sense. Not good enough, Rory. I don't know you very well, but surely you can do better than the "woman-in-business-has-to-be-tough-to-get-ahead" line?'

'Actually, I'm giving you every chance to dispel the myth. I'm putting it forward as a stereotype and asking you to show me that it's not an accurate portrayal of you. I'm afraid your snappy little tirade confirmed rather than dispelled my image of the intellectual harridan carrying her blue stockings around in her Gucci handbag.'

'Gucci! Can't you even tell the difference between Gucci and Hermès? If you had any sense you wouldn't ask questions – you'd use the stereotypes. Doesn't it make life easier? Especially in your line of business. You just get the outline and fill in the rest yourself. Like painting by numbers.'

'Why are you so reluctant to let me dispel it? Does it give you a camouflage? Do you like hiding behind it?'

Alex laid down her knife and fork, smiling. 'Off the record?'

'Of course,' Rory replied, leaning forward.

'Well, it *is* uncomfortable sometimes,' she conceded. 'These questions – perhaps you think they're impersonal and that by wrapping them up in psychological terms I won't notice. I'm caught between two stools here. I'm not going suddenly to burst out with a long emotional tirade about my relationship with my father and how it affected me. In fact there was nothing wrong with my relationship with my father – or anyone else, for that matter. There are no skeletons in my emotional cupboard. But if I don't show you some kind of chink in my armour then the stereotype persists: I'm repressed. Hard as nails, I think you said.'

'Hold on. Let's not confuse the issue here. I was asking – on behalf of a curious readership – for a fresh perspective on someone who is high profile in a sector which doesn't develop the cult of the personality. If you'd been a well-known advertising executive we would have seen profiles of you and your dog in the *Mail on Sunday* by now. All I'm doing is giving you a forum you don't have working in the City.'

'I don't have a dog.'

'Why not?'

Alex burst out laughing. 'I don't have a dog because I live in a flat and I travel a lot! No scoop there, I'm afraid.'

Rory sat back and sighed. 'I give up. You're perfect.'

Alex felt a surge of excitement, a blend of anticipation and warning.

When Rory continued his voice was slow, his smile provocative. 'Maybe you're right. Maybe I should believe that there is no interesting little chink in your armour. Hard to believe, though. Come on, Alex, give me a little something, one little confession.'

'A little something . . .' She sighed, tempted to shock him and tell him exactly what she was thinking. About the desire to lean over the table and take hold of him, to feel that hot brown skin. She wanted to put her hands round his neck and feel the strong pulse, to hold him tight.

After a moment she found the equanimity to deflect his question.

'How damn boring. I have no confessions of the kind you'd like but I do have one flaw, a major flaw which colours my life and my work.' She stopped and looked at him, teasing him with her reticence, trying to regain her composure.

'What?'

'Sloth.'

'That's it? You're lazy?'

'That's it. But if you really thought about it, it's about as significant a statement as I could make about your damn stereotypes. I'm lazy, not driven. I sleep in. I miss meetings. I do not read the *Financial Times* every day . . .'

'This is hot stuff,' he mocked. 'I had no idea . . .'

'No, wait. It *is* hot stuff. Maybe you don't know any, but I do know some women who would fit your profile of the single-minded career woman. They're very strong, very focused and very fit—'

'Alex. This is you. Perhaps you don't see yourself in this light, but you are all of these things. So

252

you miss some meetings – hardly surprising if you travel round the world then go to receptions at the Russian Embassy. So you don't read the *FT* every day. So what? This woman, the City woman you clearly despise, she sounds an awful lot like you.'

Alex felt a moment's annoyance. She knew how she had felt in the Belorussian smelter. Hardly the reaction of a hard-bitten business woman. But it was not an experience she wanted to cheapen and relate to Rory in emotional self-defence, to be trotted out, with tears in her eyes, to prove that she was not cold. Why should she have to defend herself?

She was caught in her own trap. She *did* care what Rory thought about her and was tempted to explain to him how she felt. He was looking at her expectantly and she was suddenly confused. Part of her *was* this hard-bitten businesswoman, part of her the sensitive bleeding heart. How could she sum that up in a neat soundbite?

'Well?' he prompted.

'OK, I give in. I have my *FT* here in my bag along with my blue stockings and my horn-rimmed glasses. My favourite film was *Wall Street*. My favourite drink is Badoit. Favourite food – sushi. I do aerobics three times a week and run for an hour three times a week.'

Rory laughed. 'Well, if ever you needed to dispel the myth – that little speech did it.'

'Just don't quote me on any of that. Bonus time soon. Now, I need a coffee. Will you have one too?' She signalled for the waiter. 'And I'll get the bill.'

'Just a moment, I invited *you*. You can pay next time.'

She accepted graciously. 'Well, next time, I grill you on the stereotypical journalist, the tabloid hack making up the headlines, the paparazzo poking his lens under the bedroom door. I know nothing about *your* background, Rory.'

'No headlines there, I'm afraid. If you're counting on the dirt from my background to sustain a conversation throughout dinner we'd better go to McDonald's.'

'I think you may just have attempted to side-step the issue. I warn you, I can be ruthless.'

They drank their coffee and stayed on neutral territory until they left. On the pavement he leant forward to kiss her cheek before she could begin to think about a gracious withdrawal.

'Get a good night's sleep. You need it.' He looked at his watch. 'Cup of cocoa, straight into bed.'

'I will. And thank you for dinner.'

'My pleasure.'

After the quasi-intimacy of the evening's conversation it was an oddly formal farewell, but Alex took off down the road with a smile. She looked at her watch. Barely ten o'clock; she'd call Sol when she got home.

Sol. She felt a twinge of guilt which had been absent earlier in the evening, when she could still pretend that her reasons for seeing Rory were purely professional. She could no longer make that claim.

She had been surprised by her desire for Rory; it was not a feeling she'd registered in the office when he'd interviewed her. It was as if the intellectual challenge had suddenly transformed itself into a physical recognition; as if the urge to engage had simply moved from one area of the body to another.

And he was interested in her. Sol knew what she was going to say before she said it, could anticipate every thought, every emotion. She was enjoying the attention from Rory. She hugged her jacket around herself as she walked along King's Road.

On the top step she searched in her bag for her keys, moving to the side to allow an approaching figure to pass into the building. Suddenly she realized that the presence had stopped right behind her and she swung round in a moment of panic, her shoulder colliding with the door frame, the rush of fear as strong as a physical blow to her heart.

The man was smiling, but there was a wolfish, predatory relish in his grin. He was elegant and relaxed, leaning forward slightly as if about to whisper a secret. His whole manner was inappropriately familiar and Alex recoiled from the confidence that permitted this man to act with such lack of concern for convention.

Slowly, he took his hand from his pocket. Her throat tightened and she knew she was unable to shout, although in her ears a shrill scream of panic deafened her. Her whole body convulsed against the door, as far away from his as possible. Her head jerked backwards and hit the door; the buzz of fear now overwhelming.

'What do you want?' she whispered.

'Miss Brookes?' He extended his hand towards her. 'What a coincidence! I wasn't sure it was you. My name is Roman. Professor Vichevsky has been trying, without success, to arrange a meeting. How amazing that I should spot you like this!'

'How did you know where I live?' Alex asked, ignoring his proffered hand, taking in none of his words, her mind racing.

Roman shrugged, his smile widening. 'I cannot claim any credit for having solved that mystery. I am living in a serviced apartment near here and am on my way back from Sloane Square. The professor *did* tell me that he had met you for coffee and that he believed you lived near here, so perhaps I was a little extra vigilant. But there is no more to it than that.'

'Leave me alone. Please . . .' She clutched her bag against her like body armour.

'Miss Brookes, I can imagine how this must seem, and although I am extremely happy to have bumped into you, I am beginning to regret having spoken out. I should perhaps have simply dropped a note through your letterbox. But I was so surprised to recognize you I gave no thought to how it would look. You are quite right to be alarmed and I apologize.'

He moved back slightly and Alex straightened up, her hand feeling the door behind her as if the solid wood could anchor her.

'There's nothing I can do for you. I made it quite clear to the professor that I could not take on any new customers at the moment.'

Roman nodded and Alex felt again a tremor of

mistrust. He was so urbane, so relaxed. He had Western manners; she had never witnessed this polished insincerity in a Russian and wondered where he had learnt both the language and the demeanour. For a second it occurred to her that he was not Russian at all. When he had smiled his broad, disarming smile she'd noticed that he had perfect teeth, not a common feature among his countrymen.

'Since you deal with business on an apparently chronological basis, first come first served, I had better reconcile myself to waiting. Or does the size of the potential customer have any relevance?'

Alex acknowledged the barb. But she didn't care what he thought of her, simply wanted him to go.

'I really don't want to discuss this ... I'm handling so much business already. The professor seems to have decided that I am the only possible broker for this project – whatever it is – but I can assure you that there are plenty of other people who can help.'

The man's expression remained attentive and pleasant. In the seconds of silence that followed Alex knew that she wanted nothing more than to shut the door and lock him out.

'Look, I'll ask my assistant to deal with the initial stages and I'll supervise—'

'Perfect,' Roman interjected. 'This will give us a chance to show you the extent of our interests. May I give you my card?'

Alex flinched as he put his hand into his pocket and he caught her eye, making her blush at the demonstration of her fear. She took the heavy embossed card from him and shoved it into her bag.

He bowed and retreated down the steps, turned the next corner and disappeared, leaving Alex standing on the top step, still clutching her bag. The story of having simply bumped into her was implausible; she believed he had, somehow, discovered her address but would not admit to the subterfuge. She shrugged. She had never done it but it was probably not too difficult to find someone's address. Professor Vichevsky was certainly determined. It was their insistence on having *her* as a broker that mystified and alarmed her. This was too *personal*. There was nothing sinister about the professor, but Mr Roman Annansky was in a different league. She looked at his card. He was using the professor's office in Dover Street but there was no explanation of what Mr Annansky did for a living. Uneasy, she put the card in her pocket.

The phone rang as soon as she walked into the flat. It was Sol.

'So, where have you been?'

'Out for dinner with a journalist, talking about regulations. Sol, there was a guy on my doorstep when I got back—'

'Listen, Alex, I had a good meeting with Mitchell, the merchant bank, today. He's ready to go ahead on the Brazilian thing. You want to come over and go through the deal?'

Alex groaned. 'No, no! I can't face another plane. Let me try to do it by phone. Could we manage a conference call?'

'No way. Jump on Concorde, Alex. You'll be here in no time. I need you here, face to face.'

'Jump on a plane yourself, then, if it takes no time!' she snapped, surprising even herself with her anger. Where had this word 'need' come from? It was the second time he had used it; the first time he had 'needed' information about Maxim.

'Alex, Alex, what's happening to you?'

'Nothing's happening to me. I'm busy, that's all. I have all this Russian stuff to do. I want to talk to you about finding finance. It all seems to have dried up over here. I'll do whatever has to be done for the Brazilian deal from here. Look, Sol, I have to tell you about this guy on the doorstep—'

'I have another call. I'm going to call you tomorrow. Get a good night's sleep.'

Alex slammed the phone down. She lay back on the bed and went through the conversation in her mind. Had they said one word, either of them, of a personal nature? Had there been a single word of affection between them?

He had not been interested when she began to tell him about Annansky, so he had simply cut her off. No interest. She thought back to her earlier conclusions. Did Sol really know her every thought, or was he simply not interested in hearing them? There was a big difference.

Before she got into bed she looked at the card again. Annansky.

The man was dangerous. She would have to warn Libby.

* * *

259

'I can look after myself!' Libby laughed, turning the card over in her fingers. 'Anything to get the professor off my back. You know, he started by asking if he could take you for dinner, but ended up prepared to settle for thirty seconds in the lift.'

'Libby, I mean it. There was something menacing about this guy. It was so intimate, the way he spoke to me. He was absolutely in control, standing so damn close to me.'

'Point taken. I'll make sure we're in a crowded environment at all times.'

Alex sighed. 'No, Libby, I'm not joking,' she reiterated slowly. 'I *mean* it. This man is really dangerous.'

Libby stopped. 'I see . . . OK, Alex, I'll be careful.'

Alex carried on riffling through her papers. She looked at the crumpled wad of receipts. 'I'll have to try and do something with these. I'll be in my office.'

'Before you go – two more messages. A Mr Freeman. Wants to know if you're free for dinner on Thursday.'

Alex smiled. 'Do me a favour. Call him and tell him to come to my flat at seven thirty. OK?'

'Done. The last one . . . You're not going to like this. Were you counting on a quiet night?'

'I don't care who it is!' Alex snapped, rummaging on her desk for a pen. 'I'm not going out tonight. I'm exhausted.'

'Maxim's just flown in. Very urgent,' she imitated his growl. ' "Must see Alex for dinner. I send car to take her from office at seven." '

'God, Libby. I never get anything done. So

much pressure and I never have any time . . .'

'Can I help?'

'No, you're doing enough as it is. I just need a couple of days without a phone ringing. I'm off to my office.'

A dark Mercedes was waiting outside the front door of Wellington's building when Alex left a few minutes after seven, and the uniformed driver rushed round to open the door as soon as she stepped onto the pavement.

'I'm to take you to the restaurant, Miss Brookes. Mr Volkov will meet you there.'

The Mercedes swung soundlessly alongside the Thames, weaving in and out of the traffic. The curve of the Embankment gave a clear view of Big Ben and the Houses of Parliament as they swept past the Savoy Hotel, the panorama of the swerving Thames offering up one well-known landmark after another.

Five minutes later they turned into a narrow cobbled mews, stopping outside what appeared to be a shop, with a dramatic blue fish logo on the window and the name 'Kaspia'. Although she had eaten in the steak restaurant further up the mews, Alex had never noticed this place.

Inside was an array of caviar the length of the shop, with an equally impressive display of vodka. A Russian restaurant in London. Alex was amazed both that the place existed and that Maxim had found it. She thought back to the real Russian restaurants she had visited in Moscow and found the contrast laughable. Here every surface shone, the bright halogen lights proudly accentuating the gleam of the new chrome and wood surfaces. In Moscow dirt was so ingrained it was unnoticeable. The universal pollution made dirt as natural an element as water or air. Even the restaurants were grubby, the glasses cloudy, the waiters dishevelled and uncaring. There was no point in being fastidious when dust and disorder were endemic, as unavoidable as an airborne virus.

Yet there had been charm lying dormant under the heavy soiled layers of Moscow life; a bright red tablecloth faded into brown with age had a different character from a new brown fabric. And this designer restaurant, so breathtaking in its spartan cleanliness, had a different kind of appeal. Alex looked around. Different, but not better.

Maxim stood as she walked into the restaurant, which was hidden behind the shop. The head waiter took her coat and she sat down, delighted and surprised by the delicacies on the table in front of her – quails' eggs, glistening black caviar, blinis, smoked salmon.

Maxim raised a glass of champagne. '*Nasdarovya.*'

'Your health. I just wish we had something to celebrate. I'm finding the finance issue very problematic.'

Ignoring her, he leant forward. 'Alex. I have important matter to discuss. Listen and give me your proposal. I have spoken with Mintov. You know big problems in Russia today. Very difficult times. Here is my idea. If I buy aluminium, price go up. But then, if I don't sell, there is panic, people buy even if they don't want. Then we sell and protect price of Russian aluminium industry.'

'Oh, Maxim . . .' she began. He wanted to corner the aluminium market. The plan was unworkable but she knew Maxim too well to laugh in his face. 'You can't. You simply can't. The world market for aluminium is too big. If you buy and the price goes up, someone else will sell and the price will go down. To control a market you have to be able to control almost all the available metal, otherwise . . .'

Maxim was nodding and it took a moment to sink in. Jesus. He *did* have control. He had the Russian government behind him.

'Even if you control every ton of Russian aluminium . . .'

'Yes?' He egged her on. 'If you control every ton of Russian aluminium . . . ?'

Alex stared at him, slowly coming to terms with the scale of his idea. 'My God . . . if you can . . .'

Maxim smiled.

Kartchak swung his chair round to the window and watched the activity outside the Palace Hotel. The narrow street was congested with limousines, Mercedes and BMWs, each with a taciturn driver slouched in the front seat, somehow all looking too big for the space. The drivers were professional killers, heavily armed, but they were wary now, afraid of becoming involved in a fight and losing their livelihoods, soft and spoiled. Kartchak knew that the drivers of the ancient Ladas parked further down the road were far more dangerous. From his vantage point he had watched drug deals, muggings and two murders, one of which would never be discovered. These men were brutal and vicious. Lawless. Kartchak enjoyed watching them. Today he recognized Volodya, one of his former employees, and wondered what he was doing there.

The phone rang and he swivelled back to answer it.

'It's Roman. I can't get near the Brookes woman. Says she's too busy. Put me on to her assistant, though. I'm nearly there.'

'I don't want her fucking assistant. I want *her.*'

Roman hesitated. 'What are we talking about here? What do you want me to do?' He knew what Kartchak liked to do with women but was unsure about this one. 'If she won't come to a meeting, do you want me to go and see her? In her flat? You know . . .'

'Just get her to a fucking meeting, Roman. Arrange it then call me.'

Roman lost patience. 'You just don't understand. It would be easier for me to make her dance naked than get her to a meeting. She won't come voluntarily. She doesn't want the business. Now answer me this question. Do I *make* her come or not?'

Kartchak looked out of the window again, watching Volodya pace up and down in front of the filthy car. Business had been easy in the beginning – Kartchak gave an order and it was executed. Now he had to play psychological games with Roman, try to work out why he was behaving as he was, why he had chosen not to complete this one simple task.

'Make her,' he ordered then put the phone down.

Beneath Kartchak's office Volodya was watching every passing van. Kartchak guessed he was waiting for a delivery, probably antibiotics. He liked that business and for a moment considered going down into the street himself. Dealing with Volodya would be easier than dealing with Roman. He felt a stab of anger. Although his home was in Moscow Roman need never come back; he could live quite happily in London, especially since he had become complacent, typically Western in his insolent impatience. He acted as if speaking English had elevated him above Kartchak and had forgotten that he was only a part of the complex deal which *Kartchak* had created and implemented, not him.

There was a scuffle at the door of the Palace Hotel and Volodya began to drift forward, attracted by the possibility of involvement in a theft. A group of foreign businessmen were leaving the hotel and one of them was arguing with a driver. He was wearing a distinctive thick green coat with a pleat running from the collar to the hem at the back.

Volodya circled nimbly, like a wolf looking for the weakest of the group. Kartchak felt another urge to be part of his operation and act out of pure mindless greed and aggression. He could hear the big man's voice; he was outraged, shouting with the strange strangled pitch of a man not used to shouting. Ironically, he had had more authority when silent. Now he was bleating and the others in his party were moving forward, ready to receive orders.

Suddenly the big man bent double as if he had received a massive blow to the stomach. His colleagues looked at him in confusion, not understanding what had happened. Volodya darted forward and Kartchak strained to see what he would do, excited by the sudden bloody violence. By now everyone had realized that the tall man had been stabbed in the stomach. His coat hung open and his trousers were drenched with blood yet he was still standing, bent over, mouth open, as his life poured away.

Volodya spotted a briefcase, turned and looked round. No-one had seen him, bar the hotel doorman, whose expression remained blank and incurious, and Kartchak, invisible five stories above him.

Volodya looked back at the corner where he had been standing. Kartchak knew the van he had been waiting for would not stop now; there was no way they would risk being involved in a scene like this and the police were sure to be on their way. Volodya would be angry. Pot luck with one briefcase instead of a van full of drugs which would have made him twenty thousand dollars.

The dying man was now on the ground with two colleagues kneeling beside him. Volodya grabbed the briefcase, leant over as if offering assistance, then thrust the blade of his knife into the back of one of the kneeling men. He grinned, a sudden flash almost of pain, as if the effort had been taxing, then turned and ran up the steps of the hotel.

Now the sounds were of alarm, cries of disbelief and fear as the remaining foreigners realized their own vulnerability. In shock they turned away, their bodies swaying, backing off, leaving the two bodies grotesquely angled, the only movement the slow steady spread of their blood like a shadow around them on the pavement.

Kartchak smiled, deeply satisfied by events although he had only been a spectator, understanding Volodya's actions; he had been cheated out of his legitimate earnings, thwarted and angered. He had restored the balance by taking the briefcase and assuaged his murderous resentment of the foreigners' intervention by randomly killing one, driving his blade into his unsuspecting back, just to the left of the spine, carefully and fatally aimed. Volodya would try to reschedule the delivery, maybe he would be successful, maybe not. But the memory of the afternoon would be of action, success and achievement rather than of passive futility.

Kartchak remembered that feeling. Control. He had had it back in the early days but he had certainly lost it now. Perhaps it was because he had moved outside his territory. Again he cursed his lack of English.

Normally he would have gathered his men together, listened to their summaries of the situation, then taken charge. The scheme depended on Vichevsky and Roman remaining in London, but at the moment the whole picture seemed fragmented and he could not draw it together. He knew the aluminium industry had enormous potential and he was nearly there, nearly in position. The groundwork was done. He had to move fast now but his orders were not being obeyed. Roman felt it was quite acceptable to tell him that what he wanted was simply not possible.

Kartchak wanted control back. And he wanted Alexandra Brookes.

He picked up the phone, dialled and had a brief conversation. Then he told his secretary to book a flight to London.

Somehow the concept of cornering the aluminium market seemed less ridiculous in the morning. Alex lay in bed and played with the idea. Maybe it could be done.

She pulled the phone over to the bed and called Libby. 'Are you coping?'

'Yes. Things are quiet. Where are you?'

'I'm at home, but I'm going into the library at City University. Let's meet in Raoul's at one thirty.'

'Fine. See you then.'

Alex took a shower, alternating between hot and cool water, trying to wake herself up. Back in her bedroom she selected a soft black silk knit jumper and black linen trousers, loose unstructured clothes in which she felt comfortable. She pulled on flat suede boots, picked up her bag and left.

At the library she checked out three reference

books then settled down to read the case of Bunker Hunt, who had decided to use his resources to corner the world silver market.

At first the article read like any economic treatise, dry and uninteresting. But the flamboyant Hunt brothers came alive as Alex read about their disastrous operations.

There definitely was something foolhardy about the brothers. They'd tried twice. In 1973 they had bought 38 million ounces of silver. But then the Mexican government sold 50 million ounces and smashed the price right back down again leaving the brothers high and dry. Or *long and wrong* as the market commented at the time.

In August 1979 they'd decided to try again.

The silver price, which had begun the year at $6 per ounce, began to rise spectacularly to $10, then $12, then $18 per ounce.

Nobody knew what was going on. The market was awash with rumours. There was talk that Arab investors were behind the move. Or South Americans. And they all made sense. The world was in chaos and money was looking for a 'safe haven'.

When the US Embassy in Tehran was seized and the Soviet invasion of Afghanistan took place, the Hunt brothers must have been ecstatic. The market went up even further – to $35 per ounce. Everything was going their way.

But then the tide began to turn.

No-one could have anticipated how willing people would be to melt down heirlooms, coins and jewellery. But the brothers stuck with it, mopping up all the new metal, borrowing more and more money, but it was only a matter of time. The money was running out. To maintain their massive positions they had to pay ever-increasing deposits to their brokers. But still they continued to buy, opening new accounts and spreading the positions between them. The silver price moved above $50 per ounce.

In January the Exchanges announced that no new positions could be established – the Hunts could buy no more, they could only sell. The price fell to $30 per ounce.

Thursday, 27 March 1980 became known as 'Silver Thursday'. By midday the price had fallen by $5 per ounce.

The following day the market closed at $12 per ounce.

It was all over.

It was depressing reading but instructive. Alex sat back. Now she knew how *not* to do it. A corner implied a certain kind of madness – a price rise that picked up momentum and almost had a life of its own. You had to get in, then hope everybody else followed you. Then you had to get out without bursting the bubble.

She took notes for twenty minutes, then looked at her watch. Nearly one. She gave back the books and headed slowly for the office, oblivious to the bright spring weather. She walked across Finsbury Circus and stopped for a moment in the garden in the centre, suddenly noticing that people were walking around without their coats and that some intrepid couples were even lying on the grass. She sat on the bench for a moment and smelt the warm wood.

Every fibre of common sense told her that the scheme should not even be considered. She was being asked to implement the most audacious plan she had ever been presented with.

She had no idea whether she had the flair to devise the scheme Maxim requested of her, but then she felt that perhaps caution was the one element that had been missing in similar previous schemes and that the frenzy of Bunker Hunt had elbowed out all common sense and all discipline.

Maybe this was just the kind of thing she *could* do well. Then she wondered whether she had the luxury of choice. She thought of her position at Wellington. Maybe this was the kind of thing she *had* to do. Dammit. Just because an Establishment bank didn't like the idea why should she allow herself to be put off? And Neville was nervous of anything that didn't come with an audited balance sheet. *She'd* been there. Actually seen the plant and spoken to the managers. She'd seen the assay certificates for the metal. Surely she knew best? Russia *was* viable.

Libby was already in the dark corner alcove, a large bottle of mineral water and a selection of sandwiches on the table in front of her.

Alex reached over and took a sandwich before sitting down, suddenly realizing that she was starving. She drank a glass of the cold, sparkling mineral water.

'God, these sandwiches are good. Let's have some more.'

Libby pulled out her notebook and pen. 'Come on, Alex, tell me what's going on.'

Alex leant across the table, impatient for Libby's reaction to the impact of her words. 'Aluminium. Let's corner the market.'

Libby stared back. '*Corner* it? What, like Bunker Hunt?'

'Exactly!'

Libby said nothing for a moment, her face showing no emotion.

'Have you decided to do it? I mean, you didn't say shall we, or could we ... You said, let's do it, *let's* corner the aluminium market.'

Alex said nothing. Had she decided?

Libby continued. 'I mean, God, there's millions of tonnes of the stuff out there, Alex, and they keep producing it. The Russians can't get the stuff out fast enough. Corner it? They can hardly give it away!'

'I know. It's a ridiculous plan, isn't it? And you're right to think of Bunker Hunt. What a spectacular failure.'

'... and tulips and the South Sea Bubble ...'

'All right, Libby, I get the point! I haven't decided we should do it in spite of the obvious Freudian slip you pounced on. I'm considering the logistics of it, that's all.'

'And just where have the logistics got you so far? Fill me in.'

Alex repeated the points she had learned from the Hunts, detailing the preparations necessary and the various stages of implementation.

'Hold on, hold on. Let's do a little research before we go any further, OK? I have some very basic questions I'd like answered.' Libby leant over the table. 'And the first question is why. *Why* are we doing this?'

'It's a damn good deal. It'll keep everybody happy,' Alex answered shortly, turning away from Libby, running her fingers up and down the icy surface of her glass.

'Come on, let's be honest here. Sol's in the States, Neville's putting you under pressure. You *are* sure your evaluation of this deal is ... objective? I mean—'

'I know exactly what you mean.' Alex's voice hardened. 'Is this bravado rather than brains? Am I just trying to prove something? Or maybe I've gone soft? Is this just an act of altruism on behalf of the poor old Russians?'

She turned and faced Libby, aware that this issue could lead to confrontation. For a moment they looked at each other, weighing up the differences between them, aware that a relationship founded on affection and tolerance now seemed full of conflict.

Alex sighed. 'I can't deny that the fact that we'll be helping the Russians has an appeal, but it's the icing on the cake, that's all. The numbers are good, Libby. It's a good deal.' It was suddenly very important to her that Libby understand. She tried again.

'If you'd seen the plant in Belorussia ... the faces ... It's impossible not to be moved. But why should the fact that people will benefit mean the deal is flawed? Can we only make money if we're cheating someone? Is a project only viable if it's polluting the environment?'

'No, of course not,' Libby answered, her anger

273

growing. 'But this deal is different. *You're* different. I've never seen you so ... frenzied. What happened to the analyst in you? Will you run this deal through the computer – make your usual projections? Examine every aspect of it?' She pulled back from Alex. 'Or have you made up your mind already?'

'I give you my word, Libby. If the numbers don't work I'll drop it. Listen, *you* do the research, have a look at the numbers. *You* decide. And if you say no then that's it. No questions, no recriminations. We'll drop it and move on. How's that?'

Libby smiled and extended her hand. 'It's a deal. But one last thing, Alex. If we do this we'll be manipulating the market. And that's illegal.'

'Ironic, isn't it? After I gave that interview about regulations. Alexandra Brookes, the great moralist.'

'But you *are* a moralist. I've never known you do anything that was the slightest bit ... dodgy. Nothing.'

'You know my views on the law and business. Window-dressing. Irrelevant. Insincere. It's all right for some speculator to sell a currency because he thinks he knows better than the government and the central bank – that's legitimate. The man with the money calls the shots.

'Look, I know I'm rationalizing, Libby, but somehow it just seems ... *fair*. Isn't that what the law should embody, rather than making grandiose but empty gestures at small-time crooks, while allowing massive manipulations for profit every day? I'll have to deal with this at some stage, Neville will pick up on the volume and feel he should report us to the authorities, but I'll deal with that – somehow.'

Alex straightened, her voice firm. 'Anyway. The answer to your question is yes. It is illegal. Very illegal.'

TEN

'Want to join us for a drink?' Libby asked.

Alex bit back the automatic refusal. Maybe it was time, especially after everything she had said about Spike recently.

'Love to. But will you come with me? I've arranged to meet Maxim at the Ritz at eight and I want to dump all this stuff in the car.'

They drove along the Embankment, up St James's and on to Piccadilly, where Alex jumped out and waved to the doorman. He ran over and took the car keys from her with a grin.

'I'll put it in the Arlington Street garage. Want it cleaned?'

Alex looked at the dust and mud and nodded. 'But I'll only be about an hour.'

'No problem.'

She led the way into the lobby and straight through to the bar, which hosted gracious afternoon teas before subtly changing into a cocktail bar in the early evening. There was a sense of delicacy in the refined charm of the Ritz which Alex instantly knew would be anathema to

Spike. In addition to the rose bower in the corner and the fussy latticework dividing the bar from the hallway, the hum of conversation was predominantly female, girlish, even at that hour. Looking around with fresh eyes, Alex saw the men as uncomfortable intruders, perching on delicate gilt chairs that were too small and insubstantial, while their companions – more often mothers than lovers – chinked their glasses and laughed.

'I only arranged to meet Maxim here,' she explained. 'We can go somewhere else to have a drink if you like.'

Before Libby could answer, Maxim appeared and Alex introduced him to Spike. She had anticipated that the language barrier would prevent any real conversation between them; surprisingly few people had the ability to scrub their language free of colloquialisms and Alex had assumed that Spike would make no effort.

'Right then, let's go somewhere else,' Spike announced. 'Place is full of fucking fairies.'

There was a pause as Maxim took in his words. 'Fairies?'

'Come here, my son.' Spike took him by the arm and led him away from Alex and Libby.

'I'm sorry, Alex . . .' Libby began. 'Maybe this isn't a good idea.'

'Too late now. And it was *my* idea.' She watched Spike's shaved head cocked to one side as he spoke, his fists clenched, then a sharp gesture as if heading a ball. Both men laughed. As they walked back to join Alex and Libby, Spike wiped his mouth with the back of his hand.

'Good bloke that.'

They crossed Piccadilly and turned right into Dover Street, where Alex led them down into a small basement bar. Spike ambled in, looking around suspiciously. Although the bar was decorated with photographs of celebrities, there were sufficient sportsmen among them to win his approval and the smoky darkness of the bar reassured him. When the waiter appeared and asked the men what they would like to order for the ladies, Spike beamed triumphantly at Alex.

'Pink gin for you, madame?' he asked in mock stilted English.

'No, I'll have a glass of dry white wine.'

'Oh, jolly good. Two white wines, then. And for you?' He turned to Maxim.

'Bloody Mary.'

'Make that two.'

Alex groaned. As ever, the pastime of drinking was more enjoyable for Maxim as a competitive event and she was sure he had recognized a contender in Spike. They had drained the first glass by the time Alex and Libby had been served.

Spike held up his empty glass. 'Nice drink. Shame about the tomato juice. Waste of space. Let's have another on its own, eh?'

There was no doubt in Alex's mind that Spike was about to try to manoeuvre her and Libby out of the evening. She did not trust Maxim to keep his mouth shut about the project, nor did she trust Spike not to use any information he gleaned to his own benefit, but if she alerted Spike to the fact that there was a confidential issue between them he would be unstoppable.

'Maxim. Spike works for Metco. Also a metal broker. We're in the same business.'

Maxim downed his second vodka and nodded. 'Metco. What do you do?'

'I'm a dealer,' Spike answered, leaning forward, and Alex felt that his bearing would have been the same if he had said 'gladiator'.

'I trade. Punt. You know, run my own book.'

Maxim nodded although Alex felt he probably understood little of Spike's terminology. There was no doubting his meaning, though. Whatever it was he did he was clearly proud of it.

'What about you?'

Before Maxim could answer, Alex turned to Spike. 'Maxim is in import export.'

'I see, I see.' He looked at Alex, assessing her, then, without letting her gaze go, continued slowly. 'And, Maxim, tell me. Is it true that Russian women are very strong? Russian men are like children?'

Alex knew she had lost that point. Once she had issued the challenge, Spike would rise to it, using weapons she could not use herself, manipulating and intimidating. His first pitch had been a bald, crass gesture to establish male solidarity and, of course, Maxim was ripe for this.

Maxim laughed a loud hearty laugh and ordered another round of drinks. 'Russian women like all women. They only women!'

Libby reached out and touched Spike's arm. 'I'm starving. Let's go and have dinner.'

'Go and have dinner,' he ordered Libby, speaking slowly, menacingly. 'Go and have dinner with

Alex like a good girl. I have some drinking to do.'
He pulled out his wallet and passed a wad of
notes to Libby.

'But I don't need this,' she protested.

'Have a nice dinner, girls. On me. I insist.'

Alex looked at Maxim. Under no circumstances could she leave him with Spike. She
cursed herself for having got into this awkward
situation. Libby looked at her helplessly.

Suddenly Alex stood up. 'OK, boys.' She
reached over and snatched Maxim's vodka glass
from his hand.

'Let's drink!' It was one of Maxim's favourite
sayings and she mimed his accent gently, slightly
lowering her tone so that he recognized the
private joke without being offended by it.

'*Nasdarovya!*'

She knocked back the vodka as Maxim had
taught her, having first emptied her lungs of air,
then she gulped the mineral water chaser. With a
show, she banged her fist on her chest and
exhaled.

Maxim burst out laughing. He stood up and
clapped her back, waving to the waiter to bring a
bottle.

'Now we teach Libby and Spike,' he
announced.

The danger had passed. Libby laughed as
Maxim began to order the waiter around in his
habitual dictatorial style.

Alex looked down at Spike. Somehow his face
had changed and she saw that his lower jaw was
forward, both rows of teeth meeting at the front,
clenched, slightly visible. It was the classic,

unconscious gesture of the fighter inviting the fight, showing his mettle. For a second she felt like accepting that invitation, bunching her fist and driving it into his face. Appalled by her instincts, she smiled at him and sat down.

The evening ended at midnight. Libby slept soundly in the corner of the bar, having gracefully lapsed after four vodkas. Each round was a battle between Alex and Spike and after each one he looked at her and she gazed back defiantly.

Finally, Maxim stood and made a toast. 'To Alex. Never I know a woman who can drink like her. A Russian woman in her soul!'

Alex looked at Spike and realized that this speech was the nail in his coffin. He could not win this fight; Maxim was too drunk to remember any point he made. She had summoned what limited weapons she had and used them with subtlety. Alex lifted her glass to him but he refused to acknowledge her gesture. He slammed his glass down and left.

Maxim looked at Libby. 'Why he leave her?'

Alex looked at her friend, beautiful in sleep, and her eyes filled with tears.

'He's forgotten her.'

Kartchak watched as Vassili circled the two men. In a way he was pleased to see that he was enjoying himself – the young man had potential, but Kartchak was cold and tired. In Moscow he would have delegated the job and it would have been achieved in a quarter of the time, but out here he knew nobody and had to make sure it was done properly.

Another piece of the puzzle, another component in the aluminium industry.

Electricity. Power.

He yawned. It had been Vichevsky who had spoken to him about the necessity of a continuous power supply, Vichevsky who knew little, understood the significance of nothing and who had unwittingly put together a very interesting operation.

Impatiently Kartchak looked at his watch. Enough. He wanted to get to bed. The food in the restaurant had been awful and it had taken two hours of subtle questioning to be sure that the two men really did run the hydroelectric power station. After the third bottle of vodka, Kartchak had nodded to Vassili and the four of them had moved outside.

In the car park, Vassili had drawn his gun.

'Over there, please.'

The men were clearly confused. The visitors from Moscow were affluent and had asked intelligent questions about the plant. They had been completely believable as entrepreneurs looking to build a warehouse outside Minsk.

And now the young man holding the gun was behaving in an oddly courteous manner.

'Hurry up,' Kartchak said again.

Vassili nodded. He had been told exactly what to do. He had to kill one of them and it didn't matter which. He could choose.

The younger man had a short unkempt beard and ginger whiskers. He reminded Vassili of his brother. The older man was fat and unattractive but he had been friendly in the bar and had asked

Vassili about his schooling. He looked from one to the other, undecided.

The fat man saw Vassili's indecision and wondered why they were being scrutinized so closely.

'Who are you?' he asked.

'Be quiet,' Vassili answered and waved his gun at them. 'Just shut up.'

Kartchak could see what was happening. He had told Vassili how to do it. Take the two men. Don't try to decide which one to bribe or how, or how much. Shoot one, then pay the other. Then you're covered for all eventualities. But somehow Vassili had missed the point. It didn't matter which one he shot but the boy was trying to make some kind of rational decision.

Kartchak walked over and took the gun from his hand. Without taking his eyes from Vassili's, he shot the older man in the head.

Then he shot Vassili.

Stunned, the younger Belorussian cowered. After a moment he looked up at Kartchak questioningly. Kartchak smiled at him. This unprepossessing young man was now the undisputed head of the Minsk electricity plant and would do exactly as Kartchak said.

Quickly Alex swept the bottles of spirits from the top of the bar into the cupboard and shut the door. Four bottles of good red wine remained and four white were on ice in the kitchen. Enough.

It had taken four days to co-ordinate the schedules, but she had finally assembled all the players in London. She had arranged dinner in the Meridien in Piccadilly, a five-star hotel with elegant private dining rooms, and wanted to be sure that Maxim would stay focused on the agenda.

She checked her make-up in the mirror, smoothed her hair then sat down at the head of the table, her hands flat on the heavy white linen, breathing deeply. She wanted to do this deal, wanted to persuade these men, these clever, sharp, experienced men, to do *this* deal. She knew everything there was to know about aluminium, about the market and about the mechanics of cornering a market. But could she persuade them?

The Kid arrived first, handsome and tanned. He looked around the room before walking over to Alex.

'You're gorgeous,' he whispered and Alex smiled at him. From anyone else the remark would be inappropriate, but the charm was so ingrained in The Kid that she could not take exception. His attention drifted and she caught him looking at his reflection in the mirror.

'You're gorgeous too.' She nudged him. 'But you know that, don't you?'

When the others arrived and the introductions had been made she asked everyone to be seated and produced copies of the report she and Libby had prepared.

Libby. Alex had been surprised by her enthusiasm once she had done the initial research. Alex had almost decided that the idea was foolish and had prepared herself for Libby's refusal.

But no. Out came the charts, the calculations, the figures. It can be done, she agreed.

Maxim, for once, had made an effort. He was wearing the same dark charcoal suit he had worn the first time she had met him, with a crisp white ironed shirt. He was pale but without the deathly yellow aura of bad health that surrounded him when he was hung over.

Sol looked up and winked and Alex found herself grinning back at him, remembering the many occasions of silent collusion, the undercurrent of mischief that made even the most serious board meetings tolerable. He would finish reading the report before anyone else, she knew, and would then try to dominate the early conversation with voluble, over-confident but prescient observations. She waited for his verdict above all else.

The Kid sat back in his chair, his arms crossed expectantly. Alex looked at his smooth, perfectly manicured hands and the elegant inch of white shirt cuff above them. She knew instinctively that he would like it. He would relish the control and the scale of the plan.

When they had settled at the table, she stood up.

'This is not my show. I am here only to explain what has been asked of me and what I have found out about the aluminium market since I was asked that question.'

She turned to Maxim and continued. 'I was lucky enough to be introduced to members of the Russian government who are concerned about the fall in the aluminium price and the fact that their revenues are dangerously low. We all understand the problem.'

She took a sip of water, knowing that what she was about to suggest had to be put in a straight-forward, no-nonsense way, as if it were just another deal – the reactions at the table were bound to be the same as hers had been: disbelief, amusement, scepticism. Her presentation of the idea was crucial.

'It has been suggested to me that an operation to corner the aluminium market would be feasible and that this would solve the problem.' She spoke more quickly than she had intended and allowed a moment to pass before she con-tinued. No doubt they expected her to lecture them for hours. Slowly she closed the folder in front of her. 'I have looked into this and I believe it *is* feasible.'

She sat down, tense and expectant. The three men picked up the report. As they read, Alex took another sip of water, her throat dry, her hands reluctant to be still.

Finally, Sol spoke.

'Alex. Your research is, as usual, flawless. But anyone'd think you were approaching some pro-ject to finance a new mine or a factory somewhere – you know, something legitimate. I can't believe you've done all this,' he waved at the folder, 'because you want to squeeze aluminium! Must be the first time anyone's done cashflow projections before manipulating a market!'

As he and The Kid laughed, Alex winced. 'The operation is rather more than that, Sol. We're try-ing to bring about market conditions that will allow the Russian smelters to lock in favourable prices for their future . . .'

'Bullshit. One law in the marketplace. Survival of the fittest. You can talk about free markets or protectionism, but don't intellectualize, Alex. If the Russians manage to persuade you, me and The Kid to put this thing together, then they *are* the fittest and they will survive. And they deserve to. End of story.'

While it was not how Alex would have preferred the concept to be presented, she allowed it to stand unchallenged. If that was how he wanted to think about it, fine, it did not negate her stance. Their two approaches could co-exist without friction. Sol snapped his folder shut and looked at her expectantly, but she had no intention of rising to his bait until The Kid had spoken; the issue of her motivation was irrelevant to the implementation of the plan.

Alex waited for The Kid to speak, knowing that he was the linchpin, the cash.

Finally he put down his pen and turned to Alex.

'Let me go through this with you. You buy the futures. Sol buys the real metal. We use my broker account and my credit lines. Yes?'

'Yes.'

'And how do we get paid back?'

'Quite simple. We buy, then we sell – hopefully at a much higher price. The trading profit will be yours.'

Sol flipped through the pages of the report. 'You've covered it all. New production, consumers, funds. Damn good job, Alex.'

'All right.' Alex stood up again. 'Let's summarize. We have a nervous market waiting for the outcome of the Russian dilemma. It would not be too difficult to begin to plant stories that appear to suggest a complete disaster. As we all know, you can't push a market indefinitely against its will, and the most important feature of the aluminium market today is that a bull move is entirely plausible.'

'OK. So we buy some futures, buy a little stock in the warehouses. Then what?' Sol asked.

'Then we hope that someone notices. That *they* come in and buy. That the Investment Funds begin to take notice.'

'And when the price has taken off we sell?'

'Yes.' Alex leaned forward. 'And this is crucial. I looked at the Bunker Hunt corner of the silver market and there is one thing I noticed. World events helped them. There was turmoil when they decided to mount the operation and there was continued turmoil throughout. We really need some kind of fresh impetus to bring in new buyers and create the atmosphere of panic needed to absorb our selling. Something *we* can control.'

There was a pause. Maxim, who had until now said nothing, suddenly stood up. 'I spoke to Mintov. He has thoughts to give shares in plants to Western producers if they give money to plants. Then they can make repairs. Is good idea, I think?'

'Russian legislation won't permit large foreign shareholdings . . .' Sol began.

The Kid took over. 'And the producers wouldn't be prepared to invest very much in Russia—'

'Wait!' Alex broke in, realizing the enormous potential of the idea. 'This could be excellent. You're both right about the limiting factors, but imagine what would happen if the Russian producers announced a credit facility, that they are closing for repairs and that they will lose, say, ten per cent of their production! If we time this right, it has to be worth a couple of hundred dollars more on the aluminium price! We can close our position *and* hedge for the Russians. This is ideal!'

'So what are you saying exactly?' The Kid queried. 'That the Russians sell shares in their plants to the two big American producers. The Russian producers partially close down, decrease production and the price goes up?'

Sol leant forward. 'Will the Americans go for it?'

'Maybe ... maybe.' The Kid mulled it over. 'They're very worried about the Russian production costs and the amount of metal they're exporting. Lower prices hit *their* bottom line too. This way, they can "even out", buy into the lower cost producer – a very capitalist solution! Yes, I'm pretty sure they'd go for it!'

'And the Russian plants,' Alex asked Maxim. 'Will they go for it? Will they co-operate? Some of them have achieved a measure of independence recently. Will they be willing to be part of this plan?'

'Yes, if told. All of them.'

Alex sensed that the tempo had changed. There was an intensity as everyone realized that the plan *could* work and that this could be the biggest operation any of them had ever encountered. Between them they had the resources and the experience to corner a massive world market, influence the entire investment community and affect the future of a country like Russia.

They began talking at the same time, interrupting each other, coming up with better ideas, bigger plans.

Alex sat back. They had taken the bait. Now it was *their* project. They would mould it and stamp it and she would implement it. But she didn't care as long as it was *on*.

Gradually the plan developed. It took several hours, but the loopholes were finally closed, the ends tied up.

The Kid yawned. 'I'm leaving, too tired to think constructively.' He kissed Alex on the cheek, shook hands with the others and left. Maxim rose and followed him.

'Thank you, Alex, for your work.' He shook her hand. 'I call Mintov tomorrow. He will say also thank you, I know.'

Sol and Alex remained, at opposite ends of the table, papers and debris strewn across the table between them.

'Well, Alex. How do you feel?'

She sighed. Exhaustion was the first emotion on the list, followed by anxiety. 'Have we forgotten anything?' she asked.

'Nothing,' he assured, lighting a cigar. 'Not a thing. It's a brilliant plan. We can retire after this one.'

Alex smiled. 'I'm not going to bring up the ethics of all this—'

'Too damn right you're not.'

'—but I am worried about the scale of this deal. It's so big, Sol, we've never done anything like this before.'

'Relax. This is not the biggest deal the market has ever seen. This kind of thing happens all the time. Remember when Klein cornered aluminium? The price went from $1800 to $2250. Amazing. Do you think he did that on his own? Did you think it was coincidental that at the time the whole world was short of aluminium and there wasn't a seller in sight? Come on, Alex. Everybody colludes. Apart from anything else, schemes like this leak out. The broker knows, the broker next door on the exchange overhears and tells his customer, who tells the Fund manager. The aluminium dealer from company A resigns and tells company B all about it. Look at a chart of the aluminium price over the last twenty years. The volatility has multiplied by ten. That's because there are so many big players. Instead of thirty smaller players who operated on their own, there are now only five and they tell each other what they're doing. And we'll use that. We'll tell Stark, knowing that he'll tell Marvin. We'll make it work for us.

'I concede that you've done a lot more home-work than most of these guys, and I concede that you're motivated by slightly more than the normal, naked greed, but apart from these two considerations – which do not alter the fabric of the plan – you're doing what has already been done twice in the copper market this year and once in zinc. Am I right?'

'You're right.'

'If I promise not to mention business can I take you home?'

'Sol, if you're not talking business you're dead. And if you're dead you're no use to me at home.'

With their arms round each other, they slowly made their way to the front of the hotel and asked the doorman to summon a taxi home.

Libby leant back in her chair and smiled. 'That was a wonderful dinner, the first unscheduled outing in many years, Mr Annansky.'

'Roman, please. And this is the first evening I have managed to escape from Professor Vichevsky.' He refilled Libby's glass. 'I feel rather guilty. He is likeable but intense. And almost completely humourless.'

'How did you manage to avoid him this evening?'

Roman shrugged. 'I didn't go back to the office after my visit to the bank this afternoon.' He glanced at his watch. 'Perhaps he's still there, waiting for me.'

Libby laughed. She was feeling mellow, marvelling at the fact that her earlier anxiety had been almost completely displaced by the euphoria of expensive champagne. She'd left three messages for Spike and had the feeling that he'd been there and listening when she'd left the stuttering, long-winded explanation of why she was having dinner with a customer at such short notice. Roman had been shown round the Wellington office and had inundated Libby with questions about metal trading. Since he had meetings scheduled for the following day, it had seemed logical to carry on at dinner.

'If the professor ever finds out we had dinner together, he'll be distraught,' she laughed.

'And if Alexandra had been with us . . .'

'He's obsessed with Alex,' Libby mused. 'Even after she made it completely clear that she couldn't meet him, he persisted. It was as if he refused to get the message. I often feel I just don't get through to him.'

Roman nodded. 'I know how you feel. The professor has little . . . empathy. He was a good academic, but has made little headway in business. Short of what you call "interpersonal skills".'

Suddenly Libby leant forward. 'How come you speak such perfect English?'

Roman signalled to the waiter who came immediately to clear the table. 'I learnt it, Libby. Simple as that. I read books, watched films, listened to the good old BBC World service.'

Libby narrowed her eyes, feigning suspicion. 'Alex thinks you're not Russian at all.'

'Oh, really? Why is that?'

'She says your teeth are too good. And you don't smoke.' Libby laughed. 'She's good that way, Alex. She's got great *interpersonal skills*.'

'I only met her once. She was rather abrupt. Understandably so. I accosted her on her doorstep.'

'Oh, I wouldn't worry about that,' Libby waved her hand. 'Alex doesn't bear grudges. And she's so busy just now she's probably forgotten all about it. Now then, tell me about this deal of yours.'

'Oh, don't ask me about business. I'd rather know all about you.'

Libby straightened. 'I can assure you, you do not want to know all about me.' To her horror, she felt the sudden warning irritation of tears behind her eyes. She rubbed the bridge of her nose.

'The deal ... tell me.' She rallied, her voice hardening more than she had intended.

'We feel that as a Russian company we should be in a better position than some of these Western merchants to put together export deals. We have done some remarkable things in oil and gas. Now we want to trade metals. Aluminium. We have some excellent contacts. What we're lacking is the expertise on the terminal markets and risk management. Libby ...' He stopped and Libby looked up quickly. 'I'm sorry. I can deliver the whole speech without thinking, but my mind's not really on it, to tell you the truth. Let's have another drink. Shall we have a Cognac?'

Libby nodded. 'I must just make a call ... Sorry.'

Libby rang the flat and listened as it rang seven times. Then the answering machine clicked on and she heard her own voice. She knew he was there. The machine was programmed to cut in after only four rings. Spike had switched it on and was listening.

'Spike? Pick up the phone, please.' She waited. 'Come on, this is stupid. I know you're there.' There was something sinister about talking to a void, being able to imagine him standing in silence, invisible.

'I'll be home shortly. In half an hour or so, I should think. Spike, please. Just . . . oh for God's sake.' Suddenly she felt uncharacteristic annoyance. What a ridiculous charade. 'Right. I'll see you later . . . or not.'

She put the phone down and made her way back to the table, feeling a smile spread over her face. She liked Roman. There was an undercurrent, but for once this was as attractive as the overt – if not more so. If she let him he would eventually declare his interest in her. He had almost done so on a couple of occasions, suddenly losing the thread of what he was saying, or hesitating halfway through a sentence. She liked this disorientation and the fact that he had not embarked on a formal seduction. When his mouth opened and shut in indecision, without a word having been said, she felt appreciated, an unusual sensation.

'Ah, Cognac. Lovely.' She sat down and smiled across the table. 'This is a really special restaurant. Good choice.'

'I should have asked you since you live here. It was rather arrogant of me to book without consulting you.'

'Not at all. Living here, we tend to go to the same places all the time. We need some new ideas. Alex tells me she's discovered a Russian restaurant. I must get the address and return the compliment by taking you there.'

'That would be nice,' he answered graciously. 'But I'm not sure I could allow you to take me to dinner. That would be too much of a culture shock.'

'But you'll let me advise you on trading metal?' she teased.

'Touché. I seem to have been partially reformed. Don't give up on me, though, I'm willing to be completely retrained.'

'Oh, I wouldn't want to do that . . .' Like Roman earlier she could not finish what she was going to say. 'Look, I have to go. I'm sorry, but as this was not planned . . .'

Briskly, Roman called for the bill. 'It was good of you to come. And I can assure you that you are a very welcome change from the professor.'

'Not the biggest compliment I've ever been paid. I'll see you tomorrow then, shall I? And we'll go to the Exchange?'

'What time?'

'Come to the office at twelve. We'll go along for the end of the session. It'll look frenetic and you'll be impressed.'

Roman reached for her hand, but instead of shaking it he held it tightly in his own. 'I'm impressed already.'

Libby turned away and hailed a cab. 'I'm going in the opposite direction, otherwise I'd suggest we share.'

'Please.' Roman opened the taxi door. 'I'll see you tomorrow. Good night.'

Libby slammed the door shut and leant forward to give the driver the address.

Roman watched the taxi disappear. Though he had thought Libby pretty when he first saw her and found her manner engaging she was not his type. Normally he preferred the cool, classic

Russian beauty – almond eyes, high cheekbones. Yet he found himself smiling when he thought about her, relaxed for the first time in many months. She was gorgeous. The short curls shot through with an almost metallic sheen, the mischief in her eyes. Luminous. He wanted to send her a dozen red roses and pay her the most outrageous compliments, to tell her how beautiful she was and how she made him act like a buffoon.

He liked the fact that she could be businesslike without adopting a hostile façade. He disliked powerful women but there was something very attractive about Libby's buoyancy; she was both confident and competent, but she did not brandish her skills as if they were weapons. He wondered who she had been calling. Whoever it was, the relationship was clearly troubled. She had been very worried about going out for dinner and it was only after the third abortive call that she had given up and agreed to join him. Roman wanted to find out without alienating her. He'd ask Vichevsky's assistant, Arkady, if he could help. Arkady knew everything and everyone. Unbeknown to Vichevsky, Arkady was now in Kartchak's pay for his regular reports.

Suddenly Roman became aware of someone behind him, too close to be accidental. Ignoring the instinctive urge to turn back and face the assailant he lurched forward, intending to escape across the road. But he was too slow. As soon as he felt the restraint of a hand on the back of his jacket he attacked, but it was as if every move had been anticipated. He felt his head swim as he was swung around, cursing the amount he had had to drink. When his head crashed back against the wall he focused on the face of his attacker.

Arkady.

Then his focus spread and the whole scenario made sense. There was only one reason for Arkady to have been there.

Kartchak had sent him.

Alex beat both her fists on the desk. The vibrations alerted the five other brokers to her mood and they looked at each other in silence.

'Lazy bugger. Marcus won't be in this morning. He's ill.' She turned to Libby, who was just arriving. 'I think he does it on purpose. Drives me to the limit. Does he want me to fire him?'

Libby turned away without answering, rummaging for a file in her desk drawer. It took Alex a moment to pick up on her reticence and less than a second to form her suspicions.

'Libby?' She put her hand on her arm. 'Libby, look at me.'

At first she thought Libby's face was normal; the colour was even and her make-up was perfect. Alex stared at her, then pulled her gently round so that she was fully facing her. She had missed the lopsided cast of Libby's features, the expression almost quizzical, her mouth pulled slightly down at one side.

Libby turned back to her desk and began to sort through the papers in the file, straightening the edges, lining them up.

'I ... I feel so many things ...' Alex began

quietly. 'I'm angry, I'm sorry . . . How could he, Libby?'

'Well, he did. End of story. Doesn't really matter why.'

'Are you OK? I mean. Why are you here?' She regretted her earlier words about Marcus. 'You should take the day off.'

'I don't want the day off.'

'But you should—'

'Don't tell me what I *should* or should not do,' Libby answered, still arranging the papers into right-angled order. 'Not today.'

Alex nodded. 'I'm sorry. It's just so unbeliev-able. This kind of thing . . . Why did he do it, Libby?'

'For God's sake, Alex, don't keep asking me why. It doesn't matter why. I did something . . . and he didn't like it. I was late. I went out . . . If I had had any sense—'

'Oh, I see,' Alex interrupted. 'In a minute you'll be telling me you asked for it. You went out and this is the result. Cause and effect.'

Libby stood up. 'I might as well stay at home with Spike. Thanks for your help, Alex.'

'Wait.' Alex grabbed her arm and took her over to the window. There was no privacy in the vast dealing room. 'I'm not angry with *you*. I know I'm saying all the wrong things but there's no point in being sympathetic. I don't want to make you feel better. I want you to feel that you've had enough.'

'Alex, will you stop trying to manage this.' She looked up. 'Tell me you're sorry—'

'You *know* I'm sorry!' Alex almost shouted. 'I'm

299

beyond sorry. I want you to *do* something.'

Libby wrenched her arm free. 'I can't.'

Behind them the phones rang and the Reuters screen buzzed. Alex heard her name being called. She looked at Libby, desperately wanting to hear her say that she had had enough.

'We'd better answer these phones, Alex,' she said softly.

'Can we go for a drink at lunchtime?'

'Not today. Maybe tomorrow.'

Dissatisfied, Alex followed her back to the desk. The Metco line flashed and she felt a sudden urge to wrench the line out of its socket. No doubt he was working as usual, and congratulating himself that he had brought Libby to heel. The big man.

'I'll be in Compliance if you need me.'

Alex pulled out the files to check the accounts she held for The Kid and make sure he was margined to do the business she anticipated.

Then she arranged a conference call between herself, Maxim and Sol in London, and The Kid, who was back in Portugal.

It was time to decide.

It was five in the evening when they sat in Alex's flat, and she led off the discussions.

'OK. The Americans have agreed to the Russian deal. We have the credit facilities and the reserve funds in place to start buying—'

'Let's get to the core of the deal, then,' The Kid interrupted. 'How do we split up this profit?'

'Let me declare my hand here,' Alex began. 'This is a big deal, Wellington will make a lot of money from it. But I also have to do a lot of work. I'm going to charge you all a dollar and a half per tonne commission. It's high, I know,' she smiled, 'but still good value.'

'I have no problem with that, Alex. I feel you deserve a little more for having brought the deal to us, but I'm not going to force you to take my money,' he laughed. 'Now, the equation for the rest of us is somewhat complicated. Cash versus influence, I guess. How do we deal with that?'

They talked for half an hour, a civilized negotiation between three successful, determined men. Eventually, a split of the profits was agreed: The Kid was to receive 45 per cent, Sol 27.5 per cent and Maxim 27.5 per cent.

'Next.' Alex took control again. 'The most important issue. We need a timetable.'

Sol groaned. 'Timetable, schedules ... Jesus, you should be running a bus station.'

Alex ignored him. 'When will the announcement be made, Maxim?'

'Not fixed. Deal will be signed in two weeks maybe.'

'That gives us an idea, but I need to know exactly when the announcement will be made. Speak to Mintov and set the date. Call me tomorrow.'

Finally, they sat in silence.

No-one seemed willing to make the next move. Alex looked at Sol. He looked back, eyebrows raised.

For a second Alex felt reluctant to ask the question. What if The Kid said no? He was her only hope. He had massive credit lines, secured by his company, and was a unique combination of cash and nerve.

'Well . . . are we in business?' Alex asked.

'Are you still sitting there?' The Kid answered. 'Go to it, Alex. Let's buy some aluminium!'

Alex jumped up. 'Yes!'

All four laughed and Sol shook Maxim's and Alex's hand.

'Time to celebrate,' he suggested. 'The American Bar in honour of our bold financier. Let's go.'

Alex looked at her watch. 'Leave me to it. I want to speak to Libby and get a schedule in place.'

Sol groaned. 'Do your schedule tomorrow, Alex. This is a big night.'

'No, Sol, I'm going to do it now.' She shut off the line to The Kid and hustled Sol and Maxim out of the flat. 'I don't feel like celebrating yet.'

When she was on her own she poured a large Cognac and sat down, her feet on the table in front of her. A wave of triumph was quickly superseded by a sense of exhaustion. So much effort to put the deal together, now came the execution. Layer upon layer of intricate manoeuvrings, deceit, subtlety.

And with three strong personalities to keep in check. She drained her glass.

At least Neville would be happy. Tomorrow she'd prepare a report on the estimated commission earnings. She reckoned that she should earn Wellington three million dollars – easily enough to pay for a whole new computer.

But Neville did not like risk and this operation could go wrong. Disastrously wrong.

* * *

The next morning Alex and Libby sat with their attention focused on the familiar format of the Reuters screen, unable to move, watching every tick of every price. Eventually the prices began to slip. Aluminium fell back five, then ten dollars.

'What's happening?' Alex asked the dealer.

'Fund selling.'

That was good. There would be more to come. She let the price slip off another five dollars to $1190 before turning to the dealer again.

'Buy me a hundred lots at ninety,' she instructed him.

'Done!' he yelled back almost immediately and Alex looked over at Libby. The first trade.

'That was a bit quick,' Libby said. 'Maybe we should wait—'

'Buy me another two hundred,' Alex called out.

This time the dealer took a couple of seconds longer. 'You're done, Alex. Any more?'

Alex glanced at Libby's stricken face and grinned. 'That's it for now. Thanks.'

She wrote the tickets, allocated the trades to The Kid's account, then tidied her desk as if nothing had happened.

Libby looked at her. 'How can you be so cool?'

'I'm not cool. I'm numb. If it goes wrong I'll be to blame.'

'How can it go wrong?'

'Any number of ways. Let's say Amcola announces a move from aluminium cans to these new steel "supercans". What would that do to the consumption figures and to the price of aluminium?'

'But they wouldn't do that. It'd cost them a fortune to switch over. And the price difference doesn't justify such a massive expenditure.'

'OK. But that's just one example, Libby. You and I both know that there are any number of things that could affect the price. Let's just hope they don't happen for the next couple of weeks.'

'Are you having second thoughts?'

Alex stood up. 'No. I'm not. And anyway it's too late to back out now.' She snapped her diary shut. 'What about that drink?'

Libby's shoulders sagged. 'I have a lot to do, but I do need to talk to you. Let's go.'

Alex watched in surprise as Libby ordered a large gin and tonic. She rarely drank anything other than wine.

'Come on, then,' she urged. 'Tell me everything.'

'I . . . I had dinner with that Russian, the guy on your doorstep. Spike was furious when I got home. You know . . . well, you know how furious he was. And then I was supposed to take Roman to the Exchange. He just didn't turn up. Vichevsky hasn't seen him either. It's all very peculiar.'

'Do you think Spike . . . ?'

'No! How could he have found out who he was, or where he worked? No, something else has happened to him. We're always hearing about the Russian mafia—'

Impatiently, Alex interrupted her. 'Not you as

well, Libby? Everyone I meet is obsessed with the idea that Russians are all murdering each other. Just because you can't reach this guy you assume he's been bumped off.'

'It's not just that, Alex. Vichevsky was strange on the phone, cagey. I'm pretty sure *he* thinks something's happened to Roman.'

Alex drained her glass. 'He looked like the type who can take care of himself. I wouldn't worry about him. I'm sure he'll turn up sooner or later. You know, you and I are going to book ourselves a weekend on a health farm, get our sanity back.'

Libby managed a smile. 'It'll take a damn sight more than a weekend on a health farm.'

Kartchak showered and dressed. In twenty minutes he had to meet Vichevsky. He had told him to choose the restaurant but then had regretted it; the place would no doubt be pretentious and formal. Dealing with Vichevsky was like dealing with a fistful of putty. He would obligingly change his shape to fit whatever was required of him, and if this banker was a formal Englishman Vichevsky would be unbearable. Occasionally Kartchak felt a certain loyalty towards his old acquaintance, but more often he felt only irritation.

He stopped outside the doorway of what he hoped was the restaurant and compared the incomprehensible English lettering to the fax Vichevsky had sent him. This was the first time he had travelled without Roman and he had not realized how difficult it would be. And Vichevsky would be no match as a translator.

Inside the restaurant Vichevsky jumped up and ran to the door. He kissed Kartchak on both cheeks and welcomed him in Russian. 'I have him here. The man who will make our fortunes. Did you receive my fax? Have you read it?'

'Yes, Vichevsky, I've done my homework. Take me to meet your great man who is going to make me a fortune.'

Macneice stood up as the two Russians approached. He took in Kartchak's Western clothes, fine, well-made, the jacket obviously tailored to fit his muscly bulk. Macneice smoothed his own jacket under him as they sat down.

Vichevsky began with traditional platitudes, easing himself into the role as translator.

Kartchak turned to him immediately. 'OK. Tell him how glad I am to be here and how honoured to be in his company. All that crap. But don't take all night.'

Vichevsky obliged.

'Now tell him if he's done business in Russia before he knows that he needs first-class security above all else. That's what I can do. I make sure the business operates like clockwork on my side of the border. Nothing goes missing, nothing gets substituted, no-one gets kidnapped, no-one gets killed. Tell him what it was like in the Urals when I started there, now no problems.'

Vichevsky nodded. 'David. Mr Kartchak has asked me to pass on his deepest respects, he is aware of the authority of your organization and yours within it.' Macneice inclined his head in thanks towards Kartchak. Vichevsky hurried on.

'He wants me to describe to you his concept of partnership and mutual co-operation. He will take upon himself responsibility for all matters inside the border of Belorussia and is doing valuable work with the Russian government to assist in rebuilding the infrastructure and transport network, and has already done sterling work in the Urals.'

Kartchak carried on. 'Now tell him that I will acquire the land and I will recruit and manage the workforce. He puts the money in and markets the foil. OK?'

Vichevsky nodded. 'Mr Kartchak would like to present his management consultancy and offer their services in a number of roles where he feels his specialist knowledge will be vital, namely, land management and personnel issues.'

'Does he have any literature on his company? A brochure, perhaps?' Macneice asked.

'Yes, indeed. I will have them sent on to you and I may say that Mr Kartchak's company comes with the highest recommendation from many top-ranking figures both in the military and in the government—'

'What are you saying? What is he saying?' Kartchak asked impatiently. Vichevsky translated.

'All right. That's it. Yes or no.'

Vichevsky embroidered and prevaricated, giving Kartchak and Macneice a chance to eat. Then Macneice responded.

'I am very pleased to be here and very excited by this project. I have already spoken to the management of the EBRD and there is considerable interest. I believe we will have the go-ahead very shortly for this operation. We will offer substantial finance to assist in the construction of the foil plant in Minsk and the production of the foil.'

'He's got the money,' Vichevsky abbreviated, then turned back.

'Your offer of help is very welcome and I am particularly happy to have had such a natural partner presented to me. Broadly speaking, I agree to your delineation, which we will formalize when the funding has officially been made available. There are some peripheral issues we should discuss. Transport of the raw materials into Belorussia and transport of the foil out. Is it workable to have a handover at the border or should we arrange this otherwise?'

Vichevsky translated and Kartchak shrugged. 'Who gives a damn?'

Vichevsky held up his hands. 'Mr Kartchak defers to you and your internal controls.'

'Excellent. Now there are two more key issues. One is currency risk. Do I presume that Mr Kartchak can arrange to pay the smelter and the transport costs in roubles?'

Kartchak agreed.

'Next. Hedging.' He smiled at Vichevsky. 'We both know the policy of the EBRD towards price risk. I understand that the price of aluminium foil is related to the aluminium price on the London Metal Exchange. We will have to address the issue of price risk management.'

'He wants to address the issue of hedging,' Vichevsky translated.

'Whatever it is, we'll handle it.'

Vichevsky informed Macneice that Kartchak supported the need for hedging.

'Fine. We'll agree the price parameters at a later stage.'

Kartchak was buoyed by the meeting. Macneice was like so many Russians he had met, career bureaucrats who had no grasp of commerce. Given the floor, Macneice had honed in on three issues of such trivia that Kartchak had barely been able to respond. No discussion of the real substance of the deal.

He wondered whether he should bribe the banker. Had they been speaking Russian he would have known immediately. In fact the whole issue would have been dealt with already and the usual euphemisms for 'incentives' and 'enhancements' introduced in the early stages. He looked closely at Macneice, who was talking to Vichevsky. What kind of man would have lunch with Vichevsky, listen to his ideas and take him seriously? For a moment he wondered how Vichevsky had stumbled on this idea. Macneice and Vichevsky. Very similar in spite of the fact that they were physical opposites.

There seemed little point in offering them money – they seemed committed to the deal without any kind of sweetener from him – but perhaps he should anyway, to lock them in. They were quite capable of taking fright, or pulling out if they felt pressure from anyone else; not the best kind of partners to have in a Russian venture when their resolve was sure to be tested at some stage. While he was in Moscow and they were here he needed to be sure they didn't drift away. He thought of Roman. He needed to be able to keep control of these two.

He looked from one to the other. Vichevsky was wringing his hands gently as he spoke and Macneice was leaning towards him, frowning in concentration. What a pair! He'd have to be careful how he secured their loyalty; if he pitched it right they would flutter and giggle like a pair of old maids before accepting, but if he got it wrong they'd bolt.

'I'm buying a controlling interest in the aluminium plant. Once I've done that I'm going to give you each five per cent of the shares. I don't care how you translate this, Vichevsky, but I don't want any problems. No remonstrations, hands up in the air, no outrage, or he might just think about pulling out of the whole thing. Tell him that this is how business is done in Russia, full stop. Tell him I won't consider carrying on if my partners will not accept this gift from me. This is a recognition of our good teamwork . . . Bullshit like that – you're good at it.'

Vichevsky nodded as Kartchak spoke, then turned to Macneice, using some of Kartchak's expressions verbatim. 'David, I know what you must be thinking and, if I may, I'd like to dispel any worries you may have. This is normal practice, as you know, but more, Mr Kartchak will be offended if he is not allowed to show us this gesture of solidarity. Perhaps we should think about it, discuss it between ourselves, then call him later?'

'I'm stunned,' Macneice answered. 'If this is

truly a gift given with such a sentiment, it would be difficult to refuse without giving offence. But then again we must be careful not to compromise ourselves. What are we agreeing to in accepting this gift?'

'Absolutely nothing at all!' Vichevsky reassured him. They looked at each other. Both understood the dilemma. They wanted the shares but wanted their existence to remain a secret. And they did not want to get too close to the wrong side of Kartchak.

'Tell him we're flattered and appreciate his gesture but we're not sure that we've done enough to justify it. That should stall him.'

Flattered to be the exclusive confidant of both sides, Vichevsky translated Macneice's words. Kartchak stood up.

'Call me,' he ordered and Vichevsky nodded, looking down, submissive. In two seemingly innocuous words Kartchak had issued a threat, like a secret code, recognized only by the victim. Vichevsky was to call Kartchak and tell him that Macneice had agreed. Nothing else would be tolerated.

After Kartchak had left, Macneice ordered another Cognac. His hand trembled as he lifted the glass to his mouth. This could be it. The chance to be an entrepreneur, to capitalize on all the groundwork he'd done, all the research and all the listening. His mind flickered over the ethical issue. The shares were destined to be Kartchak's; any damage that might result from his purchase of the shares would already have been done. The transfer to *his* ownership would not in any way compound the problem. And while he knew very well the bank's policy on accepting inducements, this would hardly be classified as such, since the deal had already been provisionally approved. It was a thank you, just as Vichevsky had said. Just rewards. Finally.

Spike leaned over and turned off the bedside lamp. 'I bumped into that Russian of yours.'

'What? Which one?' Libby blushed, then recovered. 'Maxim?'

'Yeah. Nice bloke, might do a bit of business with him. He's going to transfer some money to Metco.'

'Oh, Spike, you can't.' Libby laid her hand on his arm. 'Please, Spike. Not him.'

It was a breach of market convention to approach another broker's customer. Cold-calling was acceptable, but as soon as a client had been identified in the presence of another broker they became exempt.

'What's so special about him, then?' He brushed her hand away. 'Maybe if Alex isn't sleeping with him you are.'

Libby bristled. 'It has to be one of us, does it? He couldn't possibly have a professional reason for dealing with us?'

'You're just a pair of tarts!' Spike spat at her. 'You tell me Alex knocks back whole bottles of vodka with that bloke, goes off round the world with him and it's all just business, is it? What do you take me for?'

'It *is*.' Libby heard the whine in her voice and

stopped. While Spike hated any show of aggression, he also hated it when she sounded pathetic.

Spike closed in, leaning into Libby, taunting her. 'He told me, Libby. Told me what they get up to. In the sauna, in the woods . . .'

'Oh, Spike, he was just making it up to impress you.'

'. . . Maybe when he's in London you all get together. The three of you.'

'No, Spike. Don't—'

'In that flat of hers, she's got a big bed, hasn't she?'

'No . . . I don't know—'

'Good, is he? Bit rough, this Russian? Better than me?'

Libby turned her head away. 'Please, Spike.'

'"Please, Spike,"' he repeated, running his finger slowly up and down her cheek. 'Is that *"Please, Spike, do it to me."*? Or *"Please, Spike, don't do it to me."*?'

Libby said nothing. Suddenly Spike grabbed a handful of hair, yanking her face up to his.

'Ask me again,' he demanded. 'Properly.'

Libby knew what was going to happen. There was no right answer, no wrong answer. Years ago she had tried so hard to find the right thing to say. Now it hardly seemed to matter if she said anything at all.

'Just do it, Spike. Whatever you want, just do it.'

It was the wrong thing to say.

ELEVEN

Vichevsky had been permitted to wait for Kartchak in his office. Afraid he was being observed, he had sat stock still for half an hour and when Kartchak finally arrived he was stiff and uncomfortable.

'I think we have this business wrapped up, Vichevsky. That was a very productive trip to London. The last piece of the puzzle is the Exchange. Hedging. Roman told me we need a broker for that. A specialist.'

'What happened to Roman?' Vichevsky asked. 'He just didn't come back from the bank one day. Where is he?'

Kartchak smiled. 'I sent someone to kill him. Cut him into pieces. Dropped him in the Thames.'

Vichevsky felt his head buzz then a wave of sickness. God, he was going to throw up in Kartchak's office. Fear immobilized his nausea and he grasped the arms of his chair with frozen fingers to steady himself.

'What did he do?'

314

'He did not do what I asked, Vichevsky, so be warned. Just because London is three hours from Moscow does not mean I do not know what is happening. That's why I called you here. To remind you.'

'*I* know that,' Vichevsky began. 'I hope you feel that *I've* always done what you asked. After all, I brought you Macneice . . .'

'And that's coming along very nicely. Well done. One more thing. I want that woman, Brookes.'

Vichevsky's heart sank. Seventeen messages he'd left. Seventeen refusals. 'I believe Roman had a meeting with her assistant. Brookes is never there. She's always travelling.'

'How fortunate. We could meet in Moscow, then.'

Vichevsky inclined his head. 'I'll see to it.'

Alone in his office, Kartchak smiled. What a deal! Neither of them had any idea of the potential. The foil plant was nothing; did they believe he would content himself with a fee? It was the aluminium plant he wanted, that was where the real money was.

The first thing he had to do was buy all the shares. Then he wanted to buy all the aluminium from the plant. At any price. If the world price of aluminium rose, he'd sell what he'd bought at a profit. Stuff the foil plant. If the price went down he'd feed the expensive aluminium into the plant.

Either way, he'd win.

* * *

The head of the Belorussian plant, Belkov, had not wanted to see Kartchak and had refused to go to his office, finally agreeing to meet in the Slavyanski Bazaar, a traditional Russian restaurant in a narrow street running off Red Square.

In the space of a few weeks his plant had attracted interest from two sources. Volkov, who had brought along the Brookes woman, and now Kartchak, who also wanted a majority shareholding. It would not be possible to accommodate both. Belkov had taken a liking to the Brookes woman; she had wanted to put together a reasonable deal, but her choice of Russian partner was unfortunate. As soon as there seemed a likelihood that Western finance would be forthcoming, Volkov had flown to the plant, refusing to broker the deal unless he had a major shareholding.

And now Kartchak with the same story. Claiming that unless he was given a majority shareholding he would force the EBRD to pull out of the deal.

He peered around him in the gloomy restaurant. He remembered how impressed he had been with this place when he had first come to Moscow seven years earlier. The choice on the menu was unbelievable and he could not comprehend the logistics of having such a large number of dishes constantly available. He made out Kartchak sitting at a corner table and went to join him. They shook hands briefly and Belkov sat down.

'Well,' Kartchak began immediately. 'Have you thought about my offer?'

'I have, but let me tell you, I'm not empowered to trade the plant's future like a loaf of bread. I don't see why we have to give you the shares in order to do the deal with the EBRD.'

'Belkov. You're making a very simple issue very difficult.' He ordered lamb stew and beer. Belkov said he'd have the same. 'What we have here is a joint venture proposal. I have given you the conditions of my participation. I must have a shareholding in order to ensure the commitment of the plant to the operation. I will not commit my money to a venture without this gesture. If you want the deal, give me the shares.' He smiled and offered Belkov some bread. 'Very simple.'

'This is all pretence! It is simply your desire to have a share in a plant that will be exceptionally profitable. This is not a business plan, Kartchak, it is a dream.'

'You know I need your aluminium in order to operate the foil plant. It would not be feasible to have to buy the aluminium from somewhere else and transport it to the foil plant.'

'There's no question of that!' Belkov answered angrily. 'We have given you and the EBRD our agreement that fifty per cent of our production will be reserved for the foil plant. That's more than you will need. In any case, you don't seem to realize that there is not an inexhaustible supply of shares. Everybody who does a tonne of business wants a majority. It's a ludicrous situation.'

Kartchak sat back in his chair, his surprise evident. 'There are others who want the shares? Who?'

Belkov shrugged. 'A Western company has suggested we give them a contract. They, like you, insist that they must have shares.'

Kartchak was silent for a moment and Belkov hoped he would leave the issue alone.

'Belkov, I said you were making this more difficult than it is. There are advantages to dealing with me. On an exclusive basis.'

Belkov looked at him sceptically.

'Power, for example,' said Kartchak. 'Like most plants, I imagine you have not paid the power station for some time. And are not likely to in the foreseeable future.'

'We have an arrangement,' Belkov countered confidently. 'We have no problems with electricity supply.'

'At the moment, no. But electricity is essential. A *constant, uninterrupted* supply. The workers in the power station can be excitable. They themselves have not been paid. There were rumours that the last time the government baled the power station out the money was not evenly distributed. They could strike. Not for long, I concede. But if power to your plant were switched off for even a moment I understand the result would be catastrophic. And your precious tolling deal with this Western company would not save you.'

Belkov looked at him. He had underestimated both Kartchak's intelligence and his knowledge of the business. Kartchak had found the plant's weak spot. A power cut would close operations down – possibly for ever. And he, Belkov, had no way of protecting the power source.

'You have my terms. Yes or no.'

Belkov drew breath, afraid of the consequences of the ultimatum. The man sitting opposite him wanted the shares in his plant. Was there any point in arguing the case against him, or refusing point blank?

Kartchak stared back at him. Every bone seemed to be visible, every muscle clearly defined. The man resembled a living anatomical diagram, like the ones used by medical students. Even the fingers lying loosely on the table seemed unnecessarily sculptured.

Belkov felt his strength drain away. It was all so futile.

'I don't seem to have a choice. Give me the papers.'

Quickly Belkov signed over the shares in the plant. He tossed the contracts back and stood up. But before he could leave, Kartchak motioned for him to sit down again. One small flick of his index finger. Weakly, Belkov complied.

'One more thing. Who else wants ... wanted these shares?'

Belkov shrugged. 'Volkov. He brought an English woman, Brookes, to see the plant. She wants to put a deal together with Western finance.'

Kartchak inclined his head. 'Thank you.'

When Belkov had left Kartchak finished his beer then wiped his hand across his mouth. Alexandra Brookes again.

He minded less about Volkov; a Russian businessman was expected to do this kind of thing. And Arkady had already told him about

Vichevsky's early attempts to form some kind of joint venture with Volkov.

He made his way along the dingy passageway and out into the bright sunlight. What was it about this metals business? He never felt he had complete control. Even now, with the shares in his pocket, he felt it did not entirely belong to him.

Alexandra Brookes. He spat on the pavement then turned on his heel and walked towards his car.

On the other side of town Vichevsky walked along the pretty, tree-lined street towards Maxim's office. It made a change to be meeting as equals.

Vichevsky smiled. After so many years' hard work, he was finally in the game. He looked forward with particular relish to turning the tables on Volkov, who had not returned his calls, responded to his faxes, or in any way acknowledged his assistance in finding the Brookes girl.

The usual phalanx of guards stood outside Maxim's office, but unlike the brutish, petty criminals referred to broadly as guards in Moscow, Maxim's guards were alert and aggressive. Vichevsky felt an instinctive urge to hold out his hand in appeasement as he would to a pack of dogs. He was prepared to identify himself and ask admittance but they ignored him, obliging him to weave awkwardly between them to get to the door.

Inside, he noticed the close-circuit cameras at several locations in the massive, marble-floored hall. The area was newly renovated and completely unadorned, except for a cheap wood-veneer desk, but the lofty, sepulchral stillness of the area was more impressive than most of the recent extravagant attempts Vichevsky had seen to brighten up gloomy Soviet buildings. He walked up to the desk and stood dutifully in front of the guard.

'Professor Vichevsky to see Mr Volkov.'

The guard gestured towards the stairs.

Vichevsky climbed slowly, preparing his opening speech. At the top of the stairs Maxim's secretary met him and ushered him into the inner sanctum. She wore a tight red mohair sweater and a short skirt. As she withdrew Vichevsky's eyes followed her and he realized that he had lost the chance to dominate the moment.

He knew how he must look to Maxim as he swivelled round to face him, an awkward little man trying to regain the composure he had so easily lost.

'Maxim! Good to see you.' He strode across the room and stretched out his hand, which Maxim took without rising.

Vichevsky sat down carefully, dragging every inch from his spine.

'Maxim, we've known each other a long time and I felt I had to come to you with what I know to be a great opportunity. I've been approached by a French company who's looking to place five million dollars in Russia.' He paused, smiling. Ivan Belayev had tossed this lead at him and while it was an overstatement to claim that the French were ready to invest they clearly had both the money and the interest.

'I should say at this juncture that they know very little about Russia and will take my advice on the selection of investments. I would very much like to introduce you to them, knowing that we can develop this resource to its fullest potential.'

'Not interested.'

Vichevsky's head pulled back in a convulsive gesture of disbelief. 'What do you mean?'

'Not interested,' Maxim repeated.

'But, Maxim, this is five million dollars from investors who simply want Russian risk in their portfolio,' he explained. 'You know the kind of thing, ten per cent in Indonesia, fifteen per cent in Mexico. Perhaps you would like to see the company's brochure.' He began to unbuckle his briefcase.

'Listen to me, Vichevsky. I'm not interested.'

Vichevsky looked at him for a long moment. He wondered if he had not made himself clear.

'Perhaps I'll leave the brochure with you, then, and you can look through it when you have a moment.'

Maxim picked up a slim Tiffany pen Alex had left behind and rolled it between finger and thumb. 'Take the brochure with you when you go, Vichevsky.'

Vichevsky stiffened. He had been dismissed by this common upstart yet again. He squared his shoulders and smiled. 'Of course. It makes no difference to me. I have several other projects at the moment.'

Maxim's face remained impassive. Vichevsky's anger and humiliation grew.

'I would say I am almost *too* busy. The aluminium industry is developing very quickly, old alliances fading, new forces emerging. It's a very exciting time to be in business in Russia.'

'You find the aluminium business exciting? I suppose it is in a way.' Maxim rolled the fine silver pen between the palms of his hands. 'It depends on how you measure excitement. Or as Alex would say, it depends on your appetite.'

Vichevsky laughed. 'Alex! She speaks a different language entirely!' He stopped, trying to gauge Maxim's mood. If he made fun of Alex, would Maxim join in and let a common ground be established or be angered on her behalf? He decided to test the water. 'She can be very perceptive and sometimes very ... Western?' His voice rose at the end of the sentence, giving Maxim a chance to answer. When he did not, Vichevsky withdrew. 'Very nice girl.'

Maxim's expression did not change. 'In a way, of course, I understand how exciting this business can be.'

Vichevsky sat back down, momentarily confused by the return to the previous topic. Still, a dialogue with Maxim on any subject could be of use.

'Quickly changing ... exciting,' Maxim continued. '*I* have always found it so. But I'm surprised you do, Vichevsky.'

'Why? Why on earth should I find it otherwise?'

'Because I take risks with my money and my life for fun. Always have. I like risk. I have an *appetite* for it. I was not aware that you did too.'

Vichevsky hesitated. 'I would not say ... I would not say that I am the same, but I am not sure the aluminium business is in quite the same category as the games you play. These shooting trips in Siberia, for example, or the speed with which you drive.'

Maxim smiled. 'You are right, Vichevsky. It is not in the same category because in these games there is a chance. You can escape from your competitors by using skill and having courage. But the aluminium business is different. Those who stray into this game have no chance at all.'

But people don't get *killed* in the aluminium business, Vichevsky was about to answer, when he suddenly understood Maxim's analogy. His mind raced around like a frenzied dog looking for the prey he could sense but not see. He had to find an escape from the hole he himself had dug. He had one hope – that he had been enigmatic enough to allow a withdrawal and that he could erase the challenge to Maxim's authority.

'But surely, from your perspective there is no risk? Who would take you on? You are surely inviolate?' Vichevsky smiled shakily. A nerve in his lower eyelid suddenly twitched and he half turned away from Maxim, afraid he would think he was winking.

'Perhaps I am. But in any case, if I am not inviolate today,' he smiled slightly, 'I will be tomorrow.'

Vichevsky felt his chances of survival draining away. Maxim looked at him, the silver pen now balancing across the backs of his long fingers, which, to Vichevsky's eye, were conspicuously steady.

'I had heard that there were some new people in my business,' Maxim continued. 'Moving into Belorussia. Who are they, Vichevsky?' Suddenly, he flipped the pen above the back of his hand, let it fall, then snapped his curled fingers around it a split second later. An elegant, complete gesture, as spare and efficient as a crocodile's jaws.

Vichevsky wondered if it was too late. Did Maxim know already? Had this visit been the most monumental mistake? He was quite prepared to throw Kartchak to the wolves and give Maxim his name, but he was not convinced that he would save himself in doing so.

'Who? I have no idea! I have had some contact with them, of course, but not about aluminium. Shoes. They wanted shoes in the plant, that's all.'

'Perhaps I misunderstood you earlier. I thought you were involved in projects in the aluminium business, *exciting projects*. Is this not the case?'

Vichevsky managed a laugh. 'I did not mean to imply that *I* personally was involved in these projects.' He racked his brains for his exact words. 'And when I said the aluminium business, I did not mean aluminium. Just . . . in that field. That's all.'

'I see.' The pen now rolled, apparently of its own volition, to the end of Maxim's fingers. Vichevsky stared at it.

'Give me his name, Vichevsky,' Maxim said slowly. 'And then you can go.'

'Oh, Maxim . . . This man called Kartchak, he

threatened me and my family. I'm sure you can understand my dilemma. It's been such a strain—'

'Where can I find him?'

'Tsverskaya. Next to the Palace.'

Maxim picked up the pen with his long fingers and dropped it into his drawer. 'Get out.'

Vichevsky rose immediately and backed away from the desk. 'Thank you, Maxim. Thank you.'

He ran down the stairs, catching his foot on the third last step, falling awkwardly on one knee to the floor. He picked up his briefcase and limped across to the front door. God, how stupid he had been. How could he, of all people, have forgotten the tribal nature of business in Russia? He should have known that if he did even one deal with Kartchak he could expect no further contact with Maxim.

Kartchak and Volkov. He had once thought of putting them together, with himself as the linch-pin between them. What a ludicrous idea. They were like two predatory animals, heading towards each other, their eyes on the same prey. Of all the plants in the former Soviet Union, they had both fastened their attention on the Belorussian.

Suddenly Vichevsky recalled Alex's suggestion at the Embassy reception that he consider the Belorussian plant and realized that it had not been just a random thought. She and Volkov had some interest there. He should have known. And he had unwittingly put Kartchak in there, in parallel, in competition.

Vichevsky closed his eyes. The thought of

being caught in the middle when Kartchak and Volkov collided was terrifying.

He decided to leave Moscow as soon as possible. He had been lucky, stepping into the lion's den, teasing the lion and emerging unscathed. He had got away with a challenge to Maxim which would probably have resulted in death for anyone else.

But what if Kartchak found out that he had betrayed him to Volkov? And what of Alexandra Brookes? She was completely unaware of Kartchak's obsession. Vichevsky began to run. He could perhaps just make the evening plane to London.

'Put the phone down.'

Obediently Libby cut short her conversation and looked up at Alex expectantly.

'We've got ten days,' Alex said quietly. 'Maxim called this morning. May tenth is the date of the announcement.'

'Will ten days be enough? I'll run through the positions again. Check the margins. Can we do it, Alex?'

'We'll have to.'

She read the day's papers and reports, then sat with Larry and looked at technical indicators, poring over the charts in the way Egyptologists tried to decipher hieroglyphics.

She had ten days and as she examined Libby's figures she felt a new surge of confidence. They were on schedule.

She had booked a table for eight o'clock at the Italian restaurant in the mews behind the flat. It was cheap and unpretentious and, above all, handy.

She was ready early and sat by the open window in her bedroom, thinking about Sol. They had had it all, the friendship, the business, the fun. And now there seemed to be only the business left; it had elbowed out all the rest. Even as they had walked along Piccadilly together, their arms round each other, Sol had talked ceaselessly about aluminium. And when they had got back to her flat he had prowled around, still talking, his tie and shoes thrown negligently to the floor, oblivious to Alex's feeling of exclusion.

Alex had no idea how Sol lived in New York, what his new apartment was like, how he spent his weekends. She tried to remember conversations from the past. What had they talked about? She couldn't remember. Somehow the years of being Sol's lover had faded and when she thought back to the past her memory focused on the early years, when he had been the customer and she the junior broker.

She jumped when the doorbell rang.

'I'm early,' Rory said into the intercom. 'Shall I wait outside?'

Alex laughed. 'You can come up, but you can't have a drink for ten minutes. No conversation either.'

The early spring sunshine flooded in through the windows and sharpened the points of colour in the flat – the daffodils in the hallway, the blood-red cut-glass mirror in the living room, the gleaming mahogany of the curved banister leading to the upper floor.

'What a wonderful flat,' Rory murmured.

For a second even Alex stopped to admire the effect. A bright rectangle of sunlight lay carved on the living room floor, the distorted reflection of the shape of the window. It seemed to reach towards them with the theatricality of a stage set, which Alex had never noticed before. She suddenly had a sensation that something was going to happen, that this moment was somehow contrived and that she was at the point in a bad film when the viewer knows that the suspense is about to be shattered.

Briskly, she turned away, looking at her watch. 'You can have a drink now. What would you like?'

'Scotch, please. No ice, with a little flat water.'

Alex poured the drinks with a smile. 'Here you are. Have a seat. The table's booked for eight.'

'Half an hour, fifteen minutes per drink, then. Or seven and a half minutes per drink if we have four.'

'I have some pistachios. Deduct three minutes from the overall total.'

They smiled at each other. Alex recognized that there was a danger to the ease with which she related to Rory; there were no problems to snag and restrain the pace of their relationship, they seemed to be caught up in an extraordinarily harmonious momentum. It was both seductive and alarming.

She turned away from him. 'Tell me, how does it work being a freelancer?'

'What you mean is how do I pay my bills without a guaranteed salary? My mother asked me the same thing last week.'

'Well, how do you do it? You seem to live quite well considering you don't have a proper job.'

He laughed. 'How do you know I live well?'

Alex blushed. 'That's a Liberty jacket you're wearing. Even in the sales they cost a fortune. And your shoes. Nice.'

'I got them in Argentina. They look better than they are. But you're right about the jacket, it's my Sunday best.' He stroked the smooth fabric. 'I do quite a few routine stories, without my name on them. I get paid a lump sum and a retainer if I get sent off somewhere for a specific story, and I have my column.'

'What column?' Alex asked.

'Hunter.'

'You're Hunter? My God. I read it every Sunday. It's . . . you're very entertaining, very original. Even though I work in the City I concede that it's not the most interesting subject matter, yet your column is always imaginative. Here, let me top you up.' She refilled his drink and settled down with her own. 'I associated you just with commodities, but your column is very broad. Did you study economics?'

'God, no. I've had to learn it as I go. Come to a conclusion then find a theory to support it. Retroactive research, my assistant calls it.'

'I do the same sometimes. I can see the market looks weak, I can sense that there are sellers lurking in the wings, so I go and ask Larry why the fundamentals are so poor. He gives me the information I need.' As she finished her sentence, she hesitated. 'That's off the record, of course.'

Rory laughed. 'Can you imagine the headline?

Alexandra Brookes admits she sometimes looks for research to support her views? We'd sell quite a few newspapers with that one.'

Alex blushed. 'I just meant that the whole evening is . . . I never know when you're working or not.'

'This evening I'm not working. You can say what you like, tell me all your secrets from work, what all your customers are doing and I won't publish a word.'

Alex's mind suddenly snapped back to the deal. What a story. He'd love it. 'Come on, let's go.'

Alex knew the restaurant had a limited future. Rarely were there more than three of the twenty tables occupied. But the low vaulted ceilings and the alcoves concealed this fact from most of the diners and the head waiter managed to give the impression of bustling amiability even if he was underworked and facing redundancy.

Alex passed the wine list to Rory. 'You choose. I don't mind what. I'm going to have a huge plate of pasta with their home-made pesto, so I'll drink anything.'

'I'll join you. Shall we ask them if they have Chianti in the old-fashioned bottles? It seems that kind of place.'

'You want to take it home and make a lamp, don't you?'

'Off the record?'

They laughed and ordered.

'So tell me, Alex, any more reactions to my story on you?'

'Two headhunters and a lot of ridicule.'

'That's all?'

Alex smiled. She couldn't tell him about the chain of events that had been set in motion by his article, starting with the unknown Russian in Moscow International Bank who had shown the article to Vichevsky.

'Couple of others . . . nothing major.'

'And are you busy just now? Things were rather slow the last time I saw you.'

'Slow?' She laughed out loud. 'Everything seems to have taken off all of a sudden. My poor assistant is close to a nervous breakdown.'

'An occupational hazard, I should think.'

'I suppose it is, although I've always felt that it was a ludicrous waste for people to have health problems because of working in a stressful environment. High blood pressure trading commodities. It's ridiculous somehow. Not like sustaining an injury in wartime, or being wounded doing something meaningful. I can't understand ruining your health in the good cause of metal trading.' She picked up her fork and began to eat.

'So your job is meaningless? Is that what you're saying?'

Alarm bells began to ring but Alex carried on, keeping the conversation general. 'It's not *meaningless*, but neither is it worth human sacrifice.'

'You must have colleagues with high blood pressure, stress, all those things. What should they do? Resign?'

'If I were married to one of them I'd make them resign. If they work for me I can't sack them, that would compound the problem, but the day I begin to measure *my* self-esteem on the basis of tonnes of copper traded is the day I ask to be carted away to a luxury health farm and incarcerated for a long, long time.'

'And does all this make you a better or worse commodity broker?'

'I don't care. I have to fit my job into my blood pressure, not the other way round.' She put down her fork. 'It's tough enough in the City, you know, with deadlines, targets, backstabbing, politics. Add to that the fact that one little error can cost a couple of million quid and you realize that it's not for the faint-hearted. I take my job seriously, but it is just that – a job.'

Rory nodded and pushed his plate away. 'That was excellent. Good choice.' He poured out the remainder of the wine. 'Your life is beginning to sound flat. Very measured and controlled. Is it?'

Alex hesitated. It had been. Risk versus reward, equations, measurements. In an inherently risky business she tried to control that risk, imposing order on chaos. Discipline in an undisciplined milieu. But now?

She picked up her wine glass. 'I don't know.'

'And you seem to almost despise what you do. You compare commodity broking to good causes – it'll always come off worse. But what about commodity broking compared to banking or stockbroking. Isn't that a more meaningful comparison?'

'I don't despise it. I couldn't do it every day if I despised it. But I think people do take what we do too seriously, be it banking or stockbroking. Of course it's vital, moving money, financing industry, but I wouldn't die for it. That's the point I was making. '

'You know, when I listen to you talking I can't help thinking you should be in politics. You're so . . . realistic.'

'Not much point in going into politics, then, is there?' Alex burst out laughing.

Rory looked at his watch. 'I'm afraid I have to go. I have to be at Heathrow at five tomorrow morning. An unscheduled trip.'

Alex breathed a sigh of relief. No awkward parting, no uncomfortable double meanings tonight. 'Where are you going?'

'Moscow.'

Stupidly, Alex repeated the word. 'Moscow? What for?'

'A party at the Moscow Stock Exchange. Why are you surprised?'

'I don't know. I didn't realize . . . nothing.'

'I'm starting to have some good contacts in Russia. It's fascinating.'

'So you've overcome your fear of assassination, then?' she mocked.

'Who'd want to assassinate me?'

She asked for the bill and paid quickly.

'I'll be back on Sunday,' Rory said. 'Shall we do something next week?'

'*Something?*' she laughed. 'You'll have to be more precise.' Alex realized she was flirting. With her head cocked, her whole manner was a challenge, almost an invitation.

Rory leant closer. 'I had been thinking about dinner, but I'll have to come up with something better. Let me inject a little insecurity into this orderly life of yours.'

Alex shrugged on her jacket, standing close to him in the narrow entrance. As he passed her to open the door she smelled him. The brown skin, the hard muscle, the leather jacket. Heat. Cut grass and cinnamon. Again she wanted to run her hands over the leather, round his shoulders and over his broad back.

When he turned back to her, she knew he would be able to read the signals of her excitement. She smiled. To hell with it.

With no hesitation and no warning he moved forward and kissed her hard on the mouth. The force tipped her head backwards; one of his hands moved to the back of her head, holding her firm, allowing his mouth to completely cover hers.

Then her mouth began to move on its own, furiously; she sucked his lower lip into her mouth and, shocked by the satisfaction of the sensation, moaned and released him, then in the next instant seized him back, biting his tongue. He tensed as she bit him then thrust his tongue back into her mouth. She gasped. He was inviting her to do it again, to do anything she wanted.

After a moment she drew her head back. In the distorted intimacy of the embrace she could only see his eyes, gazing directly back into hers. When his expression softened and he rubbed his cheek lightly against hers she relaxed. It was going to be all right.

He lifted her hand to his mouth and kissed it.

'Perhaps I should cancel my flight—'

'No!' Alex answered quickly, then could think of no reason to justify her outburst. The ceaseless, impatient demands of those involved in the project would be an unbearable distraction; no-one would tolerate less than 100 per cent of her attention.

'You're right.' He turned her hand over and kissed the palm. 'It's only a couple of days. Let's do this properly.'

Relieved, Alex put her arms back around him and leant her head against his chest. It was an affectionate gesture, one usually shared by old friends who had got to know each other well. She smiled to herself, pleased that she felt she could do it and that he answered by wrapping his arms tightly around her.

'I'm tired . . . I'd like to—'

'I know. Come on, I'll walk you home.'

At the door he fastened the buttons on her jacket, a protective gesture, as if he wanted to make sure she stayed safely wrapped up until his return. Alex stood like an obedient child, smiling at him.

'Next week, then?'

'Next week,' he confirmed. 'I'll call you when I get back.'

She got into the flat and saw the message light winking on the machine. She smiled, knowing that it was likely to be Libby.

It was. 'Just to let you know I've rearranged your meetings for the morning. You don't have to come in till eleven. Bye.'

Her first meeting was with Neville.

'I'm glad to see you have some business here, Alex. The Kid is buying a lot of aluminium . . .' He flipped through the computer printout. 'This is a huge deal, Alex. You realize I have regulatory responsibilities here. I'm obliged to report it . . .'

Alex tried to control her anger. She had been worried that Neville would be scared by the volume of trading and run to the Exchange. The recent rogue trader scandals had made everyone nervous and the last thing she wanted was an official enquiry into The Kid's positions.

Strictly speaking, he was supposed to accumulate a position of this size only if he was a legitimate consumer – if he was intending to use the aluminium for a real industrial project. Since he was not, the operation came under the heading 'market manipulation' designed to drive the price up and nothing else. Pure speculation. And since the Exchange had the responsibility of protecting the interests of legitimate consumers, the canners, for example, who really did need the metal, they were obliged to step in and make sure the price represented real supply and demand.

'Yes, it's a big position and, yes, I do realize you have to report to the Exchange. But it's not the biggest he's had, is it?' It was a low blow; Alex knew that Neville would have no idea if it was or wasn't The Kid's biggest ever position. And that he wouldn't admit it.

'You know The Kid,' she continued. Another low blow. 'He firmly believes that aluminium is undervalued. And our research supports that view.'

Neville studied the papers on his desk uncertainly. 'Well . . . even so. Right or wrong. There is the question of market manipulation. Is he maintaining the price at an artificially high level for no fundamental reason?'

Alex recognized the terminology of the market regulations.

'Will he ever use this metal he's bought?' Neville continued, looking at Alex over his glasses.

'Of course not!' Alex snapped. 'He'll sell it. You know that.'

'Oh, but I know nothing of the sort. And the law states that the onus is on me to know. I may have to talk to The Kid myself. Then speak to the authorities.'

'That's fine,' Alex concluded and drew out the top sheet of figures from her file. 'Now then, Neville. You'll be pleased to know that our commission figures are forty per cent over target.' She looked up. '*Your* target.'

She handed Neville a copy. 'Not only has The Kid paid us a million and a half, our other customers are calling for comment and end up dealing with us since we are now perceived to be a big player in the market. Monty and I have extrapolated. We think we should be up three million dollars by the end of next month.'

She put the folder down and folded her hands on her lap. 'I'm pretty sure The Kid has more to do . . . I *do* hope the Exchange doesn't try to limit his activities. We'd lose a substantial amount of revenue.'

Neville took his time reading the figures. Alex

knew exactly what was going through his mind. He wanted the commission without falling foul of the authorities. It was a perennial dilemma – and it was the same for the Exchange authorities; they wanted the turnover but they also wanted an 'orderly' market. Legitimate business, buyers and sellers evenly matched, no rogue traders with unauthorized positions, no megalomaniac traders trying to control the price.

'I'm not sure about this,' Neville said, putting down the papers.

'I can understand your reservations, Neville,' Alex said sweetly. 'But I'm sure you'll be able to make it clear to the authorities that this is a legitimate investment position and that The Kid has no intention of manipulating the market.

'As our own figures show,' she produced another sheet of figures, 'he has not been the only buyer. Some of the US Funds have covered their shorts and gone long. I would suggest that the Exchange look into *their* activities rather than those of a long-standing, faithful, solvent customer.'

'Point taken, Alex. Leave it with me. I'll speak to The Kid then to Ron at the Exchange. I expect it'll be all right.'

'You'll let me know?'

'Of course.'

As she arrived back at her desk the phone was ringing.

'Maxim!' Alex was still buoyant from her conversation with Neville. 'How are things in Moscow?'

'Come to Siberia.'

Alex flinched. 'I can't possibly come now, Maxim! You know how busy I am.'

'You *must* come. Manager of Chaika plant wants to talk about LME. Very important.'

'What's wrong?' Alex's heart stood still. 'We need all these guys on our side. Has Chernikov changed his mind? Does he not want to be part of this?'

'No, no,' he answered impatiently. 'Is new manager. Chernikov dead.'

'Dead? What happened?'

'Killed by thief in Moscow. The usual. Come and speak to new manager.'

Alex felt a quick tremor of unease. She had only met the man once but she remembered his diplomacy when Maxim had tried to belittle her in front of him. And now he was dead. The scene on the staircase in Maxim's office came back to her in startling detail. Maxim had hugged Chernikov warmly as he left; they were old friends, yet his voice was cold as he casually told her of Chernikov's death. It seemed to be nothing more than a minor annoyance to him.

She had no choice but to agree to go; the Chaika plant was the second largest in Russia and was an essential piece in the jigsaw.

Alex arranged to fly to Moscow the following day, leaving messages for her mother, Rory and Sol. She was deeply disturbed. Some of her customers claimed to trade on instinct and while she would admit to having felt that disquieting suspicion, sometimes, that a trade may not be *right*, she would never act on it. But as she sat in the empty Business section of the BA

340

flight the insistent feeling gnawed at her.

Somehow death and business were incongruous. She remembered her shock when a colleague had suffered a heart attack in the dealing room. It was bizarre, the sudden frenetic activity, the doctor, the ambulancemen, the stretcher. It was not *appropriate*. This kind of thing happened in the part of one's life that took place after hours. The phones had continued to ring as the ambulancemen crouched on the floor, trying to save a life. No-one knew what to do – whether to answer the phones and silence the incessant ringing or ignore them as a mark of respect. Alex had stood with the others in awkward anxiety and when Ken had been taken away they had not been able – or willing – to settle back down to their work, although Ken had been revived and the prognosis was good. Work had seemed trivial after what they had witnessed.

And now she was travelling to Moscow to pull together the loose ends caused by the inconvenient death of Chernikov.

She went back over Maxim's words. Something *was* wrong.

TWELVE

Alex was met by Maxim at Moscow airport. He was clearly in a good mood and carried her bag to the car, talking as he went. Alex wondered what had happened to lift him out of his usual taciturn depression.

Boris drove them to the domestic airport and they boarded a flight to Irkutsk. There they spent the night before setting off the following morning for Usolye, the nearest town to the Chaika plant. As their small plane began its descent into the airport Alex looked out of the window and saw an identical plane to the one she was on, nose embedded in the ground, still smouldering. There were two cars near by but no sense of urgency among those at the scene. She looked away quickly.

At the airport the driver of a red Landcruiser introduced himself then drove them to the small hotel, where they checked in and left their bags before being driven straight on to the plant. Maxim throughout had a sense of purpose Alex had not seen before. There had been no anger at late departures, no protestations of disbelief at inefficiency and no irritation with Alex. He was lighthearted, in complete contrast to Alex's own mood.

The plant was more modern and cleaner than Alex had expected, and certainly more orderly than the others she had seen. The building was on the outskirts of the town and the urban bustle took away some of the sense of bleak decay that hung over the more remote Belorussian plant. But still Alex looked around in despair. The yellow pollutant dust lay in drifts and the vast concourse outside the plant showed the footprints of the passers-by like a cheap travesty of a snow scene. And the smell. Alex remembered the first gust of sulphuric gas she had encountered in Minsk, a smell so unhealthy and tangible she had almost been sick. She had felt the fumes assault the back of her throat and lodge there, thick and clinging.

She and Maxim were shown to the boardroom, where they were introduced to the new head of the plant, Yuri Maslenkov. Maslenkov was smaller than Alex, with a stunted, unhealthy appearance. His grin revealed five gold teeth and he fidgeted constantly, rubbing his hands together, scratching his head, at the same time extending his neck forwards and outwards like a tortoise looking out from its shell. While Alex realized that he was, perhaps, hard of hearing, she still found it annoying. He greeted Alex in halting English and she shook his hand, repulsed by the dampness of his palm.

To her surprise, he and Maxim hugged like old friends.

'He worked for me before,' Maxim explained. 'Now very important man.'

They laughed and clapped each other on the back.

Alex wondered why he had not previously mentioned this connection. It was good to have an ally in charge of the Chaika plant. Surely Maxim would have mentioned this? But she was accustomed by now to the fact that old Soviet habits died hard and that few of the Russians she had met were comfortable giving more information than was strictly necessary. The only exception to this had been Fedorov.

'Now we go on Yuri's boat,' Maxim announced. 'Very beautiful river.'

'On a boat?' Alex echoed. 'Maxim, we have things to discuss. I don't think a boat is a suitable place. Can we discuss the plan here? Now?'

'No. A boat is a good place to discuss.'

Alex recognized the tone of his voice. There would be various stages from then until he finally passed out or disappeared, the next being friendly acquiescence, but for the time being he was not to be crossed.

'OK,' Alex conceded. 'Let's go.'

They were driven to the river in a brand-new Series 8 BMW, Maslenkov sitting in the front with the driver while Maxim and Alex sat in the back. The conversation was loud and good-natured and after ten minutes Maslenkov opened the glove compartment and pulled out a pistol.

To his – and Maxim's – amusement, he held it to the driver's head and flicked off the safety catch. Alex felt from the joking tone of the conversation that he did not intend to do anything but she was nervous nonetheless, an anxiety exacerbated by the fear that Maslenkov's nervous tick would travel from his neck to his trigger finger. The back of the driver's head remained immobile and Alex felt for him but knew she could say nothing. If she registered fear or disapproval they would continue the charade with even more enjoyment, relishing her resentment.

For the whole of the afternoon Maslenkov bullied and humiliated the driver. There was no attempt to hold a conversation on the aluminium business and Alex was angry that she had been summoned there, wasting her precious time at this crucial juncture, only to be completely ignored. Maxim looked at her face and laughed.

'Is important to have relationship with plant manager,' he explained. 'Drink with us, then he trust you.'

'I don't want a drink. I want to talk about the plan. Does he know the situation?'

Maxim would not be distracted. He poured a glass of vodka and put it in front of Alex, then rose to his feet and drew himself unsteadily to his full height.

'You are now in Russia!' He shouted the last words and Maslenkov raised his hand, echoing the toast.

'*Russeeya!*'

'So you do things Russian way,' Maxim continued. 'Drink a toast to my country.'

Alex raised her glass and obediently repeated the toast. 'Maxim, I—'

'Yuri was once in Moscow, we together . . .' He lapsed into Russian to share the memory and the two burst into raucous laughter. The shouted conversation continued, neither allowing the other to finish. Finally Alex stood up.

'Maxim, please. I've come all the way from London for this meeting. Let's talk about the plan.' It was a last-ditch attempt to gain their attention and she knew that even if she were successful it was unlikely that they would be bound by any agreement reached after so much vodka. They would argue the next day and have to hold the whole meeting again.

With comic seriousness Maxim nodded his head and began to speak to Maslenkov with exaggerated solemnity.

Irritated, Alex sat back down. After two minutes Maxim burst out laughing.

'He wants to know how much,' Maxim explained.

'How much what?' she queried in a humour-less voice.

'How much to buy you. How much to make you do this deal and how much to make you do right thing for us.'

Alex sighed. 'You know how much I'll make. We worked it out together and you've seen the figures. I make the commission on the LME operation. Wellington pays me out of this.'

'If I tell him this, he will not believe.'

'I don't care whether he believes you or not.'

After a few words they burst out laughing and raised their glasses.

'We drink to the first Westerner who we did

346

not buy. Maybe you very, very honest, or maybe you very, very stupid!'

'Oh, for God's sake.' Alex got up and climbed the steps onto the deck. There was only so much compromise possible and she had reached her limit. Maxim understood the most minute details of the deal and knew exactly how much everyone was to be paid out. But since he was in Russia, with a Russian, he had to pretend to do business Maslenkov's way, posturing, mocking and boasting.

All she could do now was wait till they passed out, slept, then woke up. Irritated, she looked at her watch. Four o'clock. By her reckoning she had a chance. Had it been any later they would have slept for the whole night but at this point they would probably only sleep for an hour or two.

She settled back and watched the banks of the river pass lazily by. There was nothing she could do. And perhaps it was just as well if Maxim and Maslenkov re-established their friendship. She was not against this Russian way of getting to know a business partner. *In vino veritas*. Since it was not possible to do a credit check, it was reasonable to strip away the corporate formality of a potential partner and learn as much as possible.

But not today. Such a crucial time. And since Maxim already knew Maslenkov it seemed a very futile exercise.

She was surprised to see Maslenkov appear at the hatch half an hour later, his hands gripping the brass rail, his head lunging forward convulsively.

'Maxim sleeping,' he announced, his voice slurred.

Alex felt a moment's unease. He was smiling and rubbing his hands and although Alex knew the gestures were unconnected to her, they gave the impression of lascivious anticipation.

'I'm glad he's sleeping,' Alex answered, moving her chair back slightly. 'When he wakes up we can talk.'

'We can talk now.'

He sat beside her and peered at her myopically.

'This is my boat,' he began, pointing to himself like a child. 'Mine. I like to have boat to see the country. My country. I will not go, like other managers. They in Switzerland. I stay here. Maybe dangerous but I am home.'

'Why is it dangerous?' she asked.

'Because many people want to do business with me.'

'Yes, but why is that dangerous?' she insisted.

He shook his head and sighed.

'You understand nothing. Nothing. I will tell you. How much it cost to make aluminium, in a smelter?'

Alex thought back to the deal she had tried to put together for the Belorussian plant.

'About five hundred dollars per tonne,' she answered.

'Very good.' He clapped his hands in mock applause. 'You know how much I do it here?'

'Not exactly, but you're close to hydroelectric power, your labour costs must be—'

'I can do it for three hundred!' he bragged, looking at Alex for a reaction.

'Really! So little? I'm amazed. How do you manage to do it for so little?'

'Lower everything. Not pay electricity. Not pay workers, tell them no money.' He laughed. 'No, no, is really only three hundred dollars but I can sometimes make even lower.' He leant towards Alex and laid his hand on hers. 'What you think?'

Alex felt a wave of revulsion at this seedy little man. She pulled her hand away. Slowly, the significance of his words sank in. 'But your plant must be very profitable. I thought you were in deep financial trouble. You can't be if you produce aluminium at such a low cost. You can charge the Western merchants at least five hundred dollars for something that costs you only three hundred.'

'You understand nothing.' He puffed out his chest in childish braggadocio. 'I do this for Western companies and I charge them only three hundred. In the beginning even less.'

'But why? If it costs you three hundred dollars to convert alumina into aluminium, why on earth do you charge the same amount? You should be making a profit – a huge profit when you consider that you produce nearly a million tonnes a year . . .' Even as she asked the question she blushed at her naïveté. Of course. They had been right to say she was the stupidest person they had met.

Maslenkov was paid a backhander by the Western merchants to sign these unprofitable contracts and the workforce, who knew nothing about the world price of aluminium, continued producing in ignorance. It was the Western merchants who were making the profit. Their margins were easily big enough to take care of Maslenkov. The Western merchants were not cheating the poor Russians, they were colluding with them to cheat the workers.

'Much money I have.' He was so close that Alex could see the irregular surfaces of his gold teeth and the blackened stumps next to them. She could see the odd wrinkles running across his yellowed skin, and she could smell him, a sour smell of decay and disease. 'So good business with Maxim.'

Alex thought of the ten million dollars Maxim had sent from his Swiss bank account. 'Maxim helps you with this? He knows . . . ?'

'Very good man, good ideas.'

'And all the other plants in Russia, is it the same situation?'

'I think the same, some a little different, but all the same idea. One man from the West tell me that this is pure capitalism,' he bragged. 'Is right, we learned very quickly.'

Alex recognized the irony. 'Yes indeed. It is pure capitalism and you have learned very quickly.'

Alex's head buzzed with confusion. Why the hell had she put together this plan to corner the aluminium market, drive up the price, when the Russian plants were perfectly profitable? Why had Maxim, who knew all the numbers, told her that this was the only way to help Russian industry?

Again she cursed her naïveté. Profit, self-interest. He had well and truly conned her.

She thought immediately of Fedorov. She had been completely taken in. Now she understood the importance of his compromise, his perspectives, of trying to have principles. She looked back over the conversations she had had with other Russians and wondered if they all knew how stupid and naïve she was. And what about the government?

Beside her Maslenkov yawned as if exhausted by the length of his speech. Alex watched his eyes droop, then close. Even in his sleep his head twitched.

Alex looked up and caught the eye of the driver again. She blushed. She was in the same situation as he; a minor player, an unskilled labourer in the construction of an edifice designed by the Russians. But unlike the driver she had had pretensions. She stood up and walked away from them both, stunned by what she had learnt.

Alex prowled around the hotel room. It was two a.m., Moscow time. Her muscles were tense and she was tired but she could not sleep until she had assimilated Maslenkov's words and worked out what she had to do.

Every assumption she had made about the Russian metal business now had to be re-examined from her new perspective, every action based on these assumptions re-evaluated. She sat on the edge of the bed. Had she been wrong about everything?

The problem was not that the Western merchants were taking advantage of the Russian producers, nor that the world price of aluminium was falling. The problem was that the plant managers were skimming off outrageous profits themselves, sharing them with the Western buyers and allowing the plants to operate at unprofitable levels when they could easily be making a good profit even by Western standards.

Alex thought back over the conversations she had had with Belkov in Minsk and Fedorov in Siberia. Had they actually deceived her or was her enthusiasm to find a *cause* responsible for the view she had taken? Had they actively mis-represented their situation with the intent of deceiving her or had she been so totally absorbed in the thought of helping out that she had read something completely different into their words?

The phone rang and she was relieved to hear Libby's voice.

'Anything happening?' she asked auto-matically.

'Nothing. All quiet,' Libby answered. 'How are things with you?'

Alex drew a deep breath. 'I don't know. I spoke to the new manager at Chaika . . . Oh, I'll tell you all about it tomorrow. I need some sleep. There was a note waiting for me from Belkov of the Belorussian plant. He's coming here at twelve. I'm so tired . . .'

Exhausted, Alex lay on the bed. The irony of Maslenkov's words came back to her – this was indeed capitalism in action. The willing work-force slaving in antiquated blast furnaces while the directors sat in the boardroom dividing the spoils between their individual bank accounts. She was an accessory to one of the most depressing deceptions in history. The aluminium industry was trading on the pathetic conditions in the plants to gain help from outside, to assist in the collusion and cheat the workforce out of the support they so clearly needed.

And Maxim. Who had drawn information from her, used her, paraded her in front of the plants and the government and had told her virtually nothing. Every fact had been dragged from him or volunteered when it suited *him*. He who had stumbled onto the idea of cornering the market and then let her do the work.

She wondered for the hundredth time if Maslenkov had told Maxim about the conversation they had had. Did Maxim know that *she* knew? Nothing in his manner indicated that he did, but she could never read him. His natural reticence suppressed all but the most extreme emotions. If he did know he would conceal that knowledge easily from her.

But if Maslenkov *had* told him, what would he do? Alex was afraid. She was in Moscow, on his territory. Enclosed. He could do whatever he liked.

No. If he had known he would surely have done something by now instead of accompanying her back to Moscow and arranging to see her the next day.

Alex went back over the brief conversation she had had with him after she had spoken with Maslenkov.

Neutral. She was over-reacting.

Tomorrow she would leave Moscow as planned and decide what action to take.

It was close to midday when she woke up. She showered quickly, then dressed in black jumper and trousers. She pulled on her sheepskin jacket and made it downstairs minutes before twelve. She went to the vast mahogany reception desk and asked if there were any messages.

She was leaning on the desk when she heard the sound. At first she thought it came from one of the computers behind the desk, a rapid pap . . . pap . . . pap . . . , hardly any louder or sharper than the sound of typewriter keys. She didn't react but the reception staff did. They ran past her to the doors.

The rush of staff caused a bottleneck which the security guards tried to disperse by shouting and lashing out savagely at their own colleagues. Alex could make no sense of what was going on. She thought for a moment that there had been a car crash but the faces she watched showed fear rather than the morbid excitement of bystanders watching someone else's demise.

Eventually, the crowd stood aside to let two men carrying a body come in. They were carrying him awkwardly and there seemed to Alex to be a real danger that they would drop him, yet nobody moved to help as they staggered clumsily through the door. The body was pitched over to the side with one leg trailing along the ground. Blood poured from his head as freely as from a wide-mouthed jug. Just inside the door they laid him down and immediately began arguing with each other and the guards. Alex wondered how Belkov was going to get into the hotel and was about to make her way to the bar in search of another exit when the crowd suddenly moved and she saw the face of the man they had carried in.

The man, lying now on a thick blanket of blood, eyes wide open, was Belkov. The bullet had entered through the front left side of his skull and exited by the back of his head, the enormous pressure surrounding the bullet having blasted everything out of its way as it passed through the brain.

Alex turned away and pushed her way blindly through the crowd, elbowing the onlookers indiscriminately, viciously. She was on the pavement, panting, in seconds. Someone shouted and she half turned back – they could have been trying to stop her or be abusing her for her violent departure. She ignored them.

She took off to her left at a run, down the small street which led away from the main road. Belkov. She felt sick and stopped for a second, gulping the heavy polluted air and feeling the fumes in her mouth, gagging as she felt grit in her throat. She leant against the wall, struggling to contain the nausea and the humiliation and vulnerability it generated. She rested her forehead against the backs of her hands.

Suddenly she heard the sound of a car and swung round. With an angry surge of the engine the front wheel mounted the pavement and rolled towards her until the black wing was only inches away. In a second she would be cornered. Or crushed. She screamed, overcome with fear, real fear of an enemy she could see. Now there was no ambiguity. She was the target.

The car door opened and a figure emerged. Alex did not recognize the face. The short dark hair was brushed forward as if to emphasize the aggression of his features; not a single one seemed integrated into his face; each seemed to have been grafted on badly, each too large, too forceful.

Kartchak stood inches from Alex, looking at her, his hands loosely by his sides.

He watched as her eyes darted over his, looking behind him and around him, then back to his. Petrified.

Suddenly, Kartchak's hand shot out in a spasm of rage and spanned her throat, pinning her to the wall. Alex panicked. It would only be a matter of seconds until she passed out. Her heart accelerated to a high-pitched beat. She tried to lift her arms to fend him off, but he immediately tightened his grip and where his index finger dug into her jugular vein she felt a pulse of protest. She dropped her hands.

A bright light seemed to be shining in her eyes; she could make out the face of Kartchak inches from hers, but it was as if the frame of her vision had narrowed and she could see only a brightly illuminated, distorted photograph. Her legs relaxed and she felt her body slipping downwards, although his grip held her in the same place against the wall. Now, as her head started to be dragged down by the weight of her body, she felt both the pressure of his fingers around her throat and the span of his hand where it sat so neatly under her jaw. She felt sick again. A network of fine veins snaked across her eyes. She tried to regain her footing, urging her legs to support her.

Then she felt Kartchak's other hand undo the large buttons on her coat. For a second she felt no contact and wondered if she had been mistaken, but then she felt the coldness of his touch and her skin prickled with the sudden discomfort; he had lifted her jumper without her having felt it.

She could smell him beneath the tang of his cologne, an earthy smell, deep and menacing. His hand trailed slowly up from her waist and she closed her eyes. Again the sensation stopped. She had clenched every muscle in her body as if this would somehow repel the invader. But then she felt his hand on her breast, the palm flat at first, then slowly contracting, his fingers gradually digging in like a claw, cruelly squeezing her flesh into the mould of his hand.

He could have let go of her throat and she would have still stood there, immobile, pinned by the sharp humiliating pain, afraid that this violent invasion was a foretaste of his intent and the precursor of something far worse.

Suddenly she heard voices and opened her eyes. She couldn't see beyond Kartchak but his attention must have been distracted because his grip on her throat had loosened. His other hand was free. Abruptly, Kartchak released her and she staggered forwards, ending up on her knees on the pavement. She saw him pull a gun from beneath his jacket and swing round. In the split second before she ran she took in the black Zil and the long, dark shape of the man emerging from it.

Maxim. Beside him, the unmistakable shape of Boris.

Taking a deep breath into her bruised lungs she ran, the solid heels of her boots making a deafening sound. She had turned the corner and was running towards the edge of the main road when she dared look round.

No-one had followed her.

The traffic roared past her in Moscow's busiest thoroughfare and she looked back again, afraid that she would be unable to hear their approach over the noise of the cars. She ran across the road, weaving between the cars, confused by the fact that some lanes were stationary while some were fast-moving. One car grazed her, refusing to compromise, acting not through anger or impatience but a murderous dogged perseverance; she knew that he would have run her down if she had not jumped backwards out of his path.

She reached the other side and pushed straight on through the doors of the giant Metropole Hotel. While the Metropole was a Russian hotel it catered almost exclusively for foreign business travellers and was the nearest thing to a safe haven.

She leant against a pillar in the busy lobby and tried to take stock. Her hand flew to her breast under her jacket. She ached.

Belkov was dead. He had been coming to see her and now he was dead. And she herself had been attacked. She had been afraid of Maxim, afraid that he had found out about her conversation with Maslenkov, and now she had the second man to fear. In her mind the two were merged in the scene she had half taken in as she ran; two threats, two deadly intrigues.

She needed help, but with a shock she realized that she knew nobody in the country other than Maxim's contacts and she could not trust them to tell her the truth. He could have asked the staff at the Magyar to keep an eye on her. She should not go back for her bag.

It occurred to her that the only other person she had met in Moscow was Chernikov, the previous head of the Chaika plant, and a fresh wave of fear washed over her. Suddenly it all seemed unbearably convoluted.

She felt very vulnerable – more vulnerable than if she had known what was going on, the danger increased by the fact that she could unwittingly walk into a trap. She had watched Maxim so closely, trying to work out if he knew she had learnt of his deceit, afraid of his reaction if he did. She thought she had got away with it.

But two people were dead, two plant managers, both known to Maxim. It was not hard to imagine an explanation for the death of Chernikov, especially when he had been replaced by a close ally of Maxim's. And Belkov. Perhaps he, like Chernikov, had refused to co-operate in some way.

Who was the second man who had appeared at the Magyar moments after Belkov's murder?

Alex tried to marshal her thoughts and act logically, but she could not. She knew enough about her body to know that it was reacting to the situation by shutting down; her low blood pressure was a boon in the dealing room, but now she was cold and shivering, fighting off sleep. She yawned, knowing that her brain needed oxygen but alarmed by the sudden drowsiness when she needed to be alert.

Her throat ached and she ran her fingers over the tender skin, then wrapped her arms around her body. She had known tension and stress before, but never *fear*, and, specifically, fear of death. Her muscles began to shake uncontrollably, violent rhythmic twitches of panic and like a runner at the starting line she shook her legs and arms to encourage circulation. If she took flight now, panicked, running through the streets, she could not trust her instincts to take her away from danger. If Maxim or the other man was looking for her, they would know where she would go, they would second guess her and find her.

She had to have a strategy, to think ahead and outguess them.

She searched in her pockets and was relieved to find her passport and some money. She looked at the notes. Six dollars in one pocket, two twenty-pound notes in the other. She never spent any money in Russia and had been lazy about picking up dollars in the airport; there hadn't seemed to be any point as long as she had the small denomination notes she needed for tips. Her credit cards, insurance cards and ticket to London on the afternoon flight were all in her wallet in the Magyar. She looked again at the crumpled notes in her hand. How far would she get with this? She spoke no Russian, knew nothing about public transport, had never even used the phone system.

Her first instinct was to go to the British Embassy; it was on the opposite bank of the Moscow river to the Kremlin and she could walk there in under ten minutes. But she was afraid. She could think of no easy way of getting there other than down the wide avenues and across the huge square that surrounded the Kremlin, and then over the bridge. Hardly a surreptitious route.

She looked at her watch. Nearly one o'clock. The British Airways flight at three was the only flight she could take since she had no way of buying a new ticket.

She thought of the odd spy novel she had read; the methodical hero always had a plan which he implemented several stages in advance, incorporating bluffs and blinds. But Alex was still standing in the lobby of the Metropole an hour after Belkov's death, too scared to move from the sanctuary of the shadow.

One of the Metropole's security men passed by, looking curiously at her, and she realized she had to go. Reluctantly she made her way to the street at the back of the hotel and looked around, then stuck her arm out in the common Muscovite signal. The first car to see her screeched to a halt. There was no formal taxi system and all car drivers would pick up a fare for a couple of dollars – she was obviously a well-heeled foreigner and would have no trouble getting a lift. While she knew she was in danger, she had no choice.

'British Embassy,' she said as she got in.

The driver nodded and Alex was relieved that

he understood English. They drove around the block, passing the end of the narrow road that led to the Magyar, then across the square and over the Moscow river.

She could hear the crowd outside the Embassy as they approached. It was moving in a column, which widened into a crowd of two hundred gesticulating, screaming individuals at the entrance. There were security guards, clearly identifiable in their neat uniforms, but there seemed to be no strategy between them. Instead of forming a pattern and herding the trouble-makers in one direction or another, they were scattered inside and outside the crowd, their gestures matching those of the demonstrators, their fury seeming to mirror the crowd's.

As Alex's car stopped a guard lashed out, his baton connecting with the neck of a woman to his left. It seemed to have no effect at all on the crowd and the shouting, gesticulating and shoving continued unaltered.

Alex indicated to the driver that he should keep driving. The queue wound around the building, although the block contained other buildings and was perhaps three times the area of the actual Embassy. Alex knew that the visa department was overwhelmed; violence had broken out on a number of occasions and the Embassy had been closed. After a moment she got out of the car and ran over to a young guard standing by the main gates, seemingly detached, watching the crowd.

'I am a British citizen,' she said. 'Can I go in?'

'No-one in,' he replied. 'Closed. Open to-morrow.'

362

'Is there another entrance?' she persisted. 'For British citizens?'

'No.'

Alex looked up at the windows above her. Surely there must be a way of getting in. She tried again.

'I need to go in.' She pulled out a twenty-pound note and let him see it.

'Please. I'm British, I don't want the visa section. I want to see the Ambassador.'

The guard took a step towards her and for a second she thought he was going to take the note and open the gate. Her heart lifted at the prospect of being behind the enormous gates. Instead he raised his baton. The nonchalant passivity was gone and his face was suddenly transformed. His upper lip lifted and he spat some words, bearing down on her, blazing with anger. Alex cowered, her first instinct self-preservation, her second outrage that he should consider hitting her. Suddenly she felt a bitter resentment of all things Russian, the brutal instinctive violence and the unthinking aggression.

'You bastard,' she said, tears welling in her eyes. 'I just wanted to go in . . .'

He half smiled, showing how unconcerned he was by her behaviour, then gestured again with his baton, a curt motion of dismissal.

Alex walked back to the car.

The driver took off as soon as she shut the door. It was clear that he had been anxious for his own safety. Two blocks later he pulled over to the side of the road.

'Where?' he asked.

'Airport,' she answered automatically.

'Sheremetyevo?' He asked her if she wanted the international airport.

'Yes,' she confirmed. 'Thank you.'

From where she sat in the back of the car the strip of mirror reflected his eyes. They were not reassuring and, combined with the sparse tangles of unbrushed hair on his head, he was alarming. The car was filthy and smelt but she did not dare open the window for fear of provoking his anger. After five minutes she realized that she had not negotiated the fare. She cursed. Again, it was too late now.

The radio blared out contemporary Western music, which did nothing to calm Alex's nerves. She was still cold, still leaden, and, as she watched the skyscrapers of Moscow disappear and the scrubby wasteland between city and airport take over, she was aware that she was completely adrift from all forms of assistance. Perhaps she should not have been so quick to discard the Embassy lifeline. Perhaps she should have waited.

It began to rain but the car had only one windscreen wiper, on the passenger side. Ahead, the motorway looked as if it had been obscured by a snowstorm but the car's speed did not diminish. The driver depended on his reflexes to swing out of his lane into the next when another car's rear lights loomed up within feet of the front of his car. Alex closed her eyes.

She was surprised to see the signs indicating the airport as the car eventually slowed down and ashamed of herself for having automatically mistrusted the driver. She would have liked to press fifty dollars into his hand as a show of gratitude but could not. Instead, she raised her eyebrows when the car stopped at the terminal.

'How much?' she asked.

'Twenty dollars.'

Alex took out her wallet and took out a twenty-pound note. This was worth thirty dollars but she didn't know whether the driver would be aware of this.

He took the note and examined it. 'English?'

'Yes.'

He nodded and put the note in his pocket. Alex got out of the car. At the entrance to the terminal she hesitated. Anyone looking for a Western woman would fasten onto her in seconds. And surely this would be the first place they would think of looking. They would know she would panic and head for the airport.

But there was nothing she could do. She made her way through the automatic doors into the mêlée, which had been the same every time she had been in Moscow airport. Groups carried unfeasibly large packages wrapped in brown paper and huge, cheap plastic holdalls with red and blue stripes. The only individuals were foreign businessmen; the taxi drivers hunted in packs and the gypsy beggars, with their beautiful, dirty faces, prowled around the terminal building in small groups.

As usual Alex attracted attention, but this time she was aware of the interest and the danger attached to it. She did not fit readily into any of the moulds the Muscovites had recently learned to recognize; she was obviously wealthy, but dressed so conservatively that she was unlikely to be in the fashion or music industries. She was good-looking, strikingly so, but she wore no make-up and no jewellery. A particularly curious eye would spot that her ears were not pierced and that she wore a heavy man's watch, produced by the Viktoria factory in Moscow.

Unusually, Alex looked back at everyone who looked at her, wondering if she would be able to identify a potential attacker.

Her instincts were to find a dark corner and cower there until rescued. But there would be no rescue. No-one who could help her knew where she was. She stood against the wall and scanned the huge hall, her mind haywire with abortive plans and unworkable schemes.

She did not recognize the small dark man standing by the door, but when his eye caught hers there was a moment of engagement – too significant to be the casual interest she was used to seeing. When he looked away her eyes followed his and she saw him pinpoint another man on the opposite side of the hall. It was Boris.

Fear tightened round her heart and for the first time she felt tears in her eyes and a huge wave of desperation and self-pity.

Both men started to move towards her, negotiating their way through the groups of people, keeping their eyes on her. She knew it was only a matter of seconds until they reached her.

She looked around, then up. A gallery ran round the perimeter of the building on the first floor. Without thinking, she darted along the wall to the staircase. She leapt onto the stairs and had taken two great strides when she felt a hand on her ankle and then she came crashing down, her hands and face hitting the step simultaneously, the metal strip just missing her teeth. The step below slammed into her chest and it was this pain, on a part of her body already violated, already aching, which pushed her from fear to rage. With all her force, she cannoned her free foot backwards, the solid block of her heel connecting with bone. The hold on her other foot instantly released.

Now she had the impetus to bound up the remaining steps, her long legs driving upward, her heart pounding, hardly daring to believe that she was free. At the top she glanced quickly behind her.

Her foot had caught the first man on the cheekbone and blood was running down his face. He hesitated, trying to clear his vision, smearing the blood across his cheek. Boris was now on the bottom step.

Alex knew she had little hope. She had bought herself a couple of seconds, no more. These two men were on their home ground. She considered giving herself up, just walking up to them and conceding defeat. Maybe then they would be easier on her than if they had to bring her down . . .

Suddenly a nasal, officious voice on the public address system announced that passengers for the British Airways flight to London should report to customs.

Alex took a deep breath. She wanted to be

on that plane. She wanted to go home.

Just as she turned her mind snagged on the scene below her.

The two men were locked together. She had assumed they were working together but Boris had pinned the first, injured man to the step and was astride him, one hand on his chest. They had been aware of each other, but as competitors, not allies. When she saw Boris's hand reach across his own body, under his jacket, she froze. He was reaching for a gun.

The whole scene took only a couple of seconds.

Boris thrust the barrel of the gun against the man's throat, his mutilated hand awkwardly bent, his middle finger twisted round the trigger. Alex could see his mouth move. They were talking. Then the gun went off.

It was as if a grenade had exploded. The whole scene leapt forward two frames. The body convulsed once as the bullet exploded. Boris jumped away.

Alex felt her hand on her own throat. She was an easy target. Boris was twenty feet away with a gun in his hand. She closed her eyes and waited for the sound, the impact, the pain.

But nothing happened. The silence screamed in her ears.

After a moment she forced her eyes open. Boris had put the gun away but he was making his way up the stairs towards her.

She turned and ran.

Several corridors led off the main gallery. She careered blindly down the first, using her hand to ricochet her weight off the wall. The corridor dog-legged to the left and she stopped for a minute, sure that she was not being followed but afraid that her heartbeat was drowning out the sound of his footsteps. There was not a sound.

The door next to her bore the forbidding logo of Aeroflot. Alex looked around. If there was an Aeroflot office, there must be a British Airways office. She ran further on and spotted the familiar red, white and blue logo.

She burst through the door of the British Airways office, slammed it shut then leant back against it, gasping. The pretty blonde representative stared at her.

'The flight to London . . .' She could not get the words out. Her breath was jagged, her lungs constricted. 'Help me.'

She took a deep breath. She was shaking, her body freezing.

'My baggage and wallet . . .' She hesitated. The truth was convoluted and she wanted them to feel she was their responsibility. 'Stolen just now . . . downstairs . . .'

The representative was now on her feet, her expression concern and sympathy, her hands fluttering.

'I'm so sorry . . .' she began.

'They have all my documents . . .'

The girl opened a door to an adjoining office. When the armed security guard appeared in the doorway Alex jumped. But after a few words he opened the external door and looked down the corridor, then went out and pulled the door shut behind him. She could see his silhouette through the glass and began to appreciate the other side of the coin – that it was a comfort to have this unthinking stoicism on her side for once, knowing that if challenged, the guard would lash out – in her defence.

The stewardess moved into action, locking the door, making more calls. Alex suddenly felt protected. They would look after her now. She allowed herself to be led to the sofa.

'Don't worry. Everything will be all right.'

The BA desk confirmed that a new ticket would be issued and the old ticket blacklisted. The airport police wanted to talk to her. Everything was fine. The Russian girl reported all this gently, as if Alex was too traumatized to understand. Dazed, Alex sat on the sofa, listening to the instructions, nodding.

The paperwork complete, Alex was escorted through the staff channel to the plane. She found herself leaning against the stewardess, gripping her arm as if all the strength had been taken from her. Fifty more feet, she counted. If I can just make it onto the plane. She knew she could not escape if Boris confronted her here. She was a perfect sitting duck.

Inside the plane Alex listened to the comforting words of the pilot, then the senior steward. But the door remained open. From where she was sitting, Alex could see the girls chatting with a couple of Russian engineers, leaning against the body of the plane, waiting for the signal to close the doors.

With agonizing lethargy they began to pull the massive heavy doors into place. Alex watched them force the huge handles down. Then she heard the engines as the plane began to taxi. Surely they were too slow? They seemed to quieten slightly. Were they turning back?

The 737 swung onto the runway and the engines began to throb more loudly. Alex could hardly bear the sensation of impatience as the plane lumbered into position at the end of the runway.

Suddenly the noise increased and the plane, like a huge restrained animal, began to inch forward. A moment later they were hurtling down the runway at full speed. As the nose lifted Alex felt herself thrust back in her seat and laughed out loud. She had survived.

With no help from the Embassy. No credit card and very little money. She closed her eyes and gloried in the sensation of freedom.

When the drinks trolley appeared she asked for a large brandy and downed it in one warm, luxurious swallow.

The stewardess smiled at her in surprise. Alex smiled back, aware of the slight tremble at the corner of her mouth. With a shaking hand she held out the glass for a refill.

She was alive.

THIRTEEN

Alex took a taxi home, retrieved her spare key from her neighbour, collected some cash from the flat and paid off the cab.

Back inside the flat, she barricaded the door and switched on the burglar alarm. She looked at her watch, then picked up the phone and called Libby in the office, hoping to catch her before she left for the day.

'Can you come over? It's urgent.'

'Are you OK?'

'Yes, but I need to talk to you – now.'

Now that she was safely in her own territory, Alex felt disorientated. She wandered aimlessly round the flat, not knowing what to do. She checked the locks for the fourth time, then went into the kitchen and made a pot of strong coffee.

When the door bell rang her heart stopped and restarted again with a racing patter which deafened her.

'My God!' Libby took hold of her. 'What happened? What's wrong?'

'Nothing, nothing, it's not me, I mean, I'm OK.'

She drew a deep breath. 'I'm not injured.'

She led Libby through to the living room and sat down on the edge of the sofa. 'I'm going to try and tell you all the facts, just the facts. Then you can tell me what you think. I'm tired ... I'm not sure I'm being rational any more. I need you to tell me what's normal, Libby. I've lost touch ...'

Impatiently, Libby leant forward. 'Just tell me. What happened?'

It took Alex half an hour to explain what had happened in Siberia and then in Moscow.

Libby sat back. 'My God. We've been warned about Russia often enough. We thought we knew better, but maybe we didn't. What do we do now? We're seven thousand lots of aluminium long, and we have less than twenty-four hours until the announcement of the loan.'

'I'll speak to Sol and The Kid in a while. Let them know what's happened.'

'And what exactly are you going to tell them? What *has* happened? Do we really know?'

'The one thing I do know is that this whole plan is a charade. There's no need for the price to be higher to save the plants. The only thing we can do is close the position. Sell out and deprive them of the profit. It's all been a con—'

Suddenly she lashed out, sending the empty mug she had been holding across the room, smashing it against the far wall.

'I thought I was doing something so *right*, for once, not just the bloodless neutrality of business, not just the mechanical execution of a task. It was *real*. I thought it was a good thing and I was so damn pleased. Something to believe in. A cause. Finally I had *conviction*.'

'Alex, what *we* did was right. What has happened doesn't devalue *our* efforts or actions.'

'No, but I wonder . . . how much of what I did was because I believed in it and how much was sheer bloody-mindedness? I wanted this deal, Libby, I wanted to put it together to show Sol that I could do a whole deal on my own, that he would have to come to me for once. And I wanted to show that smug bastard Neville that he was wrong, too.'

'So? What's wrong with that?'

With a flat voice Alex went back over events. 'I should have asked questions. I should have satisfied myself that the whole thing was correct. I should have made sure—'

'Stop this.' Libby stood up and for a moment Alex thought she was going to slap her. But instead she sat down beside her. 'You couldn't have known. And Maxim probably decided to kill anyone who *was* going to tell you. Alex, I want you to get some sleep. You're exhausted.'

'You're right.' She stood up. 'Let's talk in the morning.'

When Libby left Alex checked the doors again and made her way up to her bedroom.

She paced the room for a while, knowing she was too agitated to sleep. She sat on the bed and dialled Sol's number in New York.

'Hey! You're back,' he greeted her. 'How was it?'

Alex launched again into the description of events, but this time Sol asked the questions and the tale came out in a different order. She was pleased to respond to his questions, pleased to be in a passive role for a moment and to have him on her side.

'Well,' he mused at the end. 'One hell of a mess. I'll think about it and call you in the morning. Are you going into the office?'

'Of course I am! I'm going to start selling the position as soon as I get in—'

'Hold on, Alex. Just because we find out that Maxim is not Snow White you're calling the game off? By the time you sell our positions, before the announcement, the price will be right back where it started – or lower.'

'Sol, please—'

'Alex, this is business. If you can't see it then you're living in a fairytale yourself. And may I remind you before you get completely carried away that you are not authorized to close the position.'

'You'd sue me?'

'I won't have to. You won't break the rules. Get some sleep, Alex, I'll get a flight in the morning and call you when I land.'

'Sol . . .' She hesitated. 'You say it's business, but what happened to me in Moscow was terrible. I'm frightened.'

'Oh, Alex,' he answered impatiently, as if she were a child with nightmares. 'No-one wants to kill *you*.'

Alex put down the phone with a sense of defeat. Someone must be able to help. She needed the assistance of someone practical, detached and realistic. A friend.

She scrambled for her bag and pulled out a phone number. Rory Freeman. After a moment's hesitation she dialled the number.

'Rory? It's Alex. I'm really sorry to disturb you, but I have a serious problem. A crisis and I wanted to ask your opinion.'

'I'm pleased to hear from you, even if it's only business. Go ahead.'

'Off the record . . .' she began.

In the back of her mind was the knowledge that this was a great story and that Rory could be counted on to assist with the exposé when the whole thing was finished. Like Sol, he asked questions and whistled when she had finished.

'My God, Alex. These people don't mess around, you know. You could be in serious trouble.'

Impatiently Alex answered, 'I know that already, Rory. What I need is your help in finding proof of what's going on.'

'There's nothing I – or you – can do,' he answered immediately. 'Let me tell you something, Alex. They'll have covered their tracks by using holding companies, companies registered in Cyprus and the Cayman Islands. You'll never get any proof of anything. And even if you do, what are you going to do with it? Do you think the KGB will come and take this Maxim away for being a bad boy? It doesn't work that way, Alex.'

'I know it doesn't work that way. I'm not a complete idiot. But there *are* authorities in Russia and I *do* want this scam exposed.'

'And if you take this information to the wrong person, who happens to be on Maxim's side,

376

what do you think will happen? You know how these people operate, Alex. They kill. Simple as that.'

Alex thought of Mintov in the government. Whose side was he on?

'OK, Rory, I'll take your advice. I'll do nothing and let them get on with it.' All anger gone, she put down the phone.

Slowly she dialled The Kid's number. The conversation had the same bottom line. Hang on, think about it. Leave the position open.

Alex lay down on the bed and wrapped the duvet around herself. She was shaking.

What a fool she'd been, assuming that they were all in this together. Nobody had stood by her. She was on her own.

'Alex!'

She swung round, unsure whose voice she'd heard. The office was subdued although business was good.

'Alex! Over here! Stocks.'

She looked at her watch. One minute to nine. The LME warehouses released data on metal stock levels once a week at nine a.m. and the market stopped for half a minute beforehand, every trader ready to seize the figure, everybody in the dealing room hunched over the screen as if proximity to the green glass would assist the process of absorption.

Alex walked over to Joseph's desk. She knew the aluminium stocks would be down. Sol was regularly buying metal, taking it out of the LME warehouses or buying cargoes before they could be put into the warehouse. She expected another modest decrease of around five thousand tonnes.

'Hell, look at that.' The newly updated figure, showing how much aluminium was held in LME warehouses, flashed on the screen. By the time Alex had focused on the small number in the correct column the noise had broken out of its confines as the brokers snatched the phones, anticipating their customers' questions.

Down twenty-four thousand tonnes.

'Alan. Where's Dec now? Are the forwards in?'

'Give me a hundred for Vincent. He's short.'

'Come *on* . . .'

The dealers were excited.

'Well, what do you think, Joe?' Alex sat down beside him. She valued his opinion; Joe was analytical but realistic, full of common sense. 'Is this significant or is it just a blip?'

He shrugged. 'Can't argue with the data, Alex. Demand is good. The market's on the boil. The Funds are nosing around. This is a bull market. End of story.'

Alex looked at the screen. The price was up $50 on the previous night's close to $1530.

'Alan! Vincent takes fifty at $1550. Offer me again . . .'

Alex watched the bedlam in the dealing room for a moment then walked back to her office. She had added up the huge holdings in futures, options and physical stocks and had the numbers in front of her on the desk. A 175,000-tonne position in total.

It had been a perfect execution, building up the position slowly, attracting no attention. There had been one article on Reuters, which had quoted an analyst's report that the US Funds were buying, and one report that mentioned that demand was steady. But nothing more.

Then suddenly the market had caught on that something was happening. And the frenzy had started. The plan was running almost by remote control; she had been so thorough when she developed it that it didn't need her any more.

'Alex!'

She turned again, this time towards Monty.

'What's this transfer for?' he shouted. 'Did you know about it?'

Alex ran over and took the fax from his hand. Ten million dollars to Barclays. She ran her eye over the details. Maxim's money. Going to Metco.

'Shit.'

'Value today. What's going on, Alex? Why has he pulled his money?'

'It's a long story, Monty. I'll speak to you about it later.'

Alex laid the fax in front of Libby. 'Look at this. They must have got pretty friendly.'

Libby shook her head. 'I'm sorry, Alex.'

'Not your fault.'

Suddenly she heard her name again, paged by switchboard this time. She picked up the phone. The timid voice of the operator informed her that a Mr Fedorov was on the line. Alex hesitated. She had given Fedorov little thought since she'd come back from Moscow, but of all the blows she had received the realization that Fedorov was part of the group was one of the hardest to take.

'Put him through to my office. I'm on my way.'

Seconds later she heard his voice, strong and positive despite the distance between them.

'Alex! How are you? I enjoyed our talk so much and am hoping that you will come again soon so that we may continue.'

'What can I do for you, Mr Fedorov?'

Without acknowledging the coldness of her voice he continued. 'Alex, I hear the price of aluminium is up this morning and I must tell you it will not stay up there. Be careful.'

'Why?' she asked. 'What's going to happen?'

There was a moment's hesitation before Fedorov continued. 'I cannot tell you everything, but you know some of the things happening in Russia today. Later today, as you know . . . when the announcement is made, the market will crash.'

'Thank you, I appreciate it,' Alex answered simply and hung up.

She stood up and looked out of the window at the bright scene below her. Tourists were walking along the cobble-stoned path between the Tower and London Bridge and the river teemed with small boats. Everyone was busy, going from A to B, sure of themselves. Purposeful.

In Alex's world everything had gone wrong.

Suddenly Libby appeared at the door. 'What is it?'

Alex repeated Fedorov's message. 'I believe him, Libby. In spite of the fact that my judgement has been so wrong recently. I want to get Sol and The Kid out. And I want Maxim to be left with his position when the market comes crashing down. How can I do it?'

'Are you sure about this?'

'Yes, I am.'

'Well, ideally we want Maxim to come in and buy some more. That way we can sell to him, close our position and leave him holding the baby.'

'Perfect. How do we induce him to do that?'

Without a moment's hesitation Libby answered. 'We use Spike.'

'What?' Alex stared at her.

'It's perfect,' Libby continued, a small smile on her face. 'What a stitch-up. He'll buy some himself and I'm pretty sure Maxim has given him discretion to buy for his account. Spike doesn't even need to call him. And he's got the money now.'

Alex hesitated. 'It's not necessarily the only way . . .' she began.

'I know it isn't.' Libby stood up. 'But I *want* to do it.'

'Why now? After all these years?' Alex asked. 'You've put up with him for so long. Are you really sure you want to do this?'

They looked at each other, the whole history of their friendship suddenly coming into focus, the wedge that had lain between them for so many years now about to be destroyed.

Libby's face cleared. She smiled. 'Am I sure I want to do it?' she echoed. 'I can't wait.'

Alex smiled back. 'OK. Here's the plan. We work out the story. You call Spike. I'll call Marvin and maybe the boys at Pascal. Feed them a line. Get them excited. This market's really going to skyrocket. Everyone's so bullish, it should be easy to get them to swallow another story. Then when the buyers come in I sell, squaring the boys up.'

'And then . . .'

'And then we hope to hell my information's correct.'

A few minutes later Libby picked up the phone. She chatted for a few moments then changed tack. 'Look, I've got to go. Alex's tearing around with some press release that she claims is dynamite. That new aluminium-framed car is coming into production early, and it's got that defence contract—'

Libby stared at the phone in her hand. Spike had put the phone down on her.

Alex walked over to her and put her hand on her shoulder. 'Are you OK?'

'Yes, I am, Alex. I know I've done the right thing. I could just never do it when *you* told me to.' She grinned. 'My own brand of bloody-mindedness.'

Alex picked up the phone. 'I'm going to call the boys. I need to get them out.'

She dialled The Kid's number. Annette, his secretary, was just about to put her on hold when she told her it was crucial to speak to him right away.

'Hey, Alex. What's happening?' said The Kid when he came on.

'I need to sell out your position. Now. Don't ask me why, trust me. I think I can get you out at a profit but do what I say *now* or you're looking at a very substantial loss. I need a fax from you authorizing me to sell.'

Libby listened to Alex. Alex's manner had completely changed. No-one would challenge the authority that lay behind that voice.

'I'll speak to Sol and get the fax to you right away,' The Kid answered.

'Give it five minutes. I need to speak to him first.'

She called Sol, anticipating a fight. Her mind was one step ahead of his refusal, considering threats of legal action. She told him what had happened and was surprised by his total acquiescence.

'Not bad, Alex. Almost sounds like something I'd have dreamed up myself. And have you told Spike about this already?'

'Yes. All done five minutes ago. If I know him he'll be on the phone to Maxim right now.'

'I'm leaving for the airport but I'll speak to The Kid and get back to you.'

'Make it quick.'

Libby snapped her fingers. 'Well?'

'We wait. That's all.'

'I'm going back to the dealing room.'

'I'll be there in a minute.'

Alex moved back to the window. She ran her index finger over her upper lip then pulled at a piece of skin. Her nails dug too deeply and the pain bit back, a sharp bloody flick of intensity. Ignoring it, she ran her finger over her top lip again and found herself looking for another loose end. Suddenly it became the most important thing to pare her mouth to smoothness. Her fingers skated over the skin, looking for an edge.

Her mind slid back to Maxim. Had he been

there she would have wanted to hurt him with the same cutting harsh sharpness she had just felt, not to inflict a blow on him but to stab him, to cut him and surprise him with her vehemence – the passive, compliant Alex.

In her anger she felt uncharacteristic barbarism. She liked the image of the knife, the metallic cruelty of the clean sharp blade. She even liked the word. The blade. I could do it, she realized. I could kill him.

She turned round abruptly and walked from her office along the corridor to the dealing room, her fists still clenched. She stopped at the door and looked at the chaos. Factions, ever-changing, were allying with and against other factions. Self-interest dictated where friendships took root in the dealing room; not one single individual in that room would hesitate before taking another's business to enhance his results, or blaming someone else for his own error.

Her ear picked up the sound of Marcus. He was waving his finger right in the face of Bill, the trainee, Libby's cousin.

'You come in, you do what I tell you, you bugger off,' Marcus drawled in his sing-song voice, a smug smile on his face. 'No chat, no questions, no what-did-I-think-of-the-game-last-night. Got it?'

Bill nodded. 'I'm sorry, I didn't mean to interrupt you. Sorry.'

Alex was surprised to realize how much she disliked Marcus.

'You did not interrupt me. You could not interrupt me.' He sat down. 'Get these fucking faxes done, Bill, or you'll be out of here.'

Without thinking Alex walked calmly over to them. Marcus looked up at her briefly, then back to his papers.

'Marcus, you're fired,' she said quietly, then, as an afterthought, added, 'Now *you're* out of here.'

The dealing room quietened to a level that would still have been considered deafening to an untrained ear. For a second Alex thought Marcus might hit her. He stood up and faced her, stunned, his mouth open, looking to see whether she was joking.

'Get your stuff. I want you out now.'

'But . . . why? What have I done?' Alex relished the change of roles. Marcus's voice was a tone or two higher, his demeanour slacker, unsure. The exact pose Bill had adopted moments earlier.

He inclined towards her. 'Alex. This is a joke, right?'

'You're a bully, Marcus. And I've listened to you talking to customers. You lie. Your figures are good, but you're a liar. You'll have no trouble getting another job. If you're out of here in less than ten minutes I'll even give you a reference. Now get going.'

As Alex watched him leaving the room she examined her motives. Was this simple displacement? She couldn't punish Maxim so she chose the next available substitute? What the hell, she decided, it felt damn good. And she should have sacked Marcus long ago, although perhaps in a more dignified manner. She smiled. As she looked around the room, starting with Bill, moving on to Libby then the whole of the metals desk, other smiles answered hers and she realized that, whatever her motivation, sacking Marcus had been a bloody good move.

She sat down at her desk and pulled the keyboard towards her, flicking expertly through the news, the currencies and the stock markets, watching every trade, listening to every phone call. She asked the aluminium dealer his view of the market, then she asked the others. Everyone was bullish, the price was going to hit $2000, they told her. All her own research quoted back at her. She'd done a good job.

She made a few calls, chatted casually about the market and the rumours she'd heard, planted a couple of ideas.

She looked up at the clock. Forty minutes until the announcement.

Libby nudged her. 'Reception says Professor Vichevsky's here for you. Shall I tell him you're too busy?'

Alex sighed. The professor's sense of timing was impeccable.

'No, I have some questions to ask him. Tell them I'm on my way, but call me if anything happens.'

Standing beside the professor was David Macneice. Alex shook their hands and ushered them into her office. The professor seemed to have shrunk since she'd last seen him and what little order there had been in his appearance had gone. Had she seen him in the street, she would have taken him for a tramp. Macneice was ashen, the plump sheen of self-satisfaction she'd found so obnoxious now gone. Something was obviously very wrong.

'What can I do for you, gentlemen?'

'I'm so glad to be back,' the professor began. 'In Moscow I had a meeting, a terrible time—'

'What happened?'

'Two days ago, with Maxim. He wanted to find out about the Belorussian deal. Wanted to know who I'd done it with.'

'Professor. I'm sorry, I don't know what you're talking about. What deal? And are you all right?'

'Yes, I am. No-one really wants to kill me. I'm not important enough. It's Kartchak they want.'

'Kartchak? Who's he?'

It was Macneice who answered. 'He's developing the deal with us ... in Belorussia. As a possible joint venture partner with the EBRD.'

Impatiently, Alex tried again. 'Which project in Belorussia?'

'We did *your* project, the one for the foil—' the professor chipped in eagerly.

Surprised, Alex interrupted him. 'That wasn't a *project*, it was only an idea. Did you really put it together?'

'All this business, this dirty business, it's all gone too far. I told Maxim and I wanted to warn you—' The professor gasped suddenly. His hand moved to his chest and he looked at Alex, stricken.

'Are you all right?'

'I am so frightened,' the professor whispered. He took a deep breath. 'I have never been so afraid. I was so stupid to become involved with Kartchak. I knew what kind of man he was.'

'So Kartchak is to be your partner in the project

with the EBRD to build a foil plant next to the smelter?'

'Yes. But not just that. He wanted more than that. He wanted shares in the plant and Belkov was not in favour. Kartchak wanted to buy all the aluminium they produced, knowing he could sell it to the foil plant. But Belkov didn't want to sell to him. Of course, Kartchak got it in the end.'

'Professor,' Alex began gently. 'You know that Belkov is dead?'

'Yes. I know. Arkady told me. I am very, very distressed. I had spoken to Belkov the previous day. He felt he had no choice but to give Kartchak the shares. He had threatened the electricity supply. Maxim would have been very disappointed to have lost the deal. I can only suspect—'

'What does this man Kartchak look like?'

'Small, dark hair, very fit. About fifty. He had been trying to contact you to do business. He sent Annansky. He wanted . . . oh, why should I lie? There was something very unhealthy about his interest in you. He was very determined.'

Now she understood the scene in the street beside the hotel.

Kartchak and Maxim. Both chasing the Belorussian business. Two projects destined to collide, coming to an explosive head that day in Moscow.

Kartchak had won the shareholding. Could Maxim really have killed Belkov?

And then the henchmen in the airport. One from each team. Kartchak's man wanting to bring her, like a prize, to his boss.

And Boris? He certainly had had the chance to kill her. It would have been so easy during those interminable seconds when she had stood on the stairs frozen with the horror of the mangled body at her feet. But maybe he had been instructed simply to bring her back to Maxim. To heel.

Of course. Why should they bother to kill her? As Maslenkov had pointed out, she was cheap, everyone could afford to have her in their operation. A minor cog, with no money and no influence.

In confirmation, Sol's impatient words came back to her: 'Oh Alex, no-one wants to kill *you*.'

She stood up, looked from one to the other and could not help feeling sorry for them.

The professor picked up his briefcase and shuffled to the door. 'I know you had some contact with Annansky. He was a nice young man. Cocky. Maybe a bit too clever—'

Alex looked up. 'He *was*?'

The professor shrugged. 'I'm sorry. Apparently Kartchak had him killed. Please be careful.'

'I think it's a bit late for that, professor.'

FOURTEEN

'Look what I've got.'

Alex leant over and Libby wisely released it. It was the authorization to close The Kid's and Sol's position. Alex read it over and over again.

'This is it.'

Libby nodded. 'Let's do it.'

For a moment Alex considered telling her about Roman, but decided to wait till she knew for certain.

'What's the total position?'

'Seven thousand three hundred lots.'

Alex winced. This was going to be hard work. She looked up. Thirty minutes to go.

'Alan, sell five hundred at $1500,' she instructed the dealer. He looked at her, surprised. Two minutes earlier she had seemed to agree with him that the price was going up. Now she was giving a substantial selling order. He did not question her but hit the phones.

'Five hundred at $1500,' he reported.

'Sell another five hundred down to $1480.'

This time he could not help himself. 'What are you up to, Alex?'

'A hunch,' she explained, uncomfortably aware that it was just that.

'Five hundred sold at $1480,' he confirmed.

There were still buyers in the market but the weight of her selling was beginning to move the price down. She had a decision to make with only thirty minutes till the announcement. It was a cat and mouse game. She could hold off and wait till the buyers came in, hoping to sell to them at a higher price, or offload the whole position irrespective of price.

She looked at Libby. 'Well? Shall I dump it or take my chances?'

Libby looked at her watch. 'If you haven't closed by the time the announcement's made you'll be trying to sell along with the rest of the world. But if you hit them now you might just spook the market.' Realizing that she had been no help at all she smiled apologetically. 'I don't know,' she concluded.

Alex decided to try the subtle approach one more time.

'Sell another five hundred down to $1450.'

This time she was not so lucky.

'I only sold 250, Alex,' the dealer told her. 'Next bid is $1440.'

'Sell the balance at forty then.'

Libby was beside her, filling out the tickets and keeping track of what she was doing. The market was slipping.

Alex sat back and took a sip of cold coffee. The dealing room was quiet, orderly. She looked at the clock again. Twenty minutes.

Suddenly the dealer shouted over. 'Hey, Alex! Metco bidding $1450. Want me to give him some?'

Alex felt a surge of excitement and saw Libby lean forward.

'Yeah, but only a hundred.'

With Metco in the market she had to take extra care. If Spike had, indeed, decided to buy for Maxim, he would buy a couple of thousand lots, which would be enough to get her out of the bulk of the position. But she didn't want to warn him off. If he saw that Wellington was selling volume he would smell a rat and pull out. And she had to be sure that he would never know that Wellington had been behind the move – and that Libby had set him up.

She told the dealer to sell to other brokers, even at lower prices if necessary, but not to Metco. The price held steady on the screen, then moved up slightly. She looked over at Libby's running total. Five thousand five hundred sold.

'Sell another thousand lots at market.'

Not only did the aluminium dealer look up but the copper and lead dealer too. This was a massive order and the aluminium dealer would be unable to hit the phones on his own to sell it. She saw them organize between themselves who would call whom. That way they could hit four or five brokers simultaneously before they were aware that there was such a lot of selling in the market.

The game went on for five more minutes. Seven minutes to go. Alex pored over the figures.

The market was slipping away even without their selling. $1390.

'We're not going to do it,' she told Libby quietly.

'No, I don't think we are. Hell, if only we'd had more time.'

They both turned as Steve called over to the dealer.

'Give me ten lots for Barry.' It was a small enquiry, a fraction of what they had to do, but they watched the dealer's face, using him as an indication of the market's temperature.

The dealer shrugged, reluctantly giving his bid and offer. '$1380 at $1390.'

'Shit.' Alex and Libby spoke simultaneously, seeing instantly how the market had turned against them. The dealer, although he was only quoting for ten lots, was so afraid of a market collapse that he had dropped his price ten dollars below the price on the screen. He did not want to buy and hoped that his low price would discourage the customer.

'We've had it.'

In confirmation of the dealer's judgement, the screen flickered with a new level. $1370.

For a moment Alex looked around at the faces in the dealing room. They were grim. The market was behaving uncharacteristically and each broker had picked up the unease that surrounded the price.

Suddenly she knew exactly what to do.

She stood up. There was a moment's silence as the brokers and dealers stared at her, telling their customers to wait, knowing something was about to happen.

Libby looked up in alarm. 'What are you doing?' she whispered.

Alex's steady, controlled voice carried around the dealing room. 'Alan, buy me five hundred at market.'

She was buying! The brokers hit the phones and reversed their previous commentaries. The atmosphere in the room suddenly lightened, the upset when the market faltered had wrongfooted a lot of the players but now they could discount it as a 'blip', a brief anomaly, some damn computer somewhere misreading a figure and churning out a wrong recommendation. The dealing room sighed a collective sigh of relief.

Libby grabbed her arm. 'What the hell are you doing?' she shouted. 'We'll never get out now! Alex, for God's sake—'

'Listen,' Alex instructed her and they tuned in to the buzz of the dealing room, the excited voices, the urgency. From a low of $1370 the price began to steady. She saw Steve lean over to the dealer, telling him to buy, using the open-armed gesture of the greedy child reaping an armful of illicit sweets.

'Just buy it!' he screamed and the dealer hit the phones.

Suddenly Libby understood how Alex had turned the tide. 'Alex, you're brilliant!'

'Look at the clock. What's the total?'

'You're back to two and a half thousand lots long. And look at the price. $1420 trading and bid.'

Alex leant over to the dealer. 'Alan, hit every bid. Don't offer. Don't show your hand. If someone wants to buy, sell to him. But *don't offer.'*

Alan nodded. The lights on the dealer board continued to flash and the price steadied, then began to rise. Alex had read the sentiment right.

Sentiment. The one overriding factor that could make nonsense of economic theories or scientific discipline.

The element that confounded the purists.

The aluminium market *wanted* to go up. She had heard it from the brokers and the dealers, noted the extra enthusiasm in their voices as they reeled off the supporting data. They wanted this price to go up. She had shaken them, then reinforced their commitment. Now they would go in and buy, confident that they were right again and that this was a true bull market.

Two minutes to go and Libby suddenly threw the trading sheets in the air. 'We've done it!'

Alex swept the pages from her desk, the wave of triumph dispelled by an awful sense of foreboding. All this because Fedorov had told her the price was going down.

A Russian. And she had trusted him.

'We did it, but did we do the right thing?'

The whole plan had been put in place to be crowned by the announcement due to be made in less than two minutes. Months of work and planning, all for nothing.

They were out and Maxim was not. Her calculations indicated that he must be long 4,500 lots at an average of $1420.

One of them was right, one monumentally wrong.

When the distinctive alarm from the Reuters

screen was heard announcing a market-moving story the office stopped again, a moment of suspense as unnatural and alarming as a heart suddenly stopping beating.

Alex read the article at top speed – as did the dealers – wanting to be the first to trade after they had digested the news.

THE RUSSIAN MINISTRY FOR METALLURGY HAS ANNOUNCED AN AGREEMENT WITH TWO AMERICAN ALUMINIUM PRODUCERS, AMNOR AND BASTION, TO REFIT AND OVERHAUL THREE RUSSIAN PLANTS WHOSE ENVIRONMENTAL PROBLEMS HAVE CAUSED WORLDWIDE CONCERN. THE **$300M** REVOLVING CREDIT FACILITY WILL ENABLE THE PLANTS – THE WORLD'S LARGEST – TO CARRY OUT ESSENTIAL REPAIRS. SOME ANALYSTS ESTIMATE THAT THE CLOSURE WILL LAST FOR 4 TO 6 MONTHS AND THAT TOTAL PRODUCTION LOST MAY BE AS MUCH AS **500,000** TONNES.

Alex scanned the rest of the article. This was, verbatim, the press release she had drawn up with Maxim. She felt sick, a sudden wave of nausea as she realized that she had been conned again.

She stood up abruptly, knocking her chair over, causing Libby to reach out to her as if steadying a frightened animal.

She was enraged. Consumed by the violent hatred for the whole group, unreasonable in her wild impotent anger.

'Bastards!' Alex spat. 'Bastards! I could kill—'

'For God's sake, Alex. Calm down.'

Alex swung round and almost knocked Libby

out of the way as she kicked at the upended chair in her way.

'I'm so stupid, so bloody stupid.'

'No, Alex, you're not. It's them, they're devious and disloyal. Do you really want to learn to be what they are? Is that what you're saying?'

'Yes, I do!' Alex burst out. 'I *do* want to be like them. I've had enough of being the fool. God, I can see it all now. Someone must have told Fedorov that I had found out what was going on. I couldn't be trusted any more so he called to persuade me to sell. I sold. They bought. They've got me out of the way and kept their hold on the market. Perfect.'

'Wait, Alex—' Libby grabbed hold of her, frightened for what she would do to herself. 'Sit down, please, just for a minute.'

'Let go of me!'

Suddenly the Reuters screen flashed and they both turned round, still holding onto each other.

'THERE WILL BE NO PRODUCTION LOST FROM THE RUSSIAN PLANTS DURING THE REFITTING,' VALERI FEDOROV, HEAD OF THE GIANT GORYA PLANT IN SIBERIA TOLD RORY FREEMAN TODAY IN RESPONSE TO EARLIER REPORTS THAT **500,000** TONNES OF PRODUCTION WILL BE LOST. 'EVERY PLANT BUILDS INTO ITS OUTPUT ESTIMATE A CERTAIN AMOUNT OF DOWNTIME FOR REPAIR. THIS YEAR WE WILL BE UPGRADING RATHER THAN PATCHING UP. THE NETT EFFECT WILL BE THAT OUR OUTPUT THIS YEAR WILL BE **20%** UP ON LAST YEAR DUE TO INCREASED EFFICIENCY. THE SAME APPLIES TO THE OTHER RUSSIAN PLANTS AND WE WILL, IN EFFECT, PRODUCE OVER 3 MILLION TONNES THIS YEAR.'

Alex had not even finished reading the report when the lines started flashing and the brokers started calling. The price ticked down to $1350 without appearing to have traded, then the screen showed $1280. She gasped.

'My God!' Libby burst out. 'My God. I don't believe it! This is dynamite. Alex. You were right!'

The words danced in front of Alex's eyes. She could see Libby, sense the electricity in the room but somehow she could not take it all in.

'Libby,' she began uncertainly. 'He did it, didn't he? Fedorov? I was right to trust him?'

'You were,' Libby laughed. 'And even if you're only going to be right once, you certainly picked the right time. What a coup!'

In a daze Alex watched the Metco line flash, unheeded by the dealers. She could almost hear Spike's voice. The rasping obscenities as he punched the board, the fury as the massive loss grew.

She turned to Libby. 'We did it, didn't we?'

Libby put her arms around her and held her tight.

'We did,' she whispered into her shoulder. They stood together, immobile, for a long moment, oblivious to the frenzy around them. Alex could not bear to release Libby, her anchor and refuge. She had got everybody out of their positions with a profit, but few would know what an effort it had been.

Suddenly she thought of Sol. He had said he would call her after speaking to The Kid but had not. She thought back to his words of the previous evening when she had asked him for the authority to close the position. His words had been clipped and impatient. Decisions should be made not on the basis of right and wrong, but of profit and loss. Why had he changed his mind?

And Rory Freeman, who had not simply dismissed her but found his own way to redress the balance.

'Alex.' Libby released her and held her gently at arm's length. 'Are you OK? Your line's ringing.'

It was The Kid.

'Well, what do you think?' Alex asked.

'Well done, you both did a great job.'

'Tell me . . . Why did you do it? Why did you authorize me to close the position?'

'Because I trust you, Alex.' He seemed surprised by her question. 'Listen, I'm on the golf course. I'll speak to you later.'

Everything had been reversed. The Kid, whose values she had always suspected of being superficial and transient, was the one who had acted on emotion. Sol, her friend and lover, had examined the situation and evaluated it like a balance sheet. Pure commerce.

The price on the screen was now $1175. The aluminium dealer came over and shook her hand.

In the mayhem of the trading room Alex and Libby prepared the paperwork, doggedly counting and recounting, making sure they had tied up all the loose ends, checking and cross-checking with the back office.

They finished at seven thirty and sat in the

artificial darkness of the fluorescent evening, reluctant to move and break the spell. The New York markets were shut and the dealing room was eerily quiet, only a couple of neglected screens flashing unread headlines about midwestern agricultural markets.

Alex scanned the note Neville had written, congratulating her on a record day. What a hypocrite. He knew perfectly well that The Kid's position had been pure speculation, nothing more than a punt. And he had chosen to turn a blind eye to it for the sake of the commission. Now he was ostensibly congratulating Alex on her wonderful commission figures, but in reality he was relieved that the position was closed and he would not be summoned to the Exchange to explain what Wellington had been doing.

I knew there was business out there! Well done! Keep it up.

Alex made a paper plane of the memo and threw it across the room.

'Well,' Libby roused herself finally. 'Maxim or Kartchak? Who's your money on?'

'Libby!' Alex feigned distaste. 'Which one's alive and which one's dead, you mean? If we sit here long enough we'll find out, I suppose.'

'Does it matter?'

'Not a bit. They're the same. I thought I knew Maxim and recognized something through the tangle of language and culture, that there was something in common in spite of the fact that we had both been trained from birth not to recognize it. And I thought his posturing was just that, hiding the side of him that he considered weak, just a façade ... but it wasn't. All the pettiness, the insecurities, the prejudices and the basic evil I saw were truly a part of him. I gave him so much latitude, thought I could see more deeply. Bullshit.' She stood up suddenly and switched off the screens in front of her. 'Maxim must be in big trouble back in Moscow. Such a well-planned scheme turning out so disastrously wrong. But I don't care who kills whom. Whoever is left standing will be mown down themselves in a month or two anyway. I hope they shoot each other.'

'Alex!' Libby laughed. 'What insensitivity! I hope you don't intend to adopt their business methods at Wellington. Andrew, answer that phone. Bang. Too slow.'

Alex started laughing and their laughter grew into kind of light-headedness bordering on hysteria.

'Who killed Belkov?' Libby asked finally.

'Maxim, probably. Belkov had given in to Kartchak, sold him the shares. Maybe Maxim knew about that – or if he didn't he wanted to prevent him giving way. It seems a little too co-incidental that Maxim should be there five minutes after the shooting. Getting rid of the opposition was his way ... I assume he did the same thing with Chernikov in order to put his own man into Chaika.'

Alex's direct line rang and she picked it up, expecting Sol. But it was Rory's voice she heard a moment later.

'Alex?'

'Rory! Where are you?'

'Moscow, but I'm stuck here now till tomorrow morning. How is everything?'

Alex laughed. 'What a leading question! Everything's fine, excellent. I don't know how to begin to thank you.'

'Listen, I get back at two tomorrow. I want to talk to you.'

'Shall I come to Heathrow to pick you up?'

'No . . . let's have a late lunch, Alex. Can I come to your flat?'

'Lunch . . .' she repeated, smiling. 'That's a good idea. I deserve a day off.'

'I'll see you then.'

'OK. And thanks again, Rory.'

The line rang again as soon as she put it down.

'Buy you a drink?' Sol asked.

Alex hesitated. 'I suppose so.'

'I'll be in Raoul's in ten minutes.'

The two women stood up, switched off the screens and gathered up their bags reluctantly.

Alex smiled. 'You know, Libby—'

'Don't say anything nice to me, Alex. I don't think I could stand it.'

Alex smiled. 'Consider it said then. All of it.'

'I do.' They hugged again, more tightly than before, but more quickly. Neither had to lean on the other now. Together they left the dealing room and, in the dark, the room became just another space, empty and lifeless.

On the pavement they parted, briskly. Alex watched Libby take off down the road to the car park and saw her turn, look back and wave.

It was over.

A couple of loose ends to tie up, a couple of

questions still to be answered, but it was finished. Alex walked slowly down the steps to Raoul's.

Sol was already there, in the corner, a bottle of Alex's favourite red on the table in front of him. She sat down and he poured her a glass.

She tried not to look at him, knowing that he would stare at her sheepishly from under his fringe, the schoolboy caught out in some minor misdemeanour. He had got away with so much like this, papering over the cracks of their relationship, charming her and distracting her from the very basic differences between them.

'Tell me everything, Sol.'

He straightened. 'OK. I guess you've pretty much pieced the whole thing together by now.' He ran his hand wearily over his face. 'I knew Mintov a long time ago. He used to be in charge of the state trading body, he was responsible for the export of the surplus metal or – in the case of tin – the import of the shortfall. I'd done business with him for years.

'I think I was the first to start trading out there and it went like clockwork. So good that I went to start up the New York office to be able to sell Russian aluminium out there.'

Suddenly Alex knew what was coming.

Not that Sol had been greedy or unprincipled, nothing so trivial. He was about to tell her that he had been deeply involved from the start.

And that he had set her up.

She swallowed, wondering whether she wanted to hear, whether she would be able to bear it.

'It all started quite legitimately,' Sol continued. 'There was no insurance and no security. I had to make a good profit. If four out of five deals worked, the fifth would be a spectacular failure. I got the head of the plants on my side. A basic strategy and I paid them money in the West to ensure their loyalty to me – and to my deals. How they came up with the numbers was up to them. I just paid the consultancy fee and took the metal.'

'You just paid the consultancy fee?' she echoed. 'Never mind that the managers were taking money that should have gone to the plant. And so much! Had you no idea what you were doing?'

'One hundred or five hundred? Where's the cut-off between acceptable and unacceptable?' Sol leant towards Alex, his eyes narrowed. 'And who decides. You?'

Impatiently, Alex waved him away. 'All right. Tell me the rest.'

'You know the rest. Mintov heard about this guy who was buying metal in Siberia. Checked him out.'

'Maxim?'

'Yes. He was an annoyance, he knew some people and they did him some favours, small time, but enough to be an annoyance. Anyway, Mintov called him to Moscow and they met. Instead of deciding to make him get out of the business, Mintov decided we could use him; the people he knew could be useful to us and he had a different approach to business.' Alex knew exactly what he meant by that and was appalled that Maxim's deadly tactics could be pigeon-holed as an approach to business.

'We realized that we had control of almost all the Russian production and, of course, we wanted to turn this control into money.'

'Of course,' Alex parodied.

'I came up with the plan to sell off the shares to Western producers. Not a bad plan. You've probably worked out by now that some of the shares in the plants have changed hands ... We have a limited number but once we realized what the impact would be on the markets we decided to magnify the whole deal. It was so neat! The price goes up and the value of our shareholding goes up too. Big time. But we needed cash ...'

'... you needed The Kid so you needed me.'

'It made sense. But I knew you wouldn't go for it. The Kid might have – dangle a profit and he might have joined us, but you'd met Maxim by then. If you'd got wind of it and started bleating about the ethics of the operation he'd probably have backed off too. Anyway, we had to have a broker and who better to trust than you?'

'So you conned me with that heart-rending story of the government unable to feed its workers – all that crap Mintov fed me. "Take her to see the plants and tell her she can help." '

Sol waved his hand. 'Wasn't much point in try-ing to bribe you, was there? Anyway, that's it. We just had to wait till you worked out the plan and then let you implement it. But it's not all that bad, Alex. It's true we would've made money out of this, but so would the workers. Everyone

405

would've been better off. This is not a charity, you know.'

'I understand all this, Sol. You're talking to a capitalist, remember? The profit motive is not entirely unknown to me. But there *are* limits and you've gone beyond them.' Suddenly she remembered the night in the Savoy when he had grilled her about her trip. Every little detail. Then he had taken her home and made love to her . . .

She sipped her drink. It tasted like acid. 'I guess this is just the same as the Sinco deal, really. Let me do all the nuts and bolts, look after the mechanics while you "spice it up", make sure the profit is there and that it goes to the right people.'

Sol looked up, surprised that she seemed to be accepting it, defeatist maybe, but not outraged.

'What do you know about Kartchak?' she asked.

'Not much. Came into the game quite late. Nasty piece of work.' Sol laughed. 'He should do well.'

'One last thing, Sol. What about the killing? Did they do it? The plant manger – Chernikov. And Belkov too. Did they tell you?'

She desperately wanted him to say that he hadn't known and that one boundary at least had not been crossed. Again he paused and she licked her dry lips in the ensuing seconds of silence.

'To be honest . . .' he started and she almost laughed at the inadvisability of the words, '. . . if you play a game on someone else's pitch, you've got to allow them to play by their own rules. Did I know they would start bumping people off?

No, I didn't, but I know how they do business and I'm just glad it wasn't me. Chernikov was refusing to play ball. Belkov had kind of given in to the opposition. Maxim said he'd deal with them and we left him to it.'

After a moment Alex moved on. 'Why did you authorize me to close the position?'

'I had no choice. You told me what Fedorov had told you. I knew he must be up to something and I knew I could do nothing to stop him. You'd also told Spike to buy – it seemed like a reasonable damage limitation exercise.'

'You didn't think of warning Spike and Maxim about Fedorov's announcement?'

'Well, no. It rather suited me that they should buy and that you should be able to get me out with a profit.'

And there it was, the sheepish, lopsided grin, the hand tentatively reaching across the table. Alex pulled back her hand and stood up. Sol remained seated and for a second they looked at each other, reappraising the new people they had become.

There was nothing left between them and Alex was surprised to feel no nostalgia for what they had had. It had been an artifice. The emotions she felt were like those she experienced at the end of a film, real emotions artificially induced.

He sighed. 'I'm finished with it all now. Bunch of murdering bastards. I made a lot of money, but I'm done. I'm going to take a trip. Brazil, maybe, tie up that damn brass deal once and for all. Will you come with me?'

'Not a chance, Sol. Why would I go halfway across the world with a complete stranger?'

At the door she turned and smiled at him. 'I'm surprised you're so casual about all this, Sol. Sitting here in a public place. Aren't you worried?'

She saw the uncertainty flash over his face, the confidence begin to drain away.

'Remember, Sol, nobody wants to kill *me* . . .'

The blood ran smoothly down the lacquered walls like rain down a window. Kartchak sat on the floor, legs splayed, head bowed, dying.

Costya stepped over him and walked along the corridor to the last door on the left. Brazenly, he turned on the light. He had left four armed men outside the apartment and two more on the pavement – there was no need to be careful.

Kartchak had been understandably confident about the security in his own domain, but no-one could have defended themselves against such a team – Costya had charged over half a million dollars for this operation. And working for a government minister meant guaranteed payment.

There were no locks on the desk or on the filing cabinets. Costya smiled. God, Kartchak had been complacent.

He started pulling out the desk drawers. In the third he found what he was looking for. The fabricated police report implicating Mintov in the death of the child. He tore it up and set the pieces alight in the ashtray on the desk. Had it been anyone else, he would have considered pocketing the report, but Mintov was an extremely valued client.

As he turned to go something caught his eye.

Slowly he pulled the glossy paper from the drawer and laid it on top of the desk. He flipped the torn edge with one finger. Odd. These drawers held Kartchak's most important documents, yet this was part of a magazine article. He looked more closely at the woman's face. She looked familiar. He had seen her with Volkov. What a coincidence.

He looked at his watch. Volkov was his next job.

THE END

THE MIRACLE STRAIN
by Michael Cordy

'*Jurassic Park* meets the quest for the Holy Grail meets
Raiders of the Lost Ark'
Mail on Sunday

A heart-pounding international thriller of retribution and
redemption. One man battles for the life of his daughter
in the face of seemingly unbeatable odds. But to save
her he must first reach for the ultimate knowledge . . .

Doctor Tom Carter, surgeon, geneticist, husband, father,
needs a miracle. As the inventor of a revolutionary
machine, the Genescope, he has the power to read a
person's genes, predicting the onset of disease . . . their
lifespan . . . their future.

But at the moment of his greatest triumph, the Nobel
Prize for Medicine, Carter's world is shattered by the
assassination of his wife. He knows that the killer's
bullets can only have been meant for him. In the aftermath
of her death, a scan reveals that his daughter Holly has
an incurable brain disorder and less than a year to live.
Even the most advanced conventional science cannot
save her. Something more radical is required.

A secret brotherhood, two thousand years old, may have
the answer. They need his new technology to complete
their own sacred quest. In return they offer Carter the
chance to look beyond the genes of man . . . and into the
genes of God.

0 552 14578 5

SHADOW DANCER
by Tom Bradby

'Taut, purposeful and above all else human . . . a compelling story of love and torn loyalties . . . Exceptional'
Daily Telegraph

Colette McVeigh: widow . . . mother . . . terrorist. A woman who has lived the Republican cause for all of her 29 years. A woman whose brothers are both heavily involved at senior levels in the IRA, whose husband was killed by the British security forces. A woman who is now an informer for MI5.

Apprehended by the police in an aborted bombing attempt in London, Colette is given two choices: talk and see her children again or stay silent and spend the rest of her life watching them grow up from behind the bars of a prison cell.

Unwillingly she is led to betray her past by her young MI5 handler, David Ryan, who always knew where his loyalties lay. But when he follows Colette across the Irish Sea to Belfast, the values are quickly sacrificed on the pyre of the province's history. And, as he watches Colette put herself in increasing danger to keep her side of the bargain, he realises that his professional integrity is irrevocably and fatally compromised . . .

'A remarkable first novel . . . Bradby handles the tension with skill to produce a gripping tale'
The Times

'The best book on the northern conflict since *Harry's Game* . . . An excellent read on any level'
Irish Independent

0 552 14586 6

KINGDOM OF THE BLIND
by Alan Blackwood

You rescue an elderly man from being kidnapped by thugs. He tells you that if he is eventually tracked down, he'll send you a cassette. Listen to its instructions and make your own decision. It could bring you things you never even dreamed of. The cassette arrives . . .

Micky Frasier's reward for his good Samaritan act in saving Dr Lügner is, literally, mind-blowing. Micky, whose ambitions up to now have been modest, begins to see his horizons expand with dazzling rapidity. But more than one group of sinister and violent men are after Lügner. As the body-count rises, and the reasons behind the manhunt gradually reveal themselves, Micky is pulled helter-skelter into a deadly game which writes its own rules and offers the most extraordinary prize of all . . .

Fast-paced, witty, sexy, *Kingdom of the Blind* is an original and audacious thriller which takes the reader on a dizzying journey into the farthest reaches of human genius – and beyond.

0 552 14645 5

CAUGHT IN THE LIGHT
by Robert Goddard

On assignment in Vienna, photographer Ian Jarrett
falls in love with a woman he meets by chance, Marian
Esguard. Back in England, he leaves his wife and goes
to meet Marian, only for her to vanish from his life as
mysteriously as she entered it.

Searching for the woman for whom he has sacrificed
everything, Jarrett comes across a Dorset churchyard
full of gravestones of dead Esguards. He also meets a
psychotherapist, Daphne Sanger. She too is looking for
someone: a former client who believes she is the
reincarnation of Marian Esguard, who may have
invented photography ten years before Fox Talbot. But
why is Marian Esguard unknown to history? And who
and where is the woman Jarrett met in Vienna?

Jarrett sets out to solve a mystery whose origins lie amid
the magical-seeming properties of early photography.
But at the end of his search a trap awaits him. He is
caught in a web of deception, woven between the enigmas
of the past and the revenges of the present. And there is
no way out.

0 552 14597 1

UNHALLOWED GROUND
by Gillian White

Once upon a time, it is said, the devil walked in this valley . . .

On a snowbound February day, when Georgina first saw Furze Pen – a picturesque thatched cottage in a peaceful valley on Dartmoor – she thought it just the place to recover from the recent nightmare of her job in London. True, the cottage was cold and isolated, and the neighbours weird and strangely threatening. But Georgie needed to work out her life, and Furze Pen seemed as good a place as any – until the terrors started.

There was the lone watcher on the hill – at first she thought it was a scarecrow, so stark and still was it standing – and then the unexplained fire, with the remains of a child's doll smouldering in the ashes. But there had never been a child at Furze Pen. And as the seasons turned and snow once again blocked off the remote valley, the frightening began in earnest . . .

In this truly terrifying novel Gillian White has created a world of dark secrets which hide behind the seemingly ordinary lives of her characters. It is a world which is scarier than most people's worst imaginings.

0 552 14563 7

REMOTE CONTROL
by Andy McNab DCM MM

Nick Stone left the Special Air Service in 1988, soon
after the shooting of three IRA terrorists in Gibraltar.
Now working for British Intelligence on deniable
operations, he discovers the seemingly senseless murders
of a fellow SAS soldier and his family in Washington, DC.
Only a seven-year-old daughter, Kelly, has survived –
and the two of them are immediately on the run from
unidentified pursuers. Stone doesn't even know which of
them is the target.

On his own, Stone stands a chance of escape. But he
needs to protect the girl and together they plunge into a
dark world of violence and corruption in which friend
cannot be told from foe. As events draw to their blazing
and unexpected climax, Stone discovers the shocking
truth about governments, terrorism and commerce –
and the greed that binds the three together . . .

Remote Control is a new kind of thriller, gritty, vivid
and menacing, with a pace that never lets up. Other
thriller-writers talk the talk. Only McNab has walked
the walk.

'It's a corker'
Independent

'An enjoyable gritty thriller'
The Scotsman

'Proceeds with a testosterone surge'
Daily Telegraph

0 552 14591 2

A SELECTED LIST OF FINE WRITING AVAILABLE FROM CORGI BOOKS

14242 5	THE LEGACY	*Evelyn Anthony*	£5.99
14168 2	JIGSAW	*Campbell Armstrong*	£5.99
14169 0	HEAT	*Campbell Armstrong*	£5.99
14496 7	SILENCER	*Campbell Armstrong*	£5.99
14645 5	KINGDOM OF THE BLIND	*Alan Blackwood*	£5.99
14586 6	SHADOW DANCER	*Tom Bradby*	£5.99
14578 5	THE MIRACLE STRAIN	*Michael Cordy*	£5.99
14654 4	THE HORSE WHISPERER	*Nicholas Evans*	£5.99
13823 1	THE DECEIVER	*Frederick Forsyth*	£5.99
12140 1	NO COMEBACKS	*Frederick Forsyth*	£5.99
13990 4	THE FIST OF GOD	*Frederick Forsyth*	£5.99
13991 2	ICON	*Frederick Forsyth*	£5.99
14512 2	WITHOUT CONSENT	*Frances Fyfield*	£5.99
14525 4	BLIND DATE	*Frances Fyfield*	£5.99
14223 9	BORROWED TIME	*Robert Goddard*	£5.99
13840 1	CLOSED CIRCLE	*Robert Goddard*	£5.99
14224 7	OUT OF THE SUN	*Robert Goddard*	£5.99
54593 7	INTO THE BLUE	*Robert Goddard*	£5.99
14225 5	BEYOND RECALL	*Robert Goddard*	£5.99
14597 1	CAUGHT IN THE LIGHT	*Robert Goddard*	£5.99
13678 6	THE EVENING NEWS	*Arthur Hailey*	£5.99
14376 6	DETECTIVE	*Arthur Hailey*	£5.99
13691 3	WHEELS	*Arthur Hailey*	£5.99
14622 6	A MIND TO KILL	*Andrea Hart*	£5.99
14584 X	THE COLD CALLING	*Will Kingdom*	£5.99
14591 2	REMOTE CONTROL	*Andy McNab*	£5.99
14136 4	THE WALPOLE ORANGE	*Frank Muir*	£4.99
54535 X	KILLING GROUND	*Gerald Seymour*	£5.99
14605 6	THE WAITING TIME	*Gerald Seymour*	£5.99
14391 X	A SIMPLE PLAN	*Scott Smith*	£4.99
10565 1	TRINITY	*Leon Uris*	£6.99
14561 0	THE SLEEPER	*Gillian White*	£5.99
14563 7	UNHALLOWED GROUND	*Gillian White*	£5.99